Sweet Sorrow

Kregg P.J. Jorgenson

BookLocker
Trenton, Georgia

Copyright 2025 Kregg P.J. Jorgenson

Print ISBN: 978-1-959621-17-1
Ebook ISBN: 979-8-88531-847-1

All rights reserved. No part of this publication may be reproduced, stored in a retrieval system, or transmitted in any form or by any means, electronic, mechanical, recording or otherwise, without the prior written permission of the author.

Published by BookLocker.com, Inc., Trenton, Georgia.

This is work of fiction. While there were 13 separate U.S. Army Ranger-75th Infantry Long Range Reconnaissance Patrol (LRRP/Lurp) Companies serving during the Vietnam War, there was no R or Romeo Company-75th Infantry LRRP/Ranger (MAC-V) unit, nor was there a Camp Mackie forward operating Base Camp to house them. All names, characters, places, events, and incidents in this book are either the product of the author's imagination or used in a fictitious manner.

BookLocker.com, Inc.
2025

First Edition

Library of Congress Cataloging in Publication Data
Jorgenson, Kregg P.J.
Sweet Sorrow by Kregg P.J. Jorgenson
Library of Congress Control Number: 2024927687

This one is for Pat and Andy Brown and crew at War Horses for Veterans because the long road home is always easier in better company.

And for those who served as LRRP/Rangers during the Vietnam War, as well as to the helicopter Gunship, Huey, and Scout pilots and crews, with a nod to Jeff Cromar for tolerating my seemingly never ending gunship questions.

To my Brother Pete.

I love you.

6/4/25

AB

Sweet Sorrow
Book 3 in the Jungle War series

"Mostly, it is loss which teaches us about
 the worth of things."
                                    -Arthur Schopenhauer

Prologue

MAC-V was the acronym for the U.S. Military Assistance Command-Vietnam, the joint service operational command center for the Department of Defense in South East Asia. The Headquarters complex that some referred to as *The Pentagon East* served as the nerve center for all ground, naval, and air operations in the Republic of South Vietnam during the drawn-out war.

The massive two-storied, multi-million dollar facility, that sprang up on the site of an old soccer field on the north edge of Saigon, consisted of twelve acres of modern prefab, wax-floored, comfortably air-conditioned offices, briefing rooms, and a myriad of other working spaces, nooks, and crannies dedicated to a lengthy list of military functions, purposes, and services. If a particular office wasn't located inside the complex proper then it could be found in one of its many supplementary annex buildings on the expansive grounds.

Self-contained, it had its own power plant, telephone exchange, mess hall, barracks, snack bar, theater, swimming pool, and layered levels of officious bureaucracy all surrounded by cyclone fencing topped with protective rolls of concertina razor wire, and guarded by strategically placed Military Police checkpoints, manned watch towers, and fortified fighting positions.

The 1968 TET Offensive saw coordinated surprise attacks against 100 cities and towns by over 80,000 North Vietnamese Army and Viet Cong forces also targeted the major command hubs and installations, including MAC-V Headquarters. After the failed enemy Offensive that still saw major damage to the battered sites, security measures and fortified safeguards were beefed-up and bolstered. The lessons learned and changes made sought to insure that the once thought *safe,* or at least *safer,* cities, towns, and the rear area military command centers and depots hit in the lunar New Year attacks, wouldn't be caught off-guard again or, at least, would fare better in the next big enemy push.

The MAC-V Headquarters Command that was a third of the size of the actual Pentagon was now a better and more secured fortress for its new Commander, four-star General Creighton Abrams, and his staff. While the 1968 Tet Offensive was little more than a propaganda victory for the Viet Cong and North Vietnamese, the coordinated attacks did show the intel failures and vulnerabilities of the Saigon government and military operational commands. The previous intelligence gathering efforts in place prior to the enemy Offensive revealed there just wasn't enough boots on the ground intelligence in the field to better alert the command against large scale enemy build ups and pending attacks. Lessons were learned and the criticisms and recommendations in the After Action Reports would not fall upon deaf ears.

In that regard General Abrams gave the nod to reorganize and reactivate the 75th Infantry Ranger Regiment for this latest war. On 1 February 1969 the U.S.

Army's thirteen existing long range reconnaissance patrol companies, conducting combat operations in the four Corps Tactical Zones of the Republic of South Vietnam, were formally reorganized, and reflagged as the 75th Infantry Ranger Regiment under the Department of the Army's Combat Arms Regimental System. With the changeover, the U.S. Army brought thirteen new alphabetical Ranger companies into play, C thru P or in Army speak, Charlie thru Papa. Two additional Ranger Companies, designated Alpha, and Bravo, were brought into being outside of the warzone.

The previously authorized Long Range Reconnaissance Patrol (LRRP) units, reorganized and rebranded as Ranger Companies would remain within their assigned Division and separate Brigade-sized commands throughout South Vietnam's four military Corps Tactical Zones. They would continue their sneaking and peeking patrols from the not so Demilitarized Zone up in I (Eye)-Corps along the 17th Parallel down to the swamps and mud-slogging marshes of the Mekong Delta in IV (Four)-Corps. Like the Detachments or Companies, they sprang from, the new Ranger Companies would operate independently of each other while carrying the lineage and legacy of the 75th Ranger Infantry Regiment from previous wars. As stand-alone Ranger Companies they didn't fall under the 75th Ranger Regimental Chain-of-Command due to the fact that there was no actual Ranger Regimental command, let alone a Ranger Battalion operating in Vietnam.

Still, as U.S. Army 75th Infantry Rangers they would sport unique Black Berets with a *Sua Sponte* crest, and the red, white, and black Ranger scroll patches on the left shoulders of their rear area jungle fatigues. The unique crest heralded its link and ties to the 5307th Composite Unit, the long range special operations warfare detachment that operated deep in the jungles of China, Burma, and India during World War Two. The 5307th was more famously known as *Merrill's Marauders*.

Like their Long Range Reconnaissance Patrol predecessors, the new Ranger Companies would continue to operate in four, five, and six-man team configurations, or if a particular patrol called for more fire power, they created *'heavy teams'* of eight to ten men. As they patrolled deep into known enemy-held territory, quietly lurking in the shadows of the North Vietnamese Army and Viet Cong hidden jungle Base Camps and strongholds, they conducted surveillance operations, ambushes, snatch missions, or directed artillery strikes.

Boots-on-the-ground, and especially small tactical teams patrolling over enemy ground, often yielded valuable hard intelligence findings for the higher command's critical decision-making plans and strategies. If the finer-minded tacticians knew where the North Vietnamese Army and Viet Cong battalions were marshalling their forces in the millions of acres of jungle throughout the Republic, it made it easier to take out those targets with significantly fewer friendly casualties. Conversely, if the enemy forces were no longer in those remote jungle areas of concern then there wouldn't be a need to chopper in a grunt company or larger battalion-size force to aimlessly go looking. The Army's new Ranger Companies enhanced the small unit strategy.

In doing so, they earned dual recognition and status, not just as Rangers but also as *Lurps*, a bastardized acronym and accepted pronunciation of the letters, LRRP. By adopting the hit-and-run tactics of the Viet Cong and making them their own, the small teams soon began to out-guerilla the guerillas. They became known to their enemy as the *Nhung Nguoi Linh Ma, The Ghost Soldiers,* who suddenly appeared out of the rainforest shadows, attacked with hit-and-run strikes like snarling green and black camo face-painted demons, and then disappeared back into the cover and concealment of the jungle.

However, by 1971, after six years of direct combat action the U.S. was drawing down its ground forces, including the Army's LRRP/Ranger units. Five of the original thirteen lettered Ranger Companies had also been stood down, one being from the Indiana National Guard unit that were already back in the Hoosier State, while the 82nd Airborne Division's O Company was deactivated only to be reactivated and sent to Alaska and relabeled as '*Artic Rangers.*'

It was also about that time when MAC-V Headquarters realized the need for additional Lurp operations, especially as North Vietnamese Army units and Viet Cong Battalions once again began flooding into the great expanse of jungle-covered countryside from neighboring Cambodia and Laos.

To meet that LRRP/Ranger need, MAC-V designated a new Ranger Company to be formed, albeit Detachment in size, Company R, or *Romeo*, in the phonetic vernacular of the military, came into existence. They were late to the game.

Unlike the other LRRP Ranger Companies operating under Field Force or Division-sized commands, Company-R's hierarchy and place in the uniformed pecking order fell directly under the MAC-V Headquarters command. Loaned out to assist the forward combat elements assigned to Camp Mackie in, quite literally, the troubled hinterland, the unit was housed in a small, barbed-wire wrapped compound on the outpost-like Base Camp that was surrounded by jungle in the upper reach of a highly contested Province bordering the neighboring Khmer Republic of Cambodia. Just over the border of the remote Fishhook region of Tay Ninh Province of South Vietnam, COSVIN, the Communist forces of the Central Office for South Vietnam headquarters command, operated out of a hidden location in and around the Memot Rubber Plantation and in nearby Kratie, Cambodia.

Those on Camp Mackie knew that their dust blown base was set smack dab in the middle of a major off-ramp for the infamous Ho Chi Minh Trail, and purposely positioned to be the latest toll road in the infiltration route for the thousands of North Vietnamese Army soldiers flowing into the south each month from Laos and Cambodia. The price of that toll which was being paid on a daily basis was extracted from the human coffers of the opposing forces on both sides of the fight. Because of its remote location Camp Mackie was also thought of by many on it as being located smack dab in the middle of downtown nowhere with no adjacent or even nearby village or town. Truth be told, it was a military island surrounded by a seemingly endless stretch of primordial jungle that would've made even a Vietnamese version of Tarzan proud.

Two veteran Green Berets had been drawn from the 5th Special Forces command in Nha Trang and tasked with setting up, organizing, and running the new Ranger unit. West Point graduate Captain Johnston Bennett Robison, and his E-7 (promotable) Acting First Sergeant, Walter *'The Brick, as in wall, just don't ever fucking call me Walt*er,' Poplawski took the call. Both were seasoned professionals with several combat tours of duty under their Green Beret belts and were more than qualified to carry out the newly assigned task.

Robison, the son of a Baptist Minister, was the calm, quiet, steady professional while Poplawski was the proverbial bull in this Southeast Asian China Shop. The street smart son of a Detroit Auto Workers Union Shop Steward was tough, blunt, combat dependable, seemingly fearless, and there was no other senior NCO the new Ranger Company Commander wanted by his side in combat than Poplawski. They had made a good working team in the past on a previous tour of duty on a Special Forces A-Team, so this latest assignment held promise even if they had to switch from green berets to the Ranger black berets.

From its launch Romeo Company was promised an eighteen month operational shelf-life by MAC-V Headquarters Command, so the two got busy and soon recruited two young Lieutenants, Ryan Marquardt, and Dick Plantagenet, along with two Non-Commissioned Officers: SFC Mikhail, Mike, *'The Mad Russian'* Kozak, and Staff Sergeant Rob Shintaku. First Lieutenant Marquardt served as the unit's Executive Officer and First Platoon Leader while Second Lieutenant Plantagenet took on the job as the Second Platoon Leader. First Sergeant Poplawski also took on a dual role as the First Platoon's Platoon Sergeant, while Sergeant First Class Kozak was brought in later as the Second Platoon's Platoon Sergeant. The much younger *'Shake and Bake'* Staff Sergeant Shintaku became the Ranger Company's Training NCO after Robison and Poplawski saw how he operated and handled himself in the field on a test run patrol. This decision was a no-brainer. On a voluntary extended tour, the Staff Sergeant came from one of the Division's Recon Platoons that was reluctant to let him go. He was a natural leader with savvy combat acumen which was why he was selected to head the training program and selection process. Between them, the six comprised the unit's functioning cadre.

Housed in their small compound on Camp Mackie in three turtle shell looking Quonset huts and several other Boom Town-like out buildings and bunkers, Romeo Company was little more than a Company in name only and a fledgling

Detachment, at best. Upon taking command Robison and Poplawski immediately went to work finding and recruiting those who would take on the unit's first in-country training course to become combat Rangers. The call went out to the various Recon platoons and to new arrivals at the Replacement Centers, as well as to soldiers from other units looking to try out for the new Ranger unit. Hands were raised and volunteers stepped forward.

To turn the volunteers into combat-ready Lurps, Robison and Poplawski devised a honed-down, three week-long training course to find the kind of men they needed. The abbreviated selection course was set up to cherry pick the critical aspects of the eight week Ranger School at Fort Benning, Georgia to meet the needs of the war's jungle campaign. The training would also mirror the key elements of the recently deactivated two-week Recondo course that the 5th Special Forces Group had previously held in Nha Trang which had proved effective in fine tuning small unit patrol operations.

Any and all of the volunteers, regardless of their previous training or military occupational specialties, were required to successfully complete Romeo Company's arduous selection course training before being accepted into the unit and assigned to a team. They had to be physically fit and mentally up to the task and that was where the in-country training came into play.

The training began pre-dawn at O-Dark-30 with physical training calisthenics followed by a five-mile, 30-pound weighted rucksack run with web gear and weapon along the camp's perimeter road. Then, released to shower, shave, and hurry through breakfast at a nearby Mess Tent, it was onto classroom or outdoor practical exercises. The curriculum included map reading and land navigation, radio procedures with use and maintenance of a team's 13-pound backpacked PRC-25 radio, familiarization with U.S. and Soviet weapons, and basic medical procedures with graded competency tests. In addition, there were Ranger patrolling formations with quick reaction team drills with Australian peels and sudden contact exercises, to learn, to staging and carrying out reconnaissance missions or ambushes, rappelling, and basically, any and everything the two Special Forces veterans could think of including dangling beneath a helicopter on a 100-foot-long rope to simulate an Mcguire Rig extraction. When a landing zone wasn't available, or a team was surrounded by an enemy force a team could be yanked out of the jungle on the long ropes and flown to safety.

Tossed in the dawn to dusk mix was a healthy amount of harassment that wore into the butt-dragging drills and demanding training. And, of course, there was the daily shit burning detail from the company's four seater outhouse and the Base Camp perimeter guard duty they pulled at night. The training, harassment, and literal shit job proved to be too much for the bulk of the volunteers to overcome; those who couldn't take it dropped out.

Romeo Company's condensed selection course was physically and mentally challenging because it had to be, since the cadre only had less than three weeks to teach what the potential new Rangers would need to know to effectively function and carry out the long range behind the line combat missions. Could the new volunteers work in five to six-man teams, shouldering an 80 to 100 pound rucksack load, plus the weight of their web gear and weapons in ninety-plus degree sweltering heat humping through in the jungle maze? Could they land navigate with a map and a compass through dense rainforests, carry out recon or hit and run ambush missions, fight, and then find their way to a preplanned or hastily selected pickup zone? Then, upon extraction from the jungle with the enemy in tow, and after a one to two-day stand down, could they gear up and do it all over again? More critical lessons would come from on-the-job training one patrol after another.

The daily weeding-out process during the training cycle sent most of the volunteers packing. Of the 38 GIs who showed up for the company's inaugural course, only six successfully completed the training. Four of the seven formed Romeo Company's first official Lurp team with First Sergeant Poplawski serving as their team leader and Sergeant Shintaku as the Assistant Team Leader. Poplawski was kicking the tires to see who stood out and which techniques needed to be fine- tuned.

With R Company's radio callsign being *Valhalla*, the radio callsign for the first team became *Longboat Nine-One*. The next selection course graduates soon became team *Longboat Nine-Two*, with the numerical designators changing with each team from the course of graduates that followed. Shintaku became the unit's first team leader with other standout Rangers taking on Team Leader and Assistant Team Leader positions.

In short order, but perhaps not short enough for the impatient Headquarters command, Romeo Company had enough suitable new Rangers to field two more Longboat teams. Eventually, they would have five operational teams in total, giving the Company's combined strength at 55. Of that number, 50 were all young, enlisted volunteers in their late teens and early twenties, straight out of high school, college, big cities, and gritty inner cities, small towns, back country rural routes or farmsteads, or, as some critics believed, pirate colonies and jails. That was fine with Captain Robison and First Sergeant Poplawski who subscribed to the belief that saints generally came from good sinners.

Surprisingly, three-quarters of those new Lurps were two-year Draftees. Most were 18 to 21-year-old white kids with a sprinkling of Blacks, Hispanics, Pacific Islanders, and second and even third generation Asian Americans in this latest Children's Crusade. The religious mix here were Baptists, Methodists, Jews, Catholics, semi-Catholics, several Mormons, a Jack Mormon, one Buddhist, and when bullets flew, at least one or two not quite committed atheists.

Those who had never interacted previously with someone from a different religion, race, or social or economic background suddenly found themselves having to live, work, and fight together. Biases, doubts, and prejudices slowly gave way to the individual players whose actions would define who and what they were to each other. They didn't always have to like each other, and at times, hadn't. The commonality, the one strong link that bound them together, was the in-country Ranger Lurp training and what it took to make it into the company and onto a team. Then, any notion of genuine brotherhood began being tempered and forged in the firefights they faced as teammates.

Teamwork was essential because with only a handful of team members on patrol, when a fight came at them deep in the Viet Cong jungle sanctuaries, in Charlie's proverbial backyard, the fighting was always close-in and intense. All too often Hell was only the next push of several branches with broad leaves away when the stink of rotten egg, sulfur-smelling gun smoke and the agonizing screams from the wounded and dying came in an instant at Point Blank range. Still, the Ranger teams gambled and rolled the dice, one long range patrol mission and the next. They led the way because that was who they were.

The Ranger motto, *Rangers Lead the Way*, was born at the cliffs of Pointe du Hoc in Normandy on D-Day. Of the 225 Rangers from the 2nd Ranger Battalion who made the climb on June 6, 1944, 77 were killed and 125 were wounded in the vicious fighting. Several months earlier at the fight for Cisterna, Italy, in the Battle of Anzio, the 767 Rangers in the 1st and 3rd Ranger Battalions, and the 3rd Reconnaissance Troop who led the way suffered 311 killed with 450 taken prisoner over the course of the vicious fighting. In the Philippines a Ranger unit along with Alamo Scouts and Filipino guerrillas conducted a behind the lines raid on a Japanese Prisoner of War camp rescuing hundreds of emaciated captives.

While the end of World War II saw an end to the combat Ranger units in the Army they were resurrected five years later during the next war in Korea. 14 Light Infantry Ranger Companies were formed at Fort Benning, Georgia with six seeing combat in the distant and then land of the not so morning calm. Carrying out bold behind the line raids, critical blocking maneuvers, and ambushes these new Rangers were always at the forefront of the fight when it came to special operations.

The 1st Ranger Company destroyed the 12th North Korean Division Headquarters Command in a bold night raid, and on Hill 205, 51 Rangers from the Eighth Army held off five separate human wave assaults from six enemy battalions before their ever dwindling numbers of 10 dead, 31 wounded, and a critical shortage of ammunition forced them to retreat against the overwhelming ten to one odds. A high cost always came with being a combat Ranger, and in this latest war, the bill for wearing the red, black, and white 75th Infantry Regiment scroll shoulder patch was still being tallied.

Chapter 1

Saigon, 1971-

If the fickle gods of war zone Military Transportation hadn't actually graced them this morning, then they at least gave the two Army Rangers favorable nods.

Today it only took Captain Robison and First Sergeant Poplawski a little over an hour to get from their Ranger Company compound at Camp Mackie high up in III Corps down to Saigon and over to MAC-V Headquarters to attend a scheduled briefing.

Their commute began with a wind-whipped, open-door Huey helicopter flight down to the joint U.S. Army and Air Force base at Bien Hoa, 19 miles north of the fledgling nation's central government hub. Shortly after the helicopter touched down they caught a cage-windowed military bus that was just leaving from Bien Hoa down, to and through, the chaotic streets of Saigon over to the Tan Son Nhut Military Air Base. There it was just a short, dusty walk, in the already sweltering morning heat to their destination.

The walk laced the black leather toes of their nylon jungle boots with a pale orange patina of road dust, and left dark rings of sweat slowly spreading beneath their armpits and on the lower backs on their jungle fatigues. The morning was more than muggy. A punishing, sauna-like high heat and accompanying humidity began pushing and probing against them like invisible fat fingers making them feel like walking wet sponges. No matter where they were stationed in Vietnam, GIs felt like they were just one good shower away from actually feeling clean immediately after a shower. These two were no exception.

The military meteorologists predicted that by mid-afternoon the worst of the seasonal heat would settle and hold in the high 90s with a high humidity index level. A heat advisory was sent out warning that by 1500 hours the double hit combination of the rising heat and humidity would become life threatening. The one-two punch would stop someone from sweating, raise an individual's body temperature higher than the outside temperature, and cause cramping, dizziness, and nausea- all symptoms and deadly signs of Heat Stroke. GIs were advised to stay hydrated, wear head covers outdoors, and forego strenuous physical activity.

With little to no breeze coming out of the South China Sea, the high season hold would not give up its grip until later in the evening. To most GIs it seemed that Vietnam didn't have four distinct seasons, just a four cycle sequence of wet, wetter, hot, and really, really dog breath in your face hot. The transition today was moving into the hotter cycle, but for those in-country the war was still business as usual, sweating or no sweating.

Generally, the trip down to MAC-V Headquarters from Camp Mackie for the 1300 hours or one o'clock briefings took them ninety minutes and change, depending upon the ever changing twists and turns of the war, available outbound transportation, the weather, and, of course, the undeniable accuracy behind the military maxim that *'whatever can go wrong, will go wrong, so plan for the worst and hope for the best.'*

A rescheduled time change for today's briefing, though, had them leaving Camp Mackie earlier than normal on the morning mail run. The *best* was the better availability of morning air and vehicle traffic that got them to Tan Son Nhut sooner than their regularly scheduled meetings.

After clearing the Military Police security checkpoint at the main entrance of the Command Center, the two were making their way down the freshly waxed and buffed hallway toward their assigned briefing room when the First Sergeant gave his Company Commander a cynical side eye.

"You know, Sir," Poplawski said. "And please bear with me on this, Captain, because this is just a thought, mind you."

"A thought, is it?"

"Yes sir, it is. One that perhaps might better serve military efficiency and combat mission performance too, I might add."

"Okay, First Sergeant, in the name of efficiency and mission performance you may add," said the Captain, playing along. Robison was always amazed and appreciated how Poplawski had the uncanny knack to Occam's Razor the heck out of any issue to cut to the chase and find the simplest, if not more efficient and direct run at a solution, albeit with his usual bent toward sarcasm. "What's your observation and time saving and job enhancement suggestion? Let me hear it."

"Well Sir, I'm thinking that maybe instead of them having us come all the way down here once a month for these briefings, maybe they could just, oh, I dunno, send us a *fucking* memo."

"You think that would do it, do you?" Robison said, chuckling.

"Given all the critical wisdom they generally impart and bless our way at these Dog & Pony Shows, why Yes sir, I do."

"What? You don't like to hear about the latest prizes for Bingo Night at the Embassy or say, updating your military driver's license in one of the many offices in this giant labyrinth?"

"Hmm? Didn't know we needed them in a war zone."

"The Bingo prizes or military driver's license?"

"Either. Both."

"Well, there are war zones and there are war zones, First Sergeant."

"Yes sir, I can tell by the on-site tennis court, movie theater, and cheeseburger smelling snack bars they have here, not to mention flush toilets and these wonderfully waxed corridor floors. In fact, these floors are so shiny and mirror-like I can damn near see my petty resentment in them."

"You do realize we fall under MAC-V's chain-of-command regardless of where we're actually stationed, so…"

"Play nice?"

"Or at least, play along."

"They say what this latest get-together is about, Sir? The start time is earlier than normal."

"No, they didn't, just that they emphasized this one was mandatory and that we be here by no later than Zero-nine-thirty hours."

"They maybe forget the commute and all, and maybe that we were lucky enough to hop a ride with a helicopter making a mail run to Bien Hoa this morning without it getting shot down by those always determined pesky little yellow fellows?"

"Pesky little yellow fellows? I take it by that you mean the Viet Cong?"

"Yes sir, them, and none that I've seen lately who'll ever take gold in the Olympic high jump competition or make it in the starting line up with the Celtics, Lakers, or Pistons."

"True, but here they seem to have the home court advantage."

"That they do, Sir. And they do seem to favor technical fouls."

"And no free throws for us. But once the briefing is over and we're done here, we'll make our way over to Long Binh and check in on our people. You have the berets?"

"Right here, Sir," Poplawski said, patting both sides of cargo pants pockets. "I had the Supply Sergeant give me four new ones with the *Sua Sponte* crest patch sewn on."

"Outstanding!"

"Maybe if there're no more follow-up surgeries they'll let us see them today?"

The Ranger officer agreed with a grunt and nod. Four of their people were laid up in hospital beds in an Evacuation Hospital eleven miles away in Long Binh and Robison and Poplawski needed to check in to see how they were doing after their surgeries. This mandatory meeting at MAC-V Headquarters was getting in the way of their pre-planned visits.

The Headquarters briefings generally were in the early afternoon, so they had made plans for the hospital visits before the briefing at MAC-V headquarters until the call had come informing them of the time change for the briefing.

"Command would like you here by no later than Zero-nine thirty hours, Captain," said the junior officer making the call and passing along the message.

"Zero-nine thirty?"

"Yes sir."

"Is there any way we can get out of the briefing, Lieutenant? We have several of our people in the hospital we need to check in on."

"I'm sorry, Sir, but the Colonel said you're required to attend the morning briefing. Said it's mandatory. If it's any consolation, the briefing will be shorter than normal."

"Roger that, Lieutenant. We'll be there," said the Ranger Captain, not liking the answer but knowing the Colonel had the final say. The briefings normally ran an hour or so which would still leave plenty of time for him and his First Sergeant to make a beeline trip over to the Evacuation Hospital before catching a ride back up to Camp Mackie.

One left turn and another long corridor later they stepped through the opened doorway of their Liaison Office's briefing room. The rows of chairs normally facing the podium on the small platform had been stacked on the left and right sides of the room. The two Rangers also noticed that the audience standing in a horseshoe formation around the room was somewhat larger than any of the previously attended briefings. Odd as well, they were receiving an unusual amount of courteous smiles and almost convincing appreciative nods on their approach. That, of course, had the Captain and First Sergeant somewhat confused and more than a little suspicious of what this early morning briefing was actually about. It also had Poplawski feeling like he was in one those nature documentaries where several studly Wildebeest had just stepped into a river crossing while a line of rear area crocodiles mud-slid into the water and began closing in around them. This audience too was all smiles and teeth.

They'd been called down to MAC-V ostensibly for a command briefing, because on paper, Company R-Ranger, fell under the command of MAC-V headquarters, but not MAC-V SOG. That was something both the Captain and First Sergeant lamented over when the new Ranger Company was first formed. MAC-V SOG, *'Studies and Observations Group'* were, in reality, clandestine special operations teams that conducted daring and deadly missions deep behind the lines in Cambodia, Laos, and North Vietnam. They, at least, would've better understood the Ranger Company's true mission and purpose.

The Ranger First Sergeant was correct with his take on today's briefing. The monthly meetings at MAC-V Headquarters were mostly informational or ceremonial, and perhaps served to remind those in attendance who was actually in charge of Romeo Company's operational fate. Thankfully, the briefing coincided with their plan to check in on their wounded in the Evacuation Hospital, albeit later than the two had hoped for. To Robison and Poplawski the hospital visits held a higher, if not, more important priority than the monthly briefing. They, however, didn't dictate the play. MAC-V Command did, so first, the briefing, then, the hospital visits.

It was Colonel Lubben, their MAC-V Headquarters Liaison Commander, who acknowledged Robison and Poplawski as they entered the briefing room.

"Ah! You're early! Good! Then let's get started. Gentlemen, please," said the Colonel, calling them to the front of the room and motioning where he wanted them to stand.

Unbeknownst to the two Rangers this particular monthly briefing would not be a briefing, but a carrot and stick *thank you/fuck you* event.

The small crowd of attendees that were mostly dressed in short sleeved Class B khaki uniforms closed in behind them. A Spec-4 checking his F-stop on a Nikon camera and attached flash followed their lead before veering off to stand next to a second lower enlisted man, who was standing to the left, and a foot behind the smiling Colonel.

The carrot and *thank you* came in the form of an ATTENTION TO ORDERS command barked out by a First Lieutenant standing off to the side as those in the room came to attention. As the award orders were being read aloud by the young officer, Robison and Poplawski were surprised to hear that they would be receiving Bronze Stars for Meritorious Service. A Specialist-4 walked in from the sidelines holding a tray with the small oblong shaped medal presentation boxes. Colonel Lubben retrieved the first medal, and pinned it to the Captain's chest before doing the same to the Ranger First Sergeant.

The awards for the two Rangers, loudly announced by the junior officer reading the citation, were for their '*Outstanding leadership in combat operations*' in the III Corps Tactical Zone of the Republic of South Vietnam.' That was echoed by the smiling Full Bird Colonel who then praised the two Lurps for their *outstanding* leadership with the unit during the grip and grin photo-op right before the Colonel quietly informed them that their Ranger Company was being disbanded.

Thus, the *fuck you* stick.

"Disbanded, Sir?" said the stunned Ranger Captain.

"Yes, that's correct," said the Colonel with a dismissive, like it or not, sniff. "Due to the drawdown of U.S. troop strength here in the Republic of South Vietnam, command is shutting down your unit in the next fifty-five days, Captain. However, that should not be overshadowed by the fact that over the last ten months, you and your Rangers have done stellar work carrying out *outstanding* behind the lines surveillance work. Truly *outstanding*! Congratulations!"

"Eight months, Sir."

"What?"

"We've only been operational for eight months. We're just beginning our ninth month, Sir."

"All the more outstanding!" said the senior officer, and then not to be deterred or deflected from his rehearsed speech, the Colonel nodded, smiled, and ran with his script. "Then, the prestigious awards for you and your people are all that more impressive!"

"My people?"

"Yes, because there's more," smiled the Colonel. "We're not done yet."

The Colonel went on.

"General Abrams couldn't be here for this ceremony as he got called away to an emergency meeting with Vice President Ky, but he wanted to let you personally know how pleased and impressed he was, and *is*, for your unit's professionalism, dedication to service, and its overall *outstanding* accomplishments."

Outstanding was the latest and highest buzzword compliment the Army was using and overusing these days, thought Poplawski, since saying, *Out Fucking Outstanding* was frowned upon, and *Huzzah* had gone the way of the Dodo bird. Publicly, the Army brass didn't like the use of obscenities, and even had a regulation issued against their utterances.

At the moment Poplawski couldn't recall the exact official title or accompanying numerical designation of the regulation, let alone its full wording, only that it was officially on the books. However, he had recalled the gist of it.

'*Profane, obscene, and/or other immoderate language will not be used or permitted,*' which he thought was somewhat odd since damn near every soldier caught up a firefight in the jungle or stomach and balls deep laying in a shit-smelling rice paddy in a sudden ambush likely never uttered, "*Oh shucks, the Viet Cong are shooting at us again. I'll be darned, they just got Billy and Lamont, and hey, what do you know, my liver's bleeding, too! Gosh, golly, gee, I'm a goner!*"

Poplawski suspected the regulation regarding the use of obscenities was more than likely meant to appease and placate public sentiment or the sensibilities of mixed company discourse in social settings. Never mind, soldiers when need be were trained and encouraged to gut an enemy soldier with a cold-steel bayonet in close-quarter combat bayonet training. The training came with what was called '*the spirit of the bayonet,*' which was a three-word charging shout of '*Kill! Kill! Kill!*' so perhaps it was improper to have a GI swear when they skewered an enemy soldier, twisted the blade, and then boot-kicked the still quivering body to free the bayonet as they shook away any of the attached torn intestines or scraps of bloodied viscera before the soldier moved on to the next target. That, of course, would be unseemly.

The regulation also kept a frustrated Poplawski from angrily shouting out, '*what idiotic, cock-sucking, motherfucking, half-assed, hairbrained, sonofabitch MAC-V REMF shit for brains, decided to shut us down?*' even as the hollow sounding compliments to the two Rangers continued. Just as he was holding back his inner voice, he too was holding back his contempt, but just barely. The muscles in his square-jawed face were trembling like plucked cello strings as the Colonel continued his speech.

"That sentiment was also echoed by Brigadier General Reese, who gave glowing reports of your unit back up at Camp Mackie, which is why Romeo Company is also receiving an impressive honor," he added.

Turning to the Lieutenant who had read the orders, Lubben said, "Lieutenant, please read aloud the next citation."

"ATTENTION TO ORDERS!" called the Lieutenant, once more ordering everyone to come to the military position of Attention before he began reading the documentation he was holding.

"The Valorous Unit Award is awarded to R Company-75th Infantry, MAC-V Command for extraordinary heroism in action against an armed enemy of the United States while engaged in armed conflict..."

There was more military speak and accompanying gratuitous hyperbole, and after the junior officer finished the rest of the prepared text, he gave the date of the order, followed by the name and rank of the approving officer before he turned and handed the Colonel a small, gold framed, red, white, and blue striped ribbon pin along with an accompanying certificate.

The Colonel, in turn, presented both items to Captain Robison. Shaking the Ranger Captain's hand, he held it in place for the pose and practiced smiling for the next Public Affairs '*grip and grin*' photo-op. The enlisted photographer taking the pictures changed his angle and took several more shots until he was sure he had what he needed to chronicle the event.

There were more smiles and applause all around from those in attendance with the exception of Captain Robison and First Sergeant Poplawski, who took the news and awards a little differently than the presenter or the audience. Later, when the film was developed, the eight by ten, black and white photo would show that neither of the Rangers were smiling.

In truth, they were still bewildered by the announcement to disband the unit, poleaxed even, and it was Poplawski who even appeared to be angrily confused by the decision. He was about to offer an unfiltered response to the Colonel when Robison whispered, *"Not now,"* to his First Sergeant. Poplawski drew in a deep breath and slowly let it out. It was his way of counting to 10.

As a West Point graduate, the Captain knew better how to mask his thoughts and emotions than the now dour-looking Poplawski as he accepted the award on behalf of the Ranger Company. Robison was more resigned to acknowledge the bad news since he also knew that the decision came down from upon high, which meant well above the Colonel's pay grade. That also meant there wasn't anything he or his First Sergeant could do or say to change the outcome. Instead, his mind was racing with what all would need to be done with the remaining time they officially had left as Romeo Company. There was much to do.

"Again, congratulations," said the Colonel, drawing Robison's attention back to the moment, ending the ceremony that had also ended Romeo Company's short run.

They were dismissed.

Well, almost.

As the Colonel and the bulk of the attendees exited the office, the Colonel's red-faced Aide approached the Ranger Captain and intimidating looking First Sergeant with a quiet and awkward request.

"Sir?"

"Yes, Lieutenant?"

"I'm…I'm afraid we need the medals back."

"Say again, Lieutenant?"

"The Bronze Stars medals, Sir. They're…they're only for the ceremony, Sir," he said to the Captain in an almost inaudible apologetic tone and then quickly added, "Copies of the orders will be entered into your military personnel files and the actual medals will be issued at a later date."

"The Army giveth, and the Army taketh away," sighed the First Sergeant as he removed the medal and handed it over to the Lieutenant.

"The Valorous Unit Award, though, is yours to take back to your unit."

"Thank you, Lieutenant, because if you asked for that back then you would've had to wrestle us for it," said Robison, placing the Valorous Unit Award citation ribbon in his top pocket.

"Damn straight," muttered Poplawski, staring at the now uncomfortable Lieutenant. "And we're one tough tag team!"

The Captain and First Sergeant removed the small bronze star shaped medals with the attached red ribbons and handed them over to the now rattled Colonel's Aide who seemed to be concentrating unusually hard on carefully replacing the two medals back in their presentation boxes for future presentations.

"Then I guess we're done here," said Captain Robison to his First Sergeant who gave a slight nod and started to follow his Commanding Officer out of the room.

"Sir?"

"Yes Lieutenant?" Robison said, turning back.

"There's…there's, eh, coffee and donuts in the back of the room."

Robison nodded. "Naw, we're good. Aren't we, First Sergeant? We good?"

The Ranger Company's First Sergeant sneered and grunted something that could've easily been construed as, *'Yes sir'* or possibly, *'fuck your donuts.'*

The two Rangers exited the briefing room. Like a boxer who'd just finished a difficult twelve rounds and lost by a bad decision, Poplawski was slumped-shouldered and brooding as they made their way back down the long highly polished corridor, and back out of the building's main entrance.

Exiting the headquarters' building and stepping back out into the high heat and harsh, glaring sunlight only added to their physical annoyance. The Valorous Unit Award was welcomed even if the disbanding of Romeo Company wasn't.

As they passed several highly polished military sedans parked out front, and paralleling the modern two-storied headquarters facility, there was time and space to talk candidly.

"Sweet Jesus, Captain, what the hell was that?" said the frustrated Poplawski out of ear shot of anyone nearby.

"Our marching orders, apparently," said Robison.

"More like *wham, bam, thank you, mam, and oh, don't let the door hit you on the ass on your way out.*"

"I believe Edward Gibbon in The Rise and Fall of the Roman Empire called it, *the vicissitudes of fortune*," said the Ranger Captain. "The ups and downs."

"Definitely the downs," agreed Poplawski.

Robison nodded but there was another more pressing matter to attend to. "Come on, First Sergeant. Let's see if we can catch a ride over to Long Binh and check in on our people."

The *'our people,'* of course, were the four seriously wounded Rangers from their unit that had been Medevaced to the 93rd Evacuation Hospital in Long Binh during the previous few days. A fifth Ranger had been killed in action in a vicious fight involving one of the two teams on patrol in the jungle. The five losses were a heavy blow to Romeo Company that barely had forty Rangers they could field for combat patrols at any given time.

Among those surviving casualties were two experienced team leaders, one assistant team leader, and a new guy who had only been in Vietnam for less than a month when he triggered a booby trap explosive device on his very first long range patrol. His war ended just twenty-seven days into his 365 day scheduled tour of duty.

Because of the severity of their wounds, the likelihood of finding all four still in the evacuation hospital were, at best, low. Lower still because of the briefing they had been required to attend. Medical evacuation flights tended to go out early in the morning. Generally, the patient evacuation policy was that after emergency surgery, and once a soldier's wounds or burns were stabilized, the soldier, sailor, marine or airman was airlifted to a second military surgical hospital in Japan for the next round of surgeries, treatments, and physical therapies. Some, though, were flown stateside to the Letterman Army Medical Center in San Francisco or to the Walter Reed Army Medical Center in Bethesda, Maryland.

Still, the Captain and First Sergeant would try to track down their people in the Evacuation hospital, and that meant they would first need to find transportation for the ride from Tan Son Nhut to Long Binh.

First Sergeant Poplawski figured that given the number of military vehicles delivering typewriters, photocopying paper, paper clips, staplers, pens, pencils, five-gallon water cooler bottles, pallets of beer and soft drinks, and bucket loads of hand cream and hand towels to wipe down all the brown nosing going on at the base as well as at MAC-V Headquarters, the odds were better than good at finding a ride near the main gate area or in and around the general vicinity.

Since MAC-V was collocated at the Tan Son Nhut Air Base, it would be just a matter of thumbing a ride. The morning temperature was now pushing 90 degrees and they were sweating again as they began their search.

Chapter 2

Over the course of its operational time individual team members in Romeo Company had earned four Silver Stars for Gallantry, thirteen Bronze Stars for Heroism, and 15 Army Commendation Medals for Valor. In addition, 18 members of the unit would be awarded Purple Hearts for minor, non-life threatening wounds, the rips and tears and the near misses from incoming machine gun rounds, shrapnel from RPG blasts or grenade fragments in sudden ambushes and firefights. A number of Lurps had even received multiple Purple Hearts for additional non-life threatening wounds while remaining in the company and still shouldering rucksacks.

However, the many bumps, bruises, bug bites, sprains, fractured or broken bones, pulled muscles, cuts, scrapes, and even the suffered bouts of malaria from the grueling five-day, non-enemy contact patrols in the jungle, didn't merit Purple Hearts from the military. That was all considered par for the course, all just the expected norm of their everyday job.

Eight months in and Romeo Company hadn't lost any of their people to serious injuries or wounds. Nor had any of their people been K-I-A, Killed in Action, a rarity given the long range patrols they carried out in the enemy occupied jungles and the number of running gun battles they were involved in. Their luck was holding, but it couldn't last. War was always a gamble, and when the luck finally broke, Romeo Company bled deep.

On one day, on one agonizing afternoon, two of the Company's teams, minutes, and miles apart, took heavy hits.

Specialist-4 Jonas Warren, walking Point Man for Lurp Team Nine-Three, had just pushed aside some heavy leaves and brush away from a small rise in front of him only to step into the middle of a ten man squad of Viet Cong fighters taking a rest break on a small, unmarked trail.

In the sudden, startling moment by Warren, and the panicked shouts from two of the Viet Cong fighters seated directly in front of him that had the enemy soldiers grabbing at their assault rifles and whatever else they could find to kill the American, the fight for life was on.

"CONTACT FRONT!" the big man shouted over his shoulder to Staff Sergeant Tommy Wade, Nine-Three's Team Leader who was a few steps behind him. Warren fired on the first Viet Cong soldier who was seated but still trying to bring up his AK-47 as the close quarter firefight erupted and chaos ensued.

For Warren there was no cover, and it was too late to retreat, so the big man took on the fight screaming literal bloodied murder. Left with no choice, all he could do now was fight, and fight as ugly and as brutally savagely as he could.

The first enemy soldier he shot was down writhing on the ground as a second Viet Cong fighter sprang at him with an upraised spiked bayonet on his AK-47.

Slapping the bayonet and assault rifle aside with the barrel and frame of his rifle but unable to bring his M-16 backup on target in time, Warren kicked the enemy soldier as hard as he could to stop the assault. He was aiming at his balls, but his jungle boot missed, and the front kick slammed into the man's right hip instead. Still, it was enough to send him falling back onto the ground, but it wasn't enough to get him to drop his rifle. The Viet Cong fighter hurriedly brought it up on target.

Realizing what was coming next Warren pivoted left as he stiff armed his Team Leader, who came charging in behind him. The stiff arm hit knocked Sergeant Wade on his ass just as the fighter let loose a burst of automatic gunfire. In the staggered Ranger file formation, the team was in, the heavy rounds that just missed Warren and Wade, tore into Specialist-4 Leon Hagar behind Wade just as he too was charging forward to enter the fight. Hagar's legs were shot out from under him, and the impact of the assault rifle's heavy rounds butchered his front thigh muscles and splintered the leg bones. Hagar fell back screaming.

Warren shot the shooter, stitching him in the right hand, arm, and shoulder. Several of the rounds that had missed the enemy soldier shattered his rifle stock and sent the AK-47 flying. A scream from his left had Warren turning on the trail and firing on another of the surprised Viet Cong fighters who was still fumbling with his weapon's leaf spring lever desperately trying to flip it down from SAFE to FIRE. The soldier crumpled and the threat was gone. Warren then turned his aim in on yet one more enemy soldier ten feet away who was bringing up an RPG rocket propelled grenade launcher to his shoulder to fire. A sustained burst from his M-16 caught the soldier from his right hip to his upper chest and blew out his neck. With his finger on the trigger the momentum as he stumbled back sent the shoulder fired rocket high and wide where it exploded well up into the trees.

The big Lurp was quickly aiming in on a small group of the Viet Cong who were taking cover behind a termite mound further on only to find his rifle bolt locked back. His 20 round magazine had emptied. Reaching for a new magazine from an ammo pouch, he dumped the empty magazine and was about to slam the new one in place when the Viet Cong fighter he had only wounded rose up and swung a heavy machete blade deep into Warren's right leg. The thick blade, hammered out from a broken truck spring, caught, and stuck in the American's calf muscle and bone as the wounded Viet Cong fighter twisted the thick blade trying to free it for another strike. With an agonizing, almost feral cry, Warren turned and shot the soldier again this time killing him, only before he could turn back around to face the remaining fighters, he was hit in his chest with a burst of automatic rifle fire. Staggering back from the impact of the hits and spitting blood, Warren took a second burst of enemy gunfire. The big man died toppling over with the crude machete still stuck in his leg.

With the weight of his 95 pound rucksack countering his own body weight and still holding him down, Wade was struggling to get to his feet and stay in the fight. The best he could do, though, was sit up and shoot a lone Viet Cong fighter who was charging in on the rest of the team. While he shot and dropped the attacker Wade was hit moments later by small arms fire coming in blind through the foliage from his left. The thick brush and jungle that had obscured the unmarked trail had also hidden the remaining enemy fighters who were firing where they thought the Americans might be as they regrouped and retreated back down the trail. Had the Viet Cong known that they were only up against a five man team and that three of them were down, they might've carried on the fight. But with the two remaining Lurps laying down a storm of suppressing small arms fire, the Viet Cong survivors made their getaway dragging away their own wounded. The dead lay where they fell.

Both sides had taken too many hits to continue the fight and within minutes the small sudden firefight was over. Five of the Viet Cong and Specialist-4 Jonas Warren littered the awkwardly silent small trail. With one new team member pulling out bandages and trying his best to treat the badly wounded Team Leader and Assistant Team Leader the second surviving Lurp called in the CONTACT and sent out a request for a much needed Medevac helicopter to pull out the casualties. Both calls were immediately acknowledged with a return call saying that a Quick Reaction Force was being sent in to safeguard the Lurp Team, evacuate the wounded, and secure the site of the firefight.

Meanwhile miles away, in a neighboring Province and a third of the way down the *Nui Ba Den*-The Black Virgin mountain, Sergeant Darrell Thomas, a Team Leader for Longboat Team Nine-Four, and Private First Class Pete Norse who was on his very first Ranger patrol, were chasing after an NVA soldier who had slipped into a tunnel when Norse triggered a boobytrap.

The hidden explosive charge partially collapsed the tunnel and sent a plume of dirt, dust and rock shooting out of the channel's entrance like a giant shotgun blast startling the remaining team members who hadn't yet reached the entrance. When the dust settled and as two of the Lurps provided security Specialist-4 Harry Li, Nine-Four's Assistant Team Leader, scrambled inside the tunnel and immediately began digging his forward trying to get to the two missing team members. However, Li only managed to locate and drag out the badly injured new guy from beneath a mound of rubble and dirt in the collapsed mess.

Thomas, who was further into the tunnel than Norse before the explosion, couldn't be reached, let alone rescued. Loose rock and dirt and heavy slabs of granite came down blocking the way forward. There was no way Li nor anyone else, short of mining tools and drills, could push through the blockage to reach him, if he was still alive.

A Quick Reaction Force, including a team of Engineers, were flown in under enemy fire to help to try to locate and rescue the missing Team Leader or, fearing the worst, to extricate the body. Several attempts were made to reach Thomas without success. What remained of the tunnel was shaky at best and threatening to come down at any moment. Dirt was spilling down from the tunnel's ceiling making it look like a giant overturned hourglass. The supports that were holding up the rest of the roof and walls were bent, splintered, and worse, creaking.

After checking out the outside ground above the tunnel and crawling in and evaluating the fragile situation, the now worried Engineers voiced their concerns. What little remained of the tunnel, they said, would soon some down. The flow of the soil was increasing, and a total collapse was inevitable, if not imminent. And there was more bad news.

If Thomas hadn't died in the explosion and the initial cave in, then any further attempts to dig through the heavy stone and debris would only bring down more of the mountain on top of him and very likely, any of the rescuers. Against their advice Captain Robison needed to see it for himself. Borrowing a flashlight from one of the Engineers he crawled into what remained of the tunnel and began searching without success as the flow of dirt increased and fell. He barely managed to get out before it completely caved in. The rescue and recovery mission was called off and upon his return back to Camp Mackie the frustrated Ranger Captain would have to officially list Thomas as Missing-In-Action and Presumed Dead.

The once missing and presumed dead Team Leader, though, somehow had survived the explosion and cave in. Partially buried beneath some loose rock and dirt, he dug and crawled his way forward and found himself inside a vast tunnel complex and enemy occupied cave system. The bruised and battered Texan avoided capture and 36 hours later found a way out of the mountain where he was rescued by a passing Scout helicopter several miles away from the Nui Ba Den.

It wasn't an easy rescue either. The missing Lurp was shot in the upper right chest and shoulder in a running gun battle with the Viet Cong when the small helicopter swooped in with cover fire, touched down to a hover, and pulled in the weary and bleeding, and oh-so-thankful Ranger. Once airborne, and realizing the serious nature of Thomas' wound, the Scout pilot immediately flew him to the nearest Army Field Hospital in Tay Ninh before he was transferred that same evening to the 93rd Evacuation Hospital in Long Binh for a second, more complicated surgery.

One dead and four critically wounded Rangers in one damn day.

Captain Robison and First Sergeant Poplawski hurried their pace. The Evacuation Hospital was still eleven miles away.

Chapter 3

While there was a scheduled bus service from Tan Son Nhut to the U.S. Army's Long Binh Post, the bus hadn't yet returned to the Air Base, so rather than wait they decided to thumb a ride to get where they needed to go. Busy as the military side of the Tan Son Nhut Air Base was, it didn't take long to find an outbound vehicle. An empty three-quarter ton truck that had just made its latest supply run to Tan Son Nhut was heading back to the Post's logistics center when the driver came to a brake squealing stop next to the two hitch-hiking Rangers near the gate.

"Where you headed, Captain?" said the driver through the open passenger side window. The driver was a smiling, skinny, pimply-faced Specialist-4.

"Long Binh, if you're going that way."

"I am, Sir. Hop in!"

"Thank you. It's much appreciated."

Three men in the front seat of a three-quarter ton truck with a floor mounted stick shift would've made for a cramped and uncomfortable ride so Poplawski deferred and happily climbed up into the truck bed as the Ranger Captain climbed in the passenger's seat to ride shotgun. Sitting on a bench seat in the back of the small truck, Poplawski pulled out what was left of his half-smoked Cuban cigar and his Zippo lighter. Propping his left arm up on the wooden railing, and sat back to take in the scenery and the drive.

"Where you going on Post, Sir?"

"The Evacuation Hospital."

"Which one, Sir? There's two, the 24th and 93rd."

"The 93rd."

"No problem, Captain! I'm driving right by it. I can drop you off at its front door."

"That would be great! Thank you."

"You're welcome, Sir."

The route out of Saigon through its crowded streets was teeming with the everyday hustle and frenzied urban life that seemed so alien and out of place to Poplawski who was used to the jungle-covered domain that surrounded Camp Mackie. The war may have been going on for almost a decade but so was everyday life, and with nearly 1,500 years of one war, or another, the resilient Vietnamese carried on with their daily routines. This morning they were laughing, shouting, and calling to friends as they were hawking wares and loudly carrying on living.

The drive was stop-and-go traffic in one of Saigon's congested and cramped streets, which gave him time to take in the show. The sightseeing visuals here came with interesting odors and a unique Southeast Asian soundtrack. A swarm of buzzing motor bikes and puttering scooters that sounded like angry chainsaws set the background track for the cars, jeeps and trucks with questionable mufflers and the diesel engine trucks and buses that sputtered clouds of exhaust and knocked out the beat to the songs of the street.

Open storefronts and sidewalks were alive and bustling with an army of vendors manning makeshift stalls that lined both sides of the busy street. Every now and then Poplawski caught sight of young, willowy women dressed in miniskirts and revealing tops outside of dingy looking bars flirting with a few beer drinking GIs seated at simple outdoor tables on straight back chairs. While some of the women were attractive enough and a few even beautiful, he found himself drawn to and appreciating the more modest young women dressed in the traditional Vietnamese *Ao Dai*, the silk-like, long white trousers, and colorful flowing blouses with the ubiquitous *Non La*, slanted, rattan and bamboo conical sun hats tied down with black ribbons under their delicate chins. The women didn't so much as walk but rather sensually flowed with a certain elegant style and grace. Just down from the storefronts and bars a number of older women in black trousers and short sleeve working blouses sat on small plastic chairs on the uneven pavement or squatted on their haunches behind sidewalk displays, makeshift markets, or outdoor eateries.

The items on offer were laid out in rows on the sidewalks; packs and cartons of American cigarettes and Zippo cigarette lighters, fifths of Jim Beam or Jack Daniels, bottles of Coca Cola or Orange Crush sodas, and *Ba muoi Ba,* number *'33'* beer, rested next to stacked bars of Ivory soap, heaps of flip-flop sandals, a riot of colorful plastic bowls. There were woks, pans, and assorted spatulas, ladles, and hand-held soft fan straw brooms for sale as were lines of bamboo and coconut chopsticks, packets of nine, ten, and eleven incense sticks, small bottles of rosewater oils and perfumes, and other everyday commodities arranged for interested onlookers or prospective buyers.

Improvised produce stands held weaved baskets and colorful yellow and red plastic tubs that were piled high and overflowing with melons, limes, papayas, dried peppers, stacks of lettuce or herbs, lemon and lime leaves, garlic bulbs, bunches of cilantro, and wet green and white bulb scallions that were freshly washed and glistening in the sunlight. There were ice-filled tubs with rows of eels, fish, and newly harvested shrimp laid out as were the wicker baskets of stir-fried and flavored scorpions, crickets, bee larvae, and silkworms with nearby small bottles of the pungent *nuoc mam* sauce used to flavor the edibles. A few yards on, a Mama-san was squatting over a wooden cutting board holding down a good sized fish with one hand while scraping away the silvery scales with the other. At her side a watery tub held two of her earlier efforts while another showed there was more work to be done. Further on the truck rolled by another woman wiping her brow as she stood over a box-size coal-fired grill that spat and sizzled with spicy chunks of chicken and skewered pork. There were no barkers or advertising needed as wafting clouds of aromatic smoke promised wonderful exotic flavors only to have the choking stench of nearby open sewers the truck was passing soon took it away.

At one corner in front of a dark, twisting alley, a somewhat plump and happy woman chewing on betelnut was stirring a large, boiling pot of Pho that was resting on a grill over glowing coals in the bottom half of a rusted 55 gallon oil drum. Smiling wide though black-stained teeth and gums, her customers were milling around and waiting on the spicy soup dish. In the slow go traffic they were passed by bicycles doubling as pushcarts and delivery vehicles, that were packed high with crates and cages holding squawking chickens, ducks, or morose looking, soon to be eaten dogs, by chain-smoking men in stained white, wife-beater tee-shirts, dark trousers, and flip-flops who weaved around the slower road and pedestrian traffic.

Poplawski grinned and chuckled when he spied a five-year-old, naked from the waist down toddler laughing with great joy as he was chasing after a zig-zagging chicken trying to pee on it, hitting, but mostly missing, the startled bird.

Life, indeed, was going on, even in war zones, and those caught up in it on the streets of Saigon were doing their best to carry on living and surviving under the always ominous man-made threatening cloud of war. But then Vietnam experienced nearly two thousand years of war against the Chinese, Mongols, themselves a few times, the Khmers, Chams, French, Japanese, the French again, this time with the Republic of South Vietnam and the Americans and their anti-communist Allies. This war too would inevitably end and life to the Vietnamese people, scars, and all, would still go on.

Poplawski had always found the Vietnamese to be industrious and hardworking people, hustling too, for that matter, and while some GIs might bitch that their Vietnamese ARVN Army counterparts were slow to enter into a fight or fray at times, he suspected that perhaps when you're caught up in a seemingly forever war, you might also become a little more reluctant or cautious about rushing into a fight. He even recalled hearing something about what the number of military losses for the South Vietnamese were at, and was startled that the count was pushing over one million. For the Vietnamese on both sides of the fight there was no one-year or 13 month tour of duty. They were in it for the long haul and the haul would always be costly.

The truck rolled on and although the ride allowed for a little sightseeing and occasional gawking, Poplawski also kept a look out for any potential threats or trouble. In the crowded city it wasn't unheard of to be sniped at by a Viet Cong assassin lying in wait on a rooftop or from an open window, or someone signaling one of his or her brethren who was leaning against a second-storied French balcony railing, that it was time to drop a burning rag-fused Molotov Cocktail onto a passing American vehicle.

Any successful ambush required patience, and perhaps a better target to show itself. It was just as possible to have someone on a passing motorbike toss a grenade or make-shift bomb into the cab of the truck or the truck bed before speeding off and disappearing in the heavy street traffic. Boom! Gone! That wasn't a daily or even weekly occurrence, but it had happened enough in the past to have many of the military buses fitted with screen cages over the windows to protect against those types of attacks.

That possibility and other nasty little scenarios were playing out on the Ranger First Sergeant's mind, while the holstered Ithaca model 1911, A-1, .45 caliber semi-auto handgun he had on his pistol belt provided some additional sense of relief and personal security. If push came to shove he was ready for a little payback. A .45 caliber round or two made for big holes with the kind of knockdown power that made it an effective combat handgun. And after the eight round magazine emptied out and when there was no time to load in another magazine in a close quarter fight, he also knew the heavy handgun made for a convincing head thumper. It wasn't a hammer, but it was hefty enough to hammer the point home that the user wanted you out of commission.

However, the Detroit native soon chuckled and dismissed any notion of a serious threat happening today because he was also well aware that the Viet Cong likely wouldn't attack a few GIs in a near-empty open truck bed. Naw, the odds were better than good that any ambushers would wait for a better target of opportunity to hit, so the Ranger First Sergeant leaned back against the truck's wooden support railing and chomped and puffed on his cigar as he took in the crowded streets, shadowy alleys, balconies and rooftops, and the city's many interesting lively displays and venues.

When traffic slowed and the truck came to a slow rolling stop near a torrent of traffic at a large roundabout he caught sight of an old woman staring up at him from the cracked and uneven sidewalk. Squatting on her haunches she was pulling and separating sprigs of purple tinted basil from a pile in one basket and placing her finished efforts in another. She paused what she was doing as the truck paused, and when their eyes met, Poplawski nodded and smiled. The smile, though, wasn't returned. There was just the stare that was ladened with heavy and prolonged sadness. The traffic cleared and the truck moved on and Poplawski was relieved as it did.

Long Binh may only have been 11 miles away, but the route the driver was taking through the city and outskirts still took a little over 30 minutes. Outside of the city where the urban gave away to the more rural, the road traffic thinned out and the small truck managed to pick up speed. The paved city streets were replaced by a hard-packed gravel road, open countryside, and inevitably to a South Vietnamese Army Military Police checkpoint where some civilian travelers were stopped while their vehicle was waved on.

The small, quarter-ton truck bumped, squeaked, and bounced along the poor highway at best between 25 to 30 miles-per-hour. The only other traffic were military vehicles or farmer's carts which, at times slowed the go. Outside of the city the truck soon began passing small huts and holdings that overlooked plots of freshly ploughed ground, and a series of diked ponds and paddies. In one of the watery paddies a bored looking water buffalo was comfortably resting in the cool, mud-brown water as a barefoot farmer in another paddy was planting thin, green rice seedlings in the ankle deep water from a fat cloth pouch slung across his body. Sunlight shimmered and glistened off of the placid dark water giving it a tranquil setting.

One of four paddies were already planted in precise farmed rows with the bright emerald colored shoots spiking the surface of the flooded fields. The farmer was barely a quarter of the way through planting the second rice paddy as a troupe of Dragonflies flitted and danced across the water behind him in a haphazard ballet.

A third pond waited to be planted while the fourth and much larger pond served as a holding pond with water to service the nearby crops. There was movement in the fourth pond made by fight-for-life ripples and small waves.

"Well now!" Poplawski muttered, catching sight of a mud-brown cobra chasing after a panicking rat trying to evade it through the water. The rodent was swimming as fast as it could trying to escape from becoming the snake's lunch in the soupy ditchwater mix. The quick moving seven-foot-long snake moved in undulating S-shaped waves as it swam after its afternoon entree.

Whether the snake caught and ate the rat wasn't to be seen as the truck picked up speed leaving the environmental buffet offerings closed for the day. The truck rolled and rattled on. The next farm over revealed a circular-shaped paddy with high, mud-dried walls that served as a well-cared for and well-stocked fish pond. Sunlight flickered off of tumbling fins and tails as an weathered old man in shorts pedaled an ancient-looking water wheel to raise the water level in the pond from an adjacent irrigation channel.

With the farm fields and ponds well-maintained, Poplawski suspected the farmers were caught in the squeeze of the fighting. This close to the city the fields could be well-tended and left undisturbed because part of the crop yield would very likely be siphoned off by both sides of the fight. With what remained he would feed his family and sell what was left.

Traffic on the road outside of the city, leading to Long Binh tended to be military vehicles and the three-quarter ton truck's driver expertly avoided collision from the often much larger vehicles using the thin highway.

One advantage the countryside had over the city was that in the open expanse the air was fresh and easier to breathe, while a distinct disadvantage was the rougher, pot-holed roadway that thumped and jostled the truck and those in it, not to mention the occasional wash of diesel fumes and kicked-up dust from the passing vehicles. Poplawski's half-smoked Cuban cigar made for a better filter.

Further up and on the side of the road a burnt-out and rusted M-113 military troop carrier with torn and missing tractor looking tracks and steel scars showed some of the past efforts and accomplishments of the Viet Cong. From the looks of the damage and of what remained, anything of use or value was gone as likely were the lives of its former crew.

Further on, as the main gate at the Long Binh Post came into view, the driver downshifted the gears and the truck rolled to a stop at the security checkpoint. After being cleared by the MPs guarding the main entrance, the truck driver shoved in the clutch and eased the small truck through the gears as he wheeled it towards the evacuation hospital. Because the drive hadn't taken him out of his way, and with more deliveries to make, the truck driver checked his watch and saw that he was still ahead of schedule. He smiled knowing he had time to also stop and pick up a burger and coke at the snack bar once he dropped off the hitchhikers.

The road system on the Long Binh Post was laid out in precise small town fashion and the roads were considerably better than the Vietnamese civilian counterparts, as were the living and working conditions for the GIs assigned to the sprawling base.

This wasn't Robison's nor Poplawski's first time to Long Binh. Over their previous tours of duty, including this one, they had visited the Post at least a dozen times or so for one reason or another. Still, there were many new upgrades and changes to see and take in. The once basic looking military installation was looking more and more like a rural Southern town, sans the town square and statues of long dead generals. From what he could see of it and of its latest changes, Poplawski was thinking that the Long Binh Post made the Camp Mackie base camp look shabby and small, but then most rear area posts and bases in-country did. Army or Air Force Posts or Bases like Tan son Nhut, Bien Hoa, Da Nang, and Cam Ranh Bay were major rear area installations that came with considerably more niceties and clean, albeit low-rent creature comforts.

Camp Mackie, on the other hand, was a forward operating base where *forward* often meant *Spartan*, and where the bulk of the fighting was taking place or very near to it. While the rear area bases were less likely to experience the same kind of war the Grunts, Cannon-cockers Artillerymen, bullet-attracting helicopter pilots and crews did, the bases and those on them, occasionally took their hits. The Long Binh Post wasn't without its share of trouble or scars. A few years back on the TET Lunar New Year a team of Viet Cong saboteurs and sappers had snuck into Long Binh's massive ammo dump and planted a series of timed satchel charges. The satchel charges set off a massive explosion that not only sent debris and car-size metal fragments falling back over the Post in a Hellish rain of blistering hot, dagger-sharp shards, but also an overheated concussive wave from the initial blast that rocked the entire Post that also rattled, shattered, and broke windows as far away as Saigon.

The huge blasts also sent undetonated artillery rounds skyward and had them slamming back down deep into the ground and threatening to explode with the slightest provocation. Those rounds were later carefully picked up or dug out of the ground, made safe, and then moved by the ballsy and overworked EOD- Explosive Ordnance Techs.

Safe as it generally was, occasionally the Long Binh Post was a tempting target for enemy mortar or rocket attacks. That these attacks were nowhere near as frequent or as targeted as the forward Base Camps and Fire Support Bases, where the combat elements that occupied those bases were subjected to incoming enemy 82mm heavy mortars and devastating 122mm Katyusha rocket attacks on a more intense nightly basis, demonstrated that even the comfortable areas were not safe from the war.

In III Corps some of the forward Base Camps like those in Tay Ninh, Quan Loi, and Song Be took on *'Rocket Alley'* monikers for the frequent attacks that were sometimes accompanied by sniper fire, ground probes, or all-out ground attacks with hundreds of enemy soldiers charging the barbwire looking to overrun the smaller camps.

Long Binh was a different kind of warzone but then Vietnam was a different kind of war.

As the largest U.S. facility in the Republic of South Vietnam, the Long Binh Post was a major logistical and administration center that served as the command headquarters for USARV, the United States Army-Republic of Vietnam. It was located between Saigon and Binh Hoa, and just east of the Dong Nai river.

To many of the GIs on Post it was *'the Nam,'* but it was a nicer and cleaner *'the Nam'* than many soldiers in the field would ever know or experience during their tours of duty. Here their day-to-day battles would be wrestling with the oppressive Southeast Asian heat, day-droning boredom, and, of course, the Catch-22 of Army bureaucracy.

To call Long Binh a *Post* too, was almost a misnomer, a technically inaccurate and misleading sounding description that might give civilians back home the impression that it was, perhaps, an *OutPost* in the *Beau Geste,* French Foreign Legion sense, which wasn't the case at all.

This *Post* was a huge installation with over 150 miles of engineered roadways that fronted hundreds upon hundreds of military buildings and other less than permanent structures. For the 60,000 GIs that lived and worked on the Post, a scheduled bus service was set up to better navigate the units and services.

In a typical U.S. Army Brigade, there could be several battalions consisting of anywhere from 3,000 to 5,000 GIs, and the Long Binh Post had more brigades on-site than any other Post or Base Camp throughout the Republic of South Vietnam.

Long Binh also served as the home for a Field Force and Light Infantry Brigade, an Aviation Brigade, various supply, and maintenance depots, the Replacement Station for newly arrived soldiers, a Military Police Brigade, a Medical Brigade with two Evacuations hospitals, a number of dental clinics, and assorted Aid Stations, Dispensaries, and clinics- many of which were on view as the truck rolled along.

Poplawski saw a sign that pointed the way to the Long Binh Stockade. GIs had nicknamed it, *LBJ,* for *the Long Binh Jail*, for the former President who had transformed the once small U.S. Military Advisory role into an all-out American war before he left office. The Stockade held GIs under criminal charges awaiting trial and those completing their *'bad time'* sentences, the incarcerated time that wouldn't count towards their tours of duty or service obligations. The LBJ time was all dead time. When the GI completed his sentence he'd still have to finish up his one year tour of duty. The jail also housed prisoners of more serious crimes who would soon be transferred to the Military Disciplinary Barracks and U.S. Army Prison at Fort Leavenworth, Kansas.

Designed to house four hundred inmates at its peak in 1968, the headcount at *LBJ* then was an overcrowded 800 inmates. That overcrowding led to a deadly riot in the Stockade that fueled the already simmering racial tensions in the jail.

At the time of the riot Poplawski was assigned to the 5th Special Forces Group up north in Nha Trang. News of the riot soon reached all major commands. It was late August then in the coastal city and the summer Monsoon season, when all but ten or eleven days in the month were met with violent storms and flooding.

The Stockade riot had a storm-like violence all its own. Scores of Military Policemen and prisoners were injured in the mayhem, and one prisoner had been beaten to death with a shovel in the takeover of the facility. The riot was finally quelled days later. Over 100 of the rioting prisoners were court-martialed with additional charges and sentences levied on them that were often more serious than their previous sentences for minor crimes such as drug offenses or going AWOL.

Surprisingly, or maybe not so much, given the unpopularity of the war back home, there was little news coverage of the riot at the time. But as is always the case, word leaked out, rumors spread in-country, and *LBJ* became the dreaded jail no GI wanted to be sent to during their time in Vietnam.

The rest of the Long Binh Post, though, was another matter. The large and sprawling Post featured a number of amenities that some might not expect to find in warzones. Here there were swimming pools, handball, tennis, and basketball courts, football and softball fields, several miniature golf courses, a driving range, Bar-B-Que pits, and even an outdoor theater area showing the latest and not-so-latest Hollywood releases.

Sweet Sorrow

There were dozens of snack bars, laundromats, a halfway decent Chinese restaurant, a branch office of the Chase Manhattan Bank, Hobby and Craft shops, and an education center where a GI could take accredited extension college courses from the University of Maryland. Long Binh also had a large '*Post Exchange*' or PX retail store that could rival any large box store back home and exceed sales projections because of its near captive customers. The PX did hundreds of thousands of dollars of business in monthly sales, in everything from low to high-end jewelry, top of the line cameras, Teac reel-to-reel tape recorders, stereo systems with Pioneer box speakers, electric razors, Seiko and Rolex watches, small, compact refrigerators, folding lawn chairs, suitcases, fans and air conditioners, hardcover and paperback books, military and civilian clothing, towels, wash cloths, shaving and grooming products, coffee makers, and a shelf that was stocked with tourist related items such as Vietnam postcards, stationary, replica Montagnard crossbows, Thai fighting swords, and hand-carved, wooden elephants. There were also car salesmen who'd hook a young E-3 or E-4 up with a new car back home, if they came looking.

"Just think of it! You could have a brand new in-violet 1971 Plymouth Barracuda with a V-Code 426 V-8 hemi-engine, 737 TorqueFlight three speed beauty, with black bucket seats, and tinted glass that'll will make for some serious driving enjoyment, son, so sign right here, soldier and the monthly payment will automatically be taken out of your pay, and the car will be waiting for you to pick up when you get back to the World! You won't get a deal like this or anywhere else! Whad'ya say?"

There were bespoke tailors from Hong Kong on site who were taking measurements for new three-piece suits, sports coats, and/or custom-made dress shirts and slacks tailored to exact specifications, with the finest material from brushed leather, tweed to sharkskin, all waiting and ready within a few days! For no extra cost the tailors would also tell buyers that the word *bespoke* meant personalized tailoring in case they forgot to ask.

There was money to be made off of GIs and there were always a wide variety of salesmen around to help them spend it. There was more in Long Binh because there was always more, as each year the war wore on, the *more* became apparent.

The PX shelves also offered portable TVs for sale so GIs in their quarters could watch rerun episodes of *Star Trek* or *Burke's Law* on AFVN, the Armed Forces Vietnam Network in Viet Nam with scheduled TV programs complete with news anchors and even a good looking weather girl. Disc jockeys on the AFVN Radio network played the latest soul, country and western, rock songs, and the highly popular two minute comedy sketches of *Chicken Man* over the radio station's air waves where GIs huddled up around their transistor radios in the distant, forward bases to hear, "*Buck, buck, buck, buuuuuucccck!* CHICKENMANNNNNN! *He's everywhere! He's everywhere!*"

In the off-duty hours, there were Enlisted, NCO, and Officers clubs, with some that featured nightly live band entertainment with scantily clad Go-Go dancers. Most of the bands were Filipino or Korean bands with talented musicians and singers who could play and sing near perfect renditions of Top-40 playlists that could rival any small club or venue in New York, Motown, San Francisco, L.A., or London. Note by note, melody by melody, and with incredible harmonies. Later, and in heavily accented English, a member of the band announced the band would be back to play another set after taking a short *'blake.'*

Many of these service clubs also had first-rate kitchens.

You want a nice steak and eggs? Fresh watermelon on the side to go with it? No problem. How about a tasty burger, onions, pickle, and fresh lettuce, maybe a cold beer? Done? How'za'bout fries?

Poplawski smiled recalling a nice steak and lobster dinner he enjoyed the Post's primary NCO Club in late 1969, although not much else of the rest of the evening readily came to mind as he got hammered that night on one to many Salty Dogs, and left the Post the following morning hungover and salt sweating gin and grapefruit juice. However, he remembered that he was up $50 MPC early on in a poker game, but not what exactly happened to the winnings nor the nearly $150 Military Payment Certificates he had on him at the time. He only vaguely recalled that it might have involved six, maybe seven drinks and going all in with a pair of twos or some such hand. Poplawski sighed at the memory, knowing he couldn't bluff worth a shit.

Further on the three-quarter ton truck passed an on-base steam bath and *'Rub'n'Tug'* massage parlor which brought on a lusty grin from the First Sergeant. The GIs stationed here on Post could get more than their shoulders rubbed, and had, especially on paydays.

Taking it all in, or at least what he could see of it, Poplawski was thinking that in some respects Long Binh was far better than some stateside military posts like Fort Polk, Louisiana, or Fort Jackson, South Carolina where he had once been assigned, during his time and training in the Army. It was no wonder why some GIs here were extending their twelve-month tours of duty at the Long Binh Post simply because it was often better than many of the stateside military bases.

Yeah, he thought, Long Binh really is a *different* kind of warzone all right. The creature comforts here were considerable. But the Ranger First Sergeant shrugged it all off knowing the GIs' Military Occupational Specialties, their jobs in Army speak, dictated the where and how GIs worked and lived while in uniform. Still, he couldn't help but think those here had it nice, and that if they didn't think so and thought otherwise, then perhaps spending some time on a forward Base Camp, Fire Support Base, or humping through the boonies carrying a lower back straining, heavy rucksack that weighed damned near as much as you did might better align their thinking.

Sweet Sorrow

Anyone here or in the Replacement Station could volunteer for the Ranger unit, if so inclined, and one or two of the Company's Lurps had. Part of Staff Sergeant Shintaku's job as the Training NCO was to go down to the Replacement Station and rear area camps once a month to look for volunteers, but the volunteers were few and far in between with the FNGs, and hardly at all from anyone in the rear area posts. Why give up the many amenities and comforts for the always miserable jungle patrols, sudden and close-in firefights, and the one-in-three chance of getting a Purple Heart, which was the Romeo Company's going average.

The many amenities and comforts that came with those rear area postings, far away from the jungle, were why those with the rear area jobs were referred to as *REMFs, Rear Echelon Mother Fuckers*, by the soldiers suffering with skin-dissolving Trench Foot from water-slogged boots and aching shoulders from heavy rucksacks doing the actual fighting in the field. The *field* meant the long foot patrols outside the wire and in the bush, the jungle, and those Artillerymen, Forward Observers, helicopter pilots and air crews in the ring punching it out daily with their opponents who were determined to send them down for the count.

It was taken for granted that everyone in the front line war despised the *REMFs*, however, Poplawski suspected that most grunts or other frontline soldiers in the field, secretly or not so secretly, envied them. Some in the frontlines even reenlisted for those rear area jobs to get out of the field. In doing so, they greatly decreased their odds for not getting wounded or killed. Each person who reenlisted had their own reasons for doing so. Maybe they had enough of the deadly combat, maybe it had to do with the one-too-many times of trudging through the mud or sleeping, or trying to, in the Monsoon rain, or burning leeches off of arms, legs, groins, or armpits with matches, or maybe it was just a pain in the ass Platoon Sergeant, an incompetent Platoon Leader, or seemingly an uncaring Commanding officer who made their tours of duty and lives miserable or put them in unnecessary danger one too many times. There were some who swore that if Dante had been a battle scarred, weathered, and worn-out grunt, he would've added a few new levels of Hell to his Inferno that involved soldiering.

For others an additional benefit to reenlisting in Vietnam came with a tax-free signing bonus of up to $10,000 or less, depending upon the job title and description and shortages to fill those positions. The big money was for the combat arms categories, and everyone knew that if you went for the $10,000, the risks were higher. A lesser bonus for a non-combat specialty, though, would still put money in your pocket and get you out of the field and away from the bullets.

Like it or not, the simple truth was that REMFs were a critical necessity. The numbers showed that for every soldier doing the actual fighting in the war there were four to five soldiers in these rear areas supporting them. Whether it was ferrying in food, fresh water, fuel, ammunition, and other necessary supplies for front line GIs to function. REMFs also took care of pay problems, sorted mail, processed, and coordinated Leaves and R&Rs, or maybe it was a dentist and dental assistant that took care of a chipped or broken tooth, or treated a face swelling abscess. Rear Area Doctors, nurses, medics, and Techs in the Evacuation Hospitals qualified for the title, but didn't merit it because of their critical lifesaving work and soul sucking horrors they faced daily. REMFs performed a myriad of different important jobs and tasks or carried out services that every GI in-country replied upon. For the Ranger Company Commander and his First Sergeant, the support today came in the form of a bummed ride to the 93rd Evacuation Hospital from a good natured truck driver and it was very much appreciated.

"Here you go, Sir!" said the truck driver after rolling to a stop near the hospital's main entrance.

"Thank you, Specialist. Much appreciated."

"No problem, Captain. Have a good one!"

Good, perhaps, wasn't the first word that came to the Captain's mind for the drop-off visit to the hospital, but he appreciated the sentiment.

"You, as well."

A cloud of rising dust followed the truck as it drove off. The two Rangers turned and made their way to the hospital's Admin Office to track down the wounded Lurps from Romeo Company.

Their pace slowed. Some walks were easier than others. As they made their way into the Evacuation Hospital, the weight of the visit became apparent in their gait. There was a price of command, a cost that accompanies sending young men into harm's way that was evident here in the hospital where visits to the bleeding and dying often scarred the visitors as well.

Soldiers steel themselves to combat, just as the seriously wounded do in the spotlessly clean, disinfected, alcohol smelling, antiseptic military hospital wards where the next round of life and death battles are found and fought during the painfully long and drawn-out desperate hours confined to hospital beds.

Warzone evacuation hospital wards made for poor recruiting poster ad campaigns.

Chapter 4

This would be their second attempt to check on the post-surgery status of their people.

The first attempt was made shortly after the reports came in to Romeo Company that two of their teams suffered casualties in firefights, and that the wounded were being flown to an Evacuation Hospital in Long Binh. Captain Robison and First Sergeant Poplawski requested and got permission from Brigadier General Reese and Colonel Becker in Camp Mackie's BIG-TOC to fly down from their base camp to check in on their people. In fact, it was BG Reese who made sure they had a helicopter on standby ready to take them to Long Binh.

However, upon arrival, they weren't allowed visits. All three of the wounded Rangers were undergoing a prolonged series of surgeries, and afterward would be heavily sedated.

"Their wounds are serious, but they'll survive," explained a Doctor who'd been sent out to talk to the Ranger Captain and his First Sergeant. "If you want to see them then you might want to try again in a few days once their wounds have a chance to stabilize and they might be awake enough to know where they are. Until then, they'll be in good hands. We have some of the finest people I've ever served with working here."

The Ranger officer and First Sergeant nodded, thanked the Doctor, and said they would try again soon. Their return trip to Camp Mackie was a somber one. The following day, though, there was something to loudly celebrate. A call came in from Camp Mackie's BIG-TOC that a wounded Sergeant Thomas had been picked up from an abandoned Fire Support Base near the Black Virgin Mountain by a Low Bird Scout helicopter. He was now in the Evacuation Hospital in Long Binh. This was great news because Thomas had been listed as Missing-in-Action-Presumed Dead two days earlier.

Captain Robison and First Sergeant Poplawski were looking forward to today's visit to see how all four were doing. They had taken a beating, and this morning's news that the unit was soon to be disbanded didn't offer any actual salve to lessen the raw, scraping pain that came with it. The shutdown order might as well have been rubbed in with salt. This, though, they would keep from the wounded Rangers. There was no need to add that to their grief.

In the Hospital's Admin office, after being greeted by an Admin Specialist working behind the counter, the Ranger Company Commander explained why they were there, who they were there to see. He handed over the names, ranks, and unit designation he had written down for the clerk.

Taking the list the Admin Specialist nodded, then married up the names with the information he had hanging on two separate clipboards on the wall behind him.

The soldier returned to the counter with what he had along with an accompanying frown.

"I'm afraid Sergeant Wade and Specialist Hagar were airlifted out to the U.S. Army Hospital at Camp Zama, Japan at ten-hundred hours this morning, Sir. Sorry," he said, by way of apology.

Robison took this latest bad news with a heavy, frustrated sigh while Poplawski swore under his breath with a still audible, *'Ah, fuck!'* as he slowly shook his head. They were too late.

"However, your Private First Class Norse and Sergeant Thomas are still with us for the time being," said the Admin clerk. "They're in separate wards. Let me tell you where you can find them. I'll write it down."

"Thank you, Specialist. It's appreciated," said Captain Robison, after the Admin clerk wrote down and handed the note with the directions to the officer.

The *'thank you'* earned a chin up nod in return.

PFC Norse was in the I-C-U, the Intensive Care Unit, while Thomas went from emergency surgery to the V-S-I, the Very Seriously Injured ward.

The I-C-U was their first stop. When they found the ward they checked in at the Nurses' Station where a Major told them that the twenty-year-old was still heavily sedated. His life was no longer in danger, but that he would require extensive time and physical therapy to recover from his wounds, injuries, and burns to his neck and hands.

"Burns?" said Robison.

"Yes, it looks like they're from an explosion of some kind."

"A boobytrap in a tunnel."

"Then he must have been close to the blast," the Major said as she led them down the long, thin corridor lined on each side with hospital beds. The patient were mostly young, horribly wounded soldiers, turned woeful patients in sky blue military pajamas. Poplawski glanced at one bed where a GI who was lying back against his pillow and displaying bandaged depressions where his eyebrows and sockets should have been appearing to be staring at the nothing he would see for the rest of his life. The Ranger First Sergeant turned his attention forward again and blew air through his teeth.

Several of the patients they passed showed wrapped pus-stained gauze over amputated stumps that were still fighting serious infections, while a large number of others, with a wide array gunshot or shell fragment wounds were holding their misery in place with heavy bandages and cloth adhesive tape and bright white casts. Robison couldn't help but notice that there were only two empty hospital beds lining the ward's east and west walls.

Eight beds down the Nurse stopped on the left side of the ward where they found Private First Class Norse sleeping. An I-V drip was feeding fluids and medications into his right arm. With the extent of his injuries, a fractured back, collapsed lung, a concussion, and enough small stab-wounds from splintered wooden spikes or shards of rock from the explosion in the tunnel to make him feel like an inverted porcupine, not to mention burn patches from the intense heat from the explosion, Robison and Poplawski exchanged looks that said that perhaps the drug-induced slumber he was in wasn't necessarily a bad thing.

The Ranger First Sergeant reached into the deep cargo pocket of his jungle fatigues and pulled out a black Ranger beret that he placed on the small night stand next to the hospital bed.

"How long will he be here? We'd like to stop back and say hello when he's awake," asked the Ranger Captain only to get a small shrug from the woman.

"Can't say," she said, apologetically. "It depends on what the Chief Surgeon and his team decide. Could be he'll be flown out as early as tomorrow. Sadly, we need the beds. Sorry."

The double doors at the far end of the ward swung wide as another new arrival of the patched-up wounded was being wheeled in on a squeaking gurney. Now, there was only one empty bed left in the I-C-U and neither Robison nor Poplawski suspected it would remain that way for long. For a number of years now the wards were ever revolving doors for those thousands coming in and going out.

"Will you make sure the beret goes with him, Ma'am when he's airlifted out?"

Nodding to Poplawski the nurse said she would.

"Excuse me," said the Nurse moving off to assist the medic pushing the gurney.

"Thank you," Robison called after her and received a tired smile in return, before both he and Poplawski left the I-C-U ward and made their way over to the V-S-I ward.

Poplawski was blowing more air out through his teeth once they were out of the ward. "Jesus, that's a grim place to work, day in and day out. Not sure I could do that, Sir."

"Me neither," agreed Captain Robison. "I doubt the V-S-I ward is going to be any better. Hopefully, Thomas is."

The First Sergeant nodded. "They've been through the wringer."

Robison wasn't certain if he meant their two Lurps or the thirty or so of those other GIs in the hospital beds that had lined the walls.

Hopefully too, if he was conscious, awake, and willing to talk they would get a chance to visit with Sergeant Thomas and fill in more than a few blanks about how he survived, after they thought they had lost him in the tunnel explosion and collapse on the Black Virgin Mountain.

Miraculously though, the young Texan hadn't died. Bruised, battered, dazed and hearing Quasimodo's clanging 21bronze bells for a while after he regained consciousness after the explosion and tunnel collapse. How he survived each and how he found his way out of the mountain, and all that came afterward would fill in the gaps to the After Action Report that would now need to be modified. And that information would come from Thomas. The initial report that was relayed to the Ranger Company at Camp Mackie was that the wounded Team Leader had been found a few miles away from the mountain by a passing Scout helicopter patrol, outside of an abandoned American Fire Support Base. Rescued under fire he was whisked away to a front line Field Hospital and then to the Evacuation Hospital. That was it and that, for the moment, was enough.

When the call came into Romeo Company's Orderly Room, there were joyful grins, back-slaps, and handshakes all around. Miracles seldom happen in combat, but this one had a Lazarus effect for everyone concerned.

Plans were made to visit them all in the Evacuation Hospital prior to the rescheduled command briefing at MAC-V Headquarters. Frustratingly, the time change for the Headquarters Monthly Briefing also changed the outcome of the visits.

Two of the wounded were airlifted out of the war zone earlier that morning and a third was too sedated to know how much misery he was in. They would still make attempts to try to return to check in on Norse, but that wouldn't happen today.

At least they would get a chance to visit and talk with Sergeant Thomas to learn the rest of his story. This was something that both Robison and Poplawski wanted to hear for their own curiosity but needed to hear to officially update the team's After Action report. With any luck, they would find him awake to hear the story.

Following protocol at the V-S-I Ward they checked in at the Nurse's station. After explaining to the Chief Nurse why they were there and who they wanted to see, the young woman who was a mid-twenty-something First Lieutenant, and who had been going over several patient charts, nodded, reached behind her, and grabbed a clipboard off a nearby wall hook.

"Thomas, you said, Sir?"

"Yes ma'am, first name Darrell, November-Mike-India, Sergeant E-5, R Company-Ranger."

"N-M-I, as in No-Middle-Initial?"

"Yes, Ma'am."

"Ah yes, here we go! Your Sergeant Thomas is ten beds down on the right hand side of the ward," said the Chief Nurse, confirming the location on a clipboard chart. "I suspect he might appreciate a few visitors. However, I'll have to ask you to keep the visit brief as the Doctors will soon be making their afternoon rounds."

Glancing at her wrist watch she added, "You have about fifteen minutes, Gentlemen, if that works for you."

"Yes Ma'am, it does. That should do it. That'll be fine. Thank you."

"You're welcome, Captain. Sergeant," she said, placing the clipboard back on a hook.

"She called us both *gentlemen*," said the First Sergeant, smiling as they walked down the aisle to find their wounded Sergeant.

"The poor woman needs glasses."

"I'd be hurt by your comment Sir, if I didn't know your vision is spot on 20/20!"

A ward medic was finishing up changing the bandage on Thomas' exposed shoulder wound as they approached the hospital bed and Robison caught a glimpse of an ugly, weeping, line of bulging stitches that ran from the top of Thomas' right shoulder down into his upper chest. The bullet that hit Thomas might as well have been a meat cleaver. An involuntary shudder momentarily rattled the Ranger Captain, but he quickly composed himself, hoping that his reaction and balk had gone unseen and hadn't given his thoughts away either.

You didn't visit someone in a warzone hospital visibly cringing or by walking up and saying, "*Well, don't you look like shit*!" especially when the bulk of the beds in the Very Serious Injury ward were filled with mostly young horribly scarred GIs with life-altering crippling wounds. A quick glance, but never a stare at a double-amputee's bandaged leg stumps or a patient's missing arm or chin when many in the hospital beds were still struggling and trying to come to terms to their new and traumatically changed lives. As sterile and antiseptic as it was, there was the unmistakable putrid odor of torn flesh and seeping pus and blood that dominated the ward. Macho only went so far, pain here was going the distance.

Beside the gunshot wound the injured Lurp Team Leader had also suffered a concussion and an assorted number of nasty bruises from flying rock and shattered wooden support beams in the blast. His face and hands, recently scrubbed cleaned of dirt, rock fragments, and dried blood, revealed a number of purplish-yellow bruises, a few red welts, and enough small cuts, scrapes, and scratches that showed he might've tried to bodywash a bag of pissed-off alley cats. A head bandage covered a small wound to the back of his head.

"Shamming, I see!" barked the First Sergeant trying for humor and smiling at the wounded soldier as they approached the hospital bed.

The loud, but familiar sarcastic remark from Poplawski got Thomas' attention as he looked up at the familiar faces. It also startled the medic working on Thomas and caught the ear and ire of the Chief Nurse back at the Nurse's Station, who was now leaning over the counter, and glaring at Poplawski.

"Sorry!" the Ranger NCO said, apologizing to the medic before turning to the Chief Nurse with his hands up and backing away only to have the Nurse frown and shake her head.

"Good to see you, Sergeant Thomas," added Poplawski, a little more quietly turning back to the soldier. "Really good, Ranger!"

"We thought we lost you," said the Ranger Captain at the foot of the bed. There was genuine concern behind the words that said he was more than a little relieved to see the soldier, given that it was believed he had died in the tunnel.

"Won't lie, Sir. It felt like it at times to me too," said Thomas.

The Medic finished what he was doing and quickly excused himself. Grunts, and especially Gung Ho Rangers, made him uncomfortable.

"Have you heard anything about PFC Norse?" asked Thomas, slowly leaning back against the upraised hospital bed trying to ease away some of the pain. Medication only went so far. "Did they find him? Did...did they get him out? Is he okay? And the rest of my Team?"

The flurry of questions drew a nod from his Company Commander who purposely lowered the rate of his response to help ease the verbal angst.

"Norse is a few wards over," he said. "We just checked in on him. He's banged up a bit, but we're told the prognosis, with time and physical therapy, he should be good."

Good left a lot of room for interpretation as did the extent of Thomas' wounds.

"The rest of your team got off the mountain okay with the Quick Reaction Force."

The relief that washed over the young Team Leader's face was medicinal. A portion of his pain lessened.

"We're told that you're both slated to be sent to Camp Zama, Japan soon so maybe when you're up and moving a little better there, maybe you can check in on him?"

"Yes sir. Will do."

"Good."

"And the rest of the team, they make it out okay?"

"They did. They're good too. Oh, and just so you know, Specialist Li was the first one into the tunnel after the explosion. He and PFC Sanchez dug Norris out before Li went back in for you, but the tunnel was blocked."

"Harry's a good guy, Captain. Specialist Li, I mean."

"He also kept the team together after the explosion and during the firefight that followed. The other NVA and VC on the mountain came looking until we got a QRF in for support."

"He'll make a good Team Leader, Sir."

"He would if he could speak better English," said Poplawski, shaking his head at the thought.

"You mean because he's Chinese and Hawaiian and all?"

"No, I mean because of all of his dumbass surfer talk! '*Bro, drop-in! Bummer soup, gremmie! Pearlin,' Dude!* And what the hell is a *rail bang,* anyway? You damn near need Frankie Avalon to come in and translate all that Beach Blanket Bingo bullshit!"

Thomas guffawed and the laughter too added some medicinal value, something the Captain figured was the response the First Sergeant was going for.

"To be honest, I'm not so sure what half those terms mean, either, Top! I was just happy to have him as my Assistant Team Leader. He's a good Lurp, a good Ranger."

"Glad you feel that way because we thought so too which is why we've given him your team."

"Good call, Sir."

The conversation and what was becoming an informal debriefing moved on. The previous After-Action Report that chronicled the timeline of events and actions with the surviving team member accounts, the immediate rescue attempts, and the follow-up attempts by the Quick Reaction Force would now need to be revised and annotated once Thomas' account of the ordeal was married-up and added in the consolidated report. The speculation would be replaced with firsthand testimony. When they returned to Camp Mackie the Captain would make the necessary edits.

"You up for maybe a bedside debriefing?"

"Yes sir. As good a time as any."

"All right then. So, let's start from where you were in the tunnel after the explosion," Robison said, pulling out a small notebook and pen from his top left pocket. Memory only went so far. "How did you survive it and the cave-in? How did you get out of the mountain?" asked the Captain eager to hear the answers. "What can you tell us about all that? What do you remember?"

Thomas had been dying to get it out, to tell somebody, if only to try to make some better sense of it himself. Taking in a slow deep breath to settle his rising blood pressure he began the retelling.

"I was chasing after the NVA soldier in the tunnel and just about had the little shit before the explosion, I'm guessing from a boobytrap. It rang my bell pretty good, Sir. Something, I dunno, maybe a piece of flying rock hit me here in the blast and sent me down for the count," said the Texan, pointing to the back of his bandaged head. "Later, when I came to, I found myself in total darkness under some loose dirt and debris. I was bleeding out my ears with a headache that even made blinking my eyes hurt. It was so dark I wasn't really certain I was awake or not until some aches and pains told me I was. Pushing up on my elbows I was spitting and blowing out dirt from my mouth and nose and remembered I had my flashlight on my LBE up near my left shoulder. It was the red filtered one and I'm glad I had it. When I flipped it on it showed the tunnel, or what was left of it, was a mess. There was some room to move but not much, so I tried crawling and clawing my way back out the way I came in, only it was a No-Go. It was blocked.

To be honest, that's when I panicked a little, afraid, and thinking maybe I was trapped inside the mountain for good."

"I think we all did," said the Captain.

"The Engineers the Captain brought with us on the QRF thought so, too," added the First Sergeant about what happened afterward. "One of them crawled in what was left of the tunnel and tried to find you, only he came out shaking his head. Said there was no way to attempt a rescue without bringing in heavy equipment and that wasn't possible given the slope of the mountain and the enemy activity in the mountain. The Engineers were worried that even if they could sling in the heavy equipment they said any drilling would just bring down more of the mountain on you. The Captain here wasn't so sure so he crawled in and took a look for himself, even when the Engineers told him the rest of what was left of the roof could cave in at any moment," added Poplawski, which surprised the Texan. "We barely got him out before the rest of the tunnel collapsed."

Captain Robison shrugged it off, downplaying his role in the attempt.

"We did everything we could to dig you out. We weren't successful, but apparently you were! So, how did you manage it? The report we received back at the Company was that you were rescued a few miles away from the mountain in some kind of running gun fight!"

"More like a bad game of TAG, sir."

"How about you start at the beginning where Li said you were chasing after an NVA soldier into the tunnel, and we'll go from there?"

"Yes sir. It was a lone NVA soldier coming down a trail, so I figured we'd snatch him up and call for an extraction, only as soon as we rose up, he took off running, and like I said I chased after him and almost had him too!"

"Until he went in the tunnel."

"Uh-huh, the brush-covered tunnel entrance."

The now more animated Thomas told how he dropped down and scurried in after the enemy soldier and almost caught the enemy soldier when he heard the new guy scrambling inside the tunnel behind him, which is when it all went wrong.

"Norse came charging in after me. He was just trying to help, but…but there was a boobytrap."

"That he must have triggered?"

Thomas hesitated a bit with his answer. "Maybe," he said "or maybe the NVA soldier we were chasing set it off looking to stop us. I dunno. I can't say…"

But he did know or was reasonably certain it was Norse. He remembered yelling at him not to grab onto any of the support beams when he heard him scrambling in behind him. Maybe it was his raspy breathing from the chase or the confined space of the rock-walled tunnel that muffled the words, or maybe Norse was too new to comprehend the warning as he grabbed at one of the thick dirt filled bamboo tubes supports to help pull himself forward. One of the bamboo support tubes, though, was boobytrapped with a spring-loaded striker that set off the explosive.

Also, he left out that he hadn't wanted the new guy to follow him into the tunnel. In fact, he was even going to chew him once he caught the NVA prisoner and hauled him back out. This, though, he would keep to himself. The Captain said the new guy was badly injured and suffering enough. He wouldn't add to it.

The explosion and the thundering boom, like an ear splitting lightning strike, collapsed the tunnel three yards in from the entrance and sent a dust and rock-filled nightmare back out of the opening like a giant shotgun's blast. The concussive force, heatwave, and pressure of the blast also caught Norse, him, and even the NVA soldier who was trying to escape.

"I was out of it for a good while but when I came to in the dark and after spitting out dust and dirt and blowing it out of my nose, I panicked and prayed a bit. The only thing that came to mind while I was praying was something my Uncle used to say to me about asking for God's help."

"Which was?" said Poplawski.

"The Lord helps those who help themselves. Then he'd tell me to get off my butt and get to work, which is what I did. I had a flashlight and my knife, so I went to work digging myself out."

Thomas chuckled and the Captain and First Sergeant nodded and chuckled along with him. His adrenaline was driving the story and what followed came out in nervous streams. The Ranger Captain was trying to keep up as he was taking notes.

"Because there was no going back and there was some room ahead of me, I... I started digging and scraping my way forward. I knew it was my only best chance because as I crawled on I could see that the tunnel was slowly beginning to open up in front of me. I think what maybe...naw, there's no maybe. I'm pretty sure what saved me was that they'd set the boobytrap near the entrance..."

"Where most of the damage was," agreed the Captain. "The NVA wanted to collapse the entrance but not the rest of the tunnel."

"Yes sir, and because I was already deeper into the tunnel there was only a partial collapse. I had room to crawl and dig my way ahead a few feet at a time. I just kept scraping and pulling away what was in front of me and shoving it all behind me as I went. When I could feel some better air coming at me, I figured the tunnel must have opened up, and it did."

"To a cave?" asked Poplawski.

"More like a large rock wall chamber somebody had spent a lot of time carving out from a cave, First Sergeant. Only before I reached it I came across one last partial collapse and mess that turned out to be the guy I was chasing. He was trapped under a pile of rubble."

"Dead?" said Poplawski.

"No, he was trapped beneath it all and worse off than I was, but he was still alive. He was badly injured and had no fight left in him, so I managed to pull him clear once I squeezed by him and had a little more room and leverage to move into the chamber."

"You rescued him?" said Captain Robison looking up from his notebook from the foot of the hospital bed.

Thomas nodded and then wished he hadn't. The nod sent a pulse-like shock to his system that radiated through his body.

"Yes sir, and he was my prisoner."

"You caught him?"

Thomas grinned. "I did," he said, beaming. "He was pretty fuc…eh, messed up from the cave-in, but he was still breathing. Injured as badly as he was, he was no real threat. So, I dragged him into the chamber and propped him up against a wall. Then, I searched him for weapons and whatnot before looking after his wounds."

"You caught him and treated his wounds?" said the surprised Poplawski.

"As best I could, First Sergeant because you once said that the Captain promised any of us who brought in a live P-O-W a two-day in-country R&R to Vung Tau."

"True, I did, but…" agreed the Captain without stating the obvious, even if his face gave away what he was thinking.

"I know, Sir. It's okay," Thomas said, glancing at his shoulder bandage. "I probably won't be needing it now. Anyway, maybe you could give to Li or one of the others on the team. Sanchez, maybe."

"Done!" said the Captain. "So, what happened to him, the P-O-W, I mean, and how did you get out of the mountain to that abandoned Fire Support Base where the helicopter picked you up?"

"There was a large, spring-fed basin inside the chamber and nothing else. I think the NVA and VC were using it as a freshwater source on the mountain."

"A water basin or a well?" said Poplawski.

"A large, big ol' tub, about the size of one of those K-Mart kiddie wading pools, only a whole lot taller and deeper. They even built a drain channel to keep the water from overflowing and flooding the chamber. The drain led down to a small hole in the floor lower into the mountain."

"From the cistern?"

"Affirmative, the drain kept the water level in the basin at a consistent depth and sent the overflow to somewhere or someone else. Pretty smart setup, really, and one that had me wondering why the cistern was so big and deep while the tunnel leading into it was little more than a crawlway. That's when it hit me…'

"There had to be another way out," said the Captain, smiling.

"Yes sir. At Tigerland…"

Sweet Sorrow

"Ah, Fort Polk, Louisiana!" said Poplawski. "The land that time forgot, but the mosquitoes, snakes, and armadillos hadn't."

Thomas grinned. "Uh-huh, they told us in Advanced Infantry Training there how Charlie sometimes used waterways to go in and out of tunnel systems beneath villages, so I climbed into the water for a better look, and found a hidden passageway six feet or so beneath the water line. Since the tunnel was blocked and there was no going back, I took in a deep breath, dropped down to the bottom, and then swam and pulled my way through the opening below. It wasn't far to the other side, but it was a tight fit that had me worried a bit."

"A bit?"

Thomas gave a half smile. "A little more than a bit until I came up inside another cistern pool on the other side and found myself in a tunnel system that led deeper into the mountain. There were passageways, storage chambers, and carved out stairwells leading up and down the whole damn mountain. Some led to gun positions, hidey holes, and concealed entrances. They must have been carving out the mountain for a thousand years. They ant farmed the hell out of it."

"Storage chambers, with supplies? How many? What kind?" asked the Captain.

"Yes sir. There were chambers filled with boxes and boxes of medical supplies, stacks of 50 pound sacks of rice, ammo crates, pith helmets, uniforms, boots, and everything else they needed to set up a GI-Ho Army surplus store in Hanoi. Well, everything except anything I could use as a weapon. All I had with me was a knife and two grenades from my web gear..."

"You didn't have your rifle?"

"No, sir. I left it at the entrance to the tunnel since there wasn't much room inside to maneuver. Anyway, I didn't find any A-Ks or SKS rifles, but other than that they looked to have everything else they needed in that mountain for the long haul, all safe and secure like. Captain, we may own the top of the mountain, but they own everything in it. There's a bunch of them running around in there, too."

"Any idea how many?"

"Can't say for sure, a platoon or two maybe or more, but a lot. The Nui Ba Den is their secure Base Camp."

"So, how did you avoid getting found out and caught?"

Thomas smiled again because he knew a shrug would hurt. "I think, early on they didn't know I was there, so they weren't looking for me yet," he said. "Also, I took one of their pith helmets and an East German camo cape from a box in one of the storage chambers, figuring maybe if I hunched down a little I'd be mistaken for one of them in the dim light at a distance. They had set up some bare bulb lighting in the bigger tunnels but most of the others were pretty low light, so, when I heard someone coming I'd slip into a side tunnel or dark corner. I laid low until they passed, waited until they were gone, and then kept searching for one of those exit points I knew had to be there. I made it down three different sets of stone staircases, several slow sloping ramps, and even hid for a while in one storage chamber behind some rice bags and crates."

"Storage chamber?"

"Yes sir. And on each level I found there were a number of natural caves they'd carved out and used as storage chambers. I only went down three levels, but each level held more tunnels, caves, and chambers. In the better lighted passages and caves, there seemed to be a whole bunch of NVA coming and going inside the mountain. I figured as long as I stayed in the shadows I was good. After a good while I found a tunnel that led to one exit only the closer I got I got a whiff of something cooking and heard a few folks talking. It turned out to be an occupied gun position, so I slowly backed away and kept looking for another way out. To tell you the truth the NVA inside the mountain didn't seem to be too worried about anyone bothering them, or from the casual conversation they were having, they didn't seem worried at all."

Robison grunted with a slow nod. He suspected they weren't worried because the honeycombed mountain provided them with a natural fortress and more than a few hidden gun ports and positions to attack any aircraft foolish enough to fly close enough to their iron gun sights.

It was no secret that South Vietnamese or U.S. helicopters had used the Nui Ba Den and the road around it as a ground guide back to the Tay Ninh Base Camp and that had often taken belt-fed enemy machine gun fire if they ventured too close to the mountain. It didn't seem to matter that even when those NVA gun positions were pounded and hit with return artillery or gunship rockets, another few would soon pop up somewhere else like a bad game of whack-a-mole. Thomas was right. The local folks hiding from whatever army had been carving out the mountain as an operating base for a thousand years or more fighting a host of Chinese invading armies, Chams, or warlords closer to home. They owned the mountain. It was theirs.

"So, you hid, what? In the storage chambers or side tunnels?"

"I did. There were a number of old collapsed tunnels they'd closed off with warning signs, so I snuck into a few, hid from anyone passing by, and kept looking for a way out."

"Using your flashlight to maneuver and find your way around?" asked Poplawski.

"I did, and Top, that sucker worked well enough to work my way through the mountain without giving me away. I don't think I ever appreciated a $5 plastic piece of equipment from the lowest contractor bidder more."

"Playing Hide n' Seek from the NVA?"

"It was mostly Hide, Sir. I had a few things on me from a box of C-rations that I ate. It wasn't much but it was enough to keep me going, although I thought at times my grumbling stomach might give me away. Almost two days, you said?"

"Pretty close," said Captain Robison.

"Seemed longer, sir. I swear. My watch broke in the explosion. A piece of rock or something shattered the crystal, so I lost track of time. The medics or Docs must've cut it off when they brought me in. It doesn't matter, the watch likely saved my hand and all I got was a bruise."

Thomas held up a wrist and showed a yellowish-green oval.

"But time was on your side anyway because you found a way out."

"Yes sir, the tunnels and caves were mostly dark and dank with stale air so when I got a whiff of jungle and some fresh cooler air ahead of me a few times that told me there were a few ways out. Like I said the first one I found was an occupied gun position, so I just slowly backed away and backtracked the way I came and kept looking. I finally found another one they were using to get in and out of the mountain. It only had one guard with a field phone manning it, so I Lurped up to him close and quiet like, and thumped him a few times on the side of his head with a grenade…"

"You hit him with a grenade?"

"Yes sir. I figured I could use it as a sap and coldcock him."

"The grenade?"

"Actually two, Captain. One in each hand. Left and right roundhouses. Bam! Bam! I thumped him good. Then I scooped up his rifle, trashed his field phone, and pulled out as much of the commo wire that led back into the mountain as I could. I tossed the phone and the wire over the side of the mountain down onto a pile of boulders. After that, I took a look around trying to get my bearings and realized I was still about a third of the way down the mountain. I moved out as fast as I could down the mountain hoping the guard would be out for a while so I could be long gone. Also, dressed as I was with one of their camo capes and pith helmets and carrying the A-K I figured that maybe even if I got spotted by one of their hidden Observations Posts or gun positions they might think I was one of their own, and maybe not give me a second look. Mostly, it worked!"

"Mostly? Is that when you got shot?"

"No, sir. That was later. The alarm must've gone out inside the mountain, either when someone found the injured NVA soldier in the cistern chamber where I left him, or the guard at the entrance I thumped pretty good when I made my getaway. Lucky for me it was just getting dark, and I thought I had a good lead, only it wasn't too long after that when I looked back up the mountain I saw a line of their flashlights coming out of the tunnel opening I'd just left. An NVA squad or two were milling around like pissed-off fire ants trying to pick up my track.

"I was barely a 100 yards away behind brush and rocks trying my best to stay out of sight and kept moving until I reached the bottom of the mountain. That's when I started putting some real distance between us. I was hoping they'd maybe think I was working my way back up to our people at the Radio Relay Station on top of the mountain..."

"Because it was closer," added Poplawski.

"Roger that, Top, and hoping they'd maybe think I went that way. I didn't because I knew their trackers or maybe one of their spotters near the Relay Station would shoot my ass before I ever reached it."

"Good call," said Poplawski.

"I hoped it was, so I went down instead of up, and planned on giving the mountain a wide berth, and maybe in the first light of day in the morning I'd start heading towards the Tay Ninh Base Camp from the south. I figured a day or two walk wouldn't kill me, but I knew Charlie would, if I rushed it."

"Another good call," said Robison.

"It was until it looked up and saw that they found the way I went. A line of flashlights started snaking their way down the mountain and another one near the base of the mountain started fanning out to try to trap me."

"Which is when you...what, made your way toward the old, abandoned Fire Support Base?"

"Yes sir. I still had my mission map on me, and it showed the sites of a few of the First CAV's old, abandoned Fire Support Bases, and one that was almost in line with the road heading up to the border. I made my way towards the road in the dark to what the map showed was LZ Carolyn or maybe Grant. I dunno, could've been one of the others too. Turned out, though, the NVA had sent a few of their people in that direction too in case I showed up."

The Texan's adrenaline was still pushing the pace of the narrative as were the painkillers he was on. Thomas was eager to tell the rest, so the Ranger Captain and the First Sergeant let him talk because they were eager to hear it as well and chronicle the run.

Robison and Poplawski were well aware too that a captured American Lurp/Ranger would have made a nice prize to the North Vietnamese or Viet Cong, just as they knew that if they couldn't take him prisoner, then a dead one would suffice.

Thomas went on. "I remembered hearing a Huey crew chief once say how the helicopter pilots often used the road as a visual back to Tay Ninh, so I thought that if I could make it to one of the old Fire Support Bases along the road then by daylight maybe a helicopter flying a first light mission or flying back to the Tay Ninh Base Camp might spot me."

"Smart move because a Pink Team did."

"Yes sir, they did," said Thomas. "When the Scout helicopter came in low over the road checking out the old base, I jumped out from where I was hiding and began waving my arms like a maniac. And that's when the bullets started flying. The NVA soldiers that had been sent to monitor the old base came out of one the old partially collapsed bunkers and began shooting and I got hit. They were still firing when the Low Bird roared in, the machine gunner pulled me in, and the pilot got us the hell out of there. I was lucky."

Lucky was one word that might apply, but it was always more than that. The kid had balls, thought Poplawski. Wits too, for that matter. And what did he say before he thumped the guard with the grenades? He '*lurped up on him!*'

Yeah, you did, thought the proud First Sergeant smiling. *You sure as Hell did!*

When the Scout helicopter touched down at the Field Hospital's landing pad he was loaded onto a gurney and rushed into surgery. That much he remembered, but nothing after the Anesthesiologist stuck a needle in his arm and had him count backward from 100. He didn't make it to number 96. Hours later he woke up in a drug-induced fog on a stretcher as he was being transferred by helicopter to the Evacuation Hospital in Long Binh where the next round of surgery began. The wound, the surgeries, the hangover from the anesthesia, and the entire ordeal left him mentally and physically out of it. He was exhausted. Drained. It was the painful shoulder wound that brought him awake in the V-S-I ward after the second surgery. Then it was the timely doses of pain relievers the Nurses administered that helped him sleep and kept away the aching edge of his wound. The latest dose had also kept the story going. However, what he omitted and wouldn't say was that it was the Scout helicopter's door gunner who'd actually shot him. Excited as he was when he heard the helicopter making a low pass over the old, abandoned base, he jumped out from where he'd been hiding waving his arms trying to get the attention of the three-man crew aboard the small helicopter. He was shot because he was wearing an NVA soldier's pith helmet, an enemy poncho to keep the rain off of him, and he was holding a Russian AK-47 assault rifle in one of his upraised hands. He told himself he was lucky the door gunner hadn't killed him for the dumbass mistake. Soon after the NVA soldiers hiding in ruins of the Fire Support Base turned their fire on him as well.

"I dunno if this will help any, but I took a journal off of the NVA soldier I caught, more like a personal diary, really."

"A journal?"

"Yes sir, along with a small pencil he had. I thought it might have some good intel in it, so I held onto it. I kinda added to it a little too, jotting down a few notes of what all I found inside the tunnel complex as best I could."

"You wrote it down?"

"Yes sir, I did. I also made a few drawings of the storage chambers and staircases, thinking it would be something for the Intel people could find interesting and be of some use."

"And you did this in the dark with only the red filtered flashlight?"

"Uh-huh, but I ballparked it. I'm sure my pace count might be off a bit or even more than a bit. I kinda lost count when a dozen of the suckers went by where I was hiding or heard a few up ahead or coming up behind me. Then I did my best to hunker down and hide."

"And you hid well like a good Lurp."

"Yes sir, and I kept my head down and prayed a little. Maybe more than a little since I wasn't so sure that helping myself was enough."

"What happened to the journal?" asked Poplawski.

"I stuffed it and my mission map in my camo fatigues pants pocket. I'm pretty sure it's all still there or was when the doctors and nurses cut them off me when they brought me in. It's gotta be there somewhere."

"We'll track it and your mission map down. You just get some rest," said Captain Robison. "We'll try to stop back down to see you before you're airlifted out to Japan, but if we can't…"

The Ranger Company Commander held out his hand and the wounded Lurp shook it.

"Proud to have had you in Romeo Company, Sergeant Thomas," he said.

"Ya done good, Ranger," added the First Sergeant, pulling a black Ranger beret out of his pocket. "Oh, and I thought you might need this."

Thomas brightened at the black Ranger beret Poplawski was holding out to him. The black beret wasn't authorized headgear outside of the war zone because the Army hadn't officially recognized the 75th Infantry Ranger Companies as Rangers worthy of wearing it or the combat scrolls on their stateside uniforms. Still, the beret held important significance for those who had earned it in combat.

"Wear it proudly," Poplawski said. "Oh, and if anybody gives you any shit about it, refer 'em to me and I'll be happy to tell them to go fuck themselves."

Thomas grinned while Captain Robison chuckled and shook his head.

"Well, he's not wrong with the sentiment," said the Captain. "Although, you might want to be a little more diplomatic in your responses."

The First Sergeant shrugged and topped with a *meh*. "Toe-matoes, tah-matoes," he said.

With the conversation waning and the Ranger Captain having all he needed for his report, the hospital visit, and unofficial mission debriefing had come to an end.

"The doctors will be making their rounds soon so we're going to head out now," Robison said. "But before we go, is there anything you need? Anything we can bring you?"

"Some personal effects from my foot locker. My wallet, photo album, and such. I'd like to have them sent back home if you would."

"No problem. We'll get them identified, packed up, and shipped to your home of record. Texas, right?"

"Yes sir, East Texas. Athens."

"Count on it, Ranger," said the Captain. "We'll get it done."

"Thank you."

"Get some rest. You've earned it."

As the Two Rangers made their way back down the center aisle on their way out, they thanked the Nurses and Medics at the Nurse's Station before stepping out into the outdoor covered walkway.

"That's some ordeal he went through," Robison said as they headed back toward the Hospital's Admin office to track down Thomas' mission map and the journal.

"One hell of a war story, for sure," added the First Sergeant. "I'm glad he's around to tell it."

"We'll make a point of telling it too back at the company. Everyone needs to hear it! It'll be a good morale booster."

They walked on in silence. Neither was saying out loud how happy and relieved they were that Thomas was no longer Missing in Action or Presumed Dead, but the genuine sentiment and relief were very much there on display on their faces and how they were carrying themselves. The hospital visit had something of a medicinal effect on Thomas and the two visitors. It was a salve of sorts. For combat soldiers, other than surviving their wounds, there were few good take-aways. This visit may have been a seemingly insignificant little thing to anyone looking on, but it mattered at this moment where the history of the war was being written daily by those doing the bleeding and those who were keenly aware of the human cost of the blood that was being used as its ink.

Chapter 5

From the Evacuation Hospital they made their way over to the Aviation Brigade's Flight Operations Center hoping to find an outbound helicopter heading back up to Camp Mackie.

They were in luck. A Chinook was scheduled to make a Mail run to Mackie once it was done picking up a few passengers at Bien Hoa. There was room on the transport helicopter for them to catch a hop.

"The flight, though, doesn't leave till 1600 hours, so if you want to grab something at the snack bar down the road and be back here at 1530 hours, I can put you two on the manifest, Sir," said a First Lieutenant behind the flight terminal check-in counter.

"That'd be great, Thank you."

Over a halfway-decent cheeseburger, at least after he'd pulled out, sniffed at, frowned, and then tossed a wilted piece of lettuce from the beef patty and rearranged the extra onions and pickle, First Sergeant Poplawski continued to vent his frustration at MAC-V's decision to deactivate Romeo Company.

"It makes no sense to shut us down," he said, angrily oversalting an accompanying plastic basket of fries before dunking one in a small paper bowl of ketchup on his plate, tasting it, and then tossing it back in the basket.

"No, it doesn't," agreed the Captain, losing interest in the slice of cheese pizza he had in front of him as well. He settled back in his seat staring into his cup of black coffee as Poplawski argued the case for keeping the Ranger Long Range reconnaissance Patrol company in business.

"Small unit tactics are one of the most effective ways to find, fix, and finish the enemy in jungle combat," said Poplawski. "You'd think the finer minds at MAC-V would've learned and understood by now that this isn't a conventional war, seeing how the Viet Cong have successfully used small unit tactics against us at every opportunity! Lurps and Recon teams are just turning it back around on them. We're beating them at their own game! Shutting us down doesn't make any sense. I just don't understand it. I really don't, Sir."

"I can't say as I do either," said the Captain.

Tactically, small unit operations had proved their place on the combat chessboard. The Field Force units and Divisions were still employing the pile-on approach to enemy engagements in the war. Send smaller recon units into the jungle, whether by ground or by air, to see where the North Vietnamese Army and Viet Cong had shifted their Battalions or Regiments, and then send in more soldiers and the necessary equipment to take them on. If a heavy firefight or larger battle broke out, then fine. No problem. Send a bigger dog into the fight, instead of willy-nilly sending in a hundred-man company or two to wander around the jungles looking to find the concentrated enemy forces.

The Special Forces well understood the small team aspect as did the smaller LRRP and Ranger teams that had effectively carried out the surveillance and reconnaissance patrols, because they provided vital information back to command; information that could be better and properly assessed and acted upon. Knowing where the enemy forces were congregating, and just as crucial, knowing where they weren't, greatly aided the war effort and strategy in play.

But that play, at least for the U.S. troops under MAC-V command, was coming to an end with the steady strategic withdrawal of American forces. Under the 1970 plan that President Richard Nixon had labeled "*Peace with Honor*" the *Vietnamization* stage of the war was in play. *Vietnamization* was part and parcel with Nixon's plan to expand, equip, and train South Vietnamese forces to increase their combat role while decreasing the U.S. role. Only there was no peace or honor coming. The North Vietnamese weren't giving up the fight or settling on a two-nation divide. The war would continue, and eventually the South Vietnamese Armed Forces would be on their own to win it or lose it. Everyone knew it, even if they pretended they didn't.

Over a chance get together and more than a few beers and whisky shots with a former Special Forces team mate at the NCO Club in Bien Hoa, and after solving all of the Army's problems with some careful thought and sarcasm his friend told Poplawski just what he thought of the whole *'Peace with Honor'* plan.

"Might as well have called it, the *'adios, cutting, and running plan'* because we're leaving the Montagnards, the Nung-Chinese, and Hmong, who fought by our sides and who relied on us high and dry to die. Those people were both loyal and brave and Jesus, *Brick*, we're pissing on them."

The Green Beret, who was on his third tour of duty added, "Might be hard to find any others looking for a reliable ally from ever believing in us again."

Poplawski gave a slow frustrated nod and took another long pull of his beer. The beer tasted a lot less bitter than MAC-V Command's decision to shut down Romeo Company this morning.

Their time remaining on the clock was quickly ticking away and would soon run out. The fact remained that Robison and Poplawski had no say in the matter. Young Captains and acting First Sergeants seldom, if ever, were involved with the big brass command decision making process. Their jobs, like it or not, would be to carry out the orders they were given to accomplish the mission, whatever the mission was, and if they weren't up to the task or couldn't carry it out, then they would quickly be replaced by others who would get it done. The mission was always the higher priority to command, but that wasn't always the case on the company level. The mission was still important, but so were those carrying it out.

"I want a cadre briefing once we get back to Mackie. We'll hold back on letting the rest of the company know about the shutdown, for the moment. However, what we will do tomorrow, in the morning formation, we'll let our people know about Thomas and the Valorous Unit Award. That'll, at least, give them something to cheer about along with the official pat on the back for their efforts."

"Yes sir, and I'll get Specialist Taras to paint the award on our unit sign and maybe show everyone passing by just who the hell we are, at least for the time we have left as a Ranger Company."

Captain Robison nodded, only his nagging thoughts about all that would need to be done to officially close down the company were quickly creeping in. There were rifles, pistols, machine guns, grenade launchers, bayonets with scabbards to account for, not to mention rifle magazines, gas masks, rucksacks, web gear harnesses, canteens, canteen covers and, and other items and equipment that would need to be inventoried, turned in, and checked off. In addition, there were the assigned vehicles to return to the Army's inventory, along with desks, filing cabinets, chairs, blankets, bunks, generators, and any and everything of government value he had signed for when Romeo Company became operational. He had signed for all of it and his name was on the dotted line. If an item that was on the list wasn't found or accounted for, or written off as a combat loss, then he would literally bear the cost of the lost item or items. His pay would be docked until the bottom-line bill was paid.

A missing rucksack was one thing, but significant property loss had expensive monetary and career ending consequences. A missing M-16 ran in the hundreds of dollars, an M-60 machine gun in the thousands, and a Deuce-and-a-half truck close to $20,000. Add in any unaccounted for items such as gas masks, generators, Starlight scopes, and the rest that was issued on the inventory list, then the bill for what couldn't be found could bankrupt him! Not finding or accounting for missing ammunition, fragmentation, or concussion or White Phosphorus grenades, or blocks of C-4 could also end his career with possible Army Criminal Investigative Division agents breathing down his neck looking to possibly apply criminal charges.

There was that, of course, and a little more to think about.

There were also the '*extra*' and '*borrowed*' items the company had on hand, like their two '*extra*' generators, the '*borrowed*' jeep, the '*extra*' three-quarter ton truck, and the '*borrowed,*' four-by-four, flatbed utility vehicle, better known as a '*mule*' that was used to ferry Lurp teams to and from Camp Mackie's main flight line back to the company after their patrols.

All of the 'extra' and '*borrowed*' vehicles and equipment would need to be scrubbed clean of any of the Romeo Company's identifying markers before they would be casually dropped off or left someplace on base where they could be, '*found*'.

'*Extra*' *and borrowed*' were euphemisms for 'stolen.' Those purloined items would need to find new homes or disappear when the bean counters officially came calling. Even in warzones bean counting teams from the Inspector General's Office conducted their inspections. Neither Camp Mackie, nor Romeo Company, would get a pass.

Captain Robison had made the Major's list, and he was slated for promotion, but that might not happen if there were significant material losses of items he had signed for when he took command.

On the unit personnel side there were citations to be written up with awards and medals requested for the deserving before the company was dissolved. There would be early out requests to be asked for those ETS-ing. ETS was another of the army's many acronyms that meant the *Estimated Time of Separation* for those soldiers whose military obligations or enlistments were up and were leaving the army. For those PCS-ing, or making a *Permanent Change of Station*, that meant seeking promotions for those who qualified and finding new and hopefully better assignments in stateside bases or in Europe.

That included Sergeant First Class *'Walter, The Brick, as in wall, just don't ever call me Walter,'* Poplawski, too, who was the Ranger Company's *Acting First Sergeant*. *Acting* meant Poplawski didn't have the actual E-8 rank required to hold that position, but was serving in the top NCO position because Robison had personally requested him and made him his First Sergeant. The veteran Green Beret was more than qualified, even if he didn't have the necessary time-in-grade for the official rank. With the shutdown as an E-7, it was likely he wouldn't receive the next promotion anytime soon, and that weighed heavily on the Captain's mind. Poplawski had done an outstanding job with Romeo Company, but bureaucracy always seemed to trump proficiency. Still, he'd push for it.

"Might as well have Staff Sergeant Shintaku sit in on the cadre meeting while we're at it, seeing how we'll be shutting down his training job. Let's get the new Lurps out of the training tent and into the second platoon hootch, as soon as possible."

Poplawski nodded and took it all in, even as he was still brooding. There is always more to war than just the fighting and always more to a nod than the physical gesture.

They killed a little more time at the snack bar before they trudged back to the Flight Operations Center only to find that their outbound flight was delayed.

"How long's the delay?" Robison asked the Lieutenant. "What are we looking at time wise?"

"Can't say, Sir," said the Lieutenant, shrugging. "But I was told it's just a small maintenance issue so it shouldn't be long, though. There's coffee next to the water cooler."

"Thank you," said Robison as he and his First Sergeant headed over to the waiting area and took their seats.

"Snack bars and water coolers," said Poplawski.

"Envious, are you?"

"Oooh yeah. They even have an ice cream machine!"

The wait time was 45 minutes and the short flight over to the Army's side of the Bien Hoa Air Base to pick up the other passengers, along with the one-hour flight would put them on the ground at Camp Mackie an hour before sunset.

It had been a long day, and it was about to get longer.

Chapter 6

The two Viet Cong spies were clad in the sun-faded, drab pajama-like loose tops and black string-tied trousers, conical shaped bamboo hats, and tire tread sandals of simple farm workers. As part of their deception, they were carrying long pole hoes and partially filled cloth pouches of rice shoots as they trudged out of the dry paddy and into the cover of the nearby jungle northwest of An Loc. To anyone watching on they appeared to be taking a well-earned break in the shade away from the punishing sun.

Three yards in, though, and under the cover of the rainforest they were met by two other Vietnamese who were similarly dressed. The two replacements took their farm tools and handed them each an AK-47 assault rifle, and a chest-mounted carrying vest with three 30 round ammunition magazines. One was handed a compass, and a crude map with instructions on how to locate waypoints through the jungle to reach a scheduled meet-up site where a guide would then lead them into their destination just over the Cambodian border. The second spy was handed a canteen that was quickly tucked into one of the two cloth shoulder bags along with the items they had brought with them. Armed and ready, the two set out on the long trek in the mid-afternoon as their replacements walked back out to the farm field. To a casual observer nothing appeared out of the ordinary.

For the two Viet Cong spies it was anything but ordinary. They were carrying coordinate and targeting information that they would deliver to the COSVN Command just over the border; information that would greatly assist in an upcoming attack on the nearby military South Vietnamese Army base.

COSVN was the Central Executive Office for South Viet Nam, the field enemy command that planned, directed, and coordinated the tactics and strategies for the regiments and battalions of the People's Army of Viet Nam (NVA) and Viet Cong, against the South Vietnamese and American military targets in the south. The information the two spies carried were for specific targets in an upcoming attack in An Loc. A rendezvous location had been selected as a meet-up site where a guide would bring them into the hidden Viet Cong headquarters. It was a five-hour trek that would bring them to the meet-up site just before sunset.

Before they set out the pair were cautioned to avoid the larger, open trails and to use the more obscured infiltration paths marked on their map instead to keep from being spotted from the air by roving American helicopters that would be flying last-light hunter-killer patrols over the jungle. Once across the border the two were to rendezvous with a patrol from the People's Army of Viet Nam on the Cambodian side of the border who would lead them into the hidden COSVN Base Camp's headquarters to deliver the targeted materials.

Departing when they did, they would soon discover that the high heat of the day and lack of enough water soon would have them dry-mouthed and sweating. With only one canteen between them, they drank the water sparingly.

They were spies, not woodsmen, so three hours into the trying trek they were frantically going over their map and realizing they had taken a bad compass reading and that they were far off-course and well south of their destination. They had somehow missed the path they were supposed to take. The living jungle was always trying to reclaim itself from what had been cut, carved out, or cleared away by humans over the millennia by one army or another, so with the new growth of fresh underbrush and ever creeping branches and vines, missing the turn was understandable, but for the two Viet Cong spies, it was a frustrating and time-consuming miscalculation. With a better estimate of where they were on the map they understood that backtracking to find the trail they should've taken was out of the question and would take more time than they allotted. They needed to be at the meet-up site prior to sunset so they came up with a quick fix.

They could correct the mistake by altering their route to make up for the lost time. Taking a corrective compass heading and lining it up with their map they opted to follow a smaller, but more well-used path north that their map told them would eventually intersect with the trail they were supposed to be on. This would prove to be their second and most costly mistake.

Earlier that morning Sergeant Gus Daley, Romeo's Ranger Team Nine-Four's Assistant Team Leader, was walking point when he found the small path. Halting the team with an upraised fist he went down on one knee just inside the brush line facing the three-foot wide trail. Slowly and carefully easing out of the wall of brush he had the barrel of his M-16 ready to rock and roll. He needed to be sure the trail was deserted before he could take the time to study the path. Scanning the trail all looked good so he dropped his gaze to take in a three foot section of the well-used ground as his Team Leader, Specialist-4 Harold 'Harry' Li came up to cover him.

"What do we got, Gus?" whispered Li.

"High-speed trail, east to west," Daley said, pointing through the leaves to the many sharp-edged boot prints and bicycle tracks on the well-used trail. "And another smaller one splitting off to the northwest. They look busy."

"And recent," Li whispered, confirming the find and then made the decision to set up and monitor them. Neither one of the trails were on their map. That wasn't uncommon. Four days into their six day mission they'd found at least a dozen other small trails and paths but none that had shown any promise like these.

Daley nodded and then tilted his head skyward. The overhead canopy of leaves and vines hid the trail from any aerial observation which was why they were busy routes.

"What do you think?"

Looking around Li decided he liked what he saw for a potential ambush site and then searched for what he thought would make a good hide site for the team. It was just off of the larger trail overlooking the Y that led to a smaller offshoot path angling in from the west. With enough surrounding foliage with broad leaves and brush the site he chose could easily hide a bright yellow school bus. It would work for surveillance or to ambush a small enemy unit, if it came to it, and it would do just fine.

"I think we set up here and set out some claymores and see who comes visiting."

Daley nodded one more time and the two pulled back to where the other three members of the team were holding up and waiting. Li then moved the team into position at the hide site that was a few yards closer to the primary trail.

After dropping their rucksacks and laying out fields of fire overlooking the two routes, Li set up the team in a 360 degree defensive position before he and Daley crept back towards the targeted kill zone carrying a handful of Claymore Anti-personnel Mines. With Daley covering him Li quickly went to work placing the Claymores on the likely avenues of approach. Planting them into the rainforest floor on scissor-legged metal spikes a yard off of the trail and just inside the tree line, he angled and aimed them in to cover their kill zone. Next, he got busy arming the Claymores and daisy chaining them together with detonation cord and blasting caps which he screwed into each of the fuse wells. Satisfied with the placement and angles of the Claymores he covered the mines with bunch grass and weathered leaves to hide them from view. Unless an enemy soldier was down on his knees and carefully searching for something out of the ordinary, the camouflaged anti-personnel mines would go unnoticed by anyone using either trail. The same for the Lurps dressed in the ERDL leaf pattern jungle fatigues, floppy hats, and camo green and black face paint.

Li slowly unrolled the Claymore's charging line on their way back to the hide-site, while Daley followed, and tried to resurrect and bring the pushed aside grass and brush back in place from the tramped down path they made sneaking up to the trail. Once they were both finally back in the team's wagon wheel perimeter and down behind their rucksacks, Li plugged the charging line into the Claymore's hand-held charging device, the *'clacker,'* and then set it down beside him within easy reach. In an ambush or a sudden firefight, he didn't need to wonder or worry where it was. The closer, the better.

For Longboat Team Nine-Four the reconnaissance part of their long range recon patrol was about to begin. Like hiding in a duck blind, they were waiting to see who was using the path, and, if the opportunity presented itself, then Li would initiate the ambush on any small unit that came calling. From the fresh tracks on the trail the game was on and the tension that came with the wait became as heavy and taxing as the humidity. Patience was a key part of reconnaissance patrols. To some, who were hunters, the patient wait came naturally, while for others from big cities and towns whose time amongst the trees had only been measured in walks through city parks, it was something to be learned and adhered to one mission after another. Patience here wasn't just a virtue, it was a necessity.

An hour passed, then several more, and any initial adrenaline rush and excitement that came with finding a well-used enemy trail gave way to a patient, uncomfortable, and boring wait.

In their four days there would be no foxholes, fires, or camping comforts. There were no sleeping bags or air mattresses for the five Lurps, only cold dehydrated rations and canteen water for their meals and rucksacks for their pillows. In their hide-site, behind the small openings in the branches and leaves of the undergrowth overlooking the footpath, Sergeant Daley brushed away the latest flight of kamikaze mosquitos homing in on his right ear and neck as his thoughts drifted back to another hot summer day back home when he was happily skinny dipping with his wife, Sarah in a small, back country lake. He was smiling to himself remembering Sarah's joy and laughter only to be jolted back to the war and the jungle by the soft rhythmic tapping coming from someone further back on the trail. Craning his head toward the faint noise he was straining to make out what, if anything, it was, as his eyes scoured the trail through the underbrush, only to find it empty. No one was there.

"Calm yourself down, son," he thought. Maybe it's a woodpecker feeding on some tree bugs or maybe it's just my nerves. Any unusual sounds or even the usual ones in the jungle and especially in the enemy's backyard could sometimes have minds imagining the worst. Leaning in further, though, there was no mistaking the sound. The tapping was there. It was faint, and rhythmic, and it was growing louder with its approach.

The Montanan turned to the others on the team who hadn't yet heard the tapping and quickly snapped his fingers hard twice to get their attention. The finger snaps weren't loud and wouldn't carry outside of the team's small perimeter, but they were loud enough to get the others' attention and turn to him. With his non-shooting hand Daley pointed to his ear and then back toward where the noise was coming from as he mouthed the word, *'Gooks!'* The soft tapping soon gave way to the distinct steady slapping of metal against metal. There were no natural metal sounds in the jungle only those caused by human activity and Daley guessed it was a metal adjustment clip on a sling that was smacking against a rifle barrel or a half-emptied metal canteen banging against someone's hip as they were walking, and the slapping noise that was growing louder was coming their way. Daley slowly lowered himself to the ground and down behind the sights of his M-16. Hurried movement would catch an eye, but slower moves tended to go unnoticed. At the far end of the team's ambush line on the left and closest to the sound, Daley thumbed the Safety switch on his rifle from *Safe* to *Fire*. It was a barely audible click.

When Li saw Daley pointing to his ears and then back down the trail, he motioned to the rest of the team members down, not that the hand signal was needed since they too were quietly reaching for their weapons and readying themselves for a possible fight.

The tapping soon grew louder and now they all could hear it. Someone, or a few someones, were coming down the trail.

On his stomach and propped up on his elbows, Li reached for the Claymore *'clacker'*, ready to blow away whoever it was entering their kill zone. The tactic was to ambush a squad of enemy soldiers or less, but if it proved to be a larger unit, then Li would instead have his people lay low and watch and count the number of those passing by. They were to note the types of any heavy weapons they might be carrying, and any other pertinent things while hoping and maybe secretly praying the larger force of enemy soldiers would keep on walking.

The string of daisy-chained Claymore anti-personnel mines that Li had set out for ambush would give the team a distinct edge if a fight came. There was a *'when'* lingering to that as well because there always was. Jungle fighting was always a crap shoot, and you knew that when you entered the game. The Claymores made for better odds in a fight.

Each of the Claymores held a-pound-and-a-half of C-4, Play Dough-looking, high explosive with 700 buckshot-sized ball bearings encased inside the thick plastic covered shape charge. When detonated the Claymores would savage and shred anything in their path within fifty meters from the ground up to a high arc. The deadly destruction that came from three quick squeezes from the *'clacker'* made the imprinted placement reminder of: FRONT TOWARD ENEMY a man-made Tsunami warning.

The camouflaged, black, and green face painted Lurps, those the NVA and VC labeled as, *'Ghost Soldiers,'* were lying prone on the ground, ready for a fight, if it came to it. In their inception, the emphasis for the Long Range Reconnaissance Patrols was on the word *reconnaissance*, which meant to observe while going unnoticed. Early on, that was the job and task of the Lurps, only in the war years that followed, other tasks were assigned to the teams, including hit-and-run ambushes. Taking a note from the Viet Cong playbook, the Ranger Lurp teams began attacking the enemy patrols in their once-thought safe sanctuary areas in the jungle before disappearing back into the forever screen of foliage and trees. New tactics were being learned and employed, and the Lurp teams and command benefited from them.

Like hunters in a blind, the Lurps in their hide-site had limited, but reasonable visibility of a section of the larger path that led to the fork in the trail two yards away but well inside the kill zone. From where they were laying one or two of them had a line-of-sight view to the northwest as well. Anyone coming or going on the path wouldn't go unnoticed.

The tension was back again and amping up as the tapping grew louder. Tap, tap, tap, TAP, TAP...

There was nothing to see or hear until suddenly there was. Further down the trail an armed Viet Cong fighter was coming their way. To Li's surprise, the enemy soldier with the slapping rifle sling entered the kill zone and then stopped almost directly in front of the prone Lurps hiding only a few yards away.

The first VC stopped because a second fighter a few yards back had called for the halt. The fork in the trail appeared to have left the second soldier in a quandary. A heart-pounding Li was just about to blow them away with the Claymores when the talker came into view and shouldered his Assault rifle.

Taking out a folded map and a U.S. Army issued compass from a small shoulder bag he had looped across his chest he earnestly began studying the map and the two trails while trying to decide which one to take. With frown lines and some confusion in his eyes, he was doing his best trying to locate where he thought he was on the map. Taking a compass reading, he glanced once more at his map and back to the fork in the trail, unaware that the two of them were being watched and targeted.

The first Viet Cong soldier who had entered the kill zone and stopped kept her Assault rifle out in front of her stretched out on its sling when she turned back around and calmly used her trigger hand to slap away at the annoying mosquitoes as she frowned and waited. This was supposed to have been an easy go and so far it hadn't been. It wasn't only the mosquitoes that had her annoyed.

To Li's delight there were no more enemy soldiers in sight, just the two standing barely ten feet in front of them! And that gave the Team Leader an idea and a sudden change of plan. The numbers were on his side as would be the element of surprise. Quietly setting the Claymore clacker back down on the ground and picked up his M-16.

When Daley looked to Li for what to do next, Li used simple and slow hand signals to convey the new plan. He, Li, would step out on the trail and confront the soldier in the lead while Daley would step out and block the trail behind the Viet Cong fighter holding the map and compass. The remaining three team members, Wexler, Sanchez, and Angeles, would hold in place and cover them in the prisoner grab while keeping an eye out for any other enemy soldiers.

When Daley ran an open hand across his throat Li shook his head. The hasty plan was to surprise the two Viet Cong and capture them both alive, not kill them. Live Prisoners of War, Li knew, were always the better option, given who they were, what unit they belonged to, what direction they came from and which direction they were heading.

Sweet Sorrow

There was more to be gleaned from a captured enemy soldier who might inadvertently give away something critical under questioning, or who might explain why there were marks on their map and what they meant? More too, could be learned from what, if any, items they were carrying. Still, Daley was thinking it would be a hell of a lot easier and safer to kill them both, retrieve the weapons, map, and any other intel material they might have on them, and make a run for it. *Shoot and scoot* with Li requesting an extraction helicopter as they ran, but Daley would go with Li's decision even as the risk factor rose to a new and more dangerous level.

Daley also thought the plan had an additional benefit because of the Ranger Company's policy of awarding a two-day, in-country R&R to Vung Tau for any captured prisoner. Two times two was four glorious days at the R&R Center at Vung Tau with its dozens of bars, pretty girls in mini-dresses, dance halls, rock bands, and drunken nights and white sandy beaches even with god awful hangovers made for some pretty nice enticements.

During the French occupation Vung Tau was where the French Colonials and upper-class Vietnamese used to enjoy their own get-aways. Then it was known as *Cap Sainte Jacques.* Rumor had it that even the Viet Cong occasionally used it for their own R&Rs with nobody the wiser. Pretend you're a civilian, put the war on hold for a brief time, and blend in to party.

Yep, Daley was thinking, *that'll work for me just fine too, merci freaking beaucoup*!

Now all they had to do was successfully carry out Li's plan without getting shot or killed in the process. The same applied to their soon-to-be prisoners as well. Yeah, there was that. In addition, they would need to keep them mobile and able to walk. A wounded prisoner would only slow them down when the team made their getaway run to a pickup zone. Blindside tackle or stick the barrel of an M-16 in their noses, and the capture was complete. The impromptu scheme to capture the two VC fighters was a good one, but plans and schemes always worked perfectly on a drawing board until the ink spilled.

Oh, so quietly, raising up the two eased out of the hide-site and out onto the trail. Li slipped in directly behind the first armed Viet Cong soldier while Daley, who had a few more yards to go, hadn't yet stepped out onto the trail. Exposed as he was and because this was to be a prisoner grab, the Chinese/Hawaiian didn't fire on the woman, but instead quickly charged forward and body slammed her from behind, bowling her over just as she sensed what was happening. She had started to turn around while hurrying to bring up her AK-47 assault rifle to shoot Li, but she was a few seconds too late. The impact of the tackle knocked her off of her feet and she hit the ground with her face and chest with Li landing on her back.

That move likely saved both of their lives as the second, now shocked and surprised Viet Cong fighter who had been staring at the map and compass when it happened, looked up, saw what was happening, but was unsure what to do. Dropping the map and compass he stutter-stepped as he grabbed at his shouldered Assault rifle. Bringing the AK-47 up and around, he thumbed off the safety switch but held his fire. He couldn't shoot without hitting his comrade in what was now a wrestling match. At this distance any rounds would go through one and hit the other. But when the *Ghost Soldier* finally got the upper hand and began pinning her down with a knee, and just as he reared his head back to keep from getting punched by the woman who was wildly swinging her fists and clawing at the American, the Viet Cong fighter now had a clear target. This close he didn't need to aim; he just needed to steady the rifle barrel and pull the trigger. With his focus locked on the fight, he hadn't seen the second Lurp stepping out onto the trail behind him, but he heard him.

"Uh-uh," said Daley, shaking his head, only the enemy soldier went for the gunfight anyway. The Viet Cong fighter was turning and trying to fire on Li when the American reacted faster and with better aim.

Daley pulled the trigger and fired a three-round burst from his M-16 that ended the threat. The Viet Cong spy fell hard on the trail with gaping wounds to his chest and hips. His finger that had been on the trigger of the now badly tilted AK-47 sent a line of fire down into the dirt away from Li and the woman who were now wrestling on the ground. The bullets tore through the right side of the trail in an erratic line of fire. The wounded soldier's rifle fire emptied into the base of a nearby tree just as the assault rifle fell from his hands and he grabbed at his throat trying to find his lost breath from his punctured lungs and where one of the bullets tore out his heart.

His fight appeared over, but Harry Li's fight was still on. The woman was surprisingly strong and agile. He wasn't sure if she was a good grappler or if he was holding back. He never all-out fought a woman before and he was fighting only to stop her while she was fighting for her life, and wasn't about to give up.

Li was slapping away most of her punches and when it looked as though he finally had the upper hand the woman let out a feral cry and struck at his throat with her left hand while her right hand sent a tiger's claw-like strike clawing at his eyes. It was a vicious one-two that almost worked until Li managed to turn and lower his head at the last moment to save throat and his eyes. The left hand hit his neck but the woman's nails on her right hand clawed into the right side of his face, and scraped down to his mouth.

"Dammit!" he swore and then slapped her hard across her face and pointed a shaking finger at the monetarily stunned woman.

"DUNG LAI!" he yelled in Vietnamese and added the English equivalent. "STOP!"

The command in both languages, though, had no actual effect. She wasn't done fighting. She began wildly bucking and twisting, turning, and bucking, all the while yelling and screaming at the American. When she tried kneeing him and followed up with a haymaker punch he quickly leaned back and shifted his body weight to lessen the impact of the blows, but not by much.

The now more than a little pissed-off Team Leader didn't waste any time in slapping her harder a second time. This time, though, he put more weight behind it and swung from the proverbial bleachers. The roundhouse, open-hand slap that sounded like a dry tree limb cracking stunned the woman. Momentarily dazed, she stopped fighting and glared glazed-eyed at her captor with palpable hate as he held her down with his left elbow on her throat. The blood that was trickling down Li's cheek and chin from her claw marks mixed in with the black and green face camo paint that gave him an even more demon-looking, snarling appearance.

Still, she was still not showing signs of fear, just visceral anger.

"STOP!" he said, again, only this time a little louder.

"Wex! Gimme your rope!" Li said turning to PFC Wexler, his Rear Scout who came out of the hide-site to help restrain the woman. The *rope* Li needed was an eight-foot section of nylon rope that each team member carried on their LBE web gear harness. Wexler unhooked the D-ring that was attached to the rope and handed it to the Team Leader.

Each team member carried the eight-foot-long sections of rope on their shoulder harness for quick extractions from the jungle. If there was no open space big enough for an extraction helicopter to touch down the Lurps would untie the ropes, quickly fashion Swiss seats, or in a pinch, tie the ropes around their chests and beneath their armpits. When 90 or 100 foot nylon ropes were lowered from a hovering helicopter those on the ground would snap their D-ring carabiners into the ones on the ends of the extraction lines and the five team members would be yanked up through the trees and lifted out of the jungle. In what was called a Mcguire Rig Extraction, the Lurps would dangle beneath the helicopter and be whisked away to safety. Now the eight foot section of rope would serve another useful purpose.

"Cover the main trail!" Li said to Wexler, as he flipped the woman over on her stomach and wrenched her arms behind her back. "Sanchez! Cover the fork in the trail!"

Wexler and Sanchez kept watch on the trails, buying time and protection for Daley to search the wounded fighter's few pockets and shoulder bag for any more weapons or Intel material while Li tightly tied the woman's wrists and elbows securely behind her. Wrapping the nylon rope around her thin wrists one more time, he looped it around her neck before tying it off at her elbows to keep her from lashing out again.

When she began yelling again Li removed the olive-drab arm sling he used as a scarf and gagged the woman to shut her up.

Once an ambush or brief firefight occurred, the clock was ticking as the odds and numbers would turn against any Lurp team in enemy occupied territory, so Li and Daley were quick to finish what needed to be done so the team could make good their getaway.

Wexler's and Sanchez's eyes were locked on the trail for any more of the Viet Cong fighters they knew were bound to come running. This close to the border the exchange of gunfire would certainly bring them or any NVA soldiers hurrying to the area and that was something the Lurp team wouldn't wait around to see who it was and how many would show.

"Call in the contact!" Li said to Spec-4 Angeles, the team's radio/telephone operator still inside the hide-site area. "Tell Valhalla we got a few P-O-Ws and we're requesting an extraction. Coordinates to follow."

"On it!" said Angeles.

Kicking aside her AK-47 rifle Li stripped off the ammunition pouch she was wearing and used his bayonet to cut away a cloth shoulder bag she was carrying.

The woman was glaring at Li and her dark brown eyes were shooting bullets at the Asian-looking *Ghost Soldier* as she kicked at Li's left knee and connected with the toe of her thick tire-soled sandal.

"OW! You little shit!" cried Li, sweeping her feet out from under her and knocking her down on the hard-packed ground. When she tried kicking at him again he slapped her legs away, shoved them to the left, and then knelt on her right front thigh muscle to hold her down. The knee pressing hard into her thigh muscle had her wincing in pain and complying.

"Lady or no lady," warned Li, leaning in with a raised fist and scowling, "keep it up and I'll clock your ass, you *lolo wahini*!"

Whether she knew English, let alone the Hawaiian way of calling her a crazy woman, she understood the harsh tenor and tone of his words that successfully made the translation. The woman, who looked to be eighteen, but very well could've been thirty, stopped fighting, only while she stopped being combative her darting eyes were looking for an opportunity to strike again or make good an escape. There was no give there.

Pulling up her up to her feet Li shoved the woman toward their hide-site and kept pushing her until she was through the underbrush and well off of the trail.

"Sanchez?" Daley said, turning to the team's acting medic and tilted his head back towards the wounded Viet Cong soldier out on the path. "See what you can do to keep him alive."

Daley nodded toward the man he'd just shot.

Sanchez, the team's acting medic, nodded, and retrieved the team's Aid Bag from his rucksack, and then went to work to see what, if anything, he could do for

Sweet Sorrow

the wounded Viet Cong fighter. Meanwhile, Daley began gathering up the enemy weapons and what else that had been dropped in the melee.

"Angeles? Watch her," Li said to the R-T-O as he rearranged his floppy boonie cap that had been twisted behind his head and neck in the scuffle. "Don't let her escape."

Angeles nodded and kept watch over the woman as Li also began cleaning the blood off of his face with a First Aid bandage that he used to wipe it away. The face scratches weren't bad, just annoying. The bleeding had stopped, and the gouges stung from the sweat, but there were more important concerns on his mind. Retrieving his mission map from his cargo pants pocket he scoured it for a possible extraction location. The team needed to get away from the contact area.

The extraction site he found was a break in the rainforest 1,500-meters to their southeast. It looked to be big enough for a helicopter to land. Using his right index finger, he ran it across the coordinates on the map, eyeing the small lines and printed numbers.

"Tell them we're moving to this location for our pickup," Li said to his radioman and rattled off the map coordinates that Angeles repeated into the radio's handset.

There were seldom ever quick extractions for the teams. There were the distances to cover to the exfil locations for the Lurps, as well as the time needed for the inbound helicopters to fly out to reach those sites. Getting to those locations took time for both parties involved.

Given the gunfire and noise the brief fight had made, anyone hearing it would begin moving to the ambush site. The natural jungle clearing Li had his radioman call in for the exfil wasn't the first or second one that was previously selected at the start of the mission, nor was it the closest one to where they were. Figuring anyone who was coming their way might also send part of their force to those clearings, Li instead settled on the smaller one that would do but was a little further away.

Out on the trail Daley was still rummaging through the small shoulder bags. There wasn't much in the wounded soldier's bag beside what he had with the compass and map, and what appeared to be mostly personal effects; a small, dulled pencil, blank pad, a well-used chrome finished flashlight, and a simple folding knife. Inside the woman's bag there was a spoon, a small round tin of ointment, a box of matches, a cloth pouch with a handful of rice inside it, and a stale bread roll in a plain white paper wrapper. Opening the small tin, he sniffed the ointment and shrugged. It was a camphor/menthol herbal cream, mostly likely for scratches or bug bites. He closed the tin and dropped it back in the bag.

Inspecting the sandwich he peeled back the wrapper, pried the sliced roll apart, and saw that it was dried fish patty of some kind. It was garnished with a few day old sprigs of cilantro, some green pepper slices, carrot shavings, and a ball of rice held together by some liquid. When the pungent odor of *nuoc mam* fermented fish sauce soon rose up to greet him, he cringed, blew air out of his nostrils, and rewrapped the rice ball and the sandwich before shoving them back into the shoulder bag. Tucking the enemy map inside his right leg cargo pants pocket he looped the bag over his right shoulder and readied his rifle.

"How's he doing?" Daley asked Sanchez, while the acting medic shook his head.

The Viet Cong fighter Daley shot wasn't moving, and his lifeless eyes were fixed on a small patch of blue sky through the tops of trees and jungle canopy a hundred and twenty feet above him. A mosquito touched down on his left eyeball and when it couldn't find purchase it flitted down to the dead man's cheek. Flies and ants were already moving in to claim some of the prize.

"Let's drag the body into the brush and cover it up as best we can," Daley said to Sanchez. "No need to give anyone an easy start point to come after us."

Sanchez nodded and the two pulled the dead man off of the trail and then slipped back into the hide-site. Daley went back to cover up the paths they'd made moving onto the trail in the capture. Pulling brush and grass back into place as best he could he tried not to leave much in the way of sign.

Back inside the hide-site Daley handed the dead fighter's cloth bag and the map over to his team leader. Li took the map, looked it over and smiled at the marks that were on it before folding it up and then shoving it into his top left pocket.

"What's in the bags?" asked Li, as he opened the shoulder bag and took a look inside.

"Personal items, mostly, oh, and a rice ball and a hoagie," said Daley.

"A what?"

"A hoagie! You know, a bread roll in the woman's bag," Daley replied as Li pulled out the bread roll, peeled away the paper wrapping, and sniffed at what was in it.

"Dried fish cake."

Shrugging at the filling, he wrapped the sandwich back up and shoved it back into the shoulder bag and tied the cut straps back together for easy carrying.

"Valhalla wants us to move to an extraction site," said Angeles, the R-T-O to Li. "An ARVN helicopter will be picking us up. ARVN Rangers."

"ARVN Rangers?"

"They're some serious dudes," Daley said to Li. "Worked with a few in the CAV."

Li and the others had only heard about the ARVN Rangers and had little to go on other than Daley's word, so Li just nodded and said, "Good. That'll work!"

To the others he said, "Let's saddle up and *Di-Di Mau!*"

Di-Di Mau was Vietnamese for *'Leave quickly,'* and if they weren't fluent in Vietnamese that particular phrase was something they were familiar with and well-understood. It was time to get the hell out of Dodge.

Checking his compass heading again Li eyed the line of travel and took point and the team moved in Ranger file through the rainforest behind him. The small natural clearing he had chosen for their extraction was less than a mile away as the crow flies. But they weren't crows, and getting to it by keeping off of any paths or trails and busting brush would take some time, even if they hustled.

Angeles, the R-T-O followed Li, followed by the gagged and bound prisoner with Daley keeping an eye on her as they went. Bound as she was, she still could make a run for it. Daley's job was to make sure that she didn't run. Sanchez was next and a wary Wexler brought up the rear. Every few yards he did a slow 360 degree pivot to make sure no one was on their tail before following the others in line.

The gunfire would indeed bring attention to the ambush site, and draw in anyone nearby, especially those who were expecting two of their comrades, now overdue, to turn up soon. They would find the ambush site, the blood, the drag marks, and inevitably the body. The body of the dead spy would be easy enough to find as the dead man's bowels would vacate in the high heat, and the horrible stench, along with the cloud of frenzied black bottle flies that would swarm in to dance on the decaying corpse would lead them to their dead comrade. It would also lead an animal or two to scurry in and rip and tear off bits and pieces of the body before the noise of the approaching searchers would scare them away. Finding the body, the searchers would then become avengers and would begin hunting the *Ghost Soldier* ambushers.

Even with their 90 to 100 pound rucksacks, the fleeing Lurps wouldn't be taking any rest breaks. The clock was ticking, and they were now moving with a more immediate purpose. They were maybe 300 meters into the run when they heard the single shot of an AK-47 back the direction of their ambush hide-site.

The NVA or Viet Cong had found the takedown site. The single round fired into the sky was a signal from a Viet Cong fighter or NVA soldier telling other enemy soldiers in the area to converge on that location. It also told Li and the others that they would sooner, rather than later, be having company.

It wouldn't take long to find the way the team had gone. Any halfway decent tracker would be able to determine the direction of travel the five Lurps and their prisoner were taking through the brush, especially the prisoner, who was dragging her feet and kicking up ground as much as she could to leave scrapes and sign for her people to follow. Catching on to what she was doing Daley told her to stop it, but he was met with a defiant glare. Daley and those Rangers behind them would do their best to clean up any of her scuff marks as well any of their own sign, but there would always be tell-tale sign. It was unavoidable.

Anyone tracking them, and the Viet Cong and NVA had some good trackers, would be subject to the time and distance gap as well. The race was on, but it would be a cautious race. It had to be unless the trackers ran headlong into an ambush themselves.

The Lurp team had a good lead. Even so, they picked up their pace.

Chapter 7

Jungles everywhere have their own unique orchestrated choral symphonies and those in the border regions of South Vietnam begin with the whispered tropical breezes out of the South China Sea that play across the treetops of the ancient rainforests like trembling woodwinds. They are joined by a buzzing chorus from mosquitoes, and the endless ratcheting clicks of cicadas, crickets, and katydids that synchronize and set the tempo of the daily performance.

From the fluttering wings and squawks and cries of birds, the snorts, grunts, and barks from unseen wild boar, sun bears, or muntjac deer, and the deep guttural rumbles and growls of tigers, leopards, and civets to the occasional loud voices from Howler, gibbon, or Duoc monkeys, or the skittering runs of rats, monitor lizards, geckos, and any one or a variety of the dozens of species of venomous snakes slithering through the underbrush and across the rainforest floor, all played and contributed to the jungle's exploration of sound.

This was the natural background music of the primeval wilds during the daylight and evening hours, the expected norm telling the Lurps the surrounding jungle was momentarily safe from enemy patrols and imminent combat in their latest hide-site. The run through the jungle from the kill zone to the extraction site had left them wiping away dripping sweat and huffing and puffing, but not quite reaching for their canteens. Even after a few deliberate changes in their line of travel to throw off anyone tracking them they had made good time but there was still more to do. Before they settled in to wait for the inbound helicopter they needed to find a good place to hunker down and then do a quick recon on the pickup zone to make sure all was Good-to-Go.

For the veteran Lurps the jungle symphony was nothing out of the ordinary while for the newer team members, the lowly *'Cherries'* on their first few patrols, every distinct sound or flickering shadow was a possible deadly threat until they took notice of how the more seasoned members of the team responded and reacted. On the long range patrols, the veteran Rangers didn't let down their guard. They simply adjusted the tension.

"Keep a good look out," Li said to the others. "Hopefully, we threw them off track, but best to play it smart."

Nods and grunts followed.

Other than what little noise the team members were making, setting up a defensive posture and settling in at the edge of the pickup location of the small, grassland clearing, the jungle that enveloped them was quiet of any other human-made sounds or activity. The natural symphony was on-going and as unobtrusive and non-threatening as background elevator music.

To Nine-Four's team leader it looked as though they would avoid a running gun battle with the enemy soldiers tracking them and that was just dandy with him.

Li, though, was well-aware that looks could be deceiving, especially in a war zone, deep in enemy held territory, so he wasn't taking any unnecessary chances. Snipers tended to be quiet too, as were enemy trackers closing in on their prey, so Li positioned the team inside the depression from a large, old growth tree that had been blown down during a long-passed Monsoon storm.

The weathered bowl-like depression left behind when the roots of the tree dug out the ground was deep and wide enough to give the five Lurps and their agitated prisoner reasonable cover and adequate protection. The fallen tree made for a good bullet stopper too. An uneven carpet of bright green moss covered the top of the rotting, three foot wide trunk like a bad wig. Its five-foot high exposed root system which had been pulled from the ground when the tree fell was still partially filled in with a screen of rocks and stones encased in hard-packed orange clay. If trouble came, the natural fox hole would serve the team well.

That it was less than ten yards from the clearing also made it ideal. Now it was the *wait* after the *hurry up* and hopefully, a short wait because the game clock was still ticking.

"Find out how far out the bird is," Li said to Angeles, his RTO.

Angeles nodded and made the call as Li had the prisoner sit and told Sanchez, Wexler, and Angeles to keep an eye on her while he and Daley crept out to check out the open grassland clearing and its oblong perimeter.

Staying inside the tree line, the two carefully examined the clearing's perimeter looking for gun positions or any lone enemy soldier that might have been assigned to monitor the clearing, which wasn't an uncommon practice. A few meters to their Li pointed out an abandoned heavy machine gun pit where a Soviet DShk .51 caliber had once sat on a tripod waiting to bring down any American or South Vietnamese aircraft that came its way. The DShk or *Dish-ka*, as it was more commonly referred to, had also earned the nickname as *'the Copter Killer'* for its mile and a half maximum effective range that could easily pierce anything flying in the sky cruising within its sites and limits. Any targeted aircraft would soon become a soup strainer if the aircraft didn't blow up in a fireball from a direct hit to its fuel tank.

Just beyond the pit there were several long abandoned fighting positions that showed no signs that anyone had used or even visited them in a while, and that too was working in the team's favor. The small clearing that would serve as the PZ or Pickup Zone could easily fit their inbound helicopter. Better still, the ground was dry.

Li breathed a sigh of relief that the big gun and the squad or platoon that had once been using it were long gone. With no sign of the enemy in or around the clearing, a quick extraction was do-able.

"Looks like we're Good-to-Go here," Li whispered, and Daley agreed. When the two made their way back to the others and settled into the hollow he noticed that the prisoner's face was flushed from the run and that she was heavily sweating.

"Give her a drink from your canteen," he said to his R-T-O. "Can't have her die from heat stroke before we get our in-country R&R."

Angeles took out his canteen, unscrewed the cap, and then removed the prisoner's gag.

As she drank her eyes were locked on the radioman.

"*Ban la nguoi Viet Nam. Tai!*" she said to him, angrily.

"What?"

"She thinks you're Vietnamese," said Daley, watching on and chuckling. The woman shot Daley a nasty look that he shrugged off.

"*Xin loi, ban sai roi*," he said to the woman.

"Oh man, you speak Vietnamese?" asked the radioman, staring at the Montanan like he was a wizard.

"Enough to get the gist of what she's saying and to tell her sorry, but she's wrong."

At five-feet, five-inches in height and 130 pounds, and with his thin build, black hair, and brown eyes, and perhaps because of the floppy hat and the olive drab colored bandana wrapped around his thin neck, Angeles looked to be a fellow countryman to the woman.

"See! So, it ain't just us," Daley said as Angeles grinned and flipped him off.

Cupping his hand over the radio's handset as he waited for a call back on the status of the inbound chopper, Angeles turned back to the P-O-W.

"I'm from L.A., lady, so *no habla nuoc mam*!"

The now confused woman sat back and wondered about these Americans with a Chinese team leader, a big grinning white guy, a somber skinny Mexican, a Filipino who looked Vietnamese, and a soldier who could pass for a gangster she'd once seen in an old French movie.

"The bird's ten minutes out," Angeles said to Li.

The Team Leader acknowledged him with a nod as he sat back down and then methodically began going through the woman's cloth shoulder bag. Something was bothering him about his initial look, something that he couldn't quite pin down and it was nagging at him.

Dumping out the bag's contents he set aside the comb and pencil and then took apart the flashlight. Satisfied there was nothing beneath the two batteries or inside its plastic housing, he placed the flashlight down as well. Unscrewing the tin of the menthol smelling, tan colored balm, he stuck his finger into the dense cream to see what, if anything, was hiding beneath it. Nothing was out of the ordinary. He wiped the finger on his jungle fatigue trousers.

Next, he dumped the rice ball and the sandwich roll out on the ground before turning the small bag inside out. It was what it was supposed to be, a small, cloth bag and nothing more. Picking up the sandwich, he unwrapped it, sniffed at it, gave a *meh* shrug, and laid out its contents in front of him. He stared at the small piece of dried fish cake, wilted green leaf of some kind, and shredded carrot and hot peppers and stain of fish sauce like an ancient oracle reading some sacred, dropped bones trying hard to decipher their meaning, but got nothing.

A long moment later told him there was nothing to learn, but when he started to wrap it all back up the bread roll shifted, and he noticed a series of numbers and notes on the paper beneath the bread roll. His eyes focused on the small row of numbers, and Vietnamese *Quoc-ngu* script within the crinkled folds. The *Quoc-ngu* Vietnamese writing system that the early Portuguese and French Missionaries created to reflect the tones, consonants, and vowels of the Vietnamese language. To Li it might as well have been Greek, but he suspected it was more than just a menu item order. He picked apart the sandwich roll looking for more clues but found nothing but the food stuff that he dumped over the rice while he held onto and straightened the wrapper.

"Hey Gus! What do you make of this?" Li said, leaning over and passing the paper wrapper over to Daley.

The Montanan took the paper and studied what was on it for a moment before flipping it over and then back again. He shrugged.

"Don't know, coordinates and references of some kind, maybe," he said, in a low voice handing it back to the team leader. "Could be a code too since the numbers don't look like a sell-by date."

No poker player, the Viet Cong prisoner's eyes flashed to Daley and then quickly turned away so as not to give away her hand, but the tell was there, and it hadn't gone unnoticed. Her dark eyes were tear bright, not from fear, but renewed anger.

"Hey, what's this?" Li asked the woman, waving the paper in front of her and pointing to numbers and writing. "You understand English? You *hieu biet* English? What's this?"

The brooding woman didn't answer, but kept up her defiant, jaw-trembling glare at the Chinese/Hawaiian as Li folded the wrapper and stuck it in his jungle fatigue cargo pants right side, leg pocket.

Watching on, Daley snorted.

"Man, she really hates you!" he said. "She's got that same look my wife gave me one winter when she was trying on a pair of old jeans of hers in the mirror and asked me if I thought they made her ass look big, and I told her they wouldn't, if she used a wider mirror."

"Used to sleeping alone on couches, are you?"

"Naw Harry, my dog still loves me. However, my wife has a wonderful sense of humor, because later that same day when she had me take out the garbage, she locked the door behind me, laughed, and then asked how the jeans looked now while I was standing outside freezing my ass off in the fifteen degree winter temperature. This one here, though, I suspect would gut you and me both with a spoon right now, given the chance."

"Then we won't give her a chance."

"No, we won't."

"Fifteen degrees? Whoa! Wait a minute. How long did your wife make you wait outside in the cold?" asked Sanchez, overhearing the conversation.

"Long enough for my I-Q to damn near rise up into double-digits and for my eyesight to miraculously improve! You married?"

"No, not yet, but I am engaged. We're getting married when I get home."

"Then take my little story to the altar with you and just remember that's the last time you'll ever dress yourself without your wife shaking her head and muttering, '*Oh my God, uh-uh, no*! Don't fight it, just nod, and change into something else, preferably something she bought you."

"Yeah, especially if you ever want to see her naked and smiling at you again," said Angeles.

"I see you're married too!" laughed Daley.

"Happily, according to my wife!" Angeles said, holding up his left hand and flashing the pale, tan line where his wedding band had been before he took it off back at the company before the start of the mission. Rings glistened and all that glittered in combat could draw fire. The ring, along with his wallet and watch and other personal effects were locked in his foot locker back at the platoon hootch.

In the near distance they could hear the familiar chopping noise from the extraction helicopter's rotor blades cutting through the sky and growing in volume. The backpacked team radio had Angeles once more cupping the handset as he leaned over to Li.

"The ARVN chopper is on its short final. They want us to pop smoke."

"I'm on it," Li said, getting to his feet and grabbing a purple smoke grenade that was taped to his shoulder harness.

He pulled the pull ring on the beer can-sized canister as he walked out to the edge of the grass field, picked a spot to aim at, and then tossed it out onto the open clearing. The spoon on the mousetrap fuse sprang away in the throw and the smoke grenade made a popping sound as it flew and tumbled on the ground when it hit. A loud hissing noise came from the smoke grenade even as it was tumbling and finally rolled to a stop. A cloud of purple smoke poured out of the emission holes in the top and bottom of the six-inch canister, and sent the colored smoke rising and swirling into the sky in a massive colorful display.

"Tell them there's smoke out!"

"Roger that," said Angeles.

A moment later a call came back to the Lurps.

"They identify Purple Haze. Guess Hendrix rocks here too," Angeles said to the Team Leader.

Back into the radio telephone handset Angeles confirmed the color of the smoke to the helicopter pilot as Li had the team up and ready to move. The tension was back up to high levels because of the duality of the smoke signal that would guide the helicopter to their location while also pinpointing it to any enemy soldiers that might be nearby tracking them.

When the prisoner was reluctant to stand, Daley pulled her up to her feet by her elbows and shoved her forward.

"Ladies first," he said, and escorted her through the scrub brush towards the clearing by her left elbow. "Move!"

Chapter 8

The extraction helicopter came in fast and low over the trees before it flared to a landing in the clearing in front of the scattering cloud of purple smoke. The face of a black tiger in a red outline and white star background painted on the nose of the Huey showed who it was picking up their American counterparts.

The five Lurps and their Viet Cong prisoner, raced out of the cover of the jungle towards the awaiting Vietnamese helicopter where, to their surprise, a blond-haired, blue-eyed gringo was waving them on from the open cargo bay.

"COME ON!" yelled the gringo over the noise of the Huey's spinning rotor blades. "LET'S GO! MOVE IT! MOVE IT!"

The gringo was dressed in a South Vietnamese Ranger tiger stripe fatigues and beret. The foreign uniform was adorned with ARVN Ranger and U.S. Army combat patches. While his uniform was that of an American Advisor to the ARVN Rangers, his rank insignia showed that he was an E-7, a Sergeant First Class.

"COME ON! LET'S GO! LET'S GO!" he yelled, pulling the rucksack laden team members and their captive inside the open cargo bay because the helicopter wasn't going to be on the ground for longer than ten seconds.

When they were all aboard and bunched up in the crowded open cargo bay the gringo yelled something in Vietnamese to the helicopter's Crew Chief. The Crew Chief nodded and relayed the message to the pilot, and the Huey quickly lifted off and began its skyward climb getaway.

Green tracers from enemy machine gun fire rose out of the jungle from the west following the flight fifty yards ahead and had the pilot quickly veering away from the line of fire. The South Vietnamese Ranger Crew Chief on the left side of the cargo bay returned fire back down towards the jungle in a brass kicking fury as empty machine gun round shells and broken links landed and danced at his feet before rolling over the side of the open doorway.

The enemy soldiers tracking the Lurps failed to find their quarry in time, and in a last, desperate attempt to seek their revenge, aimed in on the noise of the helicopter that they could barely glimpse and then lost through the treetop canopy of the jungle. Several new lines of enemy machine gun rounds rose up through the trees and missed their target by the proverbial long shot. The opportunity was lost, but the frustrated Viet Cong soldiers kept up their fire. Anger was wasting a lot of rounds.

The pilot soon had the aircraft not yet out of range but out of visual sight of the incoming enemy fire, something the door gunner understood long before the enemy soldiers on the ground had finally figured it out. The Crew Chief eased back away from the bungee cord-mounted M-60 machine gun and smiled to the American Advisor with a thumbs-up. If the crew chief weighed 115 pounds then it was only because of his flight helmet, the holstered .45 pistol on his right hip, and the Nomex flight suit, gloves, and boots he was wearing. Small as he was, the Crew Chief was still lethal.

The thumbs-up elicited tired smiles and welcomed laughter of relief all around the cargo bay except for the trussed-up woman who was sitting cross-legged on the cold metal floor. Her head was lowered in resignation to her fate as a captive and what awaited her once the bird touched down.

"Romeo Company Lurps, huh?" said the gringo over the noise of the helicopter. His accent that was further down the Arkansas River from Tulsa held a honky-tonk edge.

"Yes, Sergeant," said Li. "Rangers."

"Which division?"

"No Division. We're attached to MAC-V Headquarters and work out of Camp Mackie."

"Huh? Didn't know MAC-V had a Lurp/Ranger company."

"I don't think they do either. We get loaned out a lot."

"You the Team leader?"

"Yes, Sergeant...:

"Jonsen, Lars Jonsen, E-7 Sergeant First Class, one-each. I'm an Advisor working with the ARVN Rangers."

"Spec-4 Li, Harry Li," the team leader said, nodding and happy that the mission was over, it was a success, and they were out of the jungle.

"Well, it looks like you and your boys done good," Jonsen said, nodding to the prisoner and the captured weapons. "Viet Cong P-O-Ws are always a good catch. Was she alone?"

"No, we had one enemy K-I-A, one of her buddies."

"And their friends came hunting for you."

Li gave a slow nod staring back out towards the enemy's green tracer rounds that flew high in a burning arc and fell like copper jacketed lead weights over the jungle. It had been another Hit-and-Run mission and they'd made good their escape, once again, and the spent adrenaline gave way to a sudden overwhelming weariness. Their thoughts turned inward, and it was a quiet ride.

It was a little under 25 minutes later when the helicopter touched down on the flightline of the ARVN Ranger's Base Camp. As the Huey landed on the tarmac and the bird settled on its skids, and the turbine engine wound down to a low hum, a stern-looking, Bantamweight Vietnamese Captain and a just as small but surprisingly muscular-looking older NCO senior sergeant hurried over to greet the Americans and take control of the captured combatant.

The NCO, who was the closest to the helicopter's open cargo bay, did a double take on the Viet Cong prisoner. His surprise that it was a woman quickly turned to red-faced outrage and anger, but for another reason not yet understood by the Americans. Several trembling veins in his forehead threatened to burst. There was no mistaking the thoughts the ARVN Ranger Sergeant had as to what he was feeling about the prisoner.

He lashed out at the young woman in Vietnamese in a spittle driven tirade as he brusquely yanked her out of the open cargo bay and sent her stumbling to the hard-packed ground and on her knees. Pulling her up to her feet, he screamed at her to keep her eyes staring at the ground, only the woman held her chin up defiantly and glared back up at him. The rebellious glare earned her a hard slap across the face and a second slap until she complied with his command. It looked as though he was getting ready to kick her.

"Hey now!" protested Daley only to be ignored by both the ARVN Captain and the NCO. Their focus was locked on the young woman.

"Wait one, Gus," Li said, holding him back by the elbow.

"But..."

"Dude, she was turning an A-K on us and would've killed us both, if she had the chance and hey, she really wanted that chance."

It was true and Daley didn't like it but begrudgingly held back from coming to her defense. Trussed up as she was, she wasn't a threat.

"She was carrying these," Li said, turning to Sergeant Jonsen and handing him the dead man's compass and map along with the woman's shoulder bag and her weapon.

"Found this too," he added, reaching into his pocket, and pulling the folded sandwich wrapper. "There's some writing and numbers on the sandwich wrapper that might be important. Wasn't sure, but maybe you might make something of it."

Li handed the wrapper to Jonsen, who unfolded it, and then looked over the small print and numbers.

"Hmm," Jonsen said, obviously troubled by what he saw before handing the paper over to his Vietnamese counterpart. "It's a simple code and not a good one."

His Oklahoman accent would give any Texan a run for their money when it came to the thickness of the drawl, even as he broke into Vietnamese to his counterpart.

The ARVN Ranger NCO's dark eyes narrowed even further as he figured out what was on the paper, and then turned back yelling at the woman inches from her face in a verbal tirade that said another hard slap was coming.

The ARVN Ranger NCO handed the wrapper to the ARVN Ranger officer who scanned it before he too, turned and glared at the young woman as he gave the command for the angry NCO to take her away. The two lower enlisted Vietnamese Rangers led the prisoner away.

"Wouldn't want to be her right about now," said Sanchez watching on.

Daley quietly nodded.

"No, you wouldn't, young Ranger," said Jonsen. "Sergeant Thi recognized her. Thi's the one who slapped her. She works here on our base as a cleaning lady."

"A cleaning lady!" said Daley.

"And a Viet Cong spy from the looks of it."

"That *ain't* good."

"No, it ain't, at least for her, especially with what she had on that paper and the direction she was heading on the map when you guys scooped her up."

"Cambodia?"

"Uh-huh, and more than likely to the North Vietnamese and Viet Cong COSVN jungle headquarters Base Camp just over the border."

"Yo Dude, I thought it was cleared out last year during the incursion?"

"It was, but they're back," said the Advisor. "In force. Did you just call me, *Dude*?" Jonsen said.

"Sorry, Sergeant," apologized Li while Jonsen laughed.

"What's gonna happen to her?" asked Daley watching the woman being briskly led away while he led the conversation away from the Dude remark.

"Can't say what they'll do until they interrogate her, but whatever they decide on, I can tell you this much. It won't be pretty. The sergeant lost his wife and baby girl in a mortar attack a few weeks ago. Now we know why. It's lucky for us we brought you back here."

"Lucky for us, too, seeing how Charlie was tracking us. Thanks for coming out to get us," Li said to the American Advisor. "Would you thank the pilot and crew for us as well?"

Jonsen nodded and when he passed along the '*thank you*' in '*Y'all*'- tainted Vietnamese to the helicopter's crew chief, the crew chief said something more than, '*you're welcome*' back to the Advisor and waved to Li and the others.

"He says you're very welcome and also that he just heard on the radio before the bird shut down that your people have a helicopter coming in from Camp Mackie to get you. It's 20 minutes out."

"Thank you, Sergeant."

"No problem. You folks might as well drop your rucks on the edge of the flightline and take a break," he said. "It's a lot cooler out here than it is in the Command Post. I'll be back in a bit."

Jonsen followed the Vietnamese Rangers lead and walked off towards the large, old French concrete bunker from the late 1940s that was heavily fortified and now served as the ARVN Rangers' CP, their Command Post. True to CP status, sandbagged guard positions and heavy fencing surrounded the large bunker with the iron gate protecting its entrance. Two serious-looking Vietnamese Rangers sat behind a sandbagged machine gun post guarding the CP.

Sweet Sorrow

The five Lurps set their weapons down, dropped their rucksacks, and then sat, or stretched out back against the heavy packs to relax; something that was seldom the case on the previous four days of their patrol.

Jonsen returned a short time later carrying an armful of cans of Cokes which he handed to the team members.

"Thought you guys could use these," he said, reaching into his top right pocket and handing Li a church key can opener.

While the five GIs were opening their soft drinks Jonsen pulled out a small notebook and ballpoint pen from his top left pocket and handed both to Li.

"Listen up! I need your full names and ranks," he said. "Print them nice and neat, like."

Knowing that replying, '*why*' or '*what for*?' seldom was the correct response in the military when someone with a higher rank requested or ordered you to do something, Li nodded and printed out his name and rank.

"Sanchez?" he said, turning to the Ranger seated beside him. "Your first name's Julio, right?"

"Hulio," he replied, using the Spanish pronunciation where the J took on a H sound as Li just stared back at him.

"I thought it was Julio."

"It is. It's Hulio. J-U-L-I-O."

"J?"

"Yes. *Hulio*. J-U-L-I-O. The J's silent."

Li crossed out the H and finished jotting down the name. "So did you enlist in the Army or were you drafted?"

"I enlisted."

"Which means you joined, not *hoined*. Got it, " he said and then turned to Daley, his Assistant Team Leader. "Gus is, like, short for what?"

"Gustav."

"What the fuck? Really?"

"Yep. My Mom's people were '*Ya shure ya'bet'cha*' Swedish, and my Dad's grandfather was old potato famine Irish."

"Goose-toff," Li said out loud as he was writing.

"Wexler?"

"Aaron, Private First Class."

"Private First Class? You're one of the company's original Lurps! You should've been a Spec-4 or Buck Sergeant by now."

Wexler shrugged. "I got passed over."

"Oh yeah, that's right. You and what's his name stole a jeep."

"Redmond."

"Yeah, yeah, Redmond. What an asshole!"

"He was."

"Didn't he get kicked out of the Company for that and fighting with an MP?"

"He did, and for leaving me behind after I smacked my head on the windshield. I got a small cut here," he said, pointing to a small, jagged scar above his left eye.

The small white scar earned him a nod.

"And you got to stay in the Company."

Wexler shrugged again. "Uh-huh. I didn't get kicked out because I was too drunk to realize I had climbed into a stolen jeep, and because when the MPs arrested us I didn't put up a fight. I couldn't. I was in the passenger's seat, damn near passed out, and bleeding."

"That's right! It was the Colonel's jeep! Epic, Dude! You pissed yourself..."

"And into the Colonel's fancy sheepskin seat cover too, so..."

"So, you're still a Private First Class. A righteous one, at that!" laughed Li. "Fucking legend!"

Turning to his radioman, he asked, "Angeles? What's your first name?"

"Leo."

"Rank? PFC or Spec-4?"

"Spec-4."

"Okay," Li said, finishing the list and checking it over before he handed the notebook and pen back to Jonsen.

Listening in, Jonsen chuckled as he looked over the names and ranks in the notebook, seeing if they were legible and all there. Nodding with a grunt that possibly meant, '*Okay*' or '*good*' or '*that'll do,*' he headed back to the Command bunker.

It wasn't even ten minutes later the South Vietnamese Ranger Commander, his leather-faced senior top sergeant, and Jonsen came out from the headquarters bunker towards the five Lurps seated on the flight line. Behind the three, a lower ranking ARVN Ranger followed carrying a small open box in his hands.

"On your feet, Rangers!" yelled Jonsen to the lounging Lurps. "*AHH-ten-SHUN!*"

Li and the others quickly jumped to their feet, came to the position of attention, and saluted the Colonel when the small party came to a halt in front of the team.

The Colonel returned their salutes with a crisp salute of his own, and his senior NCO barked out a command to the soldier behind them holding a box, stepped forward. The senior NCO retrieved the first item from the box and handed it to his Commanding Officer.

"Colonel Nguyen is awarding each of you the Vietnamese Ranger Badge."

The ARVN Ranger Colonel stepped forward with the small, glistening silver and gold colored qualification badge that was meant for display on a dress uniform and pinned it above the right front shirt pocket of Li's camouflage jungle fatigues.

Reaching back, the senior NCO retrieved the corresponding Republic of South Vietnam Army certificate from the box that the Colonel presented to Li with an accompanying handshake and salute.

Li and the other Americans had failed to hide their happy grins as one-by-one the Colonel pinned the Vietnamese Ranger badges to their sweat stained and filthy uniforms, presented them the matching certificates, saluted, and then shook their hands.

Once done the ARVN Ranger Colonel thanked the Americans in English before he, the senior NCO, and the lower enlisted Ranger in the officiating party walked off leaving SFC Jonsen with the Romeo Company Rangers after the brief ceremony. The thanks they received was sincere as was the reasoning behind it.

"Turns out the sandwich wrapper was important enough for the Colonel to show his appreciation. The numbers and Vietnamese script they used was a simple code with specific targeted coordinates of our camp and something more."

"More?"

"Yeah, one of them was for the Colonel's family compound right down to the welcome mat…"

"He has a welcome mat?" said Sanchez only to have Jonsen and Li shoot him a troubled look.

"It's a folksy saying to imply close proximity," explained Jonsen. "*Comprende*?"

"*Si*."

"*Muy bien*. Anyway, besides his family home, the homes or locations of his Executive Officer's and Top sergeant's families were on the list. I'm talking wives, kids, aunts, uncles, and grandparents, pigs, chickens, and hot sauce, which is why the Colonel personally wanted to award you the badges. So again, let me say one more time, Rangers. *Ya'll* done good. Wear the badges proudly. You saved some lives."

Chapter 9

For First Sergeant Poplawski it was a long, miserable helicopter ride back to Camp Mackie from Long Binh, only it wasn't the shuddering, hour-long, jet-fuel odorous flight that had soured his disposition. He was still brooding over MAC-V's decision to disband Romeo Company.

While the enclosed cabin of the CH-47 Chinook heavy-lift helicopter made conversation easier than it would've been had they been on a smaller open-door Huey, he still found himself upping his volume to be heard over the noise from the overhead tandem rotors and the high pitched whine of the twin turbine engines located on each side of the helicopter's rear pylon.

"Dumbass sonsofbitches," he growled to his Captain, doing a little whining of his own on the canvas bench seating on the port side of the helicopter.

Captain Robison, who was seated beside him and knew what was really troubling him, let him vent. They'd been bureaucratically ambushed by MAC-V and left with a stinging and scraping, rubbed-raw wound.

The trouble was that the Senior NCO's booming comment had carried, as did its harsh edge and tone. He was still pissed-off and the Captain felt he had every right to be, even if several other passengers in the aircraft seated directly across from the two Rangers were unsure why.

Of the sixteen passengers on the flight, fourteen of which were heavily sweating new arrivals from the Replacement Depot in Bien Hoa that were being ferried up to Camp Mackie to join their units for the start of their one-year combat tours of duty. However, two of them, a young *'Shake and Bake'* Buck sergeant and a wide-eyed Private First Class, mistook the intimidating looking, weathered veteran's angry criticism for possibly something that might've had to do with them.

"No, not you," Poplawski semi-apologized to the two cowed passengers, waving it off, and shaking his head. "Some other dumbasses."

The *'Shake and Bake'* Buck Sergeant cautiously nodded then turned his attention to the tops of his shiny, new jungle boots while the PFC tried to find something inside the belly of the aircraft more interesting to look at other than the angry face of the grumbling NCO.

If his thick neck and fullback frame, dark scowl, and the holstered .45 on his right hip weren't threatening enough, then his sun-faded jungle fatigues adorned with Special Forces, Ranger, and Airborne patches and other elite foreign military tabs and the weathered Combat Infantryman's Badge said he wasn't someone to be taken lightly. With the flap of the holster hiding much of the senior NCO's pistol grip, they were afraid to try for a closer look to see if there were notches carved into it, and if there was space for a few more.

Sweet Sorrow

The Ranger First Sergeant went quiet for the remainder of the flight while his disposition and attitude remained on slow smolder.

Shortly after 1800 hours the Chinook lumbered in and touched down on the Perforated Steel Planking that was the runway at Camp Mackie. It landed with a heavy back-wheel thump, settled on the front wheels, leveled, and taxied over to the Camp's small tin-roofed shack, which served as its flight terminal, where it came to a stop.

As the big helicopter's turbines wound down, the Flight Engineer lowered the back ramp, and the waning light of afternoon bathed the distant outpost in a warm amber glow that almost made Camp Mackie appear idyllic. Almost. The wafting odor and smoke from a nearby shit burning detail broke through the slowing rotor blades of the helicopter offering a different kind of welcoming setting.

Exiting the aircraft Captain Robison gave a nod of thanks to the Flight Engineer. First Sergeant Poplawski did as well, only with less enthusiasm. He was still brooding. The Flight Engineer, a tall, rangy-looking staff sergeant, nodded back to the two and motioned for the other passengers, the new arrivals, to follow before he began hauling seven large orange nylon sacks of mail from the back of the Chinook.

Chinooks were the lifelines to the camps bringing in new replacements, materials, and equipment. They were workhorses. In combat the large helicopters could easily insert and bring out a platoon of soldiers in a jungle clearing or lower a rope ladder for those same soldiers, when the Chinook couldn't land. They could lift out a downed Huey or a damaged Loach Scout helicopter to be brought back and repaired, could sling load in a howitzer cannon, or pallets of ammunition and supplies loaded into bulging nets dangling beneath the helicopter on a long cable. They also ferried in mail bags filled with birthday cards, letters, and boxes of cookies and other goodies sent from home to GIs, and for the two Romeo Company Rangers, it was their better taxi ride home.

Robison and Poplawski were just yards away from the Chinook when the first enemy heavy mortar round fell on the Camp.

The booming explosion came from the center of the Base Camp in the direction of the BIG-TOC, Camp Mackie's Command Post. The three mortar rounds that quickly followed were being systematically walked across the Base Camp, all seemingly aimed specifically on strategic and big money targets like Mackie's two artillery batteries and any aircraft parked on the air field. A loud siren warning the Camp of incoming enemy rounds began its piercing wail and served as a backdrop to the deafening blasts.

"TAKE COVER! TAKE COVER! RUN!" yelled Robison, turning back towards the new arrivals that were standing just outside of the large helicopter unsure of what was happening, let alone what to do. The pilots and crew members, though, didn't need to be told. They were already sprinting toward the cover of a heavily sandbagged bunker 20 yards away with the Flight Engineer yelling at the gaggle of FNGs to get away from the aircraft.

"RUN!" he yelled. "GO!"

The bulk of the new arrivals followed the pilots and crew while several others closer to the Ranger Captain ran as quickly as they could in the direction he was pointing, which was to a drainage ditch less than five yards away. In the scramble to reach the ditch one of the soldiers stumbled, dropped his duffle bag and packet of assignment orders, and then spent precious time trying to pick it all back up.

"NO! LEAVE IT! LEAVE IT!" yelled Robison to the panicking soldier. "THIS WAY! HURRY!"

The warning came just in time as one of the incoming rounds hit the edge of the air field and another hit the Chinook just above the forward rotor. The powerful blast severed the cockpit from the fuselage and sent its rotor blades spinning into the air like giant meat cleavers before they tore into the flightline and shattered into a number of sharp-edged pieces. The large aircraft burst into flames as swirling black smoke rose in a dark thermal column in the dying light of day.

When a second new guy, a short, heavy-set black Private First Class, tripped and fell on his way to safety, First Sergeant Poplawski raced out from his cover and scooped him up to his feet by his shirt collar with one hand.

"You're good! I got you!" he said, pushing him towards the protective ditch. "GO! GO! GO! MOVE IT! GO!"

The two GIs dove into the ditch and like the others already in it they hugged the ground staying as low as they could without removing the buttons on their recently issued jungle fatigue shirts as the last incoming mortar slammed into an empty three-quarter ton truck on the far side of the air field. The booming blast hurled spiked chunks of the broken truck high into the sky that fell like giant lawn darts across the flight line and nearby perimeter road.

The camp's incoming warning siren was still blaring its alarm even as the last mortar round exploded. The surprise attack appeared to be over. With the exception of the burning helicopter and destroyed truck the immediate surroundings became awkwardly quiet again. Bobbing heads slowly began to peer up and over the edge of the drainage ditch and out of the bunkers as the Incoming Siren wound down to a low growl and someone in the distance yelled, *'ALL CLEAR!'*

Wary soldiers slowly began coming out from their hiding places while the more experienced Ranger Captain and his First Sergeant remained down in the ditch cautioning the others around them to remain where they were.

"STAY DOWN!" ordered Robison with Poplawski repeating the command.

When the next round of muted thumps from the jungle surrounding the Camp told of the enemy's follow-up act with incoming rounds, Robison yelled out another warning.

Sweet Sorrow

"INCOMING! INCOMING! GET DOWN! STAY DOWN!" he bellowed as heads turned toward the Ranger Captain. Many who'd heard the order but hadn't recognized the distant thumps for what they were, heeded the command and hugged the ground in the dry ditch.

The Captain's warning came just in time as the Viet Cong had waited for the soldiers in the American camp to think they were safe to come out from hiding before they struck again.

Two additional mortar rounds came in from a second location in the jungle that surrounded the Camp. These new rounds coming in overhead spared the flightline and seemed to be directed with better accuracy targeting the Mackie's Command Center, the BIG-TOC.

The incoming warning Siren growled back to life over the outpost even as the Camp's Artillery Battery Howitzers began zeroing in on the location of the enemy mortar team with a battery and a barrage of cannon fire. Once the three artillery cannons had died down, a second and more convincing, *'ALL CLEAR'* call echoed across the Base Camp.

"ALL CLEAR!" yelled the Ranger Captain as he and his First Sergeant rose to their knees in the trench.

A last light helicopter Pink Team, a Bell AH-1 Cobra gunship and the OH-6 Light Observation Helicopter came out of their protective revetments and roared out over the Camp's barbwire perimeter to where the enemy mortar teams had set up and launched their attack. If the artillery fire hadn't pounded and punished them, then the Pink Team would. The OH-6 would serve as the Scout helicopter flying just above the tops of the rainforest's tree to zero in on the Viet Cong mortar crew while the AH-1 Cobra would bide its time and wait to swoop down to attack the Viet Cong or North Vietnamese Army mortar team the Scout helicopter would pinpoint.

As the two helicopters flew off Robison and Poplawski got to their feet, stepped back up and out of the ditch, and took a look at the damage as they began brushing the red dirt off of their jungle fatigues. Those new arrivals in the ditch with them, now even more wide-eyed and more than a little bewildered, cautiously followed their lead.

"ANYBODY WOUNDED?" Poplawski shouted across to the others near the burning helicopter. A heavy column of smoke was rising 100-feet in the air signaling to the enemy mortar crew they at least found one target. "ANYBODY WOUNDED? SOUND OFF!"

A cry at the far side of the burning helicopter came back at him.

"ONE DOWN! LEG WOUND!"

"If you have a First Aid pouch or kit on you, use it! Then call for a medic!" the Ranger Captain yelled back.

The call went out as Robison asked for an injury status a second time.

"ANYONE ELSE INJURED?"

"We're good!" came back one response from the Air Crew.

"We're okay, too!" said another GI standing with a handful of the Chinook's passengers.

The *goods* and *okays* came with a few thumbs-up and several nervous looking faces that slowly rose from the protective cover as other GIs emerged from their hidey holes.

A flurry of action was taking place across the Camp in the wake of the mortar attack; a familiar normalcy. This wasn't the Camp's first ever mortar of incoming rocket attack and those assigned to the remote outpost took it as just another lousy business day.

Two medics from a nearby Aid Station arrived on scene and began treating the wounded soldier. It was one of the new arrivals. Three days in-country in Vietnam, or maybe four, and his tour of duty was literally cut short.

"They're getting bolder," said the Ranger Captain, eyeing the burning Chinook helicopter.

"And smarter," said Poplawski. "They waited on the secondary strike."

"They did," agreed Robison. "Probably hoping to catch more people looking to help any of the wounded or anyone checking out the damage."

"Thank...thank you, Sergeant," said the black FNG coming up beside the Ranger First Sergeant.

"No problem, Private. You okay?"

"Un-huh. Is...is it always crazy like this?"

Poplawski shrugged. "Naw, sometimes it's worse," he said. "Just keep your head on a swivel, watch out for your buddies, and you'll be fine. Now head on over to the tower. I suspect someone from your unit will be by shortly to pick you up. Wait by the tower."

The FNG gave a thankful nod that was returned.

Because their return time from Saigon hadn't been scheduled other than an approximation, there wasn't a jeep waiting to take them back to the Company, so the Captain and his First Sergeant made the ten minute walk back to their Ranger Compound. Turning into the entrance to their compound area Captain Robison remarked on the unit sign showing which unit was there and read: '*R Company Ranger-75th INF. All visitors MUST report to the Orderly Room.*'

"Must or shall?" said the Captain.

"At the time you said *MUST* sounded better than my suggestion of, '*If you have no business here, then keep the fuck out.*'

"To be fair, you did leave out the MUST with your take on the matter."

"Yes sir, there's that."

Coming through the screen door of the front half of the Quonset Hut that served as the Unit's Orderly Room, and Commanding Officer's living quarters in the back, they found Lieutenant Plantagenet and a young Buck Sergeant they didn't recognize, manning the small office. At best the Orderly Room was twelve by fifteen, with two desks, three folding chairs, one filing cabinet, a small refrigerator, and an olive-drab folding table in the back of the room holding two coffee pots, one electric burner, and small tray with a shaker of sugar and another for the dehydrated coffee creamer.

The junior officer was bent over a PRC-25 radio on the Captain's desk. The radio's volume was turned up and white noise could be heard coming from the radio's small speaker. The Buck sergeant was seated at the First Sergeant's desk, both had M-16s close at hand.

"Ah-TEN-shun!" yelled the Buck Sergeant starting to spring to his feet to the position of attention only to have the Captain wave him and Plantagenet back down.

"As you were," said Robison, giving the command to carry on with what they were doing. "Everything good here, Lieutenant? Any injuries to any of our people or damage from the incoming?"

"No, Sir. We're good. It missed us. Sounded more like they were targeting the BIG-TOC and the airfield again. You okay?"

Robison nodded while Poplawski went over to his coffee maker and poured himself a long overdue cup.

"We are, but the Chinook that got us here isn't. It took a direct hit." Turning to other matters he asked, "How about filling me in on what was going on while the First Sergeant and I were gone? Where's Lieutenant Marquardt and why the radio?"

"Yes sir," said Plantagenet and launched into answering the Company Commander. "Team Nine-Four got in contact outside of An Loc and captured a P-O-W. They had a hot extraction from an ARVN Ranger bird that picked them up and flew them to their Base Camp."

"ARVN Rangers?"

"Yes sir, Team Nine-Four was working just west of their base."

"Whose team?"

"Specialist Li's."

"And the team's status? They good? They okay?"

"Yes sir. They're good. They had one P-O-W and one enemy K-I-A."

"NVA or VC?"

"VC."

"Outstanding! They bringing the prisoner back here?"

The Lieutenant shook his head. "No Sir, apparently the ARVNs wanted first crack at the prisoner."

"Huh? They say why?"

The Lieutenant shrugged. "No Sir, they didn't. Lieutenant Marquadt flew up to pick them up. Sergeant Shintaku's getting a mule ready from the motor pool to standby to give them a ride back here. Their bird's 15-minutes out."

"How many teams we have in the field right now?"

"Just two, at the moment. Nine-Two and Nine-Three. Nine-Seven goes out the day after tomorrow?"

"Nine-Seven? We have that many teams?" said the surprised Captain.

The junior officer smiled and said, "The X-O's idea, Sir. Nine-Seven used to be Nine-One. Lieutenant Marquardt thought of it as psychological warfare on any of the NVA or VC who might be monitoring any of our radio frequencies. Make them think we have more teams than we actually have."

The X-O, Robison's Executive Officer, was First Lieutenant Ryan Marquardt. Robison beamed at Marquardt's ruse and the First Sergeant chuckled at the ingenuity.

"Not a bad plan at that," said the Captain, approvingly before getting back to the team in the field. So, all's well?"

"Negative SITREPs, Sir. All's quiet in the hinterland."

Robison nodded. That was at least some good news.

"And today's dead rodent tally?" he asked, moving on to another matter. "How many rats in the traps?"

"Three, although one's fat enough to make it four."

"What's our total for the month so far?"

"Seventeen."

"And the three today were all properly disposed of?"

"Yes sir, drowned in a 55 gallon barrel and then tossed in the burn barrels, the ones with the orange bands around them. I'll have the end of the month report to you soon."

Robison nodded, again. "Good. Stay on it. It's a hot button issue with the BIG-TOC."

"Yes sir."

"Oh, and just in case you're wondering why it's a hot button issue and why I added rat catching and eradication to your assigned duties, it's not because I don't value you, Lieutenant. It's because it's a quiet priority from the MAC-V command."

"Quiet priority, Sir?"

"Uh-huh. It's not widely known, and believe it or not, but there's been a significant outbreak of the Bubonic plague throughout Vietnam over the last few years. From what I've been told there have been over two hundred thousand reported cases."

"The Plague?" said the startled junior officer.

"That's affirmative. The numbers, they say, are slowly dropping, but it's still very much in play. By keeping the rat population down in our humble little company compound home, you're helping to accomplish a vital task, and maybe quietly saving some of our people from serious grief, Lieutenant, so keep up the good work."

"Yes…Yes sir," the Lieutenant added hesitantly and something that the senior officer knew was troubling Plantagenet, the same as it troubled him when he was briefed on the situation at the BIG-TOC.

"By the way, the Infectious Disease Doctor they brought in to give the briefing a while back told us it's mostly treatable these days, if it's detected early enough."

Even as he was saying it the word *'mostly'* left room for imaginations to run wild, so he continued to ease some of the worry. "I've spoken with Doc Moore. Every Monday morning when he's handing out the malaria pills he's also keeping an eye out for anyone showing any signs of the plague. Not to worry, Doc is good at his job. He can recognize the symptoms."

The junior officer gave a better nod as Robison went on to other matters.

"Sergeant Kozak in the TOC?"

"Yes sir."

"Okay. When Lieutenant Marquardt and Sergeant Shintaku get back I want you to let them know I want them back here in the Orderly Room at 1900 hours for a briefing. I'll need you here as well."

Finally, the Captain turned to the Buck Sergeant he didn't recognize, who was most likely a recent graduate of the latest Lurp training class.

"And who are you, Sergeant?"

"Sergeant Colp, Sir. I'm the C-Q for tonight."

C-Q was the Charge of Quarters, the Non-Commissioned Officer assigned to man the Orderly Room after normal duty hours and throughout the night. His job was to answer the Field Phone when someone called, sweep out the office, empty any trash, start a fresh pot of coffee, wake up the Company Commander and First Sergeant at Zero-500 hours or wake them up in case of a fire or any other emergency.

"I take it you just graduated from the selection course?"

"Yes sir."

"Which Platoon have you been assigned to or are you still in the training tent?"

"We're still in the training tent but we're supposed to be moved into the Platoon hootches in the morning. I've been assigned to Team Nine-Seven in the Second Platoon, Sir."

Colp nodded and Robison nodded. A nod covered a lot of ground and its mileage often left room for better contemplation.

"Then Sergeant Kozak is your Platoon Sergeant," Robison said. "And the Lieutenant here is your Platoon Leader." Turning back to the Lieutenant he asked, "Who's the T-L for Nine-Seven?"

"Sergeant Carey," replied Plantagenet. "The Warning Order for Nine-Seven came down from the BIG-TOC this morning."

"Sergeant Carey found me earlier and introduced himself and said he'd help me draw what I needed for the mission once I've moved into the Platoon's hootch. He also ran me through a few quick reaction drills," said Colp.

"Then you're in good hands."

Colp nodded and turned to the Lieutenant with a nod.

"Because you're the CQ tonight you'll have the day off tomorrow," said the Captain. "Use that time to get settled in and in the afternoon report to your Team Leader and his Assistant Team Leader who more than likely, will have an updated Frag Order for you and the others on your mission tomorrow evening, if anything changes."

"Yes sir."

To the junior officer he said, "How many made the cut from the latest training class?"

"Six, Sir," said Plantagenet. "But one of them told Sergeant Shintaku that he wants to transfer out."

"He did, huh?"

"Yes sir."

"Well then, we'll get him gone. What's the status of the remaining five?"

"Besides, Sergeant Colp here, we're placing the other four on teams in each platoon."

"Sounds like you got that handled as well. Good job, Lieutenant. Carry on."

As the Lieutenant gathered up his things, including the backpacked radio, and started towards the screen door the Captain called to him with an afterthought.

"You taking that radio back to the TOC, Lieutenant?"

"Yes sir."

"Would you pass word along to Sergeant Kozak that I'd like him to attend the 1900 hours briefing too."

"Yes sir. Will do."

Poplawski turned to the Buck Sergeant and nodded to the Company Commander. Robison took the hint.

"Sergeant Colp."

"Sir?"

"You're dismissed until 1930 hours."

"Yes sir."

Sweet Sorrow

Colp gathered up a dog-eared paperback book and followed the Lieutenant out of the Orderly Room's squeaking screen door. The wooden framed door closed with a distinct thump from the old, but taut support springs.

After the Lieutenant and Buck Sergeant were both out the door, the Captain turned to his First Sergeant.

"The Lieutenant's working out fine," he said. "Don't'cha think?"

"Yes sir, I do. Which only makes me even more pissed off at MAC-V's decision to shut us down. Do they even know how hard it is to train a Second Lieutenant?"

Chapter 10

The scheduled 1900 hours, seven p.m. meeting time came and went. A key player was missing.

"We're waiting on the First Sergeant before we begin the briefing," Captain Robison said to the others spread out around in the Orderly Room. "He should be here shortly."

Sitting or standing around the Company's Orderly Room were Lieutenants Marquardt and Plantagenet, Platoon Sergeant First Class Kozak, and Staff Sergeant Shintaku, the training NCO.

"Go ahead and help yourselves to the coffee in the back. There's a fresh carrot cake too that Sergeant Kozak got from the Engineers' Mess Tent."

Robison pointed towards the back of the room where a pan of cake with a thin layer of cream cheese frosting sat next to a well-used electric plug-in 30 cup coffee maker and a portable burner plate on a field table. A second tray held an upside down stack of orange/brown melamine mess hall coffee cups, a 12 ounce glass sugar container with a metal pouring tube, a jar of powdered coffee creamer, and several plastic spoons.

"Thank you, Sergeant Kozak for the carrot cake," Robison said, giving a verbal nod to the Second Platoon's Sergeant. "It's much appreciated."

Kozak nodded and raised up his coffee cup in a *'you're welcome'* gesture as more thanks or nods came his way. In a place and setting where 90% of everything they ate on patrol came from small, olive drab colored cans of C-rations or pouches of freeze-dried food, where Mess Tent offered powdered milk and eggs, the freshly baked cake that was made by a cook in the Mess Tent earlier that afternoon was a nice, little treat. A small luxury.

The pot of freshly brewed coffee was half-filled while the First Sergeant's personal, eight-sided, aluminum Italian coffee pot sitting on the burner plate was full and untouched. It wasn't that any in attendance thought that the First Sergeant didn't want to share his unique percolated espresso brew, it was just well understood that few of any takers ever wanted to drink a second cup after a much abbreviated first cup. Touted as *The Moka Express,* the Alphonso Bialetti coffee pot came in different sizes so that the maker could enjoy one through nine shots of espresso. The strength of the shot of coffee depended on the person making it and Poplawski's recipe using his own Vietnamese roasted bean coffee blend may have only satisfied his personal taste, or as some speculated, could also be used to tar roofs, or repair flat tires on jeeps. That the First Sergeant always seemed to have a cup of his coffee in his hands filled with at least three shots of Espresso made some question if he ever slept.

"We might have to make another pot of coffee…well unless there's any takers for the First Sergeant's coffee."

That inside joke drew chuckles and slow shakes of the heads as several of the members of the cadre took the Company Commander up on the offer for the cake and the regular coffee from the seemingly never emptied Westbend coffee percolator.

Robison had sent the First Sergeant to the unit's Tactical Operations Center to check on the status of the two Lurp teams in the field, so until he returned, the meeting was on hold.

No one was really sure why the Company Commander had called for the impromptu briefing, so while they waited, they drank coffee and snacked on carrot cake.

Of those in the Orderly Room waiting on the briefing, it was Shintaku who couldn't quite figure out why he had been invited to sit in. He was the lesser rank on the unit's power pyramid. Something was up and maybe when the First Sergeant arrived, he'd have his answer.

Any thoughts on the reasoning or matter stopped abruptly, though, when the Orderly Room's screen door swung open, and Acting First Sergeant Poplawski came bounding in nodding to the Captain. He was trailed by a confused looking Sergeant Cantu who stood by the door as the First Sergeant gave his report.

"All's good, Sir. Oh, and I thought maybe Sergeant Cantu needed to sit in on this, too," he said as he turned towards his Italian coffee pot and poured himself a cup of quite possibly the strongest and most questionable cup of what anyone would ever classify as *'good coffee'* in Southeast Asia.

"Who's minding the store?"

The store being the Company's TOC and the radio lifelines to the teams in the field.

"Rangers Taras and two of Sergeant Shintaku's new graduates. Thought maybe we'd break them in."

"Good call. There's cake in the back, Sergeant Cantu."

"Thank you, Sir, I'm good."

When Cantu found a seat next to Shintaku and after Poplawski had finished pouring a cup of coffee, the Company Commander was ready.

"Alright then, here it is," said Robison. The West Point graduate took in a deep breath and slowly let it out. "First and foremost, there's the status of our wounded. Staff Sergeant Wade and Specialist Hagar were airlifted out to the surgical hospital at Camp Zama, Japan this morning. PFC Norse and Sergeant Thomas are both out of their initial surgeries, and for the time being, are still at the 93rd Evacuation Hospital in Long Binh. We checked in on them this afternoon. They all have a few tough roads ahead of them, and when we know more about their recoveries, we'll let you know.

"As for Sergeant Thomas, you may have already heard and celebrated the fact that he is no longer Missing in Action, let alone K-I-A."

Robison paused to let the words resonate and then went on. "He not only survived the booby trap explosion and the tunnel collapse, but when he came to and found there was no going back he dug his way forward and into an enemy tunnel system and managed to capture and even rescue the enemy soldier he was chasing."

"Out-fucking-standing!" said Marquardt, grinning as others in the Company cadre applauded as well.

"It was, and is," agreed the Captain. Because the tunnel complex was occupied, and by sneaking and peeking he knocked out a guard at one of their tunnel entrances and then avoided being captured, all the while making notes and best estimate drawings of the tunnel and cave system."

"RANGER!" bellowed Kozak.

"Ranger indeed," agreed the Captain. "He said he couldn't go back up to the Relay Station on top of the mountain because he figured he'd be captured or killed before he ever got the station's perimeter wire. Instead, he made a false trail making it look like he was heading back up to the Relay Station and then worked his way down the mountain and slipped back into the jungle just before dark. He said his initial plan was to give the Nui Ba Den a wide berth before heading toward the Tay Ninh Base Camp."

"Good plan," said Lieutenant Marquardt.

"It was until Charlie found his real trail and started tracking him. Apparently, they were eager to catch him and make him a trophy, so as their trackers chased after him they also sent some of their people to block the way back to Tay Ninh, which was when he decided he'd head for an old, abandoned Fire Support Base near the road that led up to Cambodia. He'd heard somewhere that some of the helicopter pilots returning from missions in Cambodia often followed the road that passed the mountain as a ground guide back to Tay Ninh. What he didn't know was that the abandoned Fire Support Base wasn't abandoned. The Viet Cong and their NVA cousins radioed ahead to have some of their people there just in case he showed up."

"Good Lord!" said Marquardt.

"Truly good, and a better miracle happened when a passing gunship and Low Bird helicopter team following the road spotted Thomas coming out of the brush and waving his arms trying to get their attention, which was when he was fired upon by Charlie. The gunship provided cover fire as the Low Bird swooped in and scooped him up under fire. He was wounded getting to the bird, so the helicopter flew him to the Evacuation Hospital."

"What is the extent of his injuries, Sir? How's he doing?" This from Lieutenant Plantagenet.

"A gunshot wound to his upper left chest and shoulder, a possible concussion, and a lot of small cuts and scrapes. We were told that he too will soon be flown out to Camp Zama, Japan, or Letterman Army General Hospital in San Francisco to recover. All things considered he's in surprisingly good spirits."

There were nods, sighs of relief, and smiles from those in the small audience, but the smiles were soon about to disappear with what came next.

"That's the good news. The next part, well, not so much so."

The weight of what he had to say next made the Ranger Captain pause again. The verbal hammer was coming down.

"As you know the First Sergeant and I were called down to Saigon for a briefing by MAC-V Headquarters this morning where we were informed in that meeting that Romeo Company is being shut down..."

"Wait! What? NO!" cried First Lieutenant Marquardt on his feet in protest, that was quickly followed up with the next question.

"Why?" he said, finding something that resembled a calmer tone and asking the question that was on all of their minds.

"A drawdown of troop strength apparently," replied the Captain. "Like it or not, we're just the latest casualty. They've given us just over a month to close up shop, which basically means we have two operational weeks and maybe a handful of missions left before we'll need to start accounting for, and turning in weapons and equipment. Sergeant Shintaku? Lieutenant Plantagenet?"

"Sir?" said the two almost simultaneously.

"You just graduated your last class of volunteers, so I'm going to put you to work elsewhere."

"Yes sir," said the Lieutenant.

"You had six from the recent class make the cut, but I heard one decided he didn't want to be a Lurp after all?"

"Yes sir, a PFC says he wants to transfer out. Says it's not what he thought it would be. I suspect the five people we lost in one day had something to do with his decision."

Robison nodded, paused for a brief moment, and then said, "First Sergeant?"

"Sir?"

"Find a new home for him."

"Roger that, but I doubt he'll be happy as a clam in high water with a grunt company, either."

"His call," said the Captain, thinking he'd have the other new Lurps distributed out to the teams and deployed on at least one mission in the next few weeks before Romeo Company was shut down. They had all volunteered to be Lurps, had made it through the selection training, so he'd give them a chance to be Lurps. I understand the others are still in the training tent?"

"Yes sir," said Shintaku. "They'll be moving into the platoon hootches in the morning."

"Okay, good. I'll need you to close down your training hootch and inventory what equipment you have, including the training tent and the cots in it and anything else that's on the books. You copy?"

Plantagenet and the Staff Sergeant nodded.

"And to that point the First Sergeant and I will start looking into finding better homes for you all and the Rangers we have here. Until then I'm going to want and need all of you to start thinking about who deserves awards and decorations and, just as importantly, who doesn't. Right now, MAC-V is happy with us, which means we have some leeway when it comes to meritorious awards. Same-same when it comes to awards for combat actions for anyone we might've overlooked or just taken for granted, too. In that regard I'm going to want to see recommendations on my desk in one week's time with names, ranks, dates of action, and a brief summary of what the individual did to deserve the award. You're welcome to use the typewriter here in the Orderly Room."

"Use the damn thing because I ain't gonna spend half the day trying to make out your bad penmanship and scribbles," said the First Sergeant from the back of the room. "If need be, I'll find a five-gallon bucket of White-Out and a paint brush for you to use for any of your corrections!"

"Use the typewriter," echoed the Captain, agreeing with his top sergeant. "And keep our First Sergeant happy as a clam too. Clams are happy in high water, are they, First Sergeant?"

"Yes sir. They are, except for grains of bureaucratic sand that every so often irritates the hell out of them, but that gives us senior NCOs some folksy pearls of wisdom."

That was met with more grunts, smiles, and nods.

"Finally, this," added the Captain. "Romeo Company has been awarded the Valorous Unit award. Evidently, the Department of the Army has come to understand something we already know. We're good at what we do, very good, so the honor is well earned and deserved. We'll let our people know about what they collectively earned by the Valorous Unit Award along with the shutdown in the morning formation. Let's face it, it's shit news with a better bit of thin icing, but it is what it is, and we'll deal with it and drive on. Understood?"

Each of the five responded with, '*Yes sir's*' and grunts that lacked any genuine enthusiasm. There was much to think about and even more to get done.

"Any questions?" said Robison.

"Yes sir, I have one," said Sergeant Shintaku, raising a hand.

"What is it, Staff Sergeant?"

"You said there'll probably be enough time for several more missions."

"I imagine MAC-V has already let the BIG-TOC command know what's happening, so my best guess is one or maybe two missions, tops. Could be too, the

BIG-TOC might utilize us all as a Quick Reaction Force. However, until I hear more, we're still Ranger business as usual."

"Yes sir, but since I'm now out of a job, I'd like another chance to lead a patrol."

"You would?"

"Yes sir."

"I'd like to go back out to the field as well, Sir," said Cantu.

Robison studied the two young soldiers for a long moment before he turned to the First Sergeant, who gave him a *'what the hell, why not?'* look and shrug. They were more than capable.

"Fine. You'll lead the team…"

"Nine-Eight," said the Executive Officer, smiling.

"Nine-Eight, with Sergeant Cantu as your Assistant Team Leader. The two of you can pick the rest of your team utilizing several of the new graduates."

Shintaku's and Cantu's grins lit up the room.

"Will do, Sir."

"You have three days to put together your team, and then we'll see what the next mission the BIG-TOC has slated for us."

Chapter 11

The light purple fade was giving way to a thin white-orange layer of light as sunrise was coming up over the dark horizon. After two false insertions on two natural clearings in the vast expanse of rainforest, Team Nine-Seven was boots-on-the-ground.

Their preselected grassland clearing which served as the actual starting point for their mission was in the rolling hills southwest of Fire Support Base Buttons in Song Be. The false insertions, where the helicopter touched down briefly in other clearings and then roared away without anyone leaving the aircraft made it a toss-up for any enemy unit trying to pinpoint the Lurp team's actual drop off location. Even upon insertion the Huey would only be at the edge of the clearing for a matter of seconds.

Scrambling out of the cramped helicopter's open cargo bay the three veteran Rangers and two FNGs hurried into the cover of the jungle tree line as the helicopter took off and roared away.

They were 30 feet into the cover of the rainforest when the Team Leader did a button hook turn to his right, moved a few yards in, and then paralleled the team's route back toward the clearing. Halfway back the Team Leader gave the hand signal to go to ground. This was survival math where the tactic was to *'Lay Dog'* and listen and wait.

While they waited the team's radioman would establish radio contact with the helicopter that had just dropped them off and with the Ranger Company's radio relay team, call sign, Valhalla Yankee, that was temporarily stationed at Fire Support Base Buttons. Valhalla Yankee would serve as communications support for the patrol. A backpacked PRC-25 radio didn't give a team much in the way of reach for radio calls, so the Yankee Relay teams were critical for making sure the team had good radio commo. Even with a working radio a five or six-man team in a sudden enemy encounter were vulnerable until a gunship arrived on station to aid them. Without commo, without radio communication, a team could find that they were on their own in a firefight with the Viet Cong or North Vietnamese.

'Laying Dog' also meant that the team on the ground was waiting, watching, and listening to determine if any Viet Cong or North Vietnamese Army soldiers were tracking them. It wasn't uncommon for Viet Cong or NVA trackers to quietly sneak up on a platoon or company of grunts after a helicopter insertion and attack them from behind where they least expected it. Same-same for the Lurp teams.

Longboat Nine-Seven's buttonhook countermeasure was their ace in the hole against anyone trying to sneak up on the team. The underbrush and tangle of leaves that hid the team wouldn't stop a BB from a Red Rider BB Gun, but the concealment gave the ploy some credence and gave the Lurps a momentary tactical edge.

Sweet Sorrow

Hurrying to '*Lay Dog*' also meant moving as quickly and as quietly as they could considering that each Ranger was weighed down with a 90-pound rucksack carrying five days of dehydrated or canned C-rations, a bayonet, or a personal weapon, and an LBE- Load Bearing Equipment shoulder harness attached to a utility pistol belt that supported 25 to 30 fully-loaded rifle magazines in ammo or modified pouches, a canteen pouch with three grenades, a knife, an eight-foot section of rope and D-ring, a flashlight, 1st Aid pouch, a smoke grenade, and an extra five-pound battery for the team's radio, and several canteens filled with fresh water. The overall weight was staggering and more so for one of the team members who carried the team radio and another that carried the Medic bag which made their movement look more like a fast waddle than a quick run. It wasn't the weight of the world the soldiers carried on their shoulders, just the necessary war supplies deemed necessary for failed political diplomacy.

The insertion helicopter was in and out of the clearing in less than a minute. The familiar chopping sound of the Huey's rotor blades was already diminishing in the distance even before the Rangers had safely reached the tree line. At the right angle the ankle high, dew-covered grass they'd moved through getting to the jungle from the clearing highlighted the way they went like a brightly colored beacon of light. That couldn't be helped. When the sun rose, and as the high heat of day began to rise with it, the dew would evaporate and the pressed down grass and weeds might spring back up and hide their route, but Sergeant Carey wasn't taking any chances. They would remain in place and wait to see if anyone was tracking them.

They were 15 tense minutes into the wait when Carey was reasonably certain no bad guys were sneaking up behind them. Taking out his compass and marrying up the shaking needle with his mission map, he locked in the direction of travel. Looking up he then gave a knife hand signal heading to Specialist Pettit, his Assistant Team Leader toward the direction he wanted him to take. Pettit nodded, turned, and with his M-16 at the ready he took the lead.

The compass heading would take them north toward the upper end of the patrol zone in suspected enemy controlled territory they were assigned to recon over the next five days. The BIG-TOC wanted to know who, if anybody, was there. Pettit's pace was slow and deliberate because with only five team members in enemy controlled territory, it had to be.

What the teams would take in and learn on the patrols would be brought back and disseminated to the higher ups who'd advise command on their next course of action in that particular Area of Operations. If the grid area showed no signs of a build-up of enemy activity then it could be eliminated in the *Hide 'n Seek* jungle war.

By adding the Hunter/Killer aspect to their patrols the Lurps would also turn the tables on the Viet Cong with their own just as sneaky hit-and-run ambushes.

Attack them and hit them where they least expected it, and you did more than just take out a few of the enemy patrols or captured a few prisoners of war, you unnerved the others. Silent Reconnaissance or a booming Claymore mine initiated ambush were on the menu for this patrol, and one for the situational choosing.

Pettit wasn't busting brush as much as he was cautiously moving through the thick heavy brush and tugging *wait-a-minute* vines. The going was further slowed by dense bamboo thickets, fallen trees to go up and over or around, and three-foot-high termite mounds to skirt. The large termite mounds needed to be checked out because the Viet Cong and North Vietnamese soldiers relied on tunnel systems to hide their activities and numbers and in doing so had fashioned their own termite-looking mounds with ventilation holes to cool the tunnels and dissipate smoke in the burrowed hiding areas. As he went Petite searched for man-made signs or odors as he went around the mounds. Satisfied there were no ventilation holes and that the termite mounds were actual insect mounds, he moved on. From time-to-time he used slow swipes with the barrel of his rifle to break away any annoying face-sticking spider webs.

Pettit was 500 yards on when he held up a closed fist, halting the team in place and then waved them down. A wide wash of sunlight through the trees twenty or so yards ahead of him meant there was a large clearing in the rainforest. Turning back to his Team Leader he gave a hand signal to Carey that he was going to move forward to investigate. Carey nodded and Pettit crept forward. A few minutes later he was back with Carey moving up to join him to learn what he'd found.

"Anything in the clearing?" whispered Carey.

"A trench line surrounding it," said Pettit, quietly pointing towards the curtain of light filtering through the cover of the darker, surrounding rainforest.

Carey nodded. The clearing wasn't unexpected. It was on his map. The trench line around it wasn't that much of a surprise either. The VC or NVA had often prepared trenches and fighting positions for possible insertions from helicopters. Most were old and unmanned. Some weren't. Carey decided on taking a closer look for himself to see if the trench line was occupied, and if need be, to see if it might be suitable for an emergency extraction, if or when the shit hit the fan. That metaphor wasn't as far flung as it sounded. The war was always spinning.

Carey and Pettit moved forward like thieves to steal a look at the clearing and the trench line. A hunched over Pettit brought his rifle up ready to provide protective cover fire for his Team Leader who had taken a knee at the edge of the clearing but still inside the tree line. Anyone who might be watching wouldn't have seen either of the Lurps who were well concealed in the jungle brush.

From their vantage point the two began taking in the grassland clearing that was big enough for three helicopters to comfortably set down. Many of the natural clearings in the rainforest were little more than lowland sumps where water pooled during the rainy season. This one was no different. In the rising sunlight the sun was glistening off a shallow pool of water that took up a good portion of the clearing to the southeast. Early as it was, a thin lace of pale white mist hovered over the water as dragonflies flitted and danced across the large algae-covered pool.

In the higher heat of the coming dry season the large pool of water would evaporate, the mud would dry and harden, and the clearing would offer a viable landing zone for helicopters. The Viet Cong and NVA tacticians had prepared it for an inbound Huey looking to insert a Lurp team or trio of helicopters ferrying in a grunt recon platoon into the clearing to spring an attack. As well concealed as the trench line and fighting positions were, unless you were a few feet away from them then they easily would go unnoticed even by a low flying Scout helicopter. Whoever built them had done a pretty good job of concealing them.

Carey inched closer to the trench for a better inspection. There were signs of not-so-recent enemy activity in the trench or in the old gun positions. Weathered boot prints and spider webs reigned over the well-concealed and well maintained earthwork fortifications. Only recently abandoned the trench line and gun positions were for another day, for a future fight because the enemy were playing the long game. Invading armies had come and gone throughout Vietnam's long history, but the Vietnamese remained. Over the centuries they had practice at ambushing invaders and in this latest war they had taken it to a fine art. The protected clearing would serve its purpose, one day or the next. One war, or the next.

The Bell UH-1 Iroquois helicopter, the Huey, was famous for the unique chopping sound of its twin rotor blades that made it stand out over other military helicopters. A GI waiting to get picked up after a jungle patrol could recognize the familiar sound and smile at an inbound Huey well before he could see it coming in for a landing over the trees. But then, so could the Viet Cong and North Vietnamese Army field commanders. Their smiles at the familiar sound would have darker consequences.

One or more Huey helicopters a few minutes out on their short final coming into a makeshift landing zone would signal the enemy commander it was time to have his people quickly move into the trench line and gun emplacements. Once in place they'd lay low patiently biding their time with their machine guns, A-Ks or SKS rifles, or shoulder-fired rocket propelled grenade launchers and wait for the command to fire. That would come when the helicopters were at their most vulnerable moment as the bulbed-nosed birds slowed and flared to set down. Then the Viet Cong or NVA ambushers would spring their surprise attack and bring down one or more of the choppers with heavy gunfire from several key directions at ridiculously close range. It had happened elsewhere in open spaced clearings like this and would happen again. There were only so many ways the Americans could enter or exit the hundreds of thousands of acres of jungle and with few roads or serviceable routes, the helicopters were the best drop off option. The trench and gun positions may have been empty for now but that didn't mean they wouldn't be used when the opportunity presented itself.

"Didn't see the trench line or the gun positions on the overflight," Carey whispered to Pettit, who nodded with more than a little sense of relief.

"Me neither. They hid them well."

"Yeah they did. Let's move back to the team."

The day before the mission Carey and Pettit had gone up in a helicopter to check out the recon zone from the air and mark likely landing zones and pickup zones for quick inserts and exfils from their patrol area. The pre-mission overflights were made to look like simple passing helicopter flights so as not to alert any VC or NVA units operating in an area of an upcoming insertion of an American Lurp team or Recon platoon.

This jungle clearing was one they'd considered as a probable start point, but vetoed because of the drainage water. They figured that the sump water had left the surrounding ground a little soggy or worse, maybe in ankle deep mud that would slow their run to cover from the helicopter while leaving a giant slug trail tell-tale sign of the team's direction of travel. The accidental veto now proved to be a safe call.

Back in position with the others Carey pulled out a grease pencil from his top left pocket and marked the trench line and gun positions in the clearing on his acetate-covered mission map with a red X. The clearing would be a No-Go as an insertion or extraction site for any future patrols unless the surrounding area was first prepped with artillery fire.

"We'll work our way around it. We'll move further west on a 270-degree azimuth," Carey said to Pettit.

"270, it is," Pettit said, taking out his compass, finding the new direction of travel, and once again taking the lead.

Nine-Seven continued the mission.

They were less than 100 yards on when the Pointman came to another standstill with an upraised fist to halt the rest of the team in place. There was an open space just ahead of him. A cautious half step further on and through the underbrush, less than a meter away, was a three-foot-wide trail. With a finger on the trigger of his M-16 and his hand tightly gripping the rifle's pistol grip he took another half step forward and recognized it as an East-West *runner,* a small trail that looked to be only big enough for foot traffic. Easing in closer with sweaty palms he took a knee just inside the brush cover and checked it out. The trail was empty. There were no enemy soldiers he could see so he began studying the section of the trail in front of him. Fresh ground sign was there. Judging from the deep heel marks and sharp edges of the boot and sandal imprints in the dirt the foot and bicycle traffic was heavy. His eyes turned skyward, and he gave a slow nod. Well-hidden by the jungle's overhead tarp-like living canopy, the thin route was getting a lot of use while going undetected from any aircraft that might be passing overhead.

When Carey cautiously moved up to join his Assistant Team Leader, Pettit pointed out the path. Slowly brushing aside several broad leaves to better eye the pathway, Carey took in the tire-tread sandal prints and the deep grooves that showed the bicycles they were pushing. Modified bicycles meant they were hauling heavy weapons and equipment. Carey's gut tightened. It was yet another infiltration route from the North and a busy rat line.

"VC Ho Chi's...and recent," he whispered to Pettit over his shoulder. The overlapping prints and deep and dark indentations told much of the story. The rest was calculating the numbers. Pettit took in a three-foot section of the trail, counted the footprints in it and then divided it by two. It was a rough count, but fairly close.

"I'm seeing maybe eight to ten Dinks."

"Dinks?"

Pettit shrugged. "Yeah, the sound a bullet makes when it hits the target on the range. I'm being witty and clever," he said.

"Is that right?" Carey said, staring at the trail. "However, I've seen you shoot, so I'm surprised you don't call them, Mike-Mikes."

"Mike-Mikes?"

"Yeah, *Mostly-Misses*."

Carey grinned as Pettit frowned.

"Anybody ever told you that you're an asshole?"

"Uh-huh, but it's only the people who know me. So, eight to ten of the Dinks in *Ho Chi's,* huh?"

"Yep, and fresh tracks, too."

They got that number by counting the sandal imprints inside a three-foot section of trail and then divided the number by two. That gave them a viable working number, or close enough. *Ho Chi's* was the slang term GIs used for the heavy-duty sandals the Viet Cong wore in the bush. Made from scraps of old, discarded automobile tires that had been cut and repurposed into footwear they were named after the North Vietnamese leader, Ho Chi Minh. The sandals were practical, sturdy, and effective in jungle operations. The heavy tread provided good traction and new mileage, and better still they were more than adequate protection against immersion foot, the crippling malaise from the wet feet and tropical heat that the GIs called *jungle rot.* Continuously wet feet inside wet boots led to weeping blisters and disintegrating flesh for too many GIs in the field. Left untreated, deep sores would turn to gangrene and toes and even feet would need to be amputated when the antibiotics couldn't save them. *Ho Chi's* served a useful purpose on the often wet ground and right now their tracks would serve the Lurps.

"We'll set up here," Carey said and motioned for Pettit and the others to slip further back into the jungle. Twelve feet from the trail in a site that offered a better view of the primary path, they set the three other members of the team up in an ambush position and established fields of fire.

After calling in their find to the team's Ranger radio relay station and rattling off their location coordinates for their position, Carey snaked his way back towards the trail and daisy chained four Claymores while Pettit covered him. Carey placed and planted the book-sized anti-personnel mines on their aiming stakes, and locked in the blasting caps that linked them together. Camouflaging the mines with old leaves, grass, and brush the four anti-personnel mines would go unnoticed. If, and when, a fight came, Team Nine-Seven would have a momentary tactical advantage with the anti-personnel mines that would last only as long as the blast and diminish the team's protection once they were triggered. Then it would either be shoot-and-scoot or a flat-out, haul ass run from any enemy platoon soon-to-be coming after them.

While the team settled in to employ the recon aspect of their job, they were also ready to take on a small enemy patrol by ambush, if the opportunity presented itself. That too, was their job. They were prepared and ready either way. If luck was with them, then they might be blessed with a *'Picnic Mission'* where no enemy would be encountered, and they would spend the next day or so safely sitting in place before moving on to another site for another long wait. That wouldn't be so bad either, thought Pettit. *'Picnic Missions,'* were the best kind.

With their anti-personnel mines in place, and the five Lurps in their 360 degree wagon wheel perimeter defense, the patient wait began. Small rocks, lumps of dirt, and poking branches were pushed aside, and the challenge now became trying to find some sort of reasonable comfort on the hard packed ground.

It was a little less than four hours later when Sergeant Colp heard some commotion in the trees above them. 100 feet up a troop of long-tailed monkeys were moving through the jungle on their sky train of the tree tops. He'd heard that monkeys could be loud, only this troop was moving quietly with barely a little chatter. Several others on the team watched on but soon lost interest. As long as the monkeys weren't pissing on them or flinging shit at them, they were fine.

Colp, though, was still watching with some grinning delight as one curious George stopped when he saw the brutes assembled in a semi-circle below and then slowly and carefully made his way down like a talented gymnast for a closer look. 30 feet above him the monkey drew closer, slowed its approach, and stopped. Leaning it's head forward, it craned its neck and stared at the Lurp who was staring back.

"Well, hello there to you too, little buddy," whispered Colp, smiling and trying to reassure the monkey that there was no need to worry. All was okay, they were just passing through, only the monkey knew better and rushed back up to the others who were high in the trees and hurrying on. A moment later when an unseen spotted red Tokay gecko lizard in the near distance gave a throaty *'fucccck you'* Colp surrendered a half smile and nod. He'd heard about the famous *'Fuck you'* lizard and was taken by its editorial stance and conviction.

"And there it is," he whispered to himself and chuckled.

As one of the two newest members of the team Colp had been assigned the Rear Scout position, which meant he was last in line, their six, who was covering their go. Even as the Rear Scout he was mostly still thought of by several of the others on the team as just another universally scorned and dreaded *Fucking New Guy*. Time would change that. He just didn't have enough time in yet for the label to fall away.

It wasn't long after the monkeys had passed when Colp thought he heard some more chatter further back down the trail. Craning his head towards the sound he was wondering if maybe it was more monkeys or perhaps his imagination until he reared back in alarm. It wasn't chatter. It was someone talking, in Vietnamese, and it was enough to jumpstart his adrenaline and push it into high gear. Surprisingly, even to himself, he wasn't panicking, although the pucker factor was high. Still, he was holding it together, and just as he had been taught in his LRRP training, Colp gave two quick finger snaps to alert the other members of the team.

The quick finger snaps had the others turning his way, and when they had eyes on the New Guy, Colp pointed toward his right ear and back down the trail. All ears leaned in to listen in the direction Colp had pointed. Several of the veteran Lurps who might've been skeptical about the new guy's silent report, soon made out the something and the someone or someones coming down the trail as well. With no *friendlies* in the area, the five Lurps hugged the ground and readied their weapons. The war had just arrived at their doorstep. The New Guy was proving his worth.

Keeping it together didn't mean his adrenaline hadn't spiked or that he wasn't squeezing the armguard or the pistol grip of his M-16 over and over again. But that wasn't the problem because Colp was sure his drum thumping heart beats and slow, deep breathing would give him away even though it couldn't be heard by anyone but him.

The usually quiet enemy patrols gave way to some muffled talking, a few coughs, and the squeaking strains of modified bicycles hauling heavy loads. Far removed from any South Vietnamese ARVN, American, or Allied Army bases, and with the sky free of roving helicopters, the Viet Cong and North Vietnamese soldiers believed these jungle regions were their exclusive domain, their private and safe havens, or so they were thinking today. From the casual talk at least several of the enemy soldiers coming down the trail were relaxed and unconcerned enough with their surroundings to worry about anything more than their march through the steaming jungle.

A more cautious and alert enemy soldier who was walking point five yards ahead of the others was taking his job more seriously than those that followed. The black pajama-clad Viet Cong Pointman who'd been assigned to get the North Vietnamese soldiers to where they were going suddenly was there out on the trail, his gaze slowly sweeping left, right, and center of the trail as he went. With seemingly nothing out of the ordinary and no trip wires, snakes, or enemy soldiers to be seen, he moved past the Lurp's ambush site and soon disappeared from view.

The trail remained empty for a few minutes more before a line of armed, but surprisingly a little too casual NVA soldiers began to parade on by. They walked in a single file line and were dressed in khaki colored or olive drab long sleeve uniforms with Chinese high top boots and floppy boonie caps. Several of the soldiers were pushing modified bicycles laden with mortar tubes, heavy base plates, a .51 caliber heavy machine gun, and several two-man portable SA-7 surface-to-air missiles, and a stack of wooden crates likely carrying mortar rounds and ammunition. However, unlike their more experienced Viet Cong Pointman, their individual weapons were mostly slung over their shoulders as they appeared unconcerned about their surroundings or their noise discipline. Their low and casual talk continued. The Lurps didn't need a translator to know the newly arrived soldiers were bitching about the South Vietnamese heat, the jungle, the over-ladened bikes they were pushing, and the long trek before a pissed-off veteran NCO growled at the loudest of the talkers ordering him to keep down the noise.

The pissed-off NCO walked further up the line and when he was out of hearing range one of the lower ranking enemy soldiers said something that caused a few of the others to quietly chuckle.

Inside the hide site Carey smiled. Lower ranking soldiers seemed to be the same the world over, but he held no illusions about what he'd do to the NVA parade if one of them spotted one of the Claymores or any of his people in hiding. He'd blow a squad of them away with the Claymores and then order the team to light up the kill zone on those still standing.

In ambush the team maybe could take out a quarter to a third of the enemy soldiers, but it would've immediately been followed by a vicious, close-in firefight with those remaining, which also possibly meant that some of those heavy weapons the People's Army soldiers were transporting on the bikes might very well be used against the team.

The Americans went unnoticed and there would be no ambush. Instead, Carey had the team stay low as he and Pettit silently kept count on the line of the NVA that passed by their hide site. Both were also taking in the color and kind of uniforms the enemy soldiers were wearing, how fresh or grubby they looked, and the weight of the packs they were or weren't carrying. Also, they were mentally noting if any were unusually tall for Vietnamese? Any Chinese or Russian or other Europeans among them? Boots or Ho Chi's? Any nurses or civilians in the file?

They would take in as much useful information and intel as they could to add to their debriefing back at Camp Mackie upon completion of the mission. The puzzle pieces they were taking in would provide a better look at the overall picture once they were fitted in place.

Just as quickly as they appeared, the NVA platoon was gone. And only when Carey was certain they had moved on far enough, and when his best guess told him it was all clear, he huddled up with his Assistant Team Leader to compare their numbers for a more accurate, or at least, an agreed upon, count. Carey had counted twenty-seven in total, with four modified bicycles being used as pack mules. Pettit had 26 and then remembered the Pointman. From that figure, how they looked, their casual manner, and from what they were hauling, that were more than likely a newly arrived NVA Heavy Weapons Platoon that had just crossed the border from the north and were out to contribute to some serious damage.

Carey looked to Bowman, the team's radio man, and motioned for the backpacked radio's handset. He needed to call in a SITREP, their situation report. As he was quietly establishing commo he was unfolding his map in his lap. Lining up the map coordinates with his compass, he called in the enemy sighting, their number, what all they were hauling, and the direction they were moving back to the Valhalla Yankee radio relay who, in turn, would send it all up to command. What would be done with the intel was anybody's guess. Most of the time Carey was never really sure what the *'big wigs'* did with it. That was beyond his pay grade. He just hoped that the job he and his team were doing amounted to something worthwhile on the Chess board.

His radio call had been short and succinct, and as he handed the handset back to Bowman, the radioman, he knew he'd hear back soon enough. The finer minds were thinking. And who knows? Maybe they might extract the team since the surveillance part of the mission was a success? They'd located a heavy weapons platoon moving south and radioed in their target coordinates. On the other hand, Command might decide to have Nine-Seven *Charlie-Mike*, the military phonetic speak for *Continue the Mission* by either tracking the enemy patrol or even remaining in their position to see who else might waltz down the trail. Until the order came in, the Lurps waited.

Carey's SITREP produced a *Charlie Mike* response and a momentary *'hold in place.'* A Pink Team, consisting of a Low Bird Scout Helicopter and a Cobra gunship out of Camp Gorvad in Phuoc Vinh was on its way back from another mission. The Hunter/Killer helicopter team would divert and check out the *'purported'* sighting. The sighting was *'purported'* until it could be confirmed by the Low Bird or the helicopter gunship.

Carey frowned and slowly shook his head at the *'purported'* take, wanting very much to get back on the radio and tell them they could kiss his *'purported'* ass, but opted against it. Some things, he reasoned, were just better unsaid, especially to those who represent military hammers and view you as just another nail.

Twenty minutes had passed before the next radio call came in.

"Niner-Seven, Niner-Seven, Valhalla Yankee. Over."

"Got the radio relay calling," said Bowman, handing his Team Leader the radio's handset.

"Niner-Seven actual. Go Yankee."

"Be advised, the high bird is asking you to say again your coordinates and Mister Charlie's direction of travel. Over."

"Roger that," said Carey. He was a little miffed that the Cobra pilot was calling for verification as it appeared that neither he nor the Low Bird pilot could locate the enemy platoon after a few low passes. But in the seemingly endless ocean of dense jungle, they were in, that wasn't unusual. The helicopters could be heard coming in to snoop long before they arrived on scene, which gave the NVA time to hunker down and hide. With the dense foliage and heavy overhead canopy cover hiding would be easy.

Pulling out his map, Carey found the team's position a second time, and then with his right index finger traced a likely route south the enemy platoon would've taken, allowing for the time and distance gap and the terrain features.

At best they might manage three to four miles an hour in a straight line, but the jungle paths and trails were more like dropped ropes with bends and turns. Because there was a wetlands swamp further south on his map, a river to the west, and a number of open grassland areas in the large splotch of heavy jungle to the east, Carey's best directional guess was still south using the cover of the jungle's overhead canopy. Factor in the 30 to 40 minutes since they passed by the team, he had a reasonable idea about where they might be.

"Valhalla Yankee, Valhalla Yankee, Niner-Seven. Over."

"Go. Niner-Seven."

"Our coordinates are same-same from earlier transmission. We're holding in place. The November Victor Alpha parade that passed by our viewing stand 30 to 40 mikes earlier were on a south to southwest route. Could be they reached a Base Camp closer to our present location. Have them adjust their search back toward our hide-site."

"Roger that, Niner-Seven. Wilco. Valhalla Yankee out."

Pettit looked at the frustrated Carey who was sitting nearby and listening in.

"Why do I get the feeling they don't believe us?" said Pettit.

"Could be just green needles in a green haystack. Let's stay ready, though. If the gunship finds them and hammers the piss out of them, then that might send some of them running back our way. Pass the word to the others to stay ready."

Pettit passed the word along in whispers and the Lurps next wait began, only nothing followed. There were no muffled whumps from gunship fire or zipperlike rips from machine guns or miniguns, or return fire from the enemy soldiers in the far or near distance. There was only sound of the Hunter/Killer helicopter team off working its way closer searching for the NVA Heavy Weapons platoon Carey had called in. After a while when the noise from the two helicopters grew faint and then disappeared altogether, Carey figured command might consider the enemy sighting suspect, and that left him a little soured.

The team stayed in place. Whether command didn't believe them or not, it was an active enemy trail, so Carey saw no need to move on.

Ninety minutes had passed when an F-4 Phantom jet came in low screaming low over the jungle and shattered the afternoon calm with a nearby bomb run. The jet engine's loud roar and the exploding ordnance sent everyone on the team diving for cover behind their rucksacks or anything they could find.

The huge concussive blast, was followed by a giant fireball just east of the team's hide-site. The blast violently shook and rattled the ground, the surrounding jungle, and the five shocked and surprised Lurps. Blistering hot razor-sharp shards of metal fragments from the explosion whistled and whirred through and into the surrounding trees and brush around them as a swirling cloud of black smoke sent up a beacon hundreds of yards into the sky.

Pettit howled and cried out in pain as he wildly began shaking his right hand after a piece of the orange glowing metal the size of a bent tablespoon landed between his thumb and index finger and singed the skin. He shook it off, but a red bubbled welt was rising where the hot metal had burned him. As the metal fragment on the ground began to cool, it darkened.

"You okay, Gary?"

Trying to shake away the pain and blowing on the growing burn blister, Pettit gave a not quite convincing nod. A secondary explosion told of more dropped ordnance had sent Pettit and the other Lurps back down and hugging the trembling ground.

While the thicker trees and double canopy covering the tree tops took the worst of the metal fragments, smaller slivers of burning metal shot through the underbrush like burning darts and missiles.

A heavy *whoomph* spoke of something the size of a refrigerator crashing into the tops of the trees less than twenty yards in front of them. The heavy object pinballed and bounced its way down and breaking the lighter limbs before getting lodged ten feet up in the lower and thicker boughs of a massive tree.

"Are you fucking kidding me!" growled Sergeant Carey, more than a little peeved that no one had bothered to let him know that after the helicopter team moved away the Air Force was targeting the North Vietnamese Army platoon. His anger was checked, but just barely. He was pissed and he'd damn-well let the shot callers know it.

"Gimme the handset!" he said to his radio telephone operator.

"STAY DOWN!" he yelled, turning to Colp, who was peeking above his heavy pack staring in the direction of the initial blast even as smaller explosions were rumbling the rainforest and flinging metal fragments like angry lawn darts.

Bowman reached across and handed the push-to-talk telephone on the short length of coiled cord over to the Team Leader. Whoever made the call for the air support had screwed up royally and damn near got the team killed. No one had given them a head's up for the bomb run, let alone a *Danger Close* warning.

"VALHALLA YANKEE! VALHALLA YANKEE, LONGBOAT NINER-SEVEN. OVER!" Carey yelled into the handset in a barely controlled rage.

"Valhalla Yankee, Go, Niner-Seven."

"BE ADVISED, YOU HAVE AN ALPHA FOXTROT FAST MOVER DROPPING ORDNANCE *DANGER CLOSE*. GET THEM TO STOP! IT IS FALLING *DANGER CLOSE*. GET THEM TO STOP IT, FOR CHRIST'S SAKE! I SAY AGAIN, THE ALPHA FOXTROT FAST MOVER ORDNANCE IS FALLING *DANGER CLOSE*! YOU COPY? OVER."

"Roger Niner-Seven. I copy Fast mover ordnance falling *Danger Close*. Wait one, Niner-Seven..." came the reply and the expected delay leaving Carey fuming as smaller explosions blew around the bomb site.

The Ranger manning the radio relay site in Phuoc Vinh was checking with the Officer-in-Charge of the Tactical Operations Center at Fire Support Base Buttons to find out what was going on.

The response was not long in coming and not what he, nor Carey, had expected.

"Niner-Seven. Valhalla Yankee. Over."

"Niner-Seven, Yankee. Go."

"Be advised, it is not ordnance. I say again, it is *not* ordnance. A fast mover out of Bien Hoa just went down in your immediate area. Alpha Foxtrot Papa-Juliet's are choppering into that location, but they're asking for any units in the immediate area to move to the crash site and check for survivors. You're it so far. You copy?"

Any anger the team leader had quickly subsided even if his adrenaline had not. The danger was still there but the cause negated much of it.

"Roger that, Relay. We'll move on the crash site. Let any other fast movers, gunships, and/or Quebec Romeo Foxtrots know that we're moving in with camo and face paint, and not to fire on us. We don't want to be mistaken for Charlie. Niner-Seven out."

"I copy, Niner-Seven. Valhalla Yankee out."

A less angry and maybe not so relieved Carey handed the handset back to Bowman and then waved Pettit and the others in for a quick huddle.

"It's not a bomb run," explained Carey, feeling his own jets cool. "A jet went down. The fast mover burned into the jungle. They want us to move to secure the crash site and look for any survivors until an Air Force team of PJs show up."

"What are PJs?" asked the New Guy quietly to a veteran Lurp standing next to him. What was his name? That there were no name tags on their camo fatigues didn't help until he saw the orange hair sticking out of his boonie cap and remembered that his name was Green and that there was some irony attached to it.

"Para-Rescue Jumpers, *Ironic*," Pettit said back over his shoulder to the FNG. "Badass medics with jump wings. Good shooters, I'm told too."

"Who's ironic?"

"You. Your new nickname, so shut up and listen or it'll be Dumbass. You copy?"

The new guy nodded even though he still didn't know what exactly a Para-Jumper was, but he knew he'd find out when they arrived. He wasn't sure about the nickname either, but it was also easier to nod than ask anything more only to have the Assistant Team Leader tell him to shut the fuck up one more time and just pay attention and listen to the Team Leader. What was it that he'd heard a Drill Sergeant say during his Advanced Infantry Training?

"There are no stupid questions, just stupid dumbass people who didn't listen well enough to the directions the first time."

To Pettit Carey said, "How's the hand?"

"Burns some, but I'm good."

"You good with taking Point again?"

"Yep. Towards the boom?"

Carey nodded. "Towards the boom," he said, and then gave the order to the rest of his people to saddle up as he went out to retrieve the Claymore mines he and Pettit set out. When he returned moments later, and when they were up and shouldering their rucksacks with weapons ready, Carey gave Pettit a nod to move out.

The A-T-L didn't need a compass heading or a map to find the crash site because it was easy enough to locate. The downed jet had set a wide swath of the jungle on fire, with burning trees and brush popping and crackling in a fuel-mixed inferno.

Thanks to a passing rain shower that had fallen the previous evening and dampened the already musty smelling rainforest, the fire seemed confined to the fifty meter radius of the crash site. Pettit followed the heavy fumes from the burning fuel and jungle that had sent up a roiling thermal column of black and white smoke that served as a beacon. The black smoke was from the burning fuel while intense heat had sent clouds of steam and white smoke swirling from the adjacent wet trees. It would be an easy marker to zero in on.

The secondary explosions, some louder than others, seemed to have eased off but that didn't mean Pettit, or the rest of the team wouldn't likely come across one of the many other loose bombs, or the air-to-air missiles that had been ripped and torn off the aircraft when it crashed.

Pettit took it slowly, a little slower than his normal walk. There was too much at stake to rush it because there was no telling how many of the bombs or rockets the F-4 Phantom was carrying. Any one of them accidentally nudged or bumped, could turn him into jelly or a pink mist before he could even mouth, *'Uh-oh!'*

As he reached the outer edge of the crash site, Pettit had an upraised fist stopping the team in place and took a knee as his dark eyes scrutinized the fire and the scattered debris field that littered the jungle in front of him.

The crash site was on the north end of a good size, semi-round natural clearing. The clearing was maybe 40 yards wide and 60 long, and perhaps the last hope for the pilot that hadn't ended well. There were three deep craters. Two were filled with churned up dirt and debris, and green and muddied brown sump water while the third was a deep fire pit from burning fuel around what looked to be what was left of the F-4's fuselage. The musky, earthy smell of the rainforest floor was soon replaced by the harsher irritating smoke and odor from the crash site that bullied the eyes and nose.

Pettit wasn't looking for any survivors yet as much as he was looking for any NVA soldiers or Viet Cong patrol that also might be moving on the site, or be hiding in ambush across the clearing waiting on any rescuers.

Since he hadn't been told whether the jet was brought down by enemy fire or a catastrophic mechanical failure, he sought better caution. In either case, the noise from the jet slamming into the jungle and the dark swirling beacon was sure to draw the curious and the curious in enemy territory meant well-armed enemy soldiers like the 27 NVA soldiers that had passed the team earlier.

Carey moved up to Pettit's side and after a cautious pause and look-see, he figured it was time to secure the location as best they could. Five people weren't enough to properly do it, but it would have to do until the Cavalry rode in. Carey slipped past Pettit and took the lead as the team moved into the debris field towards the primary impact area, the burning crater.

As the first *friendlies* to reach the crash site, what he found stopped him just ahead of a deep fire pit. The fire pit was the size of an empty swimming pool except that it wasn't empty. While the tail section and part of the left wing of the two-man aircraft had been ripped off in the crash and had cartwheeled and tumbled into the trees twenty yards away, what remained of the F-4's fuselage and its twin engines were only glowing orange orbs buried deep in the large, open fire pit. There was no sign of the pilot, pilots, or anyone else. He wasn't certain how many people crewed the damn thing even as his eyes turned to the trees looking for parachutes and survivors, but none were seen.

The Ranger Team Leader was just about to have the team spread out around the impact area when the team's radioman held him up.

"Sarge," Bowman said, holding out the handset. "Valhalla Yankee on the line."

Carey took the call. "Valhalla Yankee, Niner-Seven. Go."

It was a one-sided conversation. As Carey listened, his eyes went toward the crash site and the debris field area around the team.

"I copy, Valhalla Yankee. Niner-Seven, out."

Carey signaled for the others to gather around him. The two FNGs on their very first mission and humping heavy rucksacks in the ridiculous heat, were flushed, and breathing heavily.

Reaching into his trousers' left pocket he pulled out the URC-10 survival radio and activated the homing beacon as was requested in the radio call. It was the first time he'd activate the emergency radio.

"They want us to do a quick search of the crash site. We'll spread out and do a slow walk. If you come across something don't touch it. A Quick Reaction Force is on its way, but until they arrive, we're it. So, keep an eye out for the pilot and crewman and for any UXO…"

"UXO?" asked Colp.

"Unexploded Ordnance," said Carey. "Bombs and rockets. Those jets carry a shitload of them on missions. Chances are better than good some might've been knocked off in the crash. If you find any, don't fucking touch, bump or nudge them. I have 23-days left in-country and counting. I'm short, and I'm going home in one piece. So, I say again, don't fucking even breathe on them! You copy?"

Short meant he had a short time left on his tour of duty and Carey gave Colp and the new guy Pettit called *Ironic*, a hard-edged stare and held it on each of them to make sure they got the message. Pettit and Bowman didn't need to be told.

"Drop your rucks," Carey said. "Weapons and web gear only. Bow, stay here, monitor the radio."

To Pettit he said, "Take a new guy and work your way around to the burnt ground and fire pit to the left."

Pettit nodded, but when Pettit started to grab Sergeant Colp to go with him, Carey shook his head.

"Naw, take the other one. Colp's with me."

"*Ironic*, follow me!" said Pettit to Green while Carey, with Bowman and Colp stood, and prepared to move to the left of the crash site.

"You're a '*Shake and Bake*,' right?" asked Carey to Colp.

The FNG lowered his eyes and nodded. '*Shake and Bake*' was one of the derogatory terms for the Army's latest *90 day boy wonders*, this time though, instead of becoming officers at the end of the three months of training, the graduates of the Non Commissioned Officers Candidate Course became Buck or

Staff Sergeants. The 90 day stateside course was designed to produce better trained young soldiers to become competent squad leaders in a short amount of time for the inevitable combat they'd find in Vietnam. The program that brought on the speedy promotions, though, wasn't always well received by the other enlisted ranks upon their arrival in-country.

However, good squad leaders were in short supply in the war and the Infantry NCOCC, the Non-Commissioned Officer Candidate Course at Fort Benning, Georgia helped alleviate part of the problem. Many of the newly promoted young buck sergeants worked out well in combat. Others, though, hadn't. Combat was always the crucible where what wasn't forged in fire, melted as slag.

"A *'Shake and Bake,'* huh?"

Colp nodded again, waiting for the inevitable double snub that came with being an FNG and an Instant *NCO*, hence the *'Shake and Bake'* reference.

"You'll be happy to know that I too am a sterling graduate of the Harmony Church School for Wayward Boys, so here's a tip. Team members don't really give a rat's ass what rank you hold as long as you know how to do your job. So, learn as much as you can, as quickly as you can, and you should be fine...eh, with time."

Colp nodded and then followed Carey covering the jungle as they moved around the crash site. *Time would solve a lot, thought Colp. Hopefully, I'll have it.*

They were working their way across the field when the sky overhead roared with the deafening sound of a second low flying jet racing in at Mach-2 speed. By the time they heard the roar, the jet was long gone and nowhere to be seen in the immediate sky above them. With the limited view from the jungle, even in the natural open space, the surrounding tall trees obscured most of what wasn't directly overhead.

Still, Carey was looking up and smiling.

While the sound of a Cobra gunship overhead might have caused any bad guys in the immediate area to think twice about attacking or trying to overrun the crash site, the thunderous roar of a low flying F-4 Phantom jet eliminated any threat. Jets carried napalm and napalm frightened the hell into the enemy who felt its burn.

"Longboat Niner-Seven, Double-Ugly Three. Over," came the radio call. This time the call was coming over the small URC-10 backup radio Carey he was carrying. While the URC-10 was a survival radio for downed pilots and for emergency use only, when activated, it would lead rescuers in to help. For a Lurp team in *Contact* when everything went to shit in an instant, an Air Force jet overhead was a Godsend. With it a team leader could hail any nearby Air Force aircraft and request air support. Having it call him was another matter. Pulling out the UHF transistorized survival radio Carey keyed the mike, uncertain who exactly or what a Double-Ugly was.

"Niner-Seven. Go, Double-Ugly."

"Inbound Huskie and a gunship on their way. Same-same with Quebec Romeo Foxtrot. Any sign of the pilots? There should be two. Over."

"That's a negative. Double-Ugly. We'll keep an eye out."

"Roger, Niner-Seven. And I'll keep an overwatch."

Carey gave the hand signal for Pettit and Green to move back to Bowman and their rucksacks where once again they took up a defensive posture.

Because of their limited numbers the quick search constituted the immediate area. There was no sign of two parachutes hanging in the surrounding trees or crumpled up on the ground, no emergency radio call from the pilot, and no strobe light or pen-flair showing his or the second pilot's location.

"We'll hunker down here. Bowman?"

"Yeah?"

"Monitor this one as well," he said, handing Bowman the URC-10 emergency back-up radio. "The Air Force is on its own radio frequency."

In the near distance the sky chopping sound of an in-bound helicopter was getting louder.

A second call came in to the Lurps. The pilot of the small, inbound boxcar-looking HH-43, Search and Rescue helicopter, was making a request to the Ranger long range patrol.

"Roger that, wait one…" said Bowman, taking the call on the hand-held radio and then letting his team leader know what they wanted.

"An Air Force bird is two minutes out," said Bowman. "They want us to pop smoke and guide them in."

Carey nodded and frowned. "Yeah, okay," he said. "Tell them we're on it," he said. "I'll guide the bird in. The rest of you stay down."

Pulling out a smoke grenade, he pulled the pin and held the spoon in place as he walked out to the clearing. Tossing the marking grenade to his left, he held his rifle up with both hands as yellow smoke slowly rose in a swirling cloud and marked his location.

"They identify banana!" said Bowman.

"Confirm it." Carey said over his shoulder. He was 15 yards into the clearing while his eyes went from the in-bound helicopter to the surrounding tree line and then back to the approaching Huey. If there was an enemy soldier hiding and ready to shoot then he was little more than an easy pop-up target. To a Lurp specifically trained to remain unseen by the NVA and Viet Cong in the jungle, standing out in the open had his intestines churning and feeling like he badly needed to piss.

The popping blades from the inbound helicopter brought his focus skyward over the trees to his front as the helicopter grew closer.

"Yeah well, sitting ducks at least get to sit," he muttered to himself, scanning the jungle wall across the clearing from left to right.

But there was no enemy gunfire coming at him as the odd-looking helicopter came in over the grass field, flared, and then touched down. A wave of dust and ash, loose grass and twigs sent up by the swirling helicopter blades flew at Carey and had him closing his eyes, sending his chin to his chest, and spitting dirt laced phlegm.

Two rifle-toting, serious looking Airmen raced out the back of the unusual looking helicopter and towards the soldier who had guided in the bird only to stop short of the Lurp in the camouflaged jungle fatigues and the green and black face paint. The Airmen were dressed and outfitted as the Lurps, only without the green, brown, and black face paint or stench.

"You SOG?" asked the PJ in the lead. He was a tall, lean middleweight with a fighting kit ready for battle as a Para-rescue fighting medic. With his upside down rank on his sleeves, Carey knew he was an NCO of some kind but wasn't quite sure where he fell into the E-1 through E-9 categories. An E-6 or 7, maybe. The second Airman had lesser rank but could have easily been a twin in size and disposition. Both were armed with Car-15 assault rifles and web gear that mirrored that of the Army Rangers without the burdensome rucksacks.

"Naw, Lurps," Carey said. "Five of us."

Carey pointed to where Pettit and the two others in camouflage fatigues and face paint had remained unseen down behind cover. He waved them up and the remaining team members the Air men hadn't seen slowly rose up on one knee to show themselves.

"Any sign of the crew?"

Carey shook his head. "That's a negative. We did a quick search, but only found wreckage and the burning pit," he said, earning a solemn nod from the lead PJ before the two Airmen moved to the impact crater and fire pit with the Lurp Team Leader trailing.

At the large burning pit, the PJs traded hard looks at the downed jet's twin engines that were protruding at the bottom of the fire pit. The two PJs carefully moved around the burning crater with more of a learned analytical assessment than any of the Lurps had. This was their realm, and they were well familiar with what they were looking at. The heat from the flames, though, kept them from a closer inspection.

"So, did they eject in time? They like a mile down the road somewhere wondering where their taxi is?" This from Carey to the lead PJ.

"No," the PJ said, pointing to something in the pit where what looked to be a small section of F-4's canopy with what looked to be bird splatter on it. "Part of a flight helmet."

Inside the helmet scrap that wasn't a bird hit there was severed bone and a piece of scalp attached to hair.

"They rode it in," said the PJ.

"Jesus!" said Colp.

"Given how fast they were falling, the dying was quick."

A closer look at the fiery pit had the PJ move the Lurps back away from the crater. The tail fins and what could be seen of a dug-in and damaged, unexploded 500 pound bomb had him worried.

"Let's get your people moved back a little further. Maybe back into the tree line?"

"What about securing the crash site?"

"The QRF is right behind us. Maybe 10 to 15 minutes out. They'll secure the site, and we'll recover the bodies or at least as much of them as we can find. Judging from the burning hole, I don't think there's much left."

"Then we'll cover you until they clock in."

"Thanks, and thank you guys for taking the lead on this. Looks like your team is done with your patrol."

"Naw, we're only on day one."

"How long was the mission scheduled?"

"Six days. We were set up on a busy trail, lots of fresh sign of enemy activity less than a klick away. If no one's watching us now, they soon will be."

Taking a long, slow look around, the lead PJ nodded.

"The crash site is bound to draw in a bunch of looky-loo's."

"We can do a stay-behind and see who comes in to check it out."

"Negative," said the PJ. "Our command said to extract your team. You can call it in and let your people know it's our decision. Once the QRF gets flown in, and once the remains of the pilot are retrieved, and we're all out of here, they'll light it up."

The PJ pointed skyward.

"The F-4s?"

"No, it'll be an F-100 Hun coming in to do a napalm run. He'll turn this place and any and everything around it into toast. There's too much unexploded ordnance scattered around here to leave behind or try to deal with otherwise. The napalm will do the job."

"You out of Bien Hoa?"

"We are."

"Any chance you could drop us off at Lai Khe or Di An?"

"That where you're located?"

"Naw, Camp Mackie."

"Mackie! Then it shouldn't be a problem. It's in line on our way back. I'll give the Chinook a call and check with the pilot."

The PJ nodded and made the radio call while Carey called in the team's ordered extraction to Yankee Relay. Both replies came back immediately.

"We're Good-to-Go," said Carey as the lead PJ nodded.

"Our Chinook drivers are happy to drop you off. They don't often get a chance to extract a Ranger team. You're the first for them. The truth is you guys are also the first Lurps I've ever worked with in the field."

"Same-same," said Carey.

The sound of the big helicopter flying in drew their attention in the direction of the noise. The lumbering Chinook came in slow and steady, kicking up a cloud of dust and debris as it touched down. This time Colp guided it in as it dropped off the Quick Reaction Force. Per protocol the big helicopter took off and would set down at a nearby base, and return after the pilots' bodies, or what remained of them, were recovered.

Shortly after the Chinook departed another F-4 jet, part of the same squadron the dead pilot belonged to, roared overhead in a low pass over the area looking for vengeance. If any North Vietnamese or Viet Cong units were in the area they wisely remained away.

The five Rangers watched as the Air Force Quick Reaction Force and recovery team secured the area and methodically went about the gruesome task of retrieving the few bits, pieces, and chunks of the two-man crew they could locate. There wasn't much to find. Once the remains were in the body bags, the radio call went out for the Chinook to come back in for exfiltration. The big bird lumbered in a second time and set down with its turbine engines running ready to take off once everyone was inside.

The Army Lurps rode out with the PJs and the QRF. When the helicopter was safely out of range a Super Sabre jet roared in at a low attack angle and sent the thin bodied canister tumbling toward the designated target area. Never a precise bomb, the M-47 incendiary bomb, nonetheless, found and made its fiery mark.

"Check it out!" the lead PJ said to Carey pointing to one of the port side windows where the Chinook pilot had turned for a better show.

Well behind them the crash site was erupting not just in a hellish storm of orange and black rolling jellied fuel but with giant spikes of white phosphorus that blew through the sky and fell burning anything it touched. A series of violent explosions from the rockets and bombs that had been scattered in the crash accompanied the inferno. Eventually when the fire wore down and the last of the missiles or bombs had detonated, there would be nothing left in the area but fragments of scorched earth, metal, and ash.

The flight to Camp Mackie, thankfully, was uneventful and when the Chinook touched down, Carey was up and approaching the lead PJ.

"If you guys can sit tight here for a bit I've got a few of our Ranger Company scrolls for you. The pilots too!"

The PJ passed the word on to the Flight Engineer who passed the word onto the pilots. The answer came back quickly from the now smiling Flight Engineer to the PJ.

Sweet Sorrow

"No problem," said the PJ. "The pilot needs to take a piss, anyway."

Word had gone out that Nine-Seven was coming in on the Chinook so First Sergeant Poplawski had sent one of the four-by-four mules to the flight line to drive the Lurps back to the Romeo Company's compound.

As they pulled into the Company area the Unit's Executive Officer, First Lieutenant Marquardt was standing outside the Orderly Room flicking the ash from a cigarette watching on as Carey left his rucksack on the flatbed mule and quickly started toward the First Platoon's hootch.

"Staff Sergeant Carey?"

"Sir?" said Carey, stopping and turning back to the officer.

"You and your team done good securing the crash site for the Air Force. Bien Hoa expressed their thanks to the BIG-TOC who relayed it to the C.O, so why the hurry?"

"Thank you, sir, but the Air Force helicopter that dropped us off is at the airfield waiting on me. I promised some of our Ranger scrolls to them for pulling us out."

"Wait one, Ranger!" ordered the officer, snuffing out the cigarette and then field stripping it. "Don't move!"

"Sir?"

Only Lieutenant Marquardt didn't reply but held up his right index finger before he disappeared back inside the Orderly Room.

While Carey waited the rest of the team members climbed off of the mule, slipped out of their back and shoulder straining rucksacks, and were heading back to the Platoon hootch when Pettit held them up.

"Hold up!" he said to Bowman, Colp, and Green, the *Ironic*. "Gimme some of your Lurp rations."

"Which ones?" asked Bowman.

"Don't matter. We're donating them to the Air Force folks who gave us a ride and so maybe we can call on again in the future. Our patrol was cut short which means you should have a bunch left over, so hand over what you don't want and keep the rest."

The members of the team began digging into their rucksacks and soon Pettit had over a half-dozen of the now excess freeze-dried, vacuum packed Lurp rations cradled in his forearms. Pettit couldn't help but notice that there were no Beef and Rice rations in the offerings. No surprise, really. The tasty and prized Beef and Rice Lurp rations were always at a premium over others like pork with scalloped potatoes or beef hash. He smiled. Even the New guys understood that much.

Carey said, "You know the Air Force guys have an honest to God dining facility back at Bien Hoa and I'm not talking a Mess Tent, right?"

"True, but maybe they don't have genuine Lurp rations they can use to barter with."

"Good call."

Lieutenant Marquardt came out of the Orderly Room holding out a handful of shiny new Romeo Company scrolls and several Sua Sponte pocket patches.

"Here! Give them some of these!" he said, holding out the offerings. "Just got a new order in. They're nice and clean."

"Wow, Lieutenant! Thank you!"

To Carey and Pettit, he added, "Hop back on the mule. I'll drive."

The bouncing drive back to the airfield and the awaiting Chinook only took a few minutes, and as the mule wheeled over near the back ramp of the Chinook helicopter, several of the Air Force personnel were actually surprised to see that the Rangers had returned. It was a 50/50 coin toss bet that they'd keep their word.

"Appreciated bringing us out and getting us back home," Carey said, handing the lead PJ, Flight Engineer, and one of the pilots the Ranger patches as Specialist Pettit passed over the Lurp rations. The Lieutenant watched on from the Mule.

"They're a lot better than C-rations," said Pettit to the grinning Airmen. Swag was always good, and edible swag was even better.

With thanks all around, goodbyes and good lucks given, the big helicopter shook to life first with the whirring, whooshing, and high pitched whine of its turboshaft engines, followed by the growing noise of its rotor blades as it made ready for takeoff. The spinning blades of the Chinook soon sent a cloud of dust tumbling into and over the three Rangers on the mule before it turned and made the long flight south to Bien Hoa. They'd turned their heads almost in time to avoid the rotor wash.

"Never let a good deed go unpunished!" laughed the Executive Officer, wiping the dust from his eyes and spitting dirt.

Marquardt drove Carey and Pettit back to the company and dropped them off near the First Platoon's hootch and left the mule idling as they off-loaded.

"Just so you know that helicopter Pink Team out of Lai Khe took a lot of heavy fire a few klicks south of you," said the Lieutenant to Carey. "Looks like that NVA platoon that passed your team married up with a larger force. A Recon platoon and a few gunships are going in at first light to make a run at them. Oh, and once you store your weapons and gear, I'll need you two in the TOC later for a mission debriefing."

Marquardt checked his Seiko watch.

"The Engineers Mess tent should be serving lunch soon, so you and your people go eat and then meet me in the TOC at 1300 hours. That'll give you time to clean up a bit, too. You copy?"

"Yes sir," said the two Lurps.

"Sir, you want to take the mule back to our motor pool?" asked Pettit, only to have Marquardt grin and shake his head.

"Naw, I got this! This thing is a hoot to drive!" he said, pushing in the flat bed's clutch, shifted it into gear, and then sped off kicking up dirt and laughing like he was in teenager in a Go-Cart race.

Chapter 12

It was chow time, a quarter past noon by his wrist watch, and the new guy wasn't banking on anyone else still being in the Second Platoon hootch.

Of the fourteen Lurps assigned to the corrugated tin-roofed Quonset hut that housed the Platoon, eight were out on patrol with teams in the jungle, and one was on Emergency Leave in the states, which left only a handful of others that were in-between missions to worry about. Most had already left to get something hot to eat. C-rations and dehydrated Lurp rations only went so far when it came to military meals while the company cooks the Engineers had were pretty good.

The new guy took his time and waited. After the last two lingering Lurps had finally trotted off to the Engineer's Mess Tent a quarter mile down the dirt road from the Ranger Company, he quickly got busy.

"Who are you?" asked SFC Kozak, the Platoon Sergeant coming up behind the new guy with a pair of bolt cutters in his right hand and startling him. The soldier was standing over a jimmied foot locker. The bottom half of the hasp had been pried from the wooden chest. Two loose screws were left dangling with a third on the floor in a small pile of wood dust while the locked padlock was still intact. "What are you doing?"

"PFC Donald, Sergeant," said the surprised soldier. "I...I just graduated from the selection training. I'm assigned to your platoon. I was...was just moving in."

Kozak could see that Donald was also nervously smiling and fidgeting even as he casually pulled on the drawstrings of the laundry bag he had his hands before tossing the half-filled cotton bag on the bottom empty bunk to his left.

"Someone said this bunk area was empty," he said. "And I was just wondering what all this was doing here. This didn't look right to me."

"You pop open that foot locker?"

"No, Sergeant," said Donald. "It was like that when I got here."

"Is that right?"

"Yes, Sergeant."

Kozak gave a nod with a bottom lip protruding and said something that sounded like *hmm,* as he took a quick look around before turning back to the Private First Class.

"So, eh...where are your things?"

"What?"

"Your duffle bag, LBE, and web gear, Donald. Where's all your personal shit?"

"Sergeant?"

"Your belongings. You said you were moving in, so where are they, PFC Donald?"

Sweet Sorrow

"In, eh, in the training tent. I was just checking things out first to see where there was an open bunk."

"Ah, I see," said the Platoon Sergeant, nodding, as though that was a reasonable answer as he eyed the green cloth bag on the bunk. "So, what's in the laundry bag?"

"The laundry bag?"

"Yeah, the bag," said Kozak, pointing to the partially filled, lumpy cloth bag on the bed as he glanced back at the damaged foot locker and then back to PFC Donald.

As he was asking the question, the Platoon Sergeant dropped the bolt cutters into his cargo pants pocket and then positioned himself in front of Donald and between the rows of bunk beds on either side blocking the new guy in. At 6'3" and 225-pounds Kozak was a hulking, imposing figure to the 6-foot nothing, 155-pound Army Private.

"Open it."

"I…I found a few things…on…on the floor, and, and put them in his laundry bag. I wanted to safeguard them," said Donald, almost convincingly while still not complying with the NCO's order.

"Is that right? Well then go ahead and dump the contents on the bunk."

"What?"

"Dump what's in the bag. Do it. Now!" said Kozak, more than a little impatiently.

The new guy was the not-so-dear Bambi caught in the headlights of a Cossack eighteen-wheeler logging truck with a full load bearing down on him. PFC Donald was looking for a way to run, only Kozak wasn't giving him one.

Donald reached over and grabbed the bag, but was slow in loosening the drawstrings to empty it. When he did, a dirty towel, wrinkled tee shirt, a set of dirty jungle fatigues, and two loose socks fell out of the bag, followed by a gold wedding ring, a wallet, and a dress watch. Kozak recognized the Hamilton watch with the brown leather band and his eyes narrowed when he did. Reaching over he picked up the wallet and opened it to confirm his suspicions. Specialist Warren's military ID card stared back at him as did a picture of his smiling young wife in a plastic photograph holder.

Kozak's jaw muscles tensed and trembled as he angrily turned to Donald. Jonas Warren had been killed in action several days earlier on patrol. His badly shot up body was still at the Army's Mortuary unit at the Tan Son Nhut Air Base in cold storage readying to be embalmed and worked on before it would be sent stateside. Kozak had planned on inventorying the items in the foot locker after lunch. Any military items in it would be turned over to the Supply Sergeant while Warren's personal effects would be boxed up and mailed to his home of record back to his young wife who was now a young widow.

Spinning a protesting Donald around, Kozak did a quick pat down on the soldier searching for other stolen items, but only came up with the Private's own wallet, a plastic spoon in his top left jungle fatigue pocket, and a partial roll of toilet paper in his right cargo pants pocket.

"You can steal all you like from outside the company *if* it benefits the Company, but you never steal anything from the Company, and especially not from here. You don't fucking deserve our Company scroll, you little rat bastard!"

"I...I didn't steal..."

"Shut the fuck up! You're coming with me!" Kozak said, angrily, spinning him back around, grabbing the new guy just above the elbow and then squeezing the soldier's upper arm tightly as though it had been locked in vice-grips.

Donald was wincing while Kozak was fuming.

"Hey, that hurts!" cried Donald, trying to pull away only to have the *Mad Russian* shake him a few times to get him to comply and move along.

"I said, shut up! Now keep moving!"

Rattled, he was escorted from the platoon hootch and marched across the compound to the Ranger Company's Orderly Room. Pulling the screen door open, Kozak shoved Donald none to ceremoniously inside.

The Company Commander was behind his gunmetal grey desk going over the Morning Report with the First Sergeant Poplawski. Both turned to see just what the ruckus was all about.

"Caught a barrack's thief!" said SFC Kozak, tossing the laundry bag on the Captain's desk and then placing the wedding ring, watch, and wallet on the bag. "He had these in the laundry bag when I caught him. They're Specialist Warren's."

"I'm not a thief! And nobody saw me steal nothing!"

"AT EASE!" yelled Captain Robison, shutting Donald up and letting the Platoon Sergeant continue.

"Sergeant?" he said, turning to Kozak.

"While everyone else was at chow I caught him in the second platoon hootch standing over Specialist Warren's foot locker that had been broken into."

"Say again?"

"The hasp on Warren's foot locker was pried off, the screws pulled out, and Donald here was standing in front of it holding a laundry bag. When I had him empty it, some of Warren's personal effects fell out."

Kozak tilted his square head toward the ring, wallet, and watch.

"Sir, I was just moving into the hootch, and... and... I... I didn't know who's stuff it was, so I was only safeguarding it all. I..."

"I said, AT EASE!"

Properly cowed, Donald fell silent as his mind quickly went to work looking to mitigate the situation.

"He says he was moving into the Platoon but all he had with him was the laundry bag. No duffle bag, shaving kit, personal items or issued kit and gear. Nada! Nothing!"

The Platoon Sergeant glared at the new guy, as did First Sergeant Poplawski with balled-up fists at his side looking like a boxer ready and eager to come out of his corner to apply some hurt. There was no sympathy there that Donald could see. His only hope was with the Company Commander whose face appeared more judicious than those of the two senior NCOs. They were looking more like junkyard dogs staring at a tasty trespasser who'd just dropped over the fence's locked gate.

"Care to explain yourself, Private Donald?" said the now troubled Captain, opening the wallet, confirming its rightful owner, and then staring back at the soldier.

"I...I just graduated from the last Lurp training cycle and was moving into the Platoon hootch, Sir, like I had been told to do this morning. Someone said the bunk area was open, so I was checking it out and found those things from the foot locker on the floor and wondered why they were there."

"The foot locker was secure no more than 10-minutes before I confronted him," said Kozak, interrupting Donald. "I know because I was getting ready to inventory what was in it. I'd just returned from the supply room with some bolt cutters to cut off the lock. That's when I found him standing over the broken foot locker."

"It...it was already broken, Sir, I swear I didn't break it. It was already like that."

"Is that right, Sergeant?" Captain Robison asked the Platoon Sergeant.

The *Mad Russian* shook his head. "It wasn't broken before I went to the Supply Room, Sir."

"Did you see or hear him break the hasp?"

"No, Sir."

"I didn't break it," blurted PFC Donald. "And nobody can say they saw me do it either! This is crazy! I'm not a thief!"

Robison stared at the slow spinning ceiling fan of the Quonset hut for a good moment before he turned back to the PFC.

"You're in SFC Kozak's platoon?"

"Yes sir."

"Okay, then why didn't you immediately turn over Warren's personal effects to SFC Kozak when he found you, if you were just safeguarding them? He's your Platoon Sergeant. Why didn't you just hand over what you say you found?"

"I...I panicked."

"Panicked?"

"Yes sir."

"Gentlemen, he panicked," Robison said to the others.
"Un-huh, he scared me when he came up behind me like that."
"Scared you..."
"Because the hootch being so quiet and all at the time."
To Kozak he asked, "Did he have any of Warren's personal effects on him? In his pockets or anything? You do a pat down?"
"I did, and no, Sir, he didn't have anything on him that he shouldn't have," said Kozak, wishing that he had found some of Warren's personal items on the whiny little *podonok*. *Podonok* was Russian word for *bastard*. Had he found any of Warren's personal effects then it would have been an open and shut case instead of only a suspiciously pried-open foot locker and a boatload of excuses.
"Just found him with the laundry bag standing over the foot locker, Captain."
"Did he tell you what he had?"
"Not immediately, no," said the Platoon Sergeant. "He was pulling the drawstrings on the laundry bag when I confronted him and then tossed it on Warren's bunk when I asked him what he was doing."
"Like he was hiding it from you?"
"I wasn't hiding anything! I didn't steal nothing, Sir!" Donald said, again, pleading his case.
"Double-negative," said the First Sergeant, looming in closer to the FNG Lurp. "Technically, you just admitted you did, a few times actually."
"N...no, First Sergeant, I mean, I didn't. I...I was just safeguarding those things. That's all."
Captain Robison sighed and took a seat behind his desk. Staring up at the Private he said, "That's your best defense, is it? Nobody saw you steal anything?"
PFC Donald paused, rethinking what he'd just said. When he started to say more, Captain Robison raised his hands up, palms out, and cut him off.
Robison remained quiet and thoughtful as a black Solomon as he considered the arguments before pronouncing his judgment. He stared down at his desk and wiped away a speck of dust that wasn't there and then looked up and announced his decision.
"You are correct, Private," he said, finally. "There is no proof you stole the ring, wallet, or the watch, or tried to, and it's possible, too, just as you stated, and perhaps you were only just safeguarding them..."
PFC Donald gave a relieved smile.
"And no one saw you break into the foot locker, but here's the thing," added the Captain, staring coldly at the soldier. "Romeo Company, and especially a Lurp team doesn't need someone who panics. It's a serious liability to his fellow Rangers in the field. I take it that the rest of your things are still in the training tent?"
"Y...yes sir."

Sweet Sorrow

"Then SFC Kozak will escort you to the training tent and you will pack up everything that's yours. You're out of here."

To the Platoon Sergeant he said, "Let me know if you find anything else that isn't his that he's, eh, *safeguarding*."

"Yes sir," said Kozak.

"First Sergeant Poplawski, the Captain added, turning to his senior NCO. "Get on the transfer paperwork for PFC Donald, A-SAP and have it ready for my signature by the time he's done packing."

"Yes sir," said Poplawski. "You sure you don't want to court martial him or maybe have me break his fucking head?"

Robison shook his head. "No," he said. "Contact his home unit, a grunt company here on Camp Mackie, I believe?"

"Yes sir," replied the First Sergeant. "I heard they're scheduled to rotate out to the field and relieve a sister unit on some shitty little Fire Support Base near the Cambodian border in a few days."

"Good timing, then," said the Company Commander. "He'll be there in time to join them."

"Oh, and SFC Kozak?" said Robison with an afterthought.

"Sir?"

"After PFC Donald's done packing up his things, have him wait outside of our compound area on the road for the transfer order. Once he has it, then point him back to his old unit."

Finally, to PFC Donald he said, "You'll report to your Battalion Headquarters immediately or you'll be listed as AWOL. You understand me, soldier?"

"Yes sir."

"Good. Now get the fuck out of my Ranger Company and wait on the road outside. GO!"

Chapter 13

The company's field telephone was on its second, annoying metallic clicking ring before Poplawski scooped up the handset and pressed the push-to-talk button.

"Romeo Company Ranger. First Sergeant Poplawski speaking. How may I help you, Sir?" he said, quietly listening in before he gave a low grunt and said, "Wait one."

Poplawski cupped the handset as he leaned over his desk holding out the phone to Captain Robison.

"Sir, it's the BIG-TOC. Colonel Becker's Aide, Captain Schiller."

Robison grunted and took the phone.

"Captain Robison speaking," said the Company Commander, as he too listened to what was mostly a one-way conversation. Robison gave the phone a slow nod and replied, "Roger that, Captain. Romeo Company out."

"What's up, Boss?" asked the First Sergeant as the Captain was putting the field phone back on its cradle.

"The BIG-TOC has a tasking for us."

"They say what it is?"

"Good question!" he said. "No, they didn't. However, what they did say was that MAC-V is flying a civilian up from Saigon in the morning who'll be in charge of a priority mission and that our role in the tasking will be explained in full during a briefing in the BIG-TOC at 1300 hours."

"A civilian?"

"From the, eh, *'Civil Operations and Rural Development Agency,'* a Mister Robert Evans, or so I'm told."

Robison couldn't hide his smirk as he was speaking while the First Sergeant gave him a cynical side eye stare.

"Bob Evans? You mean, just like the restaurant chain?"

"Guess McDonald was already taken," said the Captain. "Could be maybe, it's more than likely, a *nom de guerre* for a CIA somebody."

"Hopefully, he'll bring fries."

Robison chuckled, nodded, and then said, "Any idea where Lieutenants' Marquardt or Plantagenet are at this moment?"

"Affirmative on both. Lieutenant Marquardt is debriefing Sergeant Carey's team in the TOC. I believe Lieutenant Plantagenet is helping Staff Sergeant Shintaku run quick reaction drills behind the supply room with some of the new people."

Robison nodded again.

"Let's have Lieutenant Plantagenet join us at the BIG-TOC briefing. Can you let him know?"

"Yes sir, will do."

That earned another nod.

"What's the status of the teams in the field?"

"All's good with Nine-Two and Nine-Three. Team Nine-Seven's being debriefed in our TOC by the X.O...."

"That the downed jet?"

"Yes sir."

"They okay? No injuries?"

"The team's A-T-L suffered a small burn from shrapnel."

"Which A-T-L?"

"Specialist Pettit. He was treated at the Aid Station and all's good."

"Nine-Seven," Robison said, chuckling at the team's new designation.

"We debriefed Nine-Four this morning."

"That Specialist's Li's Team?"

"Yes sir, it is, and they're asking about their in-country R&R for the P-O-W they captured. I told them I'd check with you on the matter."

"What did we decide, two to three days down in Vung Tau on the beach at the in-country R&R Center for capturing a prisoner?"

"Two days, plus eight-hours travel time, to and from."

"For two team members, right?"

Poplawski nodded. "Yes sir, with team members drawing straws to see who gets to go."

Robison paused, thinking something over with a set jaw and finally a nod that said he had an answer to a question that wasn't asked.

"Make it two days for each member of the team."

The First Sergeant sat back in his chair surprised by the decision.

"That's pretty generous, Sir," he said.

"I'm thinking maybe it's time to be."

Chapter 14

The BIG-TOC, Camp Mackie's Command and Tactical Operations Center, was big by any Camp's standard and while it wasn't as secure as Fort Knox, it was seemingly just as well guarded and protected. Nobody called it the main TOC and the nickname of the BIG-TOC stuck.

It began as a single, fortified Navy Quonset hut that had given way to a grander scheme. Three more of the Quonset huts had been hauled in by truck convoy on a three hour journey from Saigon to Mackie where they were set on a combined foundation of rebar-lined, reinforced concrete to form the primary directional points on a compass of North, South, East, and West.

Because the Quonset huts were originally meant for more domestic and office use stateside, but were now sitting in a highly contested part of a warzone, meant they were vulnerable, the fortification process took over and a Castle Keep began taking serious shape. If a siege came, it would be the place of last resort.

Heavy timber beams, tons of concrete mix and rebar, and twelve thousand nylon sandbags, stacked on pallets, were trucked, or flown in and sorted, as were two iron prison gates for the main entrance and emergency exit for the facility. Thick steel plates, and corrugated galvanized roofing panels were added to the construction materials and overall design. When it was all delivered and on-site, a large crew of Army Engineers went to work for several weeks making their modification blueprints and safety add-ons come to life.

The connected huts, along with the accompanying compound area for the BIG-TOC Command Post included a shower station and two outhouses, one for the enlisted men working in the BIG-TOC and another for the officers. The site was ringed by chain-link fencing and topped with rows of rolled razor wire that gave it the look of an angry, well-sharpened Slinkie.

Ten feet in from the fencing, the engineers erected an eight-foot tall wall of sandbags set three feet deep and supported by reinforced concrete to protect the perimeter of the BIG-TOC from anything the North Vietnamese Army had in their weapons inventory, which was considerable.

In addition to the concrete walls, a series of steel panels were welded into place with sandbagged buttresses that not only served as extra shielding surrounding the BIG-TOC, but had also helped support the heavy load from the many layers of its newly fortified and expanded roof.

Above the four separate roofs, the Engineers constructed a single six foot tall false roof to cover them all and to take the impact and blast from any incoming rocket or mortar fire that might accurately be aimed in on the BIG-TOC.

Because it was also the Camp's main Communications Center the denuded forest of antennas above the false roofing made good aiming stakes for targeting by the Viet Cong and North Vietnamese Army's enthusiastic heavy weapons' crews. The antennas were something that couldn't be helped. Commo was critical to Mackie's operations and survival.

Less than two days after the false roof had been installed, the BIG-TOC was hit by one of three enemy mortars that blew a hole through the false roofing and sent antennas flying like hastily strewn pick-up sticks. The fortified roofing below, though, held, but just barely, which is when the Engineers went back to the drawing board, before they went back to work, reconfiguring and refortifying it with one new learned addition.

It was a talented, keen-eyed Engineer Captain who wisely deduced that by installing and angling steel plates to the false roofing any explosive force, along with the shell fragments and splintered debris from any incoming mortars or rockets, would be deflected out and away from the primary impact point. The steel deflection plates, that had been carefully fitted and welded in place, proved their worth one month after they were installed when a .122mm Katyusha rocket slammed into the false roof and the explosion from the 40 pounds of explosives the rocket carried sent the concussive wave of heat and shell fragments blowing and whirring out and away from the blast area where they harmlessly fell into the surrounding hard-packed earth. Other than minor damage and a few more lost antennas, both the roof and much of the false roof remained intact. Repairs began immediately on the steel plates and damage and, once again, the BIG-TOC was safe from anything short of a B-52 strike.

The more recent enemy mortar rounds that had targeted the camp the day Robison and Poplawski returned from MAC-V headquarters and the Evacuation Hospital, had missed the BIG-TOC, but had left a good-sized impact crater two-yards out from the Command Post's main entrance. The displaced dirt around the mortar's impact area was tinged with dark burn marks from the intense heat of the blast and showed shards of metal fragments spiking the small crater. The exploding mortar had also sent razor sharp, blistering hot fragments flying into the MP bunker guarding the entrance along with the sandbagged wall and the outside support beams of the BIG-TOC.

The human damage of the attack was one badly wounded Military Policeman guarding the Command Post and a Teletype operator on his way into the BIG-TOC to begin his evening shift. One day later, black bottle flies and a line of insects were busy with the remaining small, dolloped patches of blood and specks of flesh that had been missed in the clean-up.

As Captain Robison, Lieutenant Plantagenet, and First Sergeant Poplawski walked toward the BIG-TOC's entrance for the briefing they noticed that one of the two MPs on duty was using pliers to pull out the larger pieces of splintered metal from a support beam of their guard bunker. Several larger fragments, impaled in the sandbags and heavy wood frame higher up and out of reach, would likely remain in place as quiet reminders to all of the perils and dangers the MPs faced guarding the Command Post.

The MPs gave the Ranger Captain and Junior Officer a salute which they returned while First Sergeant Poplawski gave the MPs a respectful nod.

The imposing iron, jail-like gate that was set on heavy hinges and welded into the steel wall panels, was held open by a bungee cord and served as the Command Center's front door. A heavy chain and lock was looped around several rungs of the gate and could secure the entrance during any potential ground assault, if required. Behind the gate a green canvas curtain acted as a dust cover that also muffled any of the noise, light, and activity inside.

Beyond the iron gate and hanging canvas curtain, and three feet inside the entrance was a hard left turn wall of sandbags that straightened out to a longer fortified corridor leading to the BIG-TOC's second and actual main door to Quonset hut number one. The design offered a wall of protection against any explosions facing the iron gate.

While the outside of the BIG-TOC had the look of a stark, Third World prison, the inside of the Command Center showed considerably more modifications and comforts. Most of the initial interiors had been gutted and divided into four specific use areas. The first hut was a radio communications center, the second was an area for command briefings, while the third and fourth had been set aside as the Camp Commander's and Assistant Camp Commander's private quarters. Rank had its privileges and also a few homey touches like good beds, desks, chairs, and well-stocked refrigerators. It wasn't the Ritz-Carlton, but it had its exclusive clientele and associated amenities.

Several rooms had been reconfigured between the working and living quarters areas for the office equipment, supplies, of course, the all-important 30-cup, silver barrel-like coffeemaker. The job of keeping the coffeemaker filled was assigned to one of the Teletype Operators. Fresh, and sometimes not so fresh, hot coffee was an Army staple, especially for those radio operators, Intelligence officers, and enlisted men working twelve hour shifts. A second area between the huts held an easy-to-get-to rack of weapons, ammunition, helmets, and flak jackets.

The communications center showed a wall of radios with working ranges that could reach Saigon and well beyond, thanks to the many antennas on the roof. There was a Teletype machine and a number of field telephones with hard wire lines to the Camp's various primary units for immediate contact. The bank of radios and Teletype machine were monitored by a team of radio operators, specialists, and Signal Corps NCOs and junior officers who could troubleshoot any commo issues that might arise. Their duties also included jury rigging an antenna system to get the radios back on line after they had been destroyed by either incoming mortars or rockets, or from any high winds that might tear out the antenna support cables during the Monsoon season.

Sweet Sorrow

Inside the briefing area sat two rows of olive-drab, metal folding chairs that faced a twelve-inch high platform with a podium set center stage. Behind the podium, were map boards covered with clear acetate for grease pencil markings that could easily be erased for security reasons. A large, rolling cork-faced bulletin board displayed a series of eight-by-ten black and white aerial surveillance photos for today's briefing.

The open back area of the briefing room nicknamed, *The Stockyard,* was where the Junior officers and NCOs, and other enlisted men who had accompanied their unit commanders to the briefings, or had some minor role in a presentation, were to stand. There were no chairs in *The Stockyard,* so those GIs quietly milled about as they attended and waited out the meetings.

One advantage of being in *The Stockyard* was the folding table along the back wall that featured a smaller coffee pot on a hot plate, jars of powdered creamer and sugar, and a glass filled with dozens of thin birch wood coffee stirrers. A tray of upside down empty and clean coffee mugs sat beside the coffee pot with a tray of freshly baked crumb cake and sugar cookies. As they waited, those in *The Stockyard* were free to drink the coffee, although sampling the crumb cake and cookies during any briefing was frowned upon, until the higher-ups had their shot at the goodies.

As Captain Robison made his way toward the front of the briefing room, Lieutenant Plantagenet, and First Sergeant Poplawski, settled in *The Stockyard* standing next to an MP sergeant, two enlisted Intel staff personnel assigned to the BIG-TOC, and one Staff Sergeant Transportation NCO.

Standing beside the doorway of the Briefing Room was Camp Mackie's Command Sergeant Major, CSM Berry, who seemed fixated on removing a piece of loose thread from the bottom of his immaculately pressed and starched jungle fatigues left breast pocket. If the BIG-TOC had a bouncer manning the briefing room then the barrel-chested soldier fit the bill. Vietnam was his third war and would be the last for the old warrior, but not before he ensured that he successfully carried out the task of overseeing the Camp as its highest ranking Non-Commissioned Officer. Berry was tough, competent, and ready to lock horns with anyone who defied Command.

Upfront, near the raised platform, Captain Robison was in a conversation with several pilots wearing black Stetson Cavalry hats, a Military Police Major, and a short, squat First Lieutenant from the Transportation Corps. They, like the Ranger Company Commander, had been ushered to front row seats for this invitation-only briefing. For the moment, all had remained standing as they talked.

At 1406 hours when Colonel Becker, Camp Mackie's Second-in-Command, along with the senior intelligence G-2 Major, and several guests entered the briefing room, the Command Sergeant Major gave a loud command directly to those in attendance.

"*HAH-TEN- Huuut!*" bellowed Berry.

The Army's command for soldiers coming to the position of Attention, chins up, chests out, stomachs in, shoulders back, standing straight with heels and feet together and hands down to the sides of their legs, was often forcefully delivered to make sure the order was loud enough to be understood.

HAH-TEN-Huuut wasn't the official version of the command, and certainly not the one that Army Drill Sergeants in Basic Training used, but no one was about to correct the Camp's seasoned and burly Command Sergeant Major.

"As you were, gentlemen. Please take your seats," said the Colonel walking towards the podium as those officers in the front immediately sat down. Following the Colonel onto the raised platform and standing behind him on the stage were the G-2 officer and two civilian guests.

Colonel Becker and the G-2 Major were familiar, but not the moderately nondescript looking white guy civilian and a not-so-civil-looking, slightly older, short, and sturdy Vietnamese civilian, who garnered most of the attention in this morning show. The Vietnamese civilian with the coal black eyes, had an ugly four inch scar on the left side of his face, and a scowl that matched the scar. The taller civilian, looking what he likely felt was South East Asia dapper, was dressed in a sporty tan leisure suit and brown leather Chukka boots while the Vietnamese was outfitted in a set of sun-faded, sterile South Vietnamese Army jungle fatigues and French military combat boots. Sterile meant no name tag or any other identification patches with the exception of a small pin attached to his collar.

Poplawski was thinking the leisure suit had to be the CIA spook or perhaps a Fayetteville Used Car salesman who was adept at drilling back odometers, while his Vietnamese sidekick, the Republic of South Vietnam's version of their lead spy agency, the *Tinh Bao Viet Nam*, had the look and charm of an icepick toting, back alley thug.

Poplawski was also thinking that the employee from the cough, cough, '*Civil Operations and Rural Development Agency*' that the Colonel introduced as Bob Evans, carried himself with an air of arrogant aristocracy, complete with a practiced fixed smile in this latest parade for the gathered crowd.

Evans was in his early 40s, had combed-back, thinning blond hair, a slight paunch that hadn't seen a sit-up in far too many years, and a bearing that was visibly smarmy.

It didn't help Poplawski's initial take on the man that when they had entered the Briefing Room, Evans gave a slight deferential nod to the small audience of officers up front while instantly dismissing the junior officers and enlisted men standing in the back of the room with a look that patently said they didn't matter. They were only the extras in this production, the *Lessers*, who were beneath his attention, and therefore held no career importance to him. They were simply *the help*.

His Vietnamese counterpart was introduced as Mister Long Quan. To the smirking Ranger First Sergeant, Quan didn't seem to be all that much better in attitude or comportment than Evans, which had Poplawski thinking the CIA apparently had a knack for matching up in-country super spook counterparts quite well.

Mister Long Quan kept his scowl as he gave a curt nod to the assembled audience when he was introduced and then quietly took everything in, the briefing room, the number of people in the small audience, their ranks, and the photos, maps, and intel materials on the cork board, and the coffee maker. If he had missed the crumb cake and sugar cookies, then it was only because he dismissed the treats as American excess.

Poplawski recognized the old scar as an old war wound that ran across the left side of Quan's face from the cheekbone down to his lower jawline. He didn't know the history of the jagged disfigurement, but the Ranger First Sergeant had a pretty good guess about an earlier war up north, even if others in the room had not.

17-years prior, on May 1, 1954, a flying piece of shrapnel from a Viet Minh heavy mortar tore a jagged hole in the cheek, and knocked out several teeth before it lodged in his upper jaw bone and had him choking on his own blood. The shrapnel had been removed by a French Army doctor, along with the broken teeth, leaving the sunken, ugly scar and deep indentation as a reminder of the fall of Dien Bien Phu six days later.

When Quan's eyes passed to each of the officers and enlisted men in the Briefing Room, Poplawski met them and nodded and that surprised the Vietnamese visitor.

"Shoulda just introduced him as Adam," Poplawski said in a low voice to Lieutenant Plantagenet standing beside him.

"What, First Sergeant?"

"Long Quan..."

"Uh-huh."

"That's the Vietnamese equivalent of their first man, their Adam without the Eve, so I'm guessing it's a secret squirrel, *nom de guerre* since he fought with the French Foreign Legion back when this country was *Indochine francaise*."

"The Foreign Legion?"

"Yes sir. See the lapel pin?"

"Lapel pin?" The Lieutenant turned and focused on the man's collar but from the distance and overhead lighting couldn't quite make out the lettering.

"It's the 3rd R-E-I."

"R-E-I?"

"The regimental insignia for the Third Foreign Infantry of the French Foreign Legion, the *Regiment etranger d'infanterie*. They fought at Dien Bien Phu in '54. My guess it's where he picked up that ugly scar that makes him look like a

Southeast Asian pirate or a pimp from Cholon. Can't imagine how Uncle Ho's boys treated him in prison after the French surrendered."

One of the two Intel people, a tall officious-looking Staff Sergeant who worked in the BIG-TOC's G-2 office and who was standing to the left side of Poplawski turned and shot the Ranger First Sergeant and Lieutenant an annoyed look for not remaining quiet as the Colonel was speaking at the podium.

Poplawski smiled and nodded which only earned another annoyed look.

Back up front, after the introductions were made the Colonel said, "Mister Evans?" as he turned to the civilian to take the podium. There was no *'good morning'* and no *'I'm pleased to meet you all'* offered, just the civilian visitor addressing the room with a short lecture.

"Two days ago, a *Dega* village seven miles west of Loc Ninh and near the Cambodian border was accidentally hit by *Friendly Fire* and nearly destroyed. That is the reason why you all are here today, because in two-days-time, you and your people will be escorting my associate and I up to what's left of that village so we can provide suitable compensation and materials to smooth things over with the village elders to win back their favor."

"*Dega*?" the Lieutenant asked the First Sergeant in a low whisper.

"The Yards, eh, Montagnards," replied Poplawski. "Think Apache and Comanche and you'll get a better working idea of who they are."

Neither was speaking loudly enough to be heard in the front of the room, let alone loud enough to be heard by most others in *The Stockyard*, nor were the two were being disruptive. Their low voices were barely above whispers. However, that buzz hadn't stopped the Intel NCO from turning a second time and shooting the Ranger First Sergeant another scowl. This time, though, Poplawski did more than smile.

The Ranger First Sergeant, who like the Command Sergeant Major, was built like a bull and his flaring nostrils had him seeing red.

"This is Intel, too, our Intel since we're the ones who'll actually be carrying out this tasking. You copy, Staff Sergeant, or do I need to spell it out for you after the briefing?" Poplawski said, staring back stone-faced and cold until the junior NCO gave a small, nervous nod and then turned away pretending he wasn't more than a little rattled.

Up front Evans was still speaking and raised his volume for better emphasis.

"This particular tribe has done some important work for us in the past, as well as to, and for, the Saigon government by tracking and keeping tabs on the thousands of North Vietnamese Army soldiers making their way into the south from Cambodia via one of the major infiltration routes along the Ho Chi Minh Trail. This was critical information that they relayed to us. That is, until the *Friendly Fire* incident…"

"Whose *Friendly Fire*?" asked the MP officer seated beside Captain Robison. A former Texas A & M Fullback and Army Major, the MP officer's tone came with an accompanying drawl.

"An ARVN unit accidentally hit the village with heavy mortars when they were chasing after an NVA Battalion that was operating along the border."

"And the village wasn't marked on their map?"

Evans frowned, and held the look. The comment was off topic, and for him, in terms of the briefing, a distraction.

"It's under investigation, so it's not our concern. But…"

"But the damage is," Captain Robison said, speaking up and getting to the crux of the matter and very much on topic for those attending the briefing.

Evans' reply was slow in coming as he had paused, slightly annoyed by the interruptions, but addressed the Ranger Company Commander's comment.

"Yes, it is. A half dozen or so of their people, mostly women and children, were killed, and a handful more wounded. Much of their village was destroyed and their livestock scattered or destroyed…"

"Which means we might not receive a warm welcome when we arrive," Robison added, interrupting Evans a second time.

Evans wasn't happy about either the *Friendly Fire* incident or the MP and Ranger officers asking about it, and the scowl on his face said as much.

"Yeah, okay. It was a critical fuck-up which is why we intend to correct that mistake by compensating them for their losses with building materials, rice, corn, medical supplies, and the like…"

"The *like*?"

"Yes Captain, whatever we think it'll take because we need to retain their services with adequate compensation and assurances which, hopefully, might help to alleviate any animosity they might hold against the Saigon government and us at the moment."

"By *us,* you mean, Americans? Why are we apologizing for the blunder? What about the ARVN unit that did it?"

Evans sighed, frustrated at the give-and-take as his tone took a slight edge.

"Mister Quan here will offer it to the village elders on behalf of the Republic of South Vietnam as will we because I can guarantee you that the Viet Cong and North Vietnamese Political cadre in their headquarters just over the border will be doing their best to convince them that it wasn't accidental, and that it was targeted fire, either from the South Vietnamese or from any passing American aircraft."

"Aircraft? Did we have any in the area at the time?" asked Robison.

"There were a few Cobra teams making a run on the NVA on the other side of the border at about the same time, so the Commies will certainly be making use of that."

"Ya think?" said an MP Major, joining in the cynicism. "So, *'Oops, sorry. Trust us, anyway, here are a few baubles,'* will be enough?'"

There were a few chuckles at that, but not from Evans who was bristling at the loss of his lectern.

It was Colonel Becker who stepped back to the podium to get the briefing back on track.

"Settle down, gentlemen. Settle down."

Robison and the MP Major both took the hint as what would come next from the Colonel would be a harsh command had they not complied.

Evans continued.

"Warm welcome or not, we'll be making the trip. Which of you is in charge of the truck transportation?"

The short, squat Lieutenant raised his hand.

To the young Transportation officer, he said. "You and your people will be bringing in four pallet loads of building supplies, one pallet of 50 pound bags of rice, along with a few other odds and ends that accompanied us on the flight here this morning. Check in with whoever you need to at the flightline to get it all loaded and ready to move upon our return in 48-hours. If you can't fit it all in one truck, then use two."

Before the Lieutenant could respond Evans moved onto the remaining key players in the task.

"You MPs, Major, and helicopter pilots will be providing the escort for our small convoy to and from the village, so we'll need gun jeeps, as well as the helicopter gunships for the appropriate convoy protection."

The MP Major and the two Pilots nodded.

To the Ranger Company Commander he said, "I'm told you and your grunts, Captain, will be providing overall security for the convoy."

"Rangers," said Robison.

"What?"

"We're a Ranger Infantry unit. Lurps."

Evans frowned, once again pausing at the interruption only this time he didn't need the Colonel to show just who was in charge.

"Don't take this the wrong way, Captain, but this is just a to and from taxi service, so I really don't care what you call yourselves as long as you adequately do your part."

What other way was there to take it, thought Captain Robison, very much wanting to smack the supercilious sonofabitch, but instead replied, "We'll do our job, Mister Evans. We're very good at it."

Evans started to say something when Colonel Becker once again stepped back to the podium.

"That's affirmative, Captain Robison. While the MPs and the gunship will be providing the convoy security on the move, you will be the overall tactical commander on the ground, should the need arise," said Colonel Becker. Becker wasn't a huge fan of the Lurp Company, but he was less impressed with the smug civilian.

"Where exactly is this village, Sir?" asked the Transportation officer, getting back to the specifics and how it would apply to his role in the delivery. "What distance are we talking about on this trip, mileage wise, I mean? That'll give me an idea about how much fuel we'll need."

Becker turned back to Evans to continue the briefing. Evan picked up a pointer and stepped towards a large map of Camp Mackie's Area of Operations on the wall map behind him.

"The *Dega* or Montagnard village is off a small woodcutter's road off of QL-13 that dead ends deep into heavy jungle up near Loc Ninh. Right about… here!" he said, whacking the pointer towards a grid coordinate on the map that was covered in green. The green on the map represented a heavy jungle with the turn off to a side road shown as a meandering dotted line highlighted in red from a grease pencil. The woodcutter's road wasn't on the tactical map.

"You can't chopper in the supplies and whatnot, Sir?" asked the Transportation officer.

"No clearing big enough for a bird, especially for what we're bringing to them or to bring in a substantial size force to adequately secure any LZ if there was, so that's why we're convoying up to the village."

"Indian country," added the MP Major and Evans nodded.

"The *Dega* like to keep their distance from other factions," he said. "That being said, we'll convoy up to the proposed meeting site. You and your individual units will be riding shotgun for Quan and I and what we're bringing. These items will go a long way towards soothing some of the hurt. It should be a simple in and out."

The remark drew a few raised eyebrows and not quite convinced looks from those seated in the front row as both the MP officer and Captain Robison eyes went to the wall map and the route that led to their destination. The route had history. Nothing was simple about it.

Quoc Lo-13, the National Road listed on the military maps as QL-13, was the north-south highway that ran from Bien Hoa all the way up to Loc Ninh at the Vietnamese/Cambodian border on broken road and sporadic hardpack. It was a troubled route where Viet Cong Companies and Battalions and the People's Army of Viet Nam, PAVN regulars, the North Vietnamese Army, had carried out so many ambushes and hit-and-run firefights over the years of the war that the GIs had nicknamed it, *Thunder Road.*

As a national highway in a war zone, *Thunder Road* was a rough, pot-holed, often contested route in the war-torn, III Corps tactical region of South Vietnam. Because of the many attacks on military convoys, three Fire Support Bases had been set up to help protect and keep the highway open, especially since it also fed to the many rubber plantations higher up in the province. The war may have been raging on, and the once prosperous local rubber industry and rubber plantations that accounted for millions of dollars in world export sales, and had been interrupted in the fighting, still held significant cache and sway over the Saigon government. The previously booming industry had given way to actual booms and bullets, but there was still business to be done as the American government was required to pay the plantation owners $600 for each rubber tree damaged by GIs in the fighting. During the war years, the rubber industry was kept on life support with these payments.

The three Fire Support Bases on the highway, Thunder I, Thunder II, and Thunder III, provided the artillery and Quick Reaction Force support for those using the route or operating in the surrounding countryside. Quick reaction came after something miserable had happened.

The Fire Support Bases and the main cities or American or South Vietnamese base camps that were stretched out over the length of the highway were noted on the wall map as was the grease penciled in turnoff for the side road that led up to the proposed meeting site with the *Dega,* which Evans pointed out as well.

That section of the map showed that the *Dega's* jungle village in the remote countryside, was out of artillery range of those Fire Support Bases and Base Camps, which explained the gunship support that was required for this tasking.

This particular *Dega* village was located so far out and into the sticks that it didn't have to be marked as a *No-man's Land,* which it essentially was, something not lost on Captain Robison.

"I take it the start point for our mission will be here at Camp Mackie," asked the MP Major. "What are we looking at for a start time?"

"That is correct, Major. Mister Quan and I will be flying in from Saigon two days from now on the day of the mission, so you all need to be lined up and ready to go by no later than 10 o'clock. Any more questions?"

When no questions came, Evans said, "Good!" and ended his portion of the briefing.

Actually, there were more questions, a lot more, but none to the civilian. The wrinkles in the details would need to be ironed out for the logistics involved and the manning. That chore fell to the MP Major and the Ranger Captain, as to how many Rangers and MPs would be needed for the task, how many vehicles and weapons they would take, which radio call signs and radio frequencies would be used, and where and when the pre-show players would need to gather to get the convoy on the actual road, something that Colonel Becker understood, even if Evans had not.

"Gentlemen," said the Colonel, closing out the briefing. "You're dismissed. However, I suggest you take the necessary time to coordinate and work out the particulars between you."

"*HAH-TEN-huuut!*" called Sergeant Major Berry from the back of the room as everyone in the BIG-TOC's briefing room came to the position of attention when the Colonel, and the V-I-Ps made their exit.

While the rest of those in the briefing were filtering out of the BIG-TOC the MP Major stopped a few steps outside the Command center and just to the left of the entrance where he waited for the Ranger Captain, the two helicopter pilots, and the Transportation Officer. When they had exited the BIG-TOC and were outside, the MP Major pulled them aside in a loose huddle around him.

"Gentlemen! Looks like we'll be escorting Mister Pleasant and company on this little outing."

"Where and when do you want us to be, Major?" said the Ranger Captain.

"What say we stage at the flightline no later than Zero-9:30 hours the day of? If, in fact, we move out at ten hundred hours, that'll give us enough time to make the run up and back before sunset."

"Sounds good, Sir," agreed Captain Robison.

To the Transportation Officer, the Major said, "How many vehicles will you bring to the parade?"

"I'll head over to the flight line when we're done here, Sir, and if it's just the three pallet loads and depending upon the weight, then it should all fit into one of our Deuce-and-a-half's. Two, depending on what other odds and ends he was talking about. I'll know better once I see what's there, but my best guess now is one."

"Good."

"Two for us," Robison said. "One jeep and a Deuce-and-a-half. We'll have a .50 cal mounted to the top of the cab and at least two M-60s in the truck bed. We'll supplement that with a few M-72 Light Anti-Tank Weapons, and an M-79 grenade launcher with a crate of assorted rounds, and all of my people will be armed with M-16s and one M-14 sniper rifle. Have guns, will travel."

The Major grinned at both the television show reference and the significant fire power.

"Since my callsign is Pistol-Six, your Paladin reference works for me. Besides the gunship support," he added, giving a nod to the pilots, "and your fire-breathing Rangers, my armored car and two gun jeeps will fit in quite nicely. We'll provide the radio frequencies later today, as well as a contingency plan in case of trouble, which will basically be we'll haul ass back to Loc Ninh with the gunship covering our getaway…"

"Can do," said one of the two pilots. "Besides my gunship we'll have a Low Bird with us as well."

"A Pink Team huh?" said the Major.

"Eyes in the sky ready to bring thunder!"

"Outstanding!" said the Major. "Then I'll see you on the fight line in two days' time at Zero-nine-thirty-hours. You all copy?"

"Yes sir," came the chorus from the principal players.

After saluting the MP Major, they made their way to their respective units, although before heading back to Romeo Company, Robison huddled up with Poplawski and Lieutenant Plantagenet.

"I want ten of our people on this road trip, and let's get some of the new people on it as well," he said to the two of them. "Lieutenant, I want you to make sure our jeep and Deuce-and-a-half are serviced and ready to go."

"Roger that, Sir."

"First Sergeant, in that regard do you think the Engineers might jury-rig some steel plates to the sides and the radiators for our jeep and Deuce-and-a-half for some better protection? Maybe even add some layered glass for the windshields?"

The First Sergeant shrugged as though the request was no big deal.

"Yes sir, especially if we barter with an SKS rifle or two, and say, toss in a Tokarov *Blackstar* semi-automatic pistol for their C.O to sweeten the deal, I'm sure they would be more amenable."

Since Romeo Company had a number of captured enemy weapons, the barter exchange would serve a useful purpose, so the Ranger Captain readily agreed. With the shutdown of the unit, they'd need to get rid of the captured enemy weapons that officially weren't on the books anyway.

"Check on it and see what you can do to make it happen."

Back to the Lieutenant the Captain said, "Lieutenant Plantagenet, I want an M-60 mounted on our jeep, too. Pick up several 1,000 round cans from the ammo depot for it and two other machine guns we'll be taking with us. Take some of the people in your platoon and get some for a .50 cal while you're at it. If the ammo depot officer gives you any crap, refer him to me, and I'll refer him to the BIG-TOC, and the word of God in the form of General Reese, the Camp Commander or Colonel Becker, his pit bull. Amen?"

"Amen," replied the Lieutenant.

"Top off the oil and fuel in both vehicles, bring along an extra five-gallon fuel can for the jeep and several cans for the Deuce-and-a-half, a case of C's and Lurp rations, and oh, a cooler with some ice and soft drinks from the PX. It's going to get hot out there. Let's make sure we have enough water and soda for our people."

"Yes sir."

"Wait one," added Robison. Reaching into his back pocket and retrieving his wallet. The Company Commander pulled out $20 worth of Military Payment Certificates and handed them to the junior officer. "Here you go. It's on me."

"Oh, and First Sergeant?" Robison said, turning to Poplawski.

"Yes sir?"

"I'm thinking a sandbagged floor for the bed of our truck, mounted steel plates along the bench lines, and make it three M-60s, in case the .50 cal can't be mounted to the cab of the roof. One for my jeep, one for the top of the cab, and one each for the sides of the trucks, hence all of the 7.72 ammo the Lieutenant will pick up. That should be easy enough for the Engineers to accommodate and offer our people some better protection."

"Yes sir. And for fireworks?"

"A few shoulder-fired LAWs, and a crate of High Explosive and Willie Pete rounds for the grenade launcher should provide us with some additional party favors to go with our small arms fire. Anything more than that and the gunship shadowing us should be able to dissuade any prolonged engagement with whatever bad guys we might encounter along the way."

"Sounds good, Sir," said the Lieutenant, knowing the M-72, Light Anti-tank Weapons and M-79 grenade launchers would come in handy, if they needed more than the small arms and machine guns to make a difference. And that brought up something else that was on his mind. "You thinking that maybe we won't be all that welcome, Captain?"

Robison didn't hesitate. "Given the route and the region, I do, not to mention that *Friendly Fire* incident," he said.

"So, the more firepower, the better?"

"What's the motto of the Boy Scouts?"

"Be Prepared."

"There you go."

Chapter 15

The rear wheels of the Chinook helicopter carrying Evans and Quan touched down on Camp Mackie's main runway a little after 0945 hours. The large helicopter danced for a moment like a plump dog on its short hind legs as it rolled forward a few more yards before the front tires finally settled on the flight line, turned, and taxied over to the holding area adjacent to the line of military vehicles.

Coming to a jerking stop the large aircraft's two jet engines wound down to a mild hum. As the back hydraulic ramp of the big helicopter slowly was lowered the Flight Engineer, a Staff Sergeant with a drooping mustache stepped out of the aircraft and off to the left of the ramp. He was trailed by two stern-faced MPs holding M-16s rifles at the ready. The military policemen quickly scrutinized those standing in the arrival party, the immediate surroundings, and the parked convoy on the nearby road. Satisfied there was no identified threat, the two stepped to the two sides of the ramp determined to keep the barbarians at the gate.

Next, from the dark bowels of the Chinook came the helicopter's crew chief pushing a dolly loaded with five sealed, ammo-size wooden crates. Following the crew chief was another heavily armed, no-nonsense looking black MP Sergeant First Class who could've easily doubled as a right tackle for the San Francisco Forty-Niners.

Spotting the MP Major, the Sergeant First Class called out a loud, "Sir!" along with a crisp salute.

"We'll take it from here, Sergeant Westin," said the MP Major, returning the salute.

The Sergeant First Class gave a curt, "Yes sir," and then stepped to the right side of the ramp. Anything that followed would be up to the MP Major, the Transportation officer, and the Rangers. Barring Butch Cassidy and the Sundance Kid riding in guns a-blazing, the escort job by the MPs from the helicopter was done.

Strolling out of the helicopter, sans his tan, secret agent Leisure Suit, came Mister Evans dressed in sterile jungle fatigues that were free of any identifying name tag and patches. Pausing on the back ramp Evans slowly put on a pair of green aviator sunglasses, adjusted his pistol belt, and followed the rolling dolly.

Behind him came the fierce-looking Quan still dressed in his washed out, but highly starched and ironed field uniform. Unlike the flat black, newly issued jungle boots Evans was wearing, Quan's French military boots were spit-shined and glistening in the sunlight. This wouldn't be a combat patrol, but a cake walk parade, so the former Legionnaire wore what he wore with practiced pride. *Legio patria nostra.*

"What say we get this show on the road," Evans called to the MP Major while giving a nod to the crates on the dolly. "Where's my vehicle?"

Sweet Sorrow

The MP Major pointed to an armored car looking vehicle with twin machine guns mounted on the turret. It was a V-100 Cadillac-Gage *Commando*, a five-speed, seven ton, Chrysler V-8 powered amphibious armored car the MPs affectionately called, the *Duck*.

"Uh-uh, no way!" bellowed Evans, vetoing the call. "That isn't going to cut it."

"Given where we're going, I thought you'd want something a little more secure," said the MP officer.

Evans made a face like he'd just tasted something sour. "What I want is something that won't heat up inside like a fucking Dutch Oven in this heat. It's a long ride to where we're going. *Comprende*, Major? So, that's a big no to your little tank and it's not a request. Now, gimme a jeep!"

With his hands on his hips, Evans arrogantly stared at the MP officer and waited. In the verbal game of Chicken, the MP Major stared back for a long moment to show his displeasure before he blinked and gave a small nod. Turning, he called out to his people in the MP jeep behind the Ranger Company's Deuce-and-a-half behind him.

"Sergeant Burke!"

"Sir?"

"I need your vehicle!"

"Yes sir."

"Your 60 gunner can ride with our other gun jeep. You're now in the *Duck* with me."

"Sir. Yes sir!"

After the machine gunner climbed out of the jeep the dutiful Sergeant Burke drove it over to the MP Major at the back of the parked helicopter. Burke switched off the engine, pulled up the parking brake, and jumped out of the vehicle.

"Thank you, Sergeant," said the MP Major. To the civilian, he said, "It's all yours for this little outing, Mister Evans."

"Fan-fucking-tastic," said Evans, visually kicking the tires before turning to the crates on the dolly.

He and his South Vietnamese counterpart weren't about to load the crates, which was why Evans then looked to the Ranger Captain.

"Well Captain, the crates aren't going to load themselves."

"First Sergeant!" Robison bellowed to Poplawski.

"Sir?"

"Let's get these crates loaded up for our guests."

"Sir. Yes sir."

Turning to his people in the Ranger's big truck, the First Sergeant called out several of the soldiers by name.

"Daley, Hernandez, and you, New Guy? Time for some muscle work," Poplawski said to the three Lurps. "Let's get at it."

"Yes, First Sergeant!" replied the trio of Rangers as they jumped down from the back of the Deuce-and-a-half and started towards the dolly near the back of the helicopter. They stood by as Poplawski was lifting the edge of one of the crates to estimate its weight to better decide how the task should, quite literally, should be handled. His best estimate was 50-pounds per crate.

Setting the crate back down, he said, "We have 250 pounds to move, so I want two of you on each crate. I know you think you're studs but no straining backs, pulled muscles, or shoulder tears, you hear me?"

"Yes, First Sergeant," said Daley and was echoed by the other two.

"Good, then let's get them loaded into the back of our truck."

The five crates would've made the cramped space in the modified truck bed even less comfortable, but it could be done with only some minor bitching.

There was another round of *'Yes, First Sergeant,'* and a grunt from Hernandez as they lifted the first heavy crate from the dolly.

"Uh-uh, cancel that! CANCEL THAT!" yelled Evans, overhearing the command and quickly countering it. "I want them in the back of my jeep, Captain. Not the truck."

"Your jeep?"

"Yes, right where I can keep an eye on them," Evans said, pointing to the jeep that the MPs had just provided for the trip. "I've signed for what's in the crates and they're not going to leave my sight until they're handed over to the *Dega* elders. It's my call."

"It is," said Robison, turning to Poplawski. "First Sergeant!"

"Sir!"

"You heard the man. Let's get the crates loaded onto the MP jeep."

"Roger that," said the First Sergeant. Turning to the makeshift work crew he added, "Stack 'em in the back of that jeep."

As Evans and Quan moved to the jeep and watched over the transfer, the MP Major strolled over and joined the Ranger Captain and his Lieutenant. The MP Major leaned in and in a low voice said, "I suspect our *'Mister Personality'* does want to keep those crates close."

"Why? What's in them?"

The MP Major looked around to make sure no one else was within listening distance before he spoke again.

"Gold," he said in a low voice and then looked around again to make sure that other than the two Ranger officers no one else had heard him.

"Gold?" said a much surprised Lieutenant Plantagenet while the Captain's surprise could only be found in his raised eyebrows. A stern look from the Major hushed the conversation.

"Gold bars, actually. Some silver too."

"That explains the extra armed guards," said Robison.

The MP Major nodded and said, "which only attracts more than a little attention when you're loading something in a vehicle, or say a helicopter. One guy loading crates, and nobody pays much attention or takes any notice. But one guy wheeling a dolly of crates with an armed security detail draws attention, and hey, secrets only go so far."

"And you're in the loop?"

"Nope. I'm just a Military Police super sleuth. Phillip Marlow in O-D green jungle fatigues."

"A little far from the Hobart Arms, aren't you?"

"And the Bristol Hotel," laughed the Major. "Gotta love Raymond Chandler whodunnit novels."

"We do indeed."

Getting back to the small mystery of the crates, the Major said, "Word has it that the Montagnards didn't want Vietnamese Piasters or military payment certificates. Some Vietnamese screwed them over a while back with old worthless MPC a month after the new script was issued and the old script was no longer valid."

"No wonder they want the shiny."

"Hard to fake, and it doesn't lose its value. Makes it easier for the *Yards* to barter too, I imagine."

"That it does," agreed the Ranger Captain watching the crates being moved.

With no name tags on their ERDL leaf pattern jungle fatigues Poplawski thought of the wide-eyed Private First Class ginger who would assist him as FNG #1.

"How much does each of these boxes weigh, First Sergeant?" asked FNG #1

"Fifty pounds each."

"So, is like the sixth box still in the helicopter, First Sergeant?" FNG #1 asked as he and the veteran NCO picked up the third crate from the dolly.

Poplawski did a double take with a troubled expression as they carried the wooden crate to the awaiting jeep.

"You thinking about going to college when you get out of the Army, are you, Private?"

"Yes, First Sergeant, with my GI Bill."

Poplawski's troubled expression mellowed into something almost sage-like. "Then here's an entrance exam question for you. 250 divided by 50, gives you how many boxes?"

The young Lurp's eyes went to the tops of his sockets as he looked to his brain for the answer that was slowly doing the math.

"Five?"
"There you go! So no, there isn't a sixth crate hiding inside the helicopter."

Chapter 16

The convoy's lineup order had been decided earlier, and after a quick briefing laid out the order of travel by the MP Major, it was followed by a short walk from the Ranger Company Commander regarding convoy security.

"We'll have a Low Bird flying out in front and just ahead of us with a Cobra gunship providing some lightning, thunder, and hellfire, if needed," said the Major. "If we encounter trouble, the Rangers will form a defensive perimeter and between the two of us we'll unleash considerable return ground fire, which for any size convoy, is significant. Saying that, once we clear the back gate, and when the order is given and only when it is given, we'll do a test fire of the primary weapons to make sure there are no malfunctions or issues. You copy?"

That produced heads nods and a chorus of, '*Yes sirs.*'

"Captain Robison?"

It was Robison's turn in this play as he passed along the SOI-Signal Operating Instructions for the primary radio frequency they would use today as well as a secondary frequency, if for any reason the primary line was compromised.

"Set them on your radios and use your callsigns," he said, assigning the two frequencies they'd be using.

The vehicle lineup that the Ranger Captain and MP Major had decided on was settled well before the Chinook helicopter had landed. The lineup had the V-100 armored car, the *Duck*, taking the lead with the truck carrying the supplies and building materials next in line, followed by the Ranger jeep mounted with an M-60 machine gunner, then the tag-team of Evans and Quan in the second MP jeep, followed by the Ranger's gun truck with the third MP gun jeep bringing up the tail end of the column.

This, of course, was before Evans, after a brief discussion with Quan, shook his head and told the Major that their jeep would follow the armored car with the other vehicles trailing. The Major, though, saw no need for the change, and said as much.

"No," he said. "I think it's best to keep you inside the fold for better protection, so let's keep you where you are in the vehicle lineup for now."

The representative from the '*Civil Operations and Rural Development Agency,*' though, still wasn't having it and shook his head again.

"This, too, is not a request, so uh-uh, no. We're following the armored car," Evans said to the Major, bluntly.

"No?"

"Yeah, no. We'll be behind your armored car. With the air support from the gunship helicopter, along with your little tank in front of us, we'll be safe enough. So, go ahead and adjust your convoy order. We'll wait."

"You'll wait?"

"Yeah. And keep in mind the clock is ticking."

"You understand this is my call."

"Major, perhaps you need to understand that I'm not going to eat road dust to and from the meet-up site and show up filthy and looking like a ragbag to the Dega Elders."

"You're saying you don't want to follow my orders?"

"What I'm saying, Major, is that as a GS-14 government employee and the V-I-P in this little parade, this isn't up for debate, not to mention, but oh, I will. Technically, I outrank you."

A Government service rank of GS-14 was the military equivalent of a Lieutenant Colonel, one rank above the Army Military Police Major. Technically, Evans was correct.

Technically. To bolster his claim he added, "I'm also saying we're going to follow your armored car to eat as little road dust as possible. End of story, or do I need to drive over to the Command Post and have a talk with General Reese or Colonel Becker to get you to better understand your role in this little show here today? That'll cause a needless delay, which will not only throw us off-schedule, but possibly insult and piss-off the Dega Elders who are already pissed-off at some military fuck-up that took out half their village."

The staring match began a second time, with Evans standing firm and smirking because he knew he held the better hand. The MP Major was well aware that this was more than just a supply run or a simple convoy. It was about winning back the hearts and minds, and more importantly, the trust of the Dega/Montagnards by bribing the hell out of them to salute the flag. Evans wouldn't win it on his charm. No, that wasn't going to happen. It was the building supplies and pallet of rice, but more importantly the silver and gold that would accomplish the mission.

Evans was a royal pain in the ass, but his trump card was knowing that both he and Quan were indeed the Very Important Persons on this Saigon approved operation. The MP Major knew it as well, just as he knew that any delay would disrupt the accompanying helicopters supporting the mission.

Rather than grabbing the annoying bastard by the lapels and smacking some sense into him, the MP Major smiled and tossed in his verbal cards. He also held back telling him to '*Go Fish,*' or something akin to it.

"Fine," he said, almost sounding gracious. "You fall in line behind my vehicle when we move out. There are several sets of goggles under the front seats if you need them."

The Major checked the time on his watch. It was 0955 hours.

"We move in five mikes."

"*Mikes*, as in minutes, Mister Quan," said Evans, explaining to the South Vietnamese V-I-P what the U.S. Army speak meant, something that Quan already well understood in English, Vietnamese, and French. "Isn't that correct, Major?"

"Yes, Mister Evans, mikes as in minutes, so why don't you return to your jeep and get ready to move out. By the way, your radio callsign today is *Eddie*. *Eddie-One*. You got it?"

Surprisingly, Evans brightened. "Yeah, like Paul Newman as *Fast Eddie*, the pool shark in *The Hustler*. Cool! I got it."

"Okay, but it's *Eddie-One* on the radio. That's how you'll identify yourself over the net when we call you or you call us..."

"Yeah, yeah. *Eddie-One*."

"The radio in the jeep is preset on the correct frequency. I'm Pistol-Six and the Ranger Captain is Valhalla-Six. Valhalla-Six will coordinate the air support. The radio traffic will go through us. Understood?"

"Yeah, yeah, Pistol and Valhalla."

"And you're *Eddie-One*. You got that?"

"I said, I got it. We ready to go?"

"Just about. I need to let the others know about the change in the vehicle line-up."

"Good, then *Eddie* is ready."

"*Eddie-One*."

"Sure, but hey, how many other *Eddie's* you got going on this little ride?"

The MP Major took it as a snotty rhetorical question and didn't respond.

Eddie wasn't the callsign he and Robison came up with before the Chinook helicopter touched down at Camp Mackie, and he'd inform Robison of the change. It was a spur of the moment decision on the MP Major's part. The *Eddie* that sprang to mind wasn't the Paul Newman character from the film, but Eddie Haskel, the annoying little shit from the TV show, *Leave It To Beaver*. Somehow it struck him as the perfect callsign for the oh-so-smug V-I-P.

"Oh, and hey! We could use some water and food for the trip," said Evans. "I was told by the Colonel you'd be providing it."

The Major sighed. No, he hadn't been told.

"I'll have one of my people drop off some C-rations and water before we depart."

"C-rations? Canned food?"

"Roger that. It's what's on the menu today."

Like the Rangers, the MP Major had brought along an ice chest filled with soft drinks and bottled water, as well as a box of assorted snacks he picked up at the PX earlier that he had planned to share, but now saw no need to play the gracious host. The Major didn't wait around for anything more that Evans might demand and instead turned and went down the convoy line explaining the new order of travel to the others. Back at the armored car he called his driver over and turret gunner. Sergeant Burke joined them.

"Specialist Ramsay?"

"Sir?" said the armored car driver.

"How many canteens do we have with us in the *Duck*?"

"Four, plus a five gallon can of fresh water."

"And how are we fixed for C-rations?"

"I drew a case this morning from the Mess Sergeant."

The MP Major nodded at what he was thinking. To the turret gunner he said, "Take two canteens and two boxes of ham and Lima beans to the jeep behind us."

"Seriously, Sir? Nobody likes the Ham and Lima bean C-rats!"

"I know," said the Major, smiling. "Get it done. Oh, and I want you on the rear jeep manning the M-60."

"Yes sir."

"Sergeant Burke?"

"Sir?"

"You want to mann the twin-30s on the *Duck*?"

"Thought you'd never ask, Sir," the MP Sergeant said, grinning.

A single Browning .30 caliber machine gun could be formidable in a firefight. Twin 30s firing in tandem, though, brought on blistering havoc in an instant. Those MPs in the convoy were all qualified with the Twin 30s but Burke was their best gunner.

Adding to the fire power was Romeo company's Deuce-and-a-half truck. With its recent custom body work done by the Engineers it was also outfitted with some additional firepower. A 'Ma- deuce' M-2 .50 caliber machine gun was mounted over and behind the rag-top cab of the two-and-a half-ton, six-by-six, multi-fueled, all-terrain, all-weather transport vehicle.

Up armored with steel plates and sandbags protecting the front, sides, and back of the big truck that gave it the look of an angry Rhinoceros ready to make a charge.

The steel plates would hold up against small arms fire, but they wouldn't hold up too well against shoulder-fired RPG rocket grenades that the North Vietnamese Army soldiers and Viet Cong fighters often used to spring their ambushes. The infamous Soviet *Ruchnoy Protivotankoviy Granatomet,* the RPG-7 that showed up in the war in early 1967 was proving its worth in jungle combat and those lessons weren't lost on those who'd been in their sights. To counter and negate it, the Rangers brought along several M-72 shoulder-fired, Light Anti-Tank Weapons (LAWs) in the bed of the truck. Combined with the three machine guns, the portable one-shot unguided anti-tank weapons, and a grenade launcher gave the Deuce-and-a-half its own version of hell on wheels.

A camouflage net had been tied down over the top of the open bed and while it would flap and pop in the wind when the truck was up to speed, it would also offer some protection from the glaring sun for the Rangers beneath it.

Lieutenant Plantagenet had his pocket-sized Kodak Instamatic camera out and was taking pictures of the gun truck and other vehicles in line to document the first ever convoy for Romeo Company. Strolling up to the front of the column he took pictures of the armored car, his C.O. and First Sergeant standing by the Ranger jeep, only as he moved on the other vehicles in line a protesting Mister Evans raised a hand to cover his face and then violently waved the young Lieutenant away.

"Whoa! Whoa! Whoa!! Uh-uh! No! What the fuck are you doing? No pictures! I don't want my picture taken. Come on! Hand it over!"

Evans was holding out a hand as he demanded the small camera.

"Sir?"

"The camera. Give it to me."

"Sir?"

"Did you hear me, soldier? I said, *'hand'* it over. What part of that don't you understand?"

A few yards away Captain Robison, who'd overheard Evans berating his Lieutenant, he made his way up to them to intervene.

"You done taking the pictures I asked you to take, Lieutenant?"

"Sir?"

"The required pictures we'll need, if by chance anyone goes missing on this mission today? You about done? We need to get moving."

Robison was covering for his Junior officer who quickly understood what his Commanding Officer was doing, and took the bait.

"Yes…Yes sir. Well, almost."

"It's Standard Operating Procedure for all of our missions," explained the Ranger Captain to the V-I-P. "Same-same for this convoy, Mister Evans. It's our required S-O-P."

It wasn't, but Robison was looking after his Lieutenant. "We need the pictures in case anyone today goes missing or is captured, then we or any other search team will have something recent and better to identify them by."

"Our people know what Mister Quan and I look like."

"From old I-D photos, sure, but we just like to stay current. Who knows? You might've worn glasses in the past, been heftier with a buzz cut, or maybe even had more hair back then."

The dig to Evans' thinning hairline touched a nerve.

"Yeah, well I do mind. What kind of security operation are you running here anyway?"

"The kind that doesn't trust a sketch artist to try to begin to capture the essence of the real you."

"Yeah well, then picture this!" Evans snarled as he turned, and flipped off the Captain as he made his way back to his vehicle.

"Thanks for your cooperation. It's appreciated."

"Fuck you!"

"I'll take that as you're working on it."

"Thank you, Captain," whispered the Lieutenant as the two Rangers turned and were making their way back to their vehicles.

"No problem, Lieutenant. Just make sure you take enough photos of everyone else in the convoy."

"Just in case anyone gets captured or goes missing, you mean?"

Robison smiled.

"That too!"

Back at the Ranger truck Sergeant Cantu, who had volunteered to drive Romeo Company's Deuce-and-a-half on the convoy run, asked a favor of the Lieutenant when he had returned from taking the pictures of those in the vehicle line up.

"Can I get you to take a picture of me behind the wheel, Lieutenant?"

"Sure, no problem at all, Sergeant," said Plantagenet as he squinted down behind the viewfinder, and clicked off several photos.

"Now, let me get one of you, Sir?"

"Thanks! That would be great!" he said handing the camera over to the young NCO.

For the photo Plantagenet reached in and grabbed his web gear and Car-15 Commando rifle and then tried for his best John Wayne Hollywood pose standing next to the gun truck while looking, or trying to look as fierce as possible. The fierce expression only made it to one shot as the second one would show a goofy, but pleased smile.

He was pleased because he had overseen the modifications the Company Commander had called for to insure there would be some better protection for the Rangers riding in it, and more so because he was proud to be in charge of the gun truck. The modifications made it formidable.

Similar modifications were made to the company's *borrowed* jeep, *borrowed,* of course meant, *stolen.* Seeing how they'd be working closely with the Military Police on this run, the First Sergeant figured they possibly might not show too much interest in the repainted I-D bumper designations.

Since First Sergeant Poplawski would be driving the jeep with Captain Robison riding shotgun, and with a Ranger standing over a mounted M-60 machine gun, it would avoid any missing log book issues with the *borrowed* jeep.

Sweet Sorrow

It was a good call because as the vehicles were shifting into position for the lineup, several of the MPs that were going along on the ride, came by to check out the vehicles' modifications and the fire power on display, appreciating what they saw.

"Major? Sir, you gotta see this!" an MP sergeant said, calling over his unit commander.

The MP Major who was on his way to speak with Captain Robison about the change in the convoy lineup headed towards the Ranger's Deuce-and-a-half where the Ranger Company Commander was talking with his young Lieutenant and his men in the truck bed. Even from six feet away he could see why one of his MPs was admiring the truck, and to a lesser extent, the modified jeep.

"Well now, that ain't exactly a gun truck, but it might as well be. It's a beast! What? Steel plates fitted in with firing ports for the side of the truck bed and the jeep?"

"Yes sir," replied Lieutenant Plantagenet. "We had the Engineers brace and bolt them into place and then added a layer of sandbags as well. We have another similar set-up covering the tailgate, too. There wasn't a ring mount for the .50 caliber machine gun, so the Engineers mounted it on a reinforced swivel."

"Nice!"

The MP Officer went from the heavy machine gun down to the steel plates on the side of the truck bed, tapping them as he went. The weight of the inch-thick plates and sandbags would reduce the truck's gas mileage, but no one would be complaining about the lower mileage aspect, if and when enemy rounds came slamming into the truck or the jeep.

"Kinda makes my armored car look a little puny. Good job, Lieutenant."

The Lieutenant was about to thank him when Mister Evans, seated in the MP jeep, reached across Quan in the driver's seat and honked the jeep's horn a few times.

"WE MOVING OR WHAT?" he yelled, turning back and tapping his watch at the MP Major.

The Major checked his own watch again and frowned. It was three minutes before ten. The civilian wasn't only getting on his nerves, he was straining the fibers.

"Captain," said the MP Major.

"Sir?"

"Seems our Mister Evans wants his jeep to follow my armored car. He's worried about the road dust."

"Now why doesn't that surprise me?"

Evans honked the jeep's horn a second time.

"Seems our V-I-P is also getting cranky," said Robison.

"Crankier," said the Major. "Let's saddle up."

Robison gave an acknowledging nod and barked out the command which was repeated down the line as those standing outside of the vehicles climbed in and readied themselves.

Back at the Ranger jeep First Sergeant Poplawski seated in the driver's seat, cranked up the engine, and revved the motor as Captain Robison climbed into the passenger's seat.

"We got goggles for any road dust?" he asked the First Sergeant.

"That's affirmative, Sir. Underneath the seats. I tossed in a few First Aid slings as well to tie into make-shift face masks."

"Outstanding, First Sergeant!"

"I am, aren't I, Captain?"

"You are indeed!"

The Ranger officer chuckled and then turned and nodded to Specialist-Four Taras, who was standing up and over a mounted M-60 machine gun in the back seat area. The 18-year-old Taras looked like a toddler determined to shoot anybody who might tell him he needed a nap. The Captain could see that rather than just loading a typical 100 round belt-fed line of ammunition into the gun, Taras had the belt-fed ammo linked into 1,000 other rounds, S-looped into a large ammo can beside the machine gun mount at its base.

"Specialist Taras?" called the Ranger officer turning in his seat and addressing the Lurp.

"Yes Sir?"

"You Good-to-Go?"

"Yes sir."

"Outstanding! You know you don't have to stand the entire way."

"Yes Sir, thank you, Sir."

"Only when things get interesting."

"Roger that, Captain."

Chapter 17

At precisely ten hundred hours, 10 o'clock civilian time, and as scheduled, and on schedule, the armored car, the MP's *Duck*, led the convoy out of the Base Camp's back gate as the MPs on duty guarding the back gate held it open for the convoy.

The morning was crisp and cool and held promise, but the morning would give way to the rising afternoon heat, and any promise in Vietnam would come with sweltering humidity and be short-lived.

They were only fifty yards out of the gate when Captain Robison called for a halt. After clearing it with the Camp's Base Operations to conduct a weapons check, the heavy machine gun and small arms were test fired with the logic being, better to know now if there were any issues rather than later, if and when they might be critically needed. The successful short bursts by the machine guns and small arms fire put any questions on the matter to rest.

Shortly after a ceasefire was called and the order was given for the convoy to proceed two helicopters took off from the Camp's flight line and roared out low and over the column of vehicles. The Cobra gunship in the lead quickly gained altitude while the smaller OH-6, the Light Observation Scout Helicopter referred to as a Low Bird, was buzzing ahead of the column barely above the nearby trees. The Scout helicopter was searching for any sign of enemy activity and clearing the way. Soon, a radio call came over the convoy net from the attack helicopter.

"Valhalla-Six, Valhalla-Six, Piebald Two-three. Over."

"Valhalla-Six. Go, Two-three."

"Roger, Six. Be advised, you now have eyes in the sky and clear vision."

"Roger that, Piebald Two-Three. Valhalla-Six. Out."

"That was the gunslinger in the gunship, I take it," said Poplawski behind the wheel of the jeep.

"It was," said the Captain. "He and his X-Ray."

"X-Ray?"

"Front seat gunner."

"Ah!"

Poplawski's eyes went skyward, and he seemed momentarily troubled by something he was holding back, but the Captain knew that he'd get around to whatever was on his mind soon enough. For the moment, the First Sergeant was concentrating on maintaining proper convoy distance between his jeep and Evans' jeep over the feeble and tenuous road.

The rain that had fallen the evening before had the tires on the vehicles kicking up mud in several of the deeper and shaded potholes leaving the sides of the roads in a pale orange spray. However, with the Southeast Asian heat rising over the countryside like a kitchen oven set on HIGH, the pockets of mud would soon dry and turn into fine, powdered dust under the weight of the passing vehicles.

Because of more recent track vehicle convoys using QL-13, the potholes and ruts of the road had expanded and made the going a little slower for this convoy run. Track vehicles tended to chew up roadways. First Sergeant Poplawski found himself spending more time in second gear dodging potholes and downshifting than he did in finding a better rolling speed. The slow convoy speed was frustrating, if not troubling.

"Well, this wagon train sucks!" Poplawski said as his eyes went to the Low Bird checking out the road in front of the convoy and the Captain's eyes followed his gaze.

"Kinda nice to have them watching over us, though," said the Captain.

Poplawski agreed with a chin-up nod and said, "No doubt his Commanding Officer's a cowboy, damn near all of these pilots are."

"Understood, given their metallic steeds."

"Okay, but...

"But what?"

"What exactly is a Piebald? I suspect it's maybe a cowboy thing, but what exactly?"

And there it was. The thing that was puzzling the First Sergeant.

"That's right, you're from *Dee-troit*. The only horsepower you know is a big block V-8."

Poplawski grinned.

"The finest kind, Sir! I have a red '67 GTO with a 389 that can muscle its way down the highway while looking studly at the same time, so yes, a V-8 makes for fine horsepower. I know Ford has its Mustang, Porsche, and Ferrari have horses on their logos, and the CAV pilots have their crossed sabers on their Stetsons cowboy hats, but what in the Hell is a Piebald?"

"A Piebald is a horse."

"What kind of horse?"

"Think black and white camouflage."

"Ah! Easier to hide from the glue factory, then?"

"Maybe. However, I noticed in your semi-soliloquy you hadn't included the Ford Pinto."

"Yes sir, because I was talking horsepower, not an oversized cigarette lighter."

Robison chuckled. "So, a '67 Goat, huh?"

"The one thing, besides my coffee maker, my second ex-wife didn't want. Lucky for me she couldn't drive a clutch or a four-on-the-floor Hurst stick shift. What do you drive, Captain?"

"These days a Ford Country Squire station wagon because my wife wanted an automatic and something big enough to cart around the kids and our new dog."

"New dog? You got a new dog? What kind of dog?"

"My daughters picked out a Poodle, I'm told."

"A poodle?"

"A small one," Robison nodded, sighed, and finished the answer with a forlorn, "I used to have a Camaro ragtop."

"When you were first married, I take it?"

The Captain nodded, sadly. "The fate of a father with babies."

"A Country Squire station wagon, huh?"

"It…it's comfortable, gets good mileage, and doesn't have oil or fluid leaks. Not so sure about the Poodle yet."

"Learn something new every day," grinned the First Sergeant.

"Well, we should. But that's not always the case."

"Yes sir, but I have learned or at least managed to grasp that our Mister Evans, from the eh, *Department of International Agency for Ducks and Squirrels*, is a real prick, so there's that too, Sir.

"Knowledge is a powerful thing indeed. But I believe you mean the '*Civil Operations and Rural Development Agency*?'"

"Damn! I got it wrong again!"

Chapter 18

The road condition of the route, with its many divots, deep potholes, and churned-up ground from the South Vietnamese Army's M-34 Patton tank tracks and those of the M-113 armored personnel carriers, and any of the overburdened wheeled vehicles, made the convoy slow to get up to speed. And further on even when the highway improved the convoy speed barely topped 30-miles-per-hour, only that speed wouldn't hold for any consistent length of time.

Fifteen yards behind the Ranger jeep, Sergeant Cantu was at the wheel of the Deuce-and-a-half with Lieutenant Plantagenet riding shotgun in the passenger seat. Their weapons, a Car-15 assault rifle and M-16, along with several bandoliers of ammo sitting between them. Their LBE web gear harnesses, stowed behind their seats were fighting ready with six individual magazine or canteen pouches holding 25 to 30 twenty-round magazines, three fragmentation grenades, a canteen holding a quart of water, a bayonet or personal knife in a scabbard, and a First Aid pouch. Higher up on shoulder straps showed one *Willy Pete*, white phosphorous grenade, that he'd secured on one side of the harness with a smoke grenade taped to the opposite strap. There were other necessary patrol items too, depending on individual preference and available room on the already crowded Load Bearing Equipment harness. Several LRRP rations were resting next to cloth bandoliers holding more rifle magazines.

For the Rangers riding in the bed of the big truck a few modifications were made to make it a slightly more comfortable trip. Instead of a canvas cover which would've made the ride stifling in the overbearing heat of the day, the truck bed was covered with camouflage netting. The netting provided a hint of shade while somewhat obscuring the Rangers beneath it and could be dropped in an instant. What direct sunlight the netting missed; their floppy bush hats and individual green towels, would cover in the hope of keeping sun burns down to a minimum. The Lieutenant had loaded a large metal cooler with enough soft drinks in chipped ice to last the day for the Rangers on the security detail. Several cans of Budweiser had been smuggled in beneath the soft drinks. A wire line secured a *church key* beer and soda can opener to the cooler.

Several of the Lurps had fashioned air mattresses and flak jackets as makeshift seat pads over the bench seats or sandbag covered floor. Over the first ten miles during the hot and bumpy ride, the seat pads proved to be a good call. Two folding chairs that seemed like a good idea at the start of the trip hadn't fared as well and had bounced and tilted or tossed the users around until the chairs were folded up and put away.

Utilizing rotating shifts, two of the Rangers would keep watch on the passing countryside on both sides of the road while the others slept or passed the time as best they could until their shifts were called. Wexler was sleeping or trying to, Doc

Sweet Sorrow

Moore was deep into a Louis L'Amour paperback novel on the Sacketts, while Specialists Bowman and Angeles were playing cards using a folded poncho liner as a table top. Two of the latest graduates from the Lurp Training Course, Sergeant Colp and PFC Green, were wide eyed with their attention fixed on the passing countryside with their weapons nervously ready for the first sign of trouble. The convoy would traverse more of the countryside than they had experienced so far as cherry Lurps. This was their first road mission outside of the wire and everything was new to them and, if not frightening, then at least suspicious or concerning. To the veterans it was only proving to be a boring ride.

Shintaku and Hernandez rotated manning the .50 cal machine gun atop the cab of the truck with many of the others eager to give it a try. Since Lurps seldom had the opportunity to man a heavy machine gun, both were eager to take on the task. The test fire of the *Ma Deuce,* as it was better known by the GIs, wasn't their first go with the big gun, but it was fun. The day before they had a chance to take the big gun out to a make-shift range and test fire it. After adjusting the headspace and timing, and fine tuning the rear drop-leaf sites, they were comfortable that there were no issues, and it was ready to fire.

They set out an old and empty five-gallon fuel can as a target fifty yards away and tied it to a thick tree to anchor it in place. Their test fire was ready. Radioing the BIG-TOC Command Center of their test fire and getting approval, the two Lurps took turns zeroing in on the mark with bursts from the heavy machine guns' thumb-sized rounds. The effective range for the heavy machine gun was 2,000 yards only that wouldn't be the case for the convoy. Any ambush would come from only a few hundred yards away or closer, so they concentrated on a more practical application. Rather than firing high, Shintaku and Hernandez took turns walking the rounds up to the target with the impact of the ball rounds hitting the ground and target like a sledgehammer on steroids. Walking the rounds up to the target also provided additional incoming with kicked up, splintered rocks and debris that slammed into the now badly ripped and torn steel container. Pleased with the result, and maybe even a little giddy after the test fire, they returned to the Camp where back at the Ranger Company they cleaned and mounted the *Ma Deuce* on the big truck. The gun truck was ready for the trip.

Hernandez had just relieved Shintaku, and the Staff Sergeant was now settling in on a folded and partially inflated air mattress as one of the FNGs made the mistake of asking Sergeant Daley how many days he had left on his tour of duty. While Shintaku, as the former Lurp Training NCO knew the new guy's name, he doubted that Daley or any of the others did.

"He's a short-timer, PFC Green," said Shintaku, which caused several in the truck bed to turn to put a name to the new guy's face which confused a few.

"Isn't that *Ironic?*" said Wexler.

"What?" said Shintaku.

"Him. His name."

"It's Green," said Green.

"Nope, and that's the irony too, that you somehow missed," said Wexler, pointing to Daley. "He's a short-timer and you ain't!"

"Eighteen days and a wake up to go, and goodbye Vietnam, and goodbye the Army," said the Montanan happily and grinning as he revealed the low number.

"Shoooooort!" yelled Hernandez over his shoulder, giving the standard and familiar happy response to those who were close to completing their tours of duty and going home.

"Why yes, I am. Thank you," Daley said, grinning at Hernandez. Back to the new guy he added, " How'za'bout you keeping an eye on the passing countryside, so we can both make it through our tours of duty?"

Unlike some others, Daley didn't generally fuck with the new guys which made him more approachable.

"Hey Sarge," said Green, "what kind of trees are those?"

"What?"

"Those trees with the little buckets strapped to them," said Green, standing and pushing aside the camo net and pointing to what he was looking at. "They're like all in rows."

Daley rose up from where he was sitting and followed the New Guy's line of sight over the left side of the truck.

"They are, because those, young Private First Class, are rubber trees."

"Rubber trees?"

"Yep."

The certainty of Daley's answer didn't seem so certain to the red haired FNG.

"But they're, like, you know, made of wood. Right?"

Daley stared at the New Guy for a long moment trying to figure out if he was serious or not, but Green's wide-eyed, skewed expression gave him his answer.

"Let me bounce this off you, Private…"

"Green."

"Right, because I'm beginning to see the irony," said Daley, "Anyway, those trees are in neat rows because that is a rubber plantation. Vietnam is, or was, famous for the amount of latex it has produced from these plantations since the 1800s."

"But you said they were rubber," replied the New Guy in a quizzical look and tone that said maybe he wasn't quite convinced they weren't pulling his leg, so Daley went on.

"It is, eventually. The trees actually produce latex."

"Latex?"

"Think raw rubber. Much like how Maple trees in Canada collect the sap that is boiled into pancake syrup, the rubber trees collect the dripping milky white latex in small buckets. That latex then is made into rubber. It's big business here, or was until all the bang-bang started."

"Rubber comes from trees?"

Daley nodded. "Yeah, eventually, but you can't just slap some on the soles of your jungle boots and think you're having a Goodyear."

PFC Green gave a slow nod, still not quite sure what his boots had to do with it or what to make of the trees.

Spec-4 Hernandez, the street smart Cuban from just outside of Miami, who had overheard the exchange and who was now staring at the new guy, recognized the confusion on his face, which was when he added something more to help him better understand what he was looking at, and of course, to fuck with him.

"You see those really thin leaves on the branches higher up?" said Hernandez to Green, pointing to the tops of plantation trees. "Up there on the tree tops PFC New Guy?"

"Yeah, I see them? And the name is Green."

"Yeah well, that's nice, but I don't fucking care. *De todos modos*, those leaves are special and bring in more money because those thin leaves are used to make condoms, the ones with the grooves."

"Really?" asked the New Guy, turning from Hernandez back to Daley and then to Doc Moore, looking for confirmation.

Moore let out a slow sigh, shook his head, and went back to reading the L'Amour novel while Daley chuckled, and Hernandez lowered and slowly shook his head back and forth like a disappointed metronome.

"*Ay, Dios mio*, New Guy," muttered Hernandez. "You're gonna have a long tour of duty."

Chapter 19

The convoy rolled on.

For the Lurps who were used to operating like Ninjas in five or six man teams on patrol in the jungle, where sneaking and peeking, caution, and stealth were not just necessary components for a successful mission, but critical, the convoy was an anomaly, a major glitch to their operational routine and any sense of survival well-being.

On the road they were now operating in plain sight, and worse still, with advance warning from the vehicles' road noise which could be heard from a hundred yards or more away. But that was what was on the menu today so the Rangers, these Lurps, would adjust to meet the potential take-out order.

There was also the matter of time and distance to and from. Perhaps on a well-paved highway in a peaceful environment, in civilian vehicles with more horsepower, better shock absorbers and springs and better padded seats, and up to Interstate highway speed, the ride to and from the Dega/Montagnard village might've only taken sixty minutes or less. But QL-13, National Route 13, the war, and the highway's troubled history in the fighting dictated caution. The *from here to there* always looked shorter on a map than the reality of the journey. A mile on paper didn't measure the likes of a ducks-in-a-row shooting gallery from an enemy ambush that was always a possibility within that God-awful 1,760 yards.

Further North, the Dega/Montagnard village, or what had been the tribe's jungle hamlet until it was heavily shelled by South Vietnamese heavy mortars, sat seven to eight miles west of QL-13 on a much lesser maintained back country trail that most would never mistake as a roadway. The thin, dark orange track that even the Vietnamese woodcutter's would only venture into so far was little more than a one-lane, back country trail that wound its way deeper into the jungle like a giant undulating snake. For security reasons for the tribe, the dirt road ended well short of the village where a narrow footpath twisted through the jungle for another 800 meters to meet it. Where the road ended would be the agreed upon meet-up site.

The hill tribe was wary of visitors. They were a proud, fierce, and independent people with emphasis on the *fierce*, so any Vietnamese woodcutters would only venture to go so far into their territory, fearing dangerous encounters or reprisals from those indigenous clans who wished to protect what was their own. In both the distant and not so distant past, woodcutter's carts had been burned and their water buffalo hacked to death or crippled by the Dega. The message was clear; *You are not welcome.*

The turnoff from the poorly maintained QL-13 onto the even more poorly maintained and unimproved route would add more time to the convoy's clock. The village that was tucked away in a remote border region dominated by dense jungle and rolling hills was well away from any Vietnamese village, town, or government authority by design. That distance displayed that there was no love lost between the two distinct ethnic groups. The Hill Tribe intensely adhered to, and protected their tribal culture lifestyle and independence, so they maintained and appreciated the physical distance from outsiders.

Going over a map of the route earlier that morning, Captain Robison, the MP Major, Lieutenant Plantagenet, and the Lieutenant from the Transportation Corps, figured the journey from Camp Mackie's back gate to the meet up site that was just a mile shy of the village would take approximately two hours and change.

The map showed that the turn off from QL-13 to the dirt road leading to the village dead ended seven to eight miles in. Then it was a winding path that led a 1,000 meters more to the Dega settlement. There were only a few natural clearings displayed on the map that might fit a helicopter or two, but none big enough to land a three helicopter Quick Reaction Force. It didn't help any that the poorly maintained road was the only way in or out of the village, either. During the planning stage, the notion of taking the back country trail in and out of the deep and dark rainforest highlighted on the map had set the hairs on the back of the Ranger Captain's neck standing up. Some called it a foreboding *Survival Sixth Sense* while others knew it to be a physiological reflex of the tiny muscles near the hair follicles brought on by an unspoken understanding of what the route conveyed and what went unsaid. Adrenaline could do that, as would a healthy dose of learned caution from previous combat tours.

Some also called it a healthy dose of learned fear.

Chapter 20

"Well, ain't this just dandy?" grumbled Poplawski, waving away the latest cloud of road dust coming at them in the convoy. He coughed up a line of gritty phlegm, and hawked it over the side of the open jeep. "I'd light up my cigar, but I'm afraid Cuba might end up tasting like mud."

The two vehicles in the lead; the MP armored car and the MP jeep that Quan and Evans had commandeered, were sending tumbling clouds of fine, powdered dust wafting in their wakes, creating an orange-colored fog that each successive vehicle in the small column only added to and kept airborne and alive well into their passing.

The three Rangers in the jeep and those in the open truck bed had fashioned face scarves out of First Aid slings to go along with the goggles they wore to keep out most of the kicked-up dust. *The goggles are nice*, thought Poplawski as the next roiling spray of dust came at them, *but it's a shame they hadn't come with tiny fucking windshield wipers.*

To better deal with the mess, he held the jeep back a better distance from the jeep in front of him. That helped and allowed for them to occasionally push up the goggles to the foreheads and lower the face scarves. The orange colored dust left their faces looking like militant racoons, but that wasn't the only problem.

The jungle-covered countryside outside the cities and villages had the Ranger Captain thinking there were many good places where *Charlie* could carry out an ambush, and over the years, successfully had.

Charlie, of course, being the GI slang for the local Viet Cong, as were the terms *Gooks*, *Dinks*, *Slopes*, *Gomers*, or whatever else the ones fighting against them could come up with to make their opponent's easier to kill. The Viet Cong and North Vietnamese had their own insults for the Americans and the Westerners in general, such as *mui to* which translated to *long or big noses*, *tay long* for *hairy westerners*, or *Thang cho de* for a *son of a bitch*.

Insults and epithets aside, with the thousands of North Vietnamese Army regulars spilling down and out of the Ho Chi Minh Trail through Laos and Cambodia every month, any ambush could easily turn into a devastating attack against the small convoy. Highway QL-13 held that kind of reputation. Any name-calling was the least of their worries.

But with the sleek Cobra helicopter gunship high above doing calculated lazy circles over the convoy, and with the small Scout helicopter flying at treetop level doing a recon of the route ahead and tree lines closer to the road, any ambush was bound to be discovered and soon dealt with. The terrible sound and fury that an attack helicopter armed with three dozen rockets mounted on lateral stub wings, and an automatic grenade launcher and a six-barreled, spinning minigun under the chin of the gunship that could automatically fire 3,000-rounds a minute into a target could turn a body into a kitchen sieve and strainer. The lesser armed Low Bird had one Observer, an *Oscar* who carried an M-16 and a pistol, but the real firepower came from a machine gunner in the back of the aircraft. That crew member was called a *Torque* and the *Torque's* job was to lean out of the back of the small helicopter and scan the jungle looking for the enemy. With his M-60 machine gun tied to the helicopter on a bungee cord, he was ready to engage a target, or from an open crate next to him, drop a smoke grenade to mark an enemy position for the gunship if he, the pilot, or the *Oscar* saw movement in an enemy bunker or a group of enemy soldiers. The smoke grenade would give the Cobra gunship an aiming point as the small helicopter quickly veered away.

The small convoy, too, carried its own share of fireworks that would also add to any *ooh* and *ahh,* or *oh shit* show.

Still, that didn't do much for the Lurps who were used to springing ambushes, and any surprise attack today would be something they would have to initially eat and respond to, hopefully without taking too many hits or too many casualties.

The game was in play, and it was early innings.

Chapter 21

One mile short of the Lai Khe Base Camp the convoy made an unscheduled stop.

The truck carrying the three pallets of lumber, building supplies, and the four foot high stack of fifty pound sacks of rice, blew out its front right tire after rolling into several deep, back-to-back potholes. This section of the lesser maintained road was a mix of asphalt and hardpack ground and the dust that was being kicked up wasn't helping matters much either when it came to the driver who was doing his best trying to keep the Deuce-and-a-half in gear and rolling.

The truck's right front tire bounced in and out of the first pothole with a distinct *thud* but when the big wheel slid into a second deeper hole the tire popped loud enough to be heard by the Rangers in the bed of the truck in front of it. The Deuce-and-a-half rolled a bit further as it dipped down to the side of the road, wobbled, and shook before it came to a brake-stomping halt. When the enlisted driver and Transportation officer got out to inspect the damage, a closer inspection showed the rim was also trashed.

"Let's get it changed out," said the Transportation Officer before he went back to the truck cab and grabbed the radio.

The Transportation Officer, radio call sign Proud Mary Six, was on the radio calling it in before the gap between the vehicles in the lead got too far out of hand.

"I copy, Proud Mary. What are we looking at, over?"

"It might take a while, but we'll get it done A-SAP. Over."

"Roger that. Break. Pistol-Six. You copy?"

"Loud and clear and standing by."

"Roger. Break. Piebald Two-three. Valhalla-Six. Over."

"Piebald Two-three. Go."

"Be advised, we have a flat tire on one of the trucks. We'll update you on the tire change status and when we're ready to move again."

"I copy, Valhalla. Piebald team standing by."

That was immediately followed by a radio call from an annoyed member of the convoy that also came across the airway loud and clear.

"Goddamn it, we're on a tight schedule here! Tell whoever is in charge of that truck to hurry it the fuck up and get it done!" he said angrily before he tossed the radio's handset down atop the wooden crates in the back of his jeep.

The caller didn't give his assigned call sign, but there was no doubt who the radio call had come from. Mister Evans was in prime form.

"Lieutenant Plantagenet!" yelled the Captain turning to the Ranger's gun truck.

"Sir?"

"Set up a defensive perimeter. No telling how long this'll take."

Sweet Sorrow

The junior officer nodded and was repeating the command to the Rangers in the truck bed as he was making his way behind the Deuce-and-a-half. Unlatching the chained tail hooks, he lowered the heavy truck bed gate. Those in the truck bed, who'd heard their Company Commander shout out the command, were already gathering up their weapons and LBE web gear and readying to make the tailgate jump even as the Lieutenant was echoing the order.

Leaving Sergeant Hernandez to man the .50 cal heavy machine gun, the rest of the Lurps climbed down from the truck where under Staff Sergeant Shintaku's critical eye they quickly began to set up the M-60 machine gun positions in tactical placement sites. Both sides of the road facing the tree lines were now covered.

With better commo etiquette than Evans displayed, the MP Major gave the order over the radio to his people in the rear of the column to reposition the trailing gun jeep to cover the convoy's six. There was no telling how long it would take to have the truck tire and wheel removed and replaced. The spare tire the truck carried was stored behind and just below the driver's side cab weighed in at well over 100 pounds.

They were twenty three minutes into the wait when an agitated Evans made his way back to the supply truck to demand how much longer it was going to take.

"We're almost done, Sir," said the Transportation officer as the truck driver began wrestling the spare tire into place.

"Well, hurry up and get it done!" whined Evans, his tone elongating his disdain. "I'm not here to get a goddamn tan!"

"Yes sir," said the rattled Lieutenant. "The ground here's not the best."

The Lieutenant's reply had some validity. The uneven ground where the truck had come to a stop wasn't helping matters at all, even if the impatient civilian wouldn't acknowledge it. Still, the truck driver and Lieutenant were making quick work of the tire change, just not quick enough for Evans.

The convoy's Very-Important-Pain-in-the-ass civilian frowned and harrumphed as he stomped back to his jeep. Considering that, in the high heat of the day, he wasn't doing any of the heavy lifting, let alone helping in any sense of the word, his annoyance was more annoying to those doing the work in the heat of the day.

"Don't sweat it. You're doing fine," said Lieutenant Plantagenet, walking back to the truck and offering more than a little verbal salve to the Transportation officer and his driver. "You need help?"

"No, Sir, we got it."

"Outstanding! Let me know when you're ready to roll and I'll let my Captain know."

By the MP Major's watch, the hold-up took twenty-three minutes. It was what it was, and while Evans' continual bitching about the delays were grating, there was little he could do about it other than show and loudly share his vocal displeasure.

"Chop chop, people. Chop chop!" he yelled and then checked something in his teeth in the rear view mirror.

Once the heavy spare tire was finally on, the lug nuts tightened, and the flat tire with its damaged rim was stored and secured, the Transportation officer gave a thumbs-up to the Ranger Lieutenant who returned the gesture. Plantagenet then gave his Commanding Officer the news at his jeep.

"We're Good-to-Go, Sir."

"Thank you, Lieutenant," replied the Ranger Captain reaching for the handset to his radio.

"Piebald Two-three. Valhalla-Six. Over," Robison said, calling the gunship helicopter that was flying in lazy circles overhead.

"Two-three, Valhalla. Go."

"We're back up and running, Two-three. Appreciate your patience."

"No problem, Valhalla. Two-three out."

"Break, Pistol-Six, You copy. Over?"

"That's affirmative, Valhalla. Forward-ho!"

Listening in on the radio call, the pilot of the Light Observation Helicopter buzzing just west of the convoy's location began checking out a suspicious looking site before he brought the small Scout bird back towards the parked vehicles before he once again flew forward on the convoy's line of travel.

The Scout pilot wasn't the only one listening in. Overhearing the conversation on the borrowed MP's jeep radio, Evans chimed in with *'About damn time!'* on the radio as the transmission also carried the sound of Quan cranking up the jeep.

"Let me guess, it's Mister Evans?" said Poplawski turning to the Ranger Company Commander.

"The very same!" said Captain Robison.

"He could do with a little attitude readjustment."

An *attitude adjustment* was Army speak for a thump on the head or a swift kick in the ass.

Robison was thinking the very same thing but instead smiled and yelled, "*Saddle up!*" to Lieutenant Plantagenet, who once again repeated the order the Lurps. The Rangers made their way back to their Deuce-and-a-half and climbed into the truck bed. The *"Saddle up"* command went out over the radio to the rest of the vehicles in the convoy and the road trip pushed on. However, the vehicle column only made it another two miles before the next radio call came in from the Gunship pilot, this time to the Ranger Company Commander.

"Valhalla-Six, Piebald Two-three Over."

"Pistol Six. Go."

"Roger. Just a head's up to let you know you have an ARVN tank column stopped on the highway a mile or so ahead of you. I say again, there is an armored convoy stopped on the highway."

"They in contact, Two-Three?"

"Negative, Valhalla-Six. Looks like they're fixing some broken track on a 1-1-3."

"I copy, Piebald…" only before Robison could finish Evans was angrily back on the radio airway.

"Any way we can go around the fucking thing?"

"This is Piebald Two-three. Last calling station. Identify yourself. Over."

"It's me, *Eddie-One*, as in the *one* reason why you're all here today, so can we go around the damn thing or not?"

"That's a negative, *Eddie-One*. Looks like one of their Command vehicles has lost one of its tracks. Given the terrain there's no room to go around it. Traffic is backed up coming and going. Could be a while. Suggest you kick back, settle in, and next time use your call sign."

"Great! Just fucking great!" groused Evans, tossing the radio's handset down a second time and stewing in his seat as the convoy rolled towards the latest wait.

The Military Police armored car soon came to a break-squealing, bobbing halt twenty yards in front of an ARVN Armored Personnel Carrier. The M-113 was turned around and covering the armored column's rear. A South Vietnamese soldier manning a .50 caliber machine gun eased back from the weapon, smiled, and waved. Sergeant Burke in the lead vehicle's open turret behind the twin .30 cal machine guns returned the smile and waved back.

Still unconvinced there wasn't room to detour around the ARVN armored column, Evans was once more out of his jeep and hurrying to the armored car to get a look for himself. Ahead of the lead vehicle heat waves were shimmering off of the surface of the partially paved road. The temperature was pushing 96-degrees with a humidity factor of a Swedish sauna.

With his arms on his hips, staring up the road at the vehicle blockage Evans stood in front of the V-100 as Captain Robison and the MP Major and Ranger Captain strolled up behind him.

Once again, the impatient Mister Evans, wasn't happy because the gunship pilot was correct. There wasn't room to go around the long line of armored vehicles. They would have to wait.

"That's some traffic jam," said the MP Major, studying the line of stationary South Vietnamese military vehicles.

"Looks like they're heading north on an operation," replied Robison.

"Yeah well, this is turning into a real shitshow!" he muttered and stomped back to his jeep.

"And to think our Mister Cheerful is the guy they're sending to patch things up with the Yards!" laughed the MP Major.

"Well, he is a real people person," said Robison as the MP Major's laugh turned into a loud guffaw.

"God help us!"

It was a little over an hour later when the South Vietnamese armored column was rolling again. The MP Convoy column, though, was holding in place. The Cobra gunship pilot was calling in to say the Pink Team would use the time to break away to refuel. When the call over the net came in and Captain Robison acknowledged it, Evans threw another fit.

"Why in the hell aren't we moving?" he said, angrily making his way back to the Ranger jeep. "Why the fucking delay this time?"

Robison pointed towards the sky. "Air support. We're waiting on our Pink Team."

"Our what?"

"Pink Team. Gunship and Low Bird helicopters. Artillery is red and scout helicopters are white,"

"…ergo pink," added Poplawski.

"Yeah well, ergo fuck yourself, we're on a tight time table here, Sergeant, whether you want to believe it or not."

"Oh, I believe it," said Poplawski with his chin set, taking a menacing step forward, and causing the civilian to take a nervous half step back. "Just like I believe in civil discourse and professional interpersonal communication, cooperation, and courtesy, if you catch my meaning. You do catch my meaning, don't you, Mister Evans?"

Turning to the Ranger Captain, Evans said, "Choke-chain your pit bull, Captain, or I will. We need to keep moving if we're to make the rendezvous with the Montagnards."

"We will when all is ready, Mister Evans. And I'll ask you kindly not to disrespect or harass any of my people, again. We're all professionals here or should be. First Sergeant?"

"Sir?"

"Play nice with our rude and upset civilian guest. However, if for some silly reason he decides to take a swing at you, then please feel free to knock him on his ass."

"Yes sir."

Poplawski's junkyard dog smile had Evans taking another step back.

"Lieutenant Plantagenet?" said Robison.

"Yes sir," said the junior officer leaning out of the gun truck's passenger side window.

"Find out how far out the Piebald Pink Team is."

"Yes sir."

It was a short wait and when Plantagenet got off the radio the Captain had his answer.

"1-5 mikes, Sir."

"Thank you, Lieutenant."

"So, like what?" said the agitated Evans. "We're going to sit here for 15 minutes and hope we don't get ambushed or sunstroke in the meantime? Is that your plan, Captain? Sit and wait?"

Evans may have been used to looking down on or bullying others in the military because of his shadowy civilian governmental standing and status with the Central Intelligence Agency or whatever other clandestine or spook organization with three initials he belonged to, but Robison wasn't all that intimidated by the berating bluster of the cocky, browbeating bureaucrat. Neither was Poplawski since both had been '*assets*' a time or two in their Special Forces careers where they had been cherry picked by the military to assist on covert intelligence Ops as *hired guns*. They were more than that, of course, but not always to the CIA's case officers that oversaw the borrowed assets from the deep pool of military subject matter experts for a particular mission.

This wasn't their first rodeo as *hired guns* with one of the shadow alphabet agencies. Some of those assigned tasks working with the agents on assisted Ops were good, and some were better and even exceptional. Conversely, other military loan outs with less than talented agents who were jerks or arrogant assholes, weren't, which is the category Evans was comfortably fitting into. All rodeos had their share of bullshit and horse's asses.

With prescribed jobs to do Captain Robison turned to the civilian V-I-P and said, "We plan for the worst and hope for the best, which means we allow for contingencies, Mister Evans. Annoying as that may be, this is one of those possibilities. Oh, and while you're in charge of glad-handing and handing over the building supplies, rice, and whatever else you have in the crates in your jeep for the Meet-and-Greet, I'm in charge of the tactical aspect of the convoy. So, like it or not, we wait. First Sergeant?"

"Yes sir?"

"Set up a perimeter!"

"Yes sir. On it!"

Evans stormed back to his jeep and as the convoy waited, the V-I-P brooded. If patience was indeed a virtue, then Evans was at a distinct disadvantage for his lack of it.

"Do you believe this shit?" Evans yelled to Quan climbing into the jeep. Knowing his role in the latest performance, Quan shrugged. Ever the pragmatist, it was what it was. More importantly, this wasn't his fight. The American had a way for annoying people.

Entertainment was always in short supply in the war zone, so to those watching or within hearing distance, taking in the exchanges, this was becoming good theater.

Chapter 22

"UN-ASS THE VEHICLES! LET'S GO, ROMEO RANGERS! MOVE IT!" yelled the Lieutenant for the Lurps to get out of the truck. "Gimme a good 360-degree perimeter. Staff Shintaku! Get on it!"

"On it, First Sergeant!"

Defensive positions away from the convoy column were more secure. The exposed, standing vehicles lined up on the road were little more than potential sitting ducks, chief among them was the armored car, the *Duck*, giving the situation more than a little ironic credence.

Two M-60 machine gun positions were strategically placed covering both sides of the road in what were deemed possible *avenues of approach* that the MPs weren't covering to the front and back of the column. Specialist Hernandez stood ready behind the truck mounted .50 caliber heavy machine gun scanning the tree line. Several other Lurps had their small arms locked and loaded and ready to fire. Sergeant Cantu was cradling an M-79 grenade launcher while Staff Sergeant Shintaku had his M-16 in his hands and an M-72 rocket launcher in its carrying case slung over his shoulder in anticipation of any surprise visits from unwanted guests. Specialist Taras was up behind the M-60 machine gun in the Ranger's jeep. Following Hernandez's lead in the elevated positions, Taras was scouring the opposite tree line for any would-be attackers too.

On his way to join the MP Major, Captain Robison momentarily balked as he passed Taras. He couldn't help but grin at the serious expression on the young Ranger's face, thinking the kid had heart, even if he did look like a member of a high school marching band behind a deadly instrument.

After checking out the vehicular security and adjacent ground defensive positions, the MP Major and the Ranger Captain returned to their vehicles to sit out the inevitable wait. The Army was always '*hurry up and wait,*' and in Vietnam, the *hurry* was always a sweat-stained sprint while any wait came with mostly boredom, a lingering cloud of angst, with nothing really to worry about except for a sudden bout of absolute terror when the world blew up in an instant.

With no terror present and only the frustration that was being felt by the primary V-I-P they were escorting, Robison and Poplawski settled back against the jeep's canvas covered seats to fight the boredom, which in a small way they knew was a win.

The wait next to the jeep, inevitably, turned to small talk.

"I'm seriously considering canceling my R&R," Robison said to the First Sergeant. "With what little time the Company has left being operational, I don't think it would be proper for me to take it now."

Poplawski turned to his Captain and stared at him open-mouthed and dumbfounded. What came next from him was preceded by a loud, exasperated exhaling breath and a chin-dropping, slow shake of his head. The audio needed to match the video if he was to get his point across.

"Don't take this the wrong way, Sir," said Poplawski, "but that is... one... serious...dumb...fucking...move!"

Poplawski stretched out and over emphasized the last five uttered words for what he'd hoped would have better impact and effect on the Captain's decision making process.

"Excuse me?"

"I will, good Sir, but I suspect maybe your wife won't if you try to cancel the R&R," said Poplawski, who then began laying out his case.

"How's that?"

"Well, I'm thinking that she has already bought her ticket to Hawaii. Correct?"

"She has, but she can probably get a refund."

The First Sergeant waved away and dismissed that part of the Captain's trial argument as trivial and inconsequential.

"And I suspect she probably also has bought herself a brand new bathing suit and a few new blouses and dainty, pretty things to look and feel her best when she sees you? It's not a real question, Sir, because believe me with wives, that's a given."

Robison had nothing to counter that but a small shrug, so Poplawski went on presenting his argument to the one-man defendant, judge, and jury.

"And just in case you don't know it, women go to great lengths and pains to find the right bathing suit and clothes and shoes and frilly whatnot, because they want to look good for their man, but according to two of my Ex's, they mostly want to look good for snarky women as well."

"Okay, but..."

"Uh-uh! Nope! And no buts, Sir, because a while back I heard you say that her mother would be watching your kids while you both were on R&R."

"Yes, I did..."

"Which also means that this R&R is a well-deserved rest and relaxation vacation for your wife, too. I know you have passed through the islands to and from Southeast Asia a time or two in your military career, and maybe even had a 48 hour stopover, so you saw some sights like Waikiki..."

"A few, last year, when I had a day or so on an emergency leave before flying stateside."

"Okay, so how about your wife? Has she ever been to Hawaii before?"

"Well, no..."

"And BOOM! There it is!" said the First Sergeant, smiling as he went with his final closing argument. "So, it's safe to also say she might really be looking forward to the R&R vacation, and might have some tropical island walks on the beach with a few other romantic scenarios playing around inside her head. She's probably even looking forward to lounging by the pool sipping on a fancy drink with one of those tiny, little umbrellas in it, too. I'd venture to guess she has even said as much in a letter or two when you proposed meeting up in Hawaii for the R&R?"

Robison emitted something low that sounded like a deflated and defeated *hmm*, indicating that possibly she had.

"True," he said, after a moment.

"So, don't disappoint her! Take the R&R. Besides, you have a competent Executive Officer who is a fellow Upper Hudson West Point graduate, and another squared-away junior officer with a great historic name who can even tie his own boots. Not to mention you also have a highly competent veteran senior NCO with our *Mad Russian*, SFC Kozak, and might I remind you, one pretty damn good, and dare I say, out-fucking-standing acting First Sergeant in me. Here Sir, about now is where you're supposed to nod."

Robison nodded.

"Then there you go! The company will be in pretty good hands for the five days you'll be gone. We'll handle things here until you return. You owe it to your wife, Sir, and to yourself to take the R&R. Besides, if we fuck up things too badly in your absence you can always chew us out when you return."

Robison had no case, and he knew it, so he chuckled instead.

"Okay, Perry Mason you win," he said, now convinced it was okay to take the R&R. "By the way, you never said how your R&R in Bangkok went."

Poplawski went uncharacteristically quiet as his R&R to Thailand's capital had been an epic failure, something he kept to himself.

"I take it you enjoyed it and had a great time? Was it everything you thought it would be?"

Poplawski wasn't saved by the bell answering the Captain's question, but instead won time by the sound of the OH-6 Scout helicopter that came buzzing in low overhead, did a half turn and then flew ahead of the convoy at treetop level. 1,500-feet above the Low Bird, the Cobra gunship lorded over the skies like a dark bird of prey as it squawked out a radio call to the convoy below.

"Valhalla-Six, Piebald Two-Three and One-Five back on station."

Robison reached in and grabbed the radio's handset. "I copy, Two-Three. Valhalla-Six," he replied. To the gunship pilot. "We're ready to move. Valhalla-Six out."

With the Pink Team back in play, it was time to get everyone back in their vehicles and once again ready to move out once the tank column was up and running again.

"Valhalla-Six. Piebald Two-Three over."

"Go. Two-Three."

"Be advised, the road looks good ahead of you."

"Roger that, Two-Three. Valhalla-Six. Out."

With this latest *wait* over, the *hurry up* was back in motion.

"*SADDLE UP!*" Robison barked out the command into the radio. The order was repeated down the line of jeeps and trucks as the soldiers returned to their vehicles to continue the journey. Plumes of black, diesel smoke shot out of the exhaust pipes of the trucks as the big engines roared to life while the jeep drivers gunned the engines like they were on the starting line of the Indy-500.

When the radio confirmation came in from each of the vehicles that all was ready, Robison radioed the MP Major in the lead vehicle they were Good-to-Go, and the small convoy rolled on. It was pushing on mid-day, and they were 90-minutes off schedule.

On this latest stretch of highway rolling, tumbling clouds of kicked-up dust had the Americans reaching for their goggles and bandanas one more time. The convoy's V-I-P, *Eddie-one,* would be eating more dust than he had thought he had weaseled out of. A lot of dust, in fact, and that had the MP Major in the armored car, smiling.

The rubber tree plantations with their precise rows of perfectly aligned trees and open ground free of undergrowth had given way to a sprawling wall of jungle and rolling hills as far as the eyes could see. While the jungle was familiar operating ground to the Lurps, it also left them more than a little leery and on edge, especially when the convoy reached the turnoff, the vehicles halted, and they watched the tank column in front of them continue on and disappear on its way to Loc Ninh.

There were no sign posts or road markers indicating the turnoff was the route to the small village but when Robison met with the MP Major behind the *Duck* to confirm the location on their maps, it was the Ranger Captain who offered to take the lead.

"No, that's alright, Captain," said the Major. "My vehicle has better protection than your jeep, so I'll take us in, but since you and your people are in your element, I'd appreciate any input if you think anything looks hinky to you."

"Roger that, Sir. Happy to oblige."

Back at his jeep Robison grabbed the radio's handset. "All convoy units! All convoy units! Be advised, we're making the turnoff to the meet-up site," he said, "Keep your heads down and eyes out for anything out of the ordinary and I do mean *anything*. Valhalla-Six. Out."

After buttoning down the hatches to the *Duck,* and with Sergeant Burke manning the twin machine guns in the open turret, the MPs' armored car left Highway QL-13 and turned onto the thin dirt road that was more used to water buffalo carts than motorized vehicles. The going now was dramatically slower and in lower gears, as one-by-one the other vehicles followed the armored car from the highway.

Sweet Sorrow

At best, the turnoff was indeed an old, wood cutter's trail, a poor pale orange dirt road that was little more than a dark side alley through an even darker jungle. Robison was uneasy by what he saw. At worst, the route provided a good setting for an enemy ambush with only one way in and one way out.

Thinned-out sections of the jungle on both sides of the back country roadway showed where trees had been cut and hauled away by woodcutters. However, that soon gave way to thicker foliage crowding the road and showed how the war and the hill tribe had suspended much of the local logging and woodcutting by intimidation to the Vietnamese loggers.

One hundred twisting yards in, the living walls of jungle with a forest of 100 foot-tall canopy covered trees and interlocking brush, foliage, and vines, began choking the ancient route. The long-neglected back country lane was jig-sawed with shadows in the filtered sunlight that was coming through the trees from above.

Any aerial observation of the backroad or the convoy by the two accompanying helicopters overhead now was sporadic and limited to a few intermittent open spaces in the double-canopied jungle awnings, and the painfully few, small natural clearings there were in the area. The Low Bird helicopter flying just above the tops of the trees scouted ahead with the pilot and observer working hard to follow the thin route to the meet up site.

This was back woods, wild country, and an open zoo, where this particular stretch of jungle was so remote that Poplawski was thinking that even if they dropped bread crumbs or even whole loaves to guarantee they could find their way back to Highway-13, chances were better than fair that the many insects, rats, snakes, host of large or small animals, monkeys, and birds, and maybe even a tiger lurking nearby spying on the interlopers would slither or dart in, scoop them up, and slip back into the cover and protection of the jungle long before the convoy made the return trip.

Because the route was in much poorer condition than the official Highway they'd just left, vehicle travel on the backroad route became slower and more mechanically strained as the occasional grinding of shifting gears and vehicle springs squeaked in protest. Over the ages, and it had been ages, the Dega pathway that became the woodcutter's trail and had accommodated oxcarts and perhaps, nothing larger than an occasional jeep or small truck, made for a daunting drive. With its many potholes, partially exposed football-sized or larger rocks, and old or newly fallen broken branches littering the lane, the vehicles trudged on along the slender route.

"We're threading the needle here and making a shit-ton of noise, Captain," Poplawski said, visibly bothered by the heavy vegetation on each side of the road that was slapping at the vehicles as they went. Side mirrors were taking the bulk of the brush beatings, especially when it came to avoiding the deeper pot holes on the old roadway. The engine noise and squeaking vehicle springs weren't helping matters any.

Poplawski didn't have to say the rest of what more he was thinking as Robison grunted his response and had one thumb ready to flick his M-16's selector switch from SAFE to FIRE.

Along the QL-13 Highway, teams of Army engineers over the years had pushed the jungle well back from the roadway with bulldozers and Rome Plows to better screen against Viet Cong or NVA ambushes. But because this was a seldom used, dead-end road that only led towards a remote Montagnard hill country village of no real economic or strategic value, the Americans and particularly, the South Vietnamese, saw no reason to maintain it or clear away encroaching brush, and that suited the Dega/Montagnards just fine. The less unwanted outsiders, the better.

Over the centuries the Vietnamese *Kinh*, the largest ethnic group in the country, had little use for the indigenous tribes that inhabited the highlands and hill regions in the remote and distant provinces. Those people were the ethnic minorities and the mountain people the French tagged, *Montagnards*, and the Vietnamese or *Kinh* acknowledged as *dong bao,* their 'compatriots.' More often than not they were quietly or not so quietly thought of as back country hillbillies or worse, referred to as '*Moi*' or '*Nguoi hoang da,*' nasty slang epithets that meant *savages* and *wild people*, and they were somehow lesser than the Vietnamese *Kinh*.

Ethnic tensions mounted and the not-so-well-hidden prejudices and discrimination had gotten overheated and out of hand. The powder-charged bias towards the Dega and the sting they felt from it had led to open revolts and uprisings against the South Vietnamese government earlier in the war. Even so, the Dega mostly remained loyal to their American Special Forces advisors, which created a new round of problems for the American government, not to mention the Green Beret soldiers stuck in the middle of the in-fighting.

With mediated promises and concessions made by the Saigon government to the various hill tribes, cooler heads prevailed, and the uprisings and associated tensions became somewhat settled. *Somewhat* being the watchword, as the historical distrust between the factions always seemed to linger as a dark, and threatening cloud.

Not to miss out on exploiting this opportunity too, the Viet Cong and North Vietnamese took advantage of those tensions and made overtures to some of the hill tribes of the leery Dega/Montagnards, Cham, and Khmer tribes in South Vietnam. At times, some of the hill tribes responded favorably, since it was in their best interest and benefit to do so. The offers were there because the hill tribes had brave fighters, knew the local jungle terrain better than anyone else, and, who, for the most part, just wanted to be left alone. Friendships, real and genuine friendships, needed to made, maintained, and honored. Sometimes, when honor was in short supply, the friendships were maintained with better incentives and bribery.

'What? The Viet Cong only gave you one water buffalo? How'za bout we give you three! Name your price, my friends. Whatever it takes!'

Like other members of the Special Forces who had worked with the Montagnards, both Captain Robison and First Sergeant Poplawski had, wore the hammered-out brass bracelets that the tribal elders had presented to them during a rice wine ceremony honoring their kinship.

Earning a tribal bracelet was an honor that signified a lifelong attachment to the tribe, something neither Robison nor Poplawski took lightly when they had served as advisors to the *Rade* people up in South Vietnam's Central Highlands on an earlier tour of duty.

The accompanying rice wine part of the ceremony honoring the Americans, though, was another matter, especially to the Green Berets watching the production of the wine. That the women, especially the grandmothers in the tribe first chewed and chomped on the rice before they spat it into a giant clay jar mix of various herbs and roots, so their saliva could help ferment the mix, had left something visually and mentally to be desired. Once seen it couldn't go unseen. The face Poplawski made when he witnessed the rice wine being made was noticed by a veteran Green Beret accompanying the new honorees.

"You like hot dogs, do you?" asked one of the veteran Green Beret.

"Sure," said Poplawski, wondering what that had to do with what was happening.

"If the package label lists *'variety meats'* then that comes from the lips, snouts, eyes, and brains of the animal, so...."

"So, drink up like it's a grill party back home and you're terribly thirsty?"

"Bingo!"

Depending on the particular brew, and how long it had been sealed in the large clay storage jars to ferment, the rice wine might have an 18 to 21% alcohol volume score, and could sometimes run as high as 40%, the same as Jameson Whiskey and Jack Daniels with maybe a dead bug or two.

The rice wine they sipped and drew through long bamboo straws definitely had a unique flavor and a kick, but the tribal honorees drank it anyway as part of the initiation ceremony and wobbled away later. The brass bracelets that had been made from old bullet or artillery shell casings carried more than the scrap metal weight in their meaning. It signified trusted friendship, a brotherhood.

Whether this particular tribe would recognize and honor that friendship or brotherhood, or their *Rade* tribal brass bracelets was a toss-up, but then the Ranger Captain and First Sergeant weren't the key players in this get-together anyway, since technically they were just the hired guns along for the ride. This was Evans' show, and that he wasn't wearing one of the bracelets from any of the *Dega* tribes spoke volumes.

The convoy pushed deeper into the dark forest. The reception they would receive from the Dega, still several miles ahead of them on the road less travelled would make all the difference.

Chapter 23

Mother Nature was doing her best to get things back in order and making great strides in taking back what had been carved out and hacked away by the woodcutters on the old road.

The slow moving convoy was passing through the narrow one-lane road in the near impenetrable jungle that was doing its best to engulf it and turn it back into a tribal trail. Whether it was the war that had interrupted the woodcutters' work or the Dega who brought a halt to it, the road was reverting back to the wild. For the remote hill tribe, the difficulty the route presented for those trying to navigate it was the proverbial *unwelcome mat* and *No Trespasser's Allowed* sign.

The convoy drove slowly on in a low gear roll, with the vehicles jostling and swaying on the uneven dirt road like agitated, over-burdened pack mules eager to pick up the pace.

When the Ranger's fortified Deuce-and-a-half bounced over a thick tree root that had pushed up into the roadway Lieutenant Plantagenet was thinking that the ride and the big truck reminded him of Conrad's steam boat in the book, *Heart of Darkness*. The novel had been required reading in his Freshman year English Lit course in college. There was much in common on this ride as with Conrad's tale, only any pop quiz here could kill you.

"*The nightmare of my choice*," he said to himself, or thought he had, while Sergeant Cantu, who was concentrating on keeping the big truck on the road and steering around the potholes, fallen branches, and exposed rocks, overheard him but hadn't quite made out what he'd said.

"Say again, L-T?"

Embarrassed by quoting the line of the novel, at least what he could remember of it, Plantagenet waved it off.

"Naw, nothing. Just a lot of trees and brush choking the road, is all," he said, turning and staring out the open passenger's window and feeling a little uncomfortable with the encroaching surroundings that looked more like a green tunnel than it did a roadway. Thin, sprouting branches scraped and slapped at the sides of the truck and had the Lieutenant leaning away from the window to keep from getting hit. "A lot of places for someone to hide."

"Yes sir, there are. Too many," replied Cantu, emphasizing the last two words.

There was more, but neither one was saying it. As the vehicles rolled along each vehicle in succession would bump and scrape up against branches and brush that pushed out towards the road. The newer and thinner branches and vines would either snap back into place or would break off, fall, and crunch under the tires from the impact of the heavier military vehicles. Combined with the brushes, scrapes, rocking and rolling, the rattling ride brought out some occasional muttered complaints and swearing, as well as some laughter from those in the truck bed. This was a bad Disney ride in another small world after all.

Because those in the truck bed had brought along air mattresses and flak jackets that they folded and used as seat cushions, the ride wasn't as bad or as uncomfortable as it could've been without them. Still, even with the makeshift pads there were more than a few hard bounces and slams that gave it a lousy carnival ride feel. Besides the occasional swearing there was some laughter as well, and for the Lurps on this mission the outcries were unique and sarcastic.

"Jesus Cantu! You drive worse than my drunk Grandmother and she only has one eye!" cried Hernandez from the truck bed after a heavy bounce.

"Yeah well, who do you think taught me to drive and when you get home why don't you ask her how she lost that eye when we were in the backseat doing it? Man, oh man was she limber!"

"She misses you!"

"So does your mama! Now shut up and let me drive!"

It didn't help that the route too wasn't just one long straightaway but a series of turns and bends where the lead vehicle, the Military Police armored car that was snaking its way forward on the eight mile drive, was out of the line of site for a troubling moment or two from the next vehicle that was following. It was out of the line of sight too because of the mandated safety distance between the vehicles in the convoy and that presented another problem.

Convoy distance in combat meant having enough '*safe*' distance between the vehicles so that if there was an ambush or attack, or if a vehicle hit a landmine, then chances were that only one or two vehicles would be taken out and destroyed leaving the others in line time to redeploy and counter attack. It was a good working strategy provided the bad guys weren't spread out in a long ambush, hiding, and biding their time.

The radio call from the Low Bird helicopter broke the commo silence.

"Valhalla-Six, Piebald One-Five. Over."

"Valhalla-Six. Go."

"Be advised, you have a small clearing and stream crossing maybe fifty yards ahead of your lead vehicle. No activity sighted."

"Roger that, One-Five."

"One-Five. Out."

On a paved road, in excellent conditions, the V-100 Cadillac-Gage armored car had a top speed of 62 miles-per-hour, but on the woodcutters trail, on this long neglected back country lane, the armored car barely rolled above ten to fifteen miles per hour. It wasn't a snail's pace, but for rolling convoy speeds, it felt like it. In several spots the heavier vehicle's undercarriages scraped away the already poor ground. Oil pans and drivelines were taking the brunt of the beatings but were still holding up.

The six vehicle convoy was a few hundred yards shy of the meet up location at the road's dead end when the armored car in the lead came to yet, one more brake squealing stop after a slow turn to its left. Facing the idling armored car was a natural clearing spilt nearly in half by a good size, slow flowing stream.

"Valhalla-Six, Pistol-Six. Over," said the MP Major calling back to Captain Robison.

"Valhalla-Six. Go."

"Hold in place. I say again, hold in place. Be advised, I am at the edge of the small clearing that's maybe thirty-by-thirty meters, with a ten to twelve-foot-wide creek cutting across our route of travel. Looks like there are some rocks that have been made into a bridge bed of some kind."

"Is it navigable, Pistol-Six?"

"It ain't the Big Muddy and this Cadillac Duck is supposed to float if the bridge bed gives. Still, I'd like to step out and get a closer look."

"Roger that, Pistol-Six. We'll move up to provide cover support."

Robison had Poplawski steer around Evans' jeep and brought the Ranger jeep up onto the sunlit glade. The First Sergeant pulled up and parked the jeep to the left of the armored car to cover the MP Major while he checked out the creek. The jeep's position also gave Specialist Taras standing up at the mounted machine gun a better field of fire. Between the twin mounted .30 caliber machine guns on the armored car, and the jeep mounted M-60, the two gun mounts could cause a lot of havoc.

Not to be left out or miss what the cause of this latest delay was, Evans had Quan move up to the right of the armored car. Quan, though, wheeled the MP jeep to the far right edge of the clearing and hugged the rainforest. Neither Quan nor Evans were manning the machine gun on the MP jeep.

The Low Bird Scout helicopter made a slow pass over the clearing before checking out more of what lay beyond the clearing.

As the Major opened the twin-hatch doors of the armored Car and climbed out of the *Duck*, he took out his holstered .45 handgun, and walked towards the crude bridge while keeping an eye on the tree line on the other side. With a nod to Sergeant Burke behind the twin .30 caliber machine guns he started forward.

From what the MP Major could see the oblong clearing was a natural wetland gap with a stream that wasn't as much deep as it was muddy and wide. Natural erosion and heavy monsoon flooding had expanded and deepened the creek, and judging by the many animal tracks, slides, and scat along its banks, it also provided a watering hole for the animals and the birds that inhabited the surrounding jungle. The MP Major made out hoof prints from small deer and a few larger cat tracks that had him looking around the clearing one more time for any snarling teeth or low growls. His eyes soon went back to the bridge.

The crude bridge was well-constructed. A series of flat stones and oblong rocks had been carefully placed and set to fashion something of a convincing bridge bed to keep foot traffic and rolling carts from sinking deeper into the mud beneath the stream as they crossed. Seeping into the creek on the far right end of the clearing was a smaller rivulet of surprisingly clear water from a natural spring that flowed into and joined the main current that washed across the rock bed before falling over a few drop off pools and back into a lower stream on the other side. The ground across the bridge ground looked to be firm and stable.

Taking in the creek, the stone bridge, and the status of the trail-like road that fed back into the jungle on the far side, the MP Major nodded to himself and gave another nod at what he could make of what he could see. If the bridge could hold the weight of the seven-ton, armored car, and the two deuce-and-a-halves didn't get mired in the mud, then the much lighter jeeps wouldn't have a problem making it across the water.

The only concern was that over time the steady flow of water that washed over the rocks and stones had also created a three-foot high drop-off into several dark pools just left of the bridge. Beyond that the lower stream disappeared deeper into the jungle. The Major was thinking the drop-off might present a problem. If one of the heavier vehicles in the convoy crossing the bridge drifted too much to the left, its weight and pressure on the stones near that edge of the crude bridge would collapse into the drop-off. The vehicle would fall with it and very likely overturn. Without a Wrecker Truck there would be no way to pull the *Duck* or a truck out of the mess. No, any vehicle crossing would need to keep to the right of the stone-bed bridge, something he would pass along to the others over the radio.

The weathered banks of the stream and the surrounding ground also showed how, in the rainy season, the water level swelled and flooded over the banks and much of the clearing. The heavy downpours during the Monsoon season pushed a heavier current that swept away a number of the supporting rocks from the makeshift bridge, which might explain the drop-off and pool, and the many varied and different sized rocks used to maintain the crossing.

Still, the MP Major was satisfied that the crude bridge would hold. More troubling, perhaps, was that beyond the stream and clearing, the dusty back road narrowed again and disappeared behind another bend to the north east. The bend and turn would temporarily remove the Duck from the line of sight for the vehicle that followed for a few rolling moments.

That could be a problem and he wasn't alone in thinking so. Recognizing the potential problem from the air, the pilot in the small OH-6 Loach observation helicopter dropped the Low Bird down to make a careful pass over the jungle to check out what the armored car couldn't see on the other side of the creek or around the next curve in the dirt roadway.

"Wouldn't mind maybe doing a little recon-by-fire," Sergeant Burke said to his boss, who was returning to the armored car. Burke was eyeing the wall of jungle on the far side of the creek thinking that maybe sending a few short bursts from his twin-machine guns into the brush and trees across the creek might not be a bad idea right about now.

"Might scare the people we're supposed to be meeting," said the Major.

Burke reluctantly nodded. It was a valid point, even if he still was convinced it wouldn't be a prudent move.

"Not far to the meet-up location," added the Ranger Captain who'd climbed out of his jeep to join the Major. The MP Major grunted in agreement.

"Are we moving or what?" Evans bellowed while the Ranger Captain held up a hand signaling for him to hold in place.

"What do you think?" asked Robison, turning his attention to the crude bridge.

"Might fishtail a little, but if we all take it slow it's do-able, provided the vehicles keep to the right on the bridge bed," said the Major.

"I said, ARE WE MOVING OR WHAT?"

It was Mister Evans, again and had the MP Major thinking, *Of course, it was.*

"Just making certain your jeep won't sink or roll over on top of you in the water, Mister Evans," the MP Major said to the civilian as he and the Ranger Company Commander returned to their vehicles.

"I've taken an old Ford pickup through deeper creeks than this!" Evans said, tapping his watch again. "Let's get a move on!"

The Major let the arrogant civilian have the last word because walking over and trying to slap some sense into him might take more than a few good swings, something that at the moment didn't seem like a bad idea.

"Let's roll," the MP Major said to the Ranger Captain.

The Scout helicopter was buzzing the treetops as the MP Major climbed back inside the armored car, and closed the heavy hatch covers.

"We're Good-to-Go," said the Major to his driver.

The armored car's driver revved its engine, shoved it into gear, and began moving toward the stone-bed bridge.

Robison gave the command over the radio to once again move out and the convoy was back in business.

"Keep a good eye on the other side of the clearing," he said over his shoulder to Taras who was up behind the mounted machine gun.

Still in the lead position the armored car rolled further out into the clearing to cross the bridge. As the weight of the heavy vehicle's steel-encased body pushed on its large front tires the big wheels flattened the small dirt bank but found the better grip and traction of the rocks and stones that had been handcrafted in place. The 15,000-plus-pound vehicle crunched and pressed the rocks and stones deeper into the mud-bottom of the stream bed. Any once rock obstructed water in the creek began to flow more freely with a better current through a newly liberated channel.

With a little downshifting and a few spinning wheels kicking up muddied water and several smaller stones, the small tank-looking armored car trudged on. It was almost across the creek bed and clearing when the MP Major called back to the Ranger Captain over the radio.

"Valhalla-Six, Pistol-Six. Over."

"Go Pistol-Six."

"Once we're across the stream we'll set up and hold on the other side of the clearing at the curve until you…"

Only the MP Major didn't finish the radio transmission. Just as the Scout helicopter turned back to a hover over the far tree line for something the Observer seated next to the Pilot spotted something below that he wanted a better look at, a line of green tracer rounds erupted out of the jungle floor, rose up to the small aircraft and tore into one of the helicopter's four rotor blades, and bulb-like fuselage. The incoming machine gun rounds missed the Pilot and the Observer, but tore through the thin metal and hit his machine gunner in the back of the aircraft. The bones in the *Torque's* right forearm were shattered and the arm left bloodied and dangling. His dropped M-60 machine gun was dangling on the bungee cord.

"BREAK-BREAK! TAKING FIRE! TAKING FIRE!" yelled the pilot's over the radio interrupting the MP Major's call. "WE'RE HIT! MY TORQUE'S WOUNDED."

The enemy gunfire that left spiked and splintered holes in the Loach failed to bring down the helicopter thanks to the pilot who pivoted the Volkswagen-sized aircraft out of the direct line of fire even as the wounded *Torque* was back behind the machine gun and returning fire to the ambushers as best he could.

"You going down, One-Five?" This from the gunship.

"NEGATIVE. Negative. I'm…I'm good! I'm good for now!' said the pilot fighting to hold trim and regain altitude. "I'm… I'm gonna try for Loc Ninh. My *Torque's* hit and bleeding bad, Two-Three."

The Low Bird helicopter was moving away from the contact area as the call went out. The small helicopter's Observer managed to drop a red smoke grenade down on what he believed was where the enemy fire originated, but with rounds coming in from several directions he'd need four to five more on the targets only there was no time. The hits the small bird had taken meant it would have to set down soon and with its wounded crew member and damage to the fuselage and rotor blades it could no longer stay on station. If it didn't go down and crash before it reached the base at Loc Ninh, then it would certainly limp its way there.

"Two-Three, One-Five."

"Two-three. Go."

Sweet Sorrow

"HAMMER THOSE SONSABITCHES!" yelled the Loach pilot to the gunship studying his gauges and fighting for the trim as he nursed the damaged bird back toward the Base Camp. Over the radio those on the frequency could hear that a second Pink Team was already being scrambled while a Quick Reaction Force was on stand-by.

The Low Bird helicopter exposed the pending ambush and the premature strike on it gave away the planned enemy attack. The bulk of the convoy was still on the far side of the clearing and not in the kill zone that was the bridge bed. The enemy attackers now had to quickly readjust their strategy.

Across the creek and coming out of the swirling red smoke an NVA soldier stepped out onto the road shouldering a rocket propelled grenade launcher. He was hurrying to line up the sites on the MP's armored car when Sergeant Burke, standing in the open turret of the *Duck* spotted the threat.

"RPG!" he screamed to the others in the V-100 as he dropped down behind the gun sights.

Like an Old West showdown gunfight, the two found themselves facing-off shortly after high noon. Burke let loose with the twin .30 caliber machine guns a split second after the enemy soldier fired the rocket. The NVA soldier, though, had rushed his shot. As the machine gun rounds bowled him over the rocket driven, shape-charged warhead swooshed off-target towards the armored car but was a little too high to hit it. The explosive projectile flew over Burke's head and missed the American by inches before the warhead slammed into the jungle ten yards behind the vehicle in a violent impact and explosion.

The blast sent splintered wood, bark, leaves, and shrapnel flying and left one of the big trees smoking. The rocket propelled grenade round was quickly followed by enemy machine gun and small arms fire from the tree line across the creek. The convoy column had driven into an ambush.

Not waiting for a second RPG to come flying at them, the armored car's driver quickly stepped on the gas pedal, downshifted to second gear, and cranked the large steering wheel hard to the right hoping to steer away from the heavy incoming fire that was now coming at the *Duck*. Incoming machine gun and small arms fire pinged and jackhammered against the armored car even as Burke was turning the twin guns on the ambush line. The ambushers, though, had planned for such an evasive move, and the armored car's right tire rolled onto a well-placed Soviet anti-tank landmine just over the bridge bed that had been planted to the right side of the road.

The buried anti-tank mine that could devastate a forty-four ton tank ripped away the armored car's large right front wheel and hub and blew it high into the air and sent the rest of the eighteen-foot long, armored car tumbling end over end in the massive explosion. Like a tarpon on a taut fishing line the *Duck* danced on the clearing before it slammed back down upside down and back across the creek.

Its intact front left wheel was left spinning in place, while the right front tire and hub that had been wrenched and ripped from its axle bounced several times before it finally settled into the drop-off pool next to the bridge bed with a loud *whump* and breaking wave of water.

Sergeant Burke had been blown out of the open turret in the explosion and he too, was sent awkwardly flying before slamming down onto the rock bed bridge. The impact on his left side cracked and broke bones on the uneven sized stones and rocks. The few inches of water flowing over the crude bridge hadn't lessened the body slam and left Burke on his back groaning and sucking for precious air.

He'd hit the rock bridge seconds before the badly damaged armored car he'd been tossed out of came down and banged into the ground five feet in front of him. The *Duck* hit and tumbled end over end barely missing him before it finally came to a stop up[side down ten yards away. With it out of the fight, both sides now continued shooting at each other.

His left shoulder was painfully broken or in the very least badly dislocated, and the arm was mostly unresponsive. A sharp pain in his left knee where his jungle fatigue pants had ripped and scraped told him he might've torn some cartilage there too. He was bleeding from a deep cut over his left eye and the heavy flow probably accounted for why no more gunfire was coming at him. He looked dead, so for the moment, he wisely played dead.

With the firefight raging and exposed in the open as he was, he knew he needed to find cover and soon before anything more serious and uglier could happen. It wouldn't take long before the ambushers saw that he was still alive and turned their aim back on him to finish the job. At less than twenty yards from the enemy ambush line he would be an easy target. Too easy.

Without turning his head, he saw that the closest thing to him that looked like it might offer any kind of protective cover was the tire and the heavy steel rim and hub that had ploughed into the drop-off pool. It wasn't much protection, but the large heavy-duty tire and steel hub in the small drop-off was better than where he was at, and it was only a few feet away. All he had to do was summon up the courage to make the attempt, and any attempt would bring on enemy gunfire.

He was left with no choice other than the obvious one. Suppressive fire was coming from the Ranger jeep with Taras up on the machine gun raking the ambush line and momentarily sending enemy heads down, slowing the rate of incoming rounds. That return fire was all that Burke needed to know it was time to move.

Rolling over on his stomach the MP sergeant got up on all fours and scrambled across the rocks and muddied water as best he could, and leapt into the small pool and landed upside down behind the cover of the large wheel. On his butt with his feet propped up and with only one good arm he was pulling in his legs and struggling as a line of incoming enemy machine gun rounds followed his route and pounded into the large wheel and hub. The torn wheel took the bulk of the hits and the bullets only thumped into the thick rubber or ricocheted off of the splintered steel and rubber wheel. Burke knew the tires on the armored car were designed to take assault rifle fire and keep rolling for another forty miles. At least, that's what he had been told. That claim now, though, was sorely being tested as was any notion of cover and actual safety. Three or four rounds missed the MP sergeant while one better aimed bullet tore into the exposed toe of his left boot just as he was trying to pull the foot in.

"NO, NO, no, nooooooo!" he cried, staring at the gaping hole in the top of his left jungle boot where his big toe should have been.

With bullets bouncing off of the torn wheel hub all around him all he could do was helplessly watch as the leather scrap of the jungle boot and the severed toe inside it tumbled and bounced on the edge of the stone bridge. The bloodied scrap briefly got hung up on a sharp-edged stone, pivoted and turned in the current, and sent the bloodied toe bobbing along in the muddied current before it reached a second drop-off and a deeper pool a few yards beyond him. The now naked toe plopped into the swirling pool below, bounced once and disappeared only to resurface seconds later. It drifted a little further on with the current, and then violently disappeared as something rose from the murky depths, thrashed wildly at the surface, and then took it underwater. And that had Burke wondering what was in the pool of water he was in.

Those thoughts gave way to a larger fear as a new round of assault rifle fire edged closer to his cover. *They're coming at me from another angle,* he thought as the incoming rounds began slamming into the other side of the heavy tire.

With the enemy soldiers knowing he was still alive and determined to take him out, he pulled himself into a tight fetal position, and that sent a shock of blinding pain through his core as he shifted his body weight. Worse still, there was screaming pain in his foot from the missing toe which made it feel as though he was stubbing it against the corner of a desk over and over and over again like a bad Ground Hog Day with no let up.

Shifting his body again to try to keep his head and torso behind the wheel, another ambusher with a better line of sight on his left sent more AK-47 gunfire coming his way which only pissed him off even more.

"YOU BASTARDS!" he yelled, remembering his .45 automatic pistol on his right hip, he drew it out of the holster and emptied the eight round magazine in the direction of the enemy shooter. The shots went low and wide, kicking up dirt and rock a few yards in front of him. Quickly replacing it with another magazine he fired off three more rounds, this time a little higher. The pistol fire sent the ambusher that had targeted him hugging the ground and provided a brief, momentary sense of relief to the MP sergeant.

The incoming fire quickly shifted from the American behind the broken wheel to the lead jeep in the open as the ambushers homed in on the new target. The rounds, though, were hitting low into the steel plates covering the jeep's radiator and wheels while the following rounds tore into protective sandbags that had been placed on the jeep's flat hood. The protective sandbags that covered a third of the windshield were now taking the brunt of the fire. While they missed the three Americans in the jeep, the impact from the incoming rounds shoved and shifted the sandbags away from the passenger's side with some sliding across and off of the hood. Realizing his mistake, the enemy machine gunner would adjust his aim once he changed out the drum magazine on the RPD Soviet machine gun in the entrenched position.

The silence from the gun position told Poplawski what was coming next. Ducking down low behind the steering wheel and what he hoped was the engine block, he leaned over and shoved his Captain out of the jeep. Robison was sent unceremoniously falling and toppling out of the passenger's seat just as a burst of machine gun fire tore through the glass windshield and ripped into the seat where the Ranger Company Commander had been sitting. Besides the several bullet holes the canvas seat covering was peppered with shards of glass from the shattered windshield.

"JUMP!" Poplawski yelled over his shoulder to Taras as the First Sergeant looked for a way to crawl out of the driver's seat without getting hit by more enemy small arms fire.

Taras, though, didn't jump. Instead, the five-foot-eight, skinny teenager remained standing in the back of the jeep behind the mounted M-60 machine gun returning the fire with ballsy intensity and the kind of grit that belied his strength and size. Taras wouldn't be anyone's first, or even second visual pick to represent an elite fighting Ranger on a recruiting poster, but he led the way in this fight still standing, shaking in his boots, and working the machine gun back and forth across the line of ambushers' positions in textbook fashion. That gave Poplawski the much needed time to deal with his own little dilemma.

If he tried to exit from the driver's side of the jeep then he'd get shot more than a few times by the incoming rounds that were still raking the steel plates on the jeep. For some reason the ambushers were firing low which told him they were in a trench line or spider hole fighting positions. Soon, they would adjust their fire with better aim.

The passenger side was his only option, but the jeep's floor stick shift was in the way blocking him. That the sandbags were being violently shoved out of the way from the impact of the incoming enemy gunfire told him he'd have to raise himself up if he was going to try climbing out behind his Captain.

"Fuck it!" he said to himself and squeezed around the gearshift lever as low as he could go. His head and upper body were over the side of the jeep, but his butt and thighs had risen up to target level when he was suddenly kicked the rest of the way out of the jeep by the 18-year-old Ranger behind the mounted machine gun.

"GO!" yelled Specialist Taras, leaning over and kicking him again to get the push he needed to get the First Sergeant over the protective steel plates. "GO!"

Taras was still yelling as a burst from an AK-47 raked across the damaged windshield and hit both the driver's and passenger's seat. The incoming rounds just missed Taras who kept up his rate of return fire.

More incoming enemy fire pinged and hit what was left of the windshield glass and sent splintered shards that hit Taras legs and thighs like a flight of darts. The young Lurp, though, gritted his teeth, screamed like a Banshee, and then silenced the shooter with better aim.

From where he was upside down and trying to right himself with the help of Captain Robison, who was also safely down behind the jeep and firing at the ambushers, Poplawski stared up in wonder at the teenage soldier manning the machine gun. Even Robison, who was crouching beside his First Sergeant changing out magazines on his M-16, couldn't believe what he was seeing.

Other enemy shooters were still trying to knock Taras out of the fight, only they couldn't get the right bead on him since the young soldier kept traversing the machine gun fire across the jungle beyond the creek bed with better targeted, short, sustained, six-round bursts. Brass was flying from the hundreds of expended 7.62mm rounds from the can of 1,000 rounds at his feet and the sustained fire was forcing the ambushers to drop back down to cover.

Taras was firing the short, six-round bursts to keep from burning out the machine gun barrel, but even then the tempered steel was heating up under the sustained fire and beginning to glow a dull orange. The short bursts would keep the barrel from warping and that had Poplawski who was firing from behind the jeep's engine block thinking the kid was playing the light machine gun like Keith Moon banging away hard on a snare drum.

With the ambushers concentrating on the lesser protected jeep, they didn't immediately take notice that the front of a large truck had just pulled into the clearing to join the fight. The enemy officer commanding the ambush hadn't counted on the amount of return fire power coming from the big truck. An American behind a 50.cal, heavy machine gun began brutalizing the hidden ambush positions as did the additional M-60 machine guns from the bed of the vehicle. It was now no longer a one-sided fight. It was now just chaos and mayhem.

The ambush was a bust because it was sprung before the bulk of the convoy had entered the kill zone. Several of the enemy soldiers literally had jumped the gun when the Low Bird helicopter spotted some suspicious movement below and threatened to give them away. But once they fired on the helicopter, the enemy commander had no choice but to give the order to the others in hiding to open fire, only now with the heavy return fire coming from the convoy, the fight had turned into a pound-for-pound slug fest.

Lieutenant Plantagenet and Sergeant Cantu were quickly out of the big truck's cab and down behind the engine block and front wheels. The two began covering the right flank of the column where Evans and Quan were out of their jeep and crouching behind the vehicle. Evans was firing his pistol blindly into the trees nearest him while Quan, wisely, held his fire, not wanting to draw fire.

The bulk of the well-armed Rangers in the truck bed were up and firing over the steel panels with everything they'd brought to the proverbial party. Sergeant Daley began dumping M-79 grenade rounds on the ambushers as the others in the truck bed punished the enemy line. The NVA soldiers, though, remained dogged in their attack even under the suppressing return fire. They were dug in and determined.

When enemy fire began coming in from their left flank, Staff Sergeant Shintaku leapt out of the Deuce-and-a-half along with Sanchez and *Ironic* Green to shore up the line.

The .50 caliber machine gun atop the Deuce-and-a-half was battering the hidden enemy positions in the jungle across the stream bed sending bark, shattered leaves, and branches, along with torn trees and very likely human limbs and body parts, flying. A .50 caliber heavy machine gun round hit you like a copper-tipped line drive baseball and tore away arms, legs, necks, and heads with fist sized holes. If you didn't die right away, the heavy blood loss that followed would count your life down in a matter of seconds. Here it didn't take three strikes to be out of the game.

On the *Ma Deuce* Hernandez quickly silenced the enemy RPD light machine gun with its two-man crew leaving them either dead, badly wounded, or hurriedly retreating. Once the heavy machine gun had found its aim, there would be no choice but to move or stay in place and die. A second two-man RPD machine gun was now carrying the ambush further on the left, but Hernandez wasn't in position enough to stop it. He didn't have the angle.

Crouched down behind the Deuce-and-a-half Sergeant Shintaku popped the end caps off of the M-72 shoulder-fired rocket launcher, extended the tube, and made it ready to fire. Stepping out from behind the bed of the truck, he dropped the end caps and sling, pulled back on the arming mechanism, sighted down the flip-up site, and aligned it on his chosen target. He pressed down on the rubber-covered trigger and sent the missile whooshing towards a second enemy machine gun emplacement. The one-shot-and-toss mini-bazooka round roared across the clearing and creek at over 400 feet-per-second and exploded on target. There was a brief flash of fire in the loud explosion followed by a dirty geyser of dirt, leaves, and body parts rising and hurriedly falling back on the fighting position. It also took out the base of a big tree that once protected the ambushers. The blast was followed by a loud crack as the big tree started to fall only to be propped but leaning at an unnatural angle by the many vines and thick branches of nearby trees. The M-72 LAW did its job, and that part of the ambush line went still for a brief moment. When the firing continued it was only from an individual shooter a few yards away to the right.

Shintaku had a second Light Anti-Tank Weapon in its carrying tube slung over his shoulder, but instead of employing it, he scooped up his M-16 and looked to see where he could do the most good with his small arms return fire. The targets were plentiful and didn't merit the M-72. At least, not yet. That one he'd save for whatever big gun came next.

The heavy battering from the .50 cal, Taras's machine gun fire, the two machine guns on the gun truck, and the shoulder-fired rocket temporarily quieted the bulk of the enemy's ambush line. However, it didn't end the fight. The firefight wasn't over. The attack just shifted. From the back of the convoy column and well away from the lead vehicles a squad of NVA soldiers were firing on the MP jeep and the second Deuce-and-a-half. The ambushers were trying to block in and choke the convoy column.

"LIEUTENANT PLANTAGENET!"

"Sir!"

"Set up a tight perimeter and send some people back to shore up our six!"

"Yes sir! On it!" said Plantagenet. "SERGEANT DALEY!" called Lieutenant Plantagenet, coming around to the bed of the big truck. Daley scurried over to the Lieutenant holding M-79 grenade launchers and a Claymore bag filled with gold-tipped high explosive rounds.

"Sir!"

"Take Wexler and go back and help the MP gun jeep!"

"Roger that, L-T!"

"Here, take this!" said Shintaku, handing the light anti-tank weapon to the forever Army Private.

Wexler took the shoulder-fired rocket tube, slung it over his right shoulder as he and Daley ran back towards the rear of the column. The LAW and the grenade launcher would bring some serious deterrent to the NVA's game plan.

"Sergeant Shintaku!" yelled the Lieutenant, "you got the left flank! Cantu and I will cover the right. Give me another man!"

"Roger that, L-T," said the Staff Sergeant nodding at the Lieutenant and Sergeant Cantu. Incoming rounds followed the dash, but none found their target.

"SANCHEZ! ANGELES! GREEN! ON ME!" Shintaku yelled for the three Lurps to jump down from the truck bed. "Angeles you're with the L-T. You two, follow me."

The chess move firefight was shifting with a hurried change of strategy, and the enemy movement through the trees caught the Staff Sergeant's attention and he moved to counter it.

"ON THE LEFT! ON THE LEFT! FIRE! FIRE! Shintaku ordered, pointing where he wanted them to fire. The three took on a squad of ambushers that were trying to flank the convoy and were about to cross the stream. The thick jungle had slowed their run, and the three Rangers took out the two NVA soldiers in the lead, wounded a third, and sent the rest falling back the way they had come and deeper back into the rainforest.

Turning back towards the ambush site Shintaku could see the attackers were still targeting the Ranger jeep. His Commanding Officer and First Sergeant were down and firing from both sides of the exposed jeep and Taras was still up behind the post-mounted machine gun, but staggering from one of the incoming AK-47 rounds that grazed his head. Blood was spilling down his head and right ear as he removed the machine gun from its mount and dropped down behind the jeep. Seeing what was happening, Shintaku knew what he needed to do.

"Sanchez? You and Green hold here and make sure they don't flank us," he said to the two nervous-looking Privates. Green was the Cherry Lurp, the FNG, but Sanchez, at least, had some combat time.

"YOU CAN DO IT! YOU'RE A FIRE TEAM! YOU GOT THIS!"

With his eyes locked on the two dead enemy soldiers, Sanchez gave a chin up nod while a nervous Green, looking to Sanchez, followed the bravado lead.

"You got this!" Shintaku said again, reassuring them in a calmer voice before he raced over to the Company Commander's jeep to bulk up their fighting position. "You got this!"

The extra weapons and doggedness had the Rangers exacting a terrible toll on the attackers. The NVA had lost any advantage they once held, and their rate of fire was now limited to a diminishing platoon of assault rifles. When two enemy soldiers tried to rush out and retrieve the dropped RPG, Hernandez turned the .50 cal on them. He missed the enemy soldiers that quickly dodged back behind cover but realizing what they were after, turned his aim on the exposed weapon. The heavy rounds blew away the wooden covering protecting the barrel and severed both the hand grip and trigger grip and sent it broken with the pieces flying high into the air.

"IT'S A PAPERWEIGHT NOW, *CABRON*!" yelled the Floridian.

The enemy soldiers kept up the fight, but the bulk of the heavier fighting was shifting to the left flank as the NVA changed the angle of their attack.

Down behind his jeep Captain Robison quickly grabbed the handset of the radio that was in the jeep to direct the aerial artillery.

"Piebald Two-Three, Valhalla-Six. Over."

"Go, Valhalla."

"I need you to hit the tree line just west of our location. I'll toss a smoke!' Robison said to the gun ship pilot as he retrieved a smoke grenade and lobbed it on the other side of the creek. The hissing grenade hit the hard pack and flipped end over end before rolling to a stop just before the thin brush of the jungle wall.

The smoke grenade sent a billowing cloud of blood red smoke rose skyward in tumbling, rolling waves.

"I identify cherry."

"Roger that, Piebald. Do your thing."

"Be advised, you are DANGER CLOSE," cautioned the gunship pilot lining up for a run.

"So are the bastards shooting at us. We're good. Take them out!"

"Your call, Valhalla. Coming in hot with the minigun. Keep your heads down."

Robison turned and yelled at the others behind him in the convoy.

"EVERYBODY DOWN! KEEP YOUR HEADS DOWN! THE GUNSHIP IS ROLLING IN HOT!"

High in the sky the attack helicopter went nose up in its attitude, rolled hard to the left until it was almost upside down, and then swooped nose down in a high angle dive. The mechanical bird of prey was locked on its target. As green tracers from several enemy machine guns rose to try to shoot down the fast moving gunship, the Cobra's front seat gunner fired a number of rockets from the aircraft's twin pods. The rockets slammed into the tree line in staggered hits. Closer to the target the gunner sent thousands of rounds from the aircraft's six-barreled, electrically driven, rotating machine minigun on the wall of jungle.

The attackers' flanking maneuver stalled and broke as the jungle erupted in violent explosions and mini gun fire producing a swirling squall of vegetation like that section of the rainforest had all been caught in a giant blender on steroids. The main line of the ambush and now the last desperate flanking attack failed, but those who'd survived were back up and still stubbornly sending small arms fire toward the Americans. The ambushers were tenacious, but foolish by remaining in place where they were.

The rocket fire that hit the section of the forest to the southwest of the glade ignited a fire in the bone dry brush and grass. The brush fire soon spiraled high into a nearby tree with its vines and branches hissing and crackling as the flames grew and quickly spread into the trees next to it. The rainforest, despite its name, was catching fire and burning, and would soon become a growing wildfire. One saving grace was that a breeze out of the southeast pushed the fire to the southwest and away from the clearing and more thankfully, away from the convoy.

The ferocity of the gunship run, and the growing forest fire brought a longer momentary lull in the fighting and in the awkward calm that followed the painful cries and moans from the two MPs trapped and injured inside the armored car were now loud enough to be heard by those few vehicles nearest to the wreckage.

The landmine that sent the armored car tumbling also had the MP Major and the driver both tumbling inside the damaged vehicle slamming into hard steel edges, exposed levers, and knobs before it finally came to rest. The *Duck* was on its side and leaking fuel. The injured MPs inside it would need to find a way out of the vehicle before the fuel tank exploded.

Enemy fire was now coming from the left center of the far tree line of the clearing as the NVA shifted their angle of attack and stubbornly went at the convoy again.

"Two-Three, Two-Three! Can I get you to do a run on the November Victor Alpha positions fifty yards ahead of the armored car?"

"Roger that, Valhalla. Setting up for a *chunker* run. Take cover."

"EVERYONE STAY DOWN!" yelled the Ranger Captain. "GET DOWN!"

High in the sky the Cobra gunship had started its rolling turn to lineup for the second gun run this time with the *chunker*, the automatic grenade launcher.

Evans and Quan were still down behind their jeep, heads bobbing up and down for a peek at the situation as the fight had unfolded. They weren't about to leave their precious crates, and since they hadn't offered any return fire they weren't being targeted, Quan leapt into action. Jumping back into the jeep behind the steering wheel he cranked up the engine.

"WE GO! COME! "WE GO! NOW!" Quan yelled at the somewhat confused Evans who wasn't about to get up behind the mounted machine gun. "WE CHARGE THE AMBUSH! ONLY WAY TO SURVIVE! WE GO!"

Although charging an ambush was the approved tactical way to break an ambush, Evans wasn't so sure that charging it was the best course of action either. Quan, though, was adamant, so Evans reluctantly jumped into the passenger's seat as the former French Legionnaire popped the clutch, shoved the jeep into gear, and floored the gas pedal. The jeep lurched forward with its tires spinning and spitting back dirt and loose rocks as it sped away.

"HALT! WHERE ARE YOU GOING! STOP!" yelled Captain Robison jumping to his feet, frantically waving them back as a new round of enemy fire came at the vehicles remaining in the open. Incoming small arms fire ricocheted off of the jeep with loud pings and whistling grazes.

Robison dropped back down behind cover of the jeep's engine block and watched as the speeding MP jeep swerved around the damaged armored car and raced on toward the rock bridge. The jeep roared by the wounded MP who was in the drop off pool down behind the broken wheel, sped over to the rock bridge bed and kept going. Enemy gunfire was coming at the jeep, but none seemed to find their mark.

When a panicked Evans tried to reach across and grab at the steering wheel and steer the jeep away from the enemy fire, Quan angrily slapped his hand away. And then as the frightened civilian tried grabbing at the steering wheel a second time, Quan pulled out his .45 pistol and thumped it against the side of Evans head as he concentrated on the evasive moves. This was no time for panic.

Just before the jeep disappeared around the dogleg bend on the far side of the creek bed, Quan was wildly firing his pistol into the surrounding jungle. But if he was actually hitting anything then it was certainly by accident. With Quan racing through the gears the jeep was out of the kill zone and soon out of sight. The enemy fire that seemed to be following the advancing jeep stopped as the jeep raced on free of gunfire. With Quan and Evans out of the kill zone and well beyond it the ambushers shifted their small arms fire back toward the convoy vehicles.

"PIEBALD TWO-THREE! HOLD YOUR FIRE," yelled Robison into the radio's handset to the approaching gunship. "I SAY AGAIN, HOLD YOUR FIRE!"

"Roger Valhalla, Piebald Two-Three making a pass."

The Cobra Attack helicopter that was already coming in fast and low with its nose down, pulled pitch and veered away hurriedly gaining altitude. The noise alone from the gunship was enough to have what was left of the ambush line turn its fire on the gunship. A line of green tracers rose in the sky but once again failed to bring down the aircraft, as did an enemy rocket propelled grenade that rose up from the jungle and arched much too late to hit the speeding helicopter. The relieved Cobra pilot also noticed something more coming at him on the run that brought on a nervous laughter over the radio airway. While fortune favors the bold and sometimes the bold are just very, very lucky.

"Fuckin-A, B and C! Did they just assault the ambush?" said First Sergeant Poplawski, unsure of what they had all just witnessed.

"Quan, maybe," said the Ranger Captain, a little unsure what to make of it. "Evans looked like he was panicking."

The incoming enemy fire had lessened considerably but there was enough to still show that the firefight was far from over.

Chapter 24

The plan was to ambush and destroy a number of the convoy vehicles *after* those in the lead crossed the creek and were in the open. A flanking force would simultaneously hit the American column from the left side in a classic L-shaped ambush. As this was happening a blocking force at the rear of the column would trap the remaining vehicles in place, and together they would overrun and take out any who had managed to survive the initial attack.

It was all to begin in the Kill Zone on a designated signal, only it didn't play out that way. The enemy commander had been forced to quickly rethink his strategy and tactics and adapt to the situation in play. He had only taken out the armored car but nothing more. The flanking maneuver had failed too, and reluctantly realizing that holding the ambush line was proving far too costly, the NVA officer angrily yelled out a new command.

From the slowing rate of small arms fire that was coming at the convoy in shifting patterns, Robison knew the bulk of the enemy soldiers were falling back. To cover the retreat, the NVA commander left a handful of fighters, either too wounded to move, or too hardcore and determined to fight on to buy the others time to escape. He also knew that they were cutting their losses and wisely choosing their next battle.

The enemy Commander hadn't counted on the small, low-flying Scout helicopter they'd nicknamed, *the flying egg,* spotting his people as they were lying in wait, nor had he imagined the overwhelming fire from the big truck that had effectively taken out much of his line, crippled the attack, and had almost killed him. The only thing that saved him in the trench line when the gunship swooped in with its rockets and Gatling-gun-like minigun fire was him leaning into the front wall of the trench and hugging the dirt wall. The rockets that exploded in the trees and ground around him sent splintered shrapnel and broken branches flying into their fighting positions while the thousands of automatic machine gun rounds from the gunship's minigun left the surrounding jungle foliage looking like a sieve. He was lucky in that it was only a piece of shrapnel that had sliced across his left tricep that left the muscle torn and bleeding, but left him alive and pissing mad.

He had anticipated the helicopter attacks and some return fire from the convoy column, just not the heavy amount of it the Americans were throwing at him from their heavily modified gun truck and that damn jeep.

The perfect trap is always perfect until it isn't.

The Rangers kept up their blistering fire on those few ambushers that remained in their dug-in fighting positions, but it was quickly turning into a one-sided fight. The Americans now had the upper hand.

Sweet Sorrow

"COVER ME!" yelled Shintaku as he raced out from behind their protective cover of the gun truck toward the badly wounded MP sergeant huddled up behind the broken wheel and torn hub in the creek bed.

Shintaku wasn't alone in a rescue attempt as Cantu took off in a broken field run toward those trapped in the overturned armored car.

"GIVE THEM SOME COVER FIRE!" yelled Captain Robison firing his rifle as the Rangers lit up the ambush line spraying the jungle to their left and right flanks with continuous fire to better protect the two rescuers.

Any enemy fire coming at the convoy now was hurried and forced, and the shooters tried and failed to hit either of the two Rangers as they charged forward, the bullets that came at them only danced and kicked up water, dirt, and debris but missed them completely. The incoming enemy gunfire was hurried and forced because it drew better aimed return fire from the Ranger's heavy machine guns, grenade launcher, and assault rifles. Newton never took in combat in his third law of motion. There was no equal and opposite reaction here. The Rangers were hitting the ambush line with overwhelming firepower and that bought time for the rescuers.

Shintaku reached the wounded MP and dropped down behind the now semi-cover of the big wheel that wasn't quite big enough for two people. It was a dance to keep exposed parts of his body out of the line of fire.

"I got you! I got you!" Shintaku said, quickly assessing the MP gunner's wounds and injuries as best he could for what he knew was coming next. "Where you hit? Can you move?"

"Broken shoulder and arm, maybe. They shot off one of my big toes," Burke said, nodding toward his boots and the missing part of one boot that was still spilling blood. "But let me tell you, man, I'll be happy to move and if the bastards don't shoot me again I'll damn near skip!" laughed the MP sergeant. Despite his injuries, and with the battle turning his spirits were high. It was bravado, and it needed to be.

With the Ranger Sergeant helping Burke to his feet, readying to run, Shintaku signaled to the Ranger Captain that he was ready to bring back the wounded MP in a mad dash.

"POUR IT ON! GET ME SOME SUPPRESSING FIRE ON THAT TREE LINE!" yelled the Captain to those in the gun truck. "KEEP FIRING! KEEP IT GOING!"

The return fire was there again, keeping those handful of hardcore enemy soldiers down behind cover, but it wasn't much of a dash for Shintaku and the wounded MP, let alone an all-out run. The two were moving like entrants in a bad three-legged sack race, but were soon assisted by Doc Moore and the First Sergeant, who ran out and took over the burden until they were all safely behind the cover of the big truck.

The cover fire had also bought Sergeant Cantu some time. He was now safely behind the upside down *Duck.* Safety in combat was never a sure thing. At the back hatches of the damaged armored car, he was greeted by a harsh smell of leaking fuel. Worse still, the petrol was pooling beneath the wreckage and spreading to within a foot from where he was crouching.

"Okay then," he muttered to himself, knowing he would need to be careful. One spark and the armored car and those in it, and maybe he as well, would go up in flames. It didn't help that the incoming fire, even as little as it was, was plinking and ricocheting bullet rounds off of the vehicle and although they were missing the American they were sending sparks flying. Worse still, Cantu could hear the spitting and hissing sparks from the torn and frayed wires inside the V-100 and got a whiff of melting plastic. Wires were shorting out.

Any of the flitting sparks could ignite it all in an ugly inferno at any moment. His adrenalin was racing, and his heart was already pounding from the run to the *Duck* and the incoming rounds that were bouncing off of the wreck and the sparks from the exposed wires amped up both to eleven when ten was the high mark. Return fire from Hernandez's .50 cal sent the two latest shooters back down, either wounded, dead, or down and hiding and rethinking their courage in the fighting positions they were holding. Bullets the size of baseballs tended to do that. He'd bear hug the Cubano if he made it safely back to the Deuce-and-a-half.

Taking in a few deep breaths to steady himself, the veteran Lurp hurriedly went to work. When the armored car drove over the landmine, the explosion sent the V-100 tumbling end-over-end before it came to rest upside down. In the bouncing roll the two sections that formed the back hatch of the vehicle were badly bent and skewed. The hinges to the upper portion of the hatch cover were wrenched and twisted. When the Ranger Sergeant tugged at the upper hatch trying to open it to get to MPs trapped inside, there was no give.

"Come on! Come on!" he said, blowing air through his teeth as he tried the lower hatch cover.

The heavy metal access door creaked, groaned, and only opened six to seven inches before it stopped. Cantu tried again but something was keeping it from opening all the way, which only told him he needed to pull harder.

Standing that couldn't happen but if he was seated on the ground he could maybe plant his boots against the vehicle's heavy frame, and use his leg and back muscles with the strength he had in his arms. It was worth a try. Sitting down he scooted his butt closer to the hatch and planted his boots on both sides of it. With a guttural grunt he tried opening the bottom hatch a second time. The steel door screeched metal-on-metal defiance before it finally gave a little bit more and left him with just enough room for him to crawl inside. Without a winch or several crowbars it wouldn't move any further.

"It's enough! It'll do!" he said to himself as he rolled onto his stomach and got his first good look inside the darkened vehicle.

The MP Major and the vehicle driver were both like tossed ragdolls. They were barely splayed out on the roof and now floor of the armored car. The two were semi-conscious and moaning. In the explosion and tumbling rollover, they were turned into human pinballs slamming against and bouncing off of the steel interior as ammo cans and a bent fire extinguisher flew at them like blunt missiles.

The MP Major who was closest to Cantu was bleeding from a deep cut to his forehead and looking more than a little dazed from an obvious concussion. Blood was dripping down his forehead, over his left eye, and spilled down his cheek and chin. His left arm was resting at an unnatural angle and the splintered bone that had pushed out just below his elbow looked like a bloodied icicle. In the deeper shadows, in a heap behind the Major with one boot stuck in the floor pedals that had the leg hanging, the vehicle driver wasn't looking all that much better. Both legs were twisted at painful angles and there were burns on his hands and face from the explosion. Broken bones, ugly cuts and burns, moans, and groans, aside, they were alive. Extracting them through the tight opening, though, wasn't going to be a cake walk. It was going to hurt.

"Major! You're gonna be okay," Cantu said to the officer trying to get his attention. "We got'cha! We'll get you out of here."

There was no '*we.*' It was just him for the moment, but others, he knew, would be coming to help. Those in the armored car wouldn't be left behind. It's not what Rangers did. It wasn't part of the creed they'd learned in their training, nor part of Cantu's own personal creed either. Even if it wasn't always possible, he and the others from Romeo Company knew they would damn well try.

Squeezing through the small opening to reach the Major, Cantu hoped he wouldn't put any more serious hurt on the officer by pulling him out of the damaged vehicle. But weighing the very real possibility of what worse could happen if the vehicle suddenly erupted in a fiery, swirling fury, he made the judgement call.

"Sir! Gimme your good hand!" he said to the officer who didn't seem to comprehend what the Ranger sergeant was saying. "Sir? Look at me! Look at me! Gimme your good hand! Your good hand!"

Finding some momentary clarity, the Major tried reaching out but was still a few inches away from the offered hand. He couldn't lift his left arm to move closer and he was struggling with his right. A lightening-like strike to a series of nerves sent a bolt of eye-closing, pain shooting through him, and had him feeling as though he was going to vomit.

"I…I think my left arm is broken," said the Major, unaware that the bone was sticking through his sleeve.

"No problem, Sir," said Cantu, scooting in a little further, grabbing the Major's right wrist, and then prying the Major up beneath the armpits.

"My...my pistol!" cried the Major.

Cantu looked around for the .45 Automatic and handed it to the MP officer.

"Okay, on three," he said to the Major who gave a hesitant nod.

Cantu began the count down and on three pulled and dragged the officer toward the opening only to find Doc Moore and the First Sergeant crouched down behind the pried open hatch, waiting to help. Although Cantu was happy to see them, he was also worried as well with good reason.

"Top, you two need to move away from here. The vehicle's leaking fuel. It could go up any minute."

"We know," said Poplawski.

"I'm going back in for the driver."

Before the First Sergeant or Medic could protest the young sergeant was already crawling back into the wreckage.

Poplawski and Doc Moore lifted the badly injured MP officer up under their arms and turned back towards the rest of the convoy as the Ranger Company Commander shouted out an order. There was still intermittent incoming fire coming at the convoy.

"I WANT COVER FIRE ON THE AMBUSH LINE," ordered Captain Robison. "DO IT NOW! HIT IT!"

The Rangers unleashed a torrent of fire from every weapon seemingly at their disposal allowing Doc Moore, with the help of the First Sergeant, to shoulder the MP Major safely back behind the cover of the two-and-a-half-ton truck.

As the cover fire was tearing up the far tree line to give the First Sergeant and Doc Moore time to get back to the Ranger's gun truck, Cantu was scurrying back inside the armored car to bring out the driver. This, though, was going to take a little doing since the driver was still half in the driver's seat and partially hanging upside down. His left arm and the left side of his neck and face were burned in the explosion and his left wrist was flopped over and unusable. Cantu, though, was more jarred when he saw that the driver's left pant leg was torn and there was a dark hole where the kneecap should have been.

"Oh, sweet Jesus," he muttered as he looked around and then found the severed bloodied patella in a lump stuck to the vehicle's dashboard. The Ranger grabbed the bloody lump and shoved it in his cargo pants pocket. Crouching to get the leverage to free him he reached under the man's armpits and pulled the injured man free. As Cantu lifted and pulled the driver cried out in pain, but it couldn't be helped.

"You're okay! You're okay!" said Cantu, easing the MP back and back towards the open hatch cover. The heat of day had the inside of the armored car feeling like an oven and the Ranger was dripping sweat. "I got'cha. I got'cha."

Sweet Sorrow

First Sergeant Poplawski was already back at the armored car by the time Cantu was backing out of the lower hatch and hauling out the injured driver. The cover fire had ceased and there was a momentary lull as the firefight became a deadly waiting game of whack-a-mole when the next and latest target on either side popped up.

"Thought you could use a hand," said the First Sergeant.

Cantu nodded with a nervous smile. He was happy to see him.

"Ready?" said the First Sergeant.

Cantu nodded again, and together the two got the driver out of the wreckage.

The extraction, though, drew a new wave of incoming fire with enemy rifle fire pinging off of the overturned vehicle in short bursts, but other than maybe chipping the vehicle's paint, the rounds weren't having the effect the shooters were hoping for. The new round of enemy small arms fire drew targeted return machine gun fire from both Taras and Hernandez once more quieting the ambushers.

Back at the Ranger's gun truck Doc Moore began making a cursory assessment of the driver's injuries and Cantu briefly pulled the medic aside.

"Doc, it's his kneecap," he whispered, handing Moore the small, severed lump. "Wasn't sure if maybe you could do something with it or not."

Moore nodded, took the kneecap, and placed it between several clean gauze pads in his aid bag. He wasn't really sure what could be done with it either, but that wasn't his primary concern at the moment. His focus was on who needed him the most and what needed to be done to keep them alive. After the cursory assessments, it was a toss-up. It was the MP Major who helped or tried to with the decision-making process.

"Doc, I'm good. See to my people first," he said, wiping away the blood from the cut on his head and waving the Medic off and gesturing toward the injured Burke. The Major had a broken arm and cut on his forehead, maybe even a possible concussion but he was conscious and seemingly handling the pain even if his face was saying otherwise.

"You sure, Major?"

"Yeah, I'm good. Head wounds always bleed like a faucet, I hear."

The Major managed a weak, unconvincing laugh.

Doc Moore stared at the Major for a long moment, nodded, and then dug out a bandage for the bleeding cut on the officer's forehead.

"Here! Place this on your head wound. I'll be back in a bit to check you out."

"Go. I'm good."

Moore wasn't sure that the Major's *'good'* was acceptable or not, but at the Major's urging he turned to the MP sergeant who'd been thrown from the open gun turret in the explosion.

Sergeant Burke was showing a broken shoulder and arm. There was a small cut over his forehead too that was badly bleeding and needed attention. Wiping away the blood Moore saw that the head wound looked worse than it was which, like the MP Major had said, was typical for head wounds. Even so, the bloodied gash would need stitches but that would have to come later at a field hospital, so Doc Moore cleaned and bandaged the wound and then turned his attention to the broken shoulder and arm. While he was applying a splint and an arm sling to lock the shoulder in place Burke told him there was more.

"I...I got shot too," said the MP sergeant.

"Where?"

Moore had done a quick scan over the injured MP when Shintaku brought him back and he hadn't seen any entry or exit wounds on the soldier or so he'd thought.

"My left big toe... it's...it's gone."

Burke's eyes turned to the hole in the top of the left boot that he had overlooked, and he was eyeing the gaping tear.

"Let's get that boot off you."

Moore gently helped Burke unlace and remove the jungle boot. There was a blood soaked hole in his olive drab colored sock revealing an ugly wound. What remained was muddied and bloodied splintered bone fragments and torn cartilage and flesh.

"The toe back out there somewhere?"

Doc Moore stared back at the torn wheel and hub in the stream.

"Naw, it bobbed along in the creek when they were shooting at me, and then it disappeared," said Burke. "I think something ate it."

"What?"

Burke nodded. "In a deeper pool further down a large catfish or a snake came up, snatched it, and disappeared."

Moore's eyes turned back to the muddy pool and he involuntarily shivered.

"How's the pain?"

"The toe still feels like it's there and someone keeps smashing it with a hammer," said the MP Sergeant, wincing while putting up a brave front, but the medic knew better. "You got anything that'll stop it?"

"Arm or ass?" said the Medic reaching back into his Aid Bag and retrieving a morphine syrette.

"Arm."

Moore nodded and then jabbed the needle of the small tube into the MP sergeant's right shoulder.

"This'll help. Let's take a look at it."

The medic went to work on the foot wound. Grabbing his canteen, he unscrewed the cap and poured water over the wound to clean it and to get a better look at the damage. When some of the dirt and mud had been rinsed away he shoved gauze inside the hole in the foot before carefully wrapping the bandage tightly in place with an elastic bandage around the foot and ankle.

"You're gonna be okay," he said to Burke.

The MP sergeant gave a slow nod. *Okay* was the actual better option, just not yet. The morphine was already going to work which added some convincing gravity to the Medic's words before the Ranger Medic moved on to the next injured MP.

The driver's left leg was a bloodied mess. Torn, angry flesh and the bloody depression where the patella didn't show a life threatening wound as much it did as life altering damage. After bandaging the knee, Moore applied a straight leg splint to hold the knee and leg steady and in place. The Ranger Medic wasn't sure what could be done about the severed knee cap. His medical training at Fort Sam Houston hadn't prepared him for half of what he had to deal with as a combat medic in Vietnam because the latest textbook procedures were still being written in the jungle amidst the bloody mayhem by the Medics and Corpsmen who were doing their damnedest to treat and keep the wounded GIs in the field alive. For the driver's burns, Doc Moore avoided creams and any greasy products he had in his Aid Bag and instead slowly poured canteen water over the driver's hands and face to clean and cool the seared flesh.

"Ah fuck! It hurts!" cried the driver.

"I know, but hang in there, man. You're gonna be good, you hear me?" Moore said to the barely conscious driver who'd managed an unconvincing and pain-filled nod.

With the two enlisted men's injuries and wounds stabilized, Moore turned back to the MP Major. The bandage the officer was holding against the deep cut on his head had slowed the flow of blood. Some of the blood had seeped through his fingers and dried. The bigger problem was the man's coloring was off. Way off. Outwardly he wasn't showing any signs of any serious injuries or wounds, with the exception of the broken left arm, but the facial contortions he displayed as he shifted his weight while he was leaning against the back wheels of the gun truck told the Medic something more was going on.

"How you doing, Major? You good?" asked the Medic, taking a closer look at the officer, easing him away from the big wheels to get a better look at his stomach, chest, and then his back to make sure he hadn't missed something.

"My...my people okay?"

"They're good, Sir," said the Medic as he began to undo the buttons on the Major's jungle fatigue shirt. "Now let's get your blouse off and take a look at your chest."

"I'm feeling a little tired...woozy."

"Then let's get you back up against the wheel again. I need you to stay awake for me now."

Moore unbuttoned the officer's jungle fatigue blouse and began carefully poking and probing the Major with the officer wincing as the Medic went. Moore wasn't liking what he was finding. The Major's stomach was swollen too, he was dizzy, and there was bruising around both sides of his abdomen. It all pointed to the troubling and telltale signs of internal injuries.

"We'll get you all out on a Medevac soon, Sir. Just hang in there. We got this. The Medevac is on its way."

Moore mentally flagged the Major to be the first to go out on the Medevac bird when it came in. They would all need to be flown to the nearest Field Hospital where the doctors, nurses, medics, and techs would take over the fight. *My job here is to just keep them alive in the early rounds.*

The ambush and firefight to their front was drawing down and it looked like the firefight was over until a loud blast from the rear of the column interrupted the temporary calm. The blast was met with return machine gun fire and a thundering boom, most likely from the rocket launcher Shintaku had given to Wexler and Daley. The second explosion sent things suddenly and eerily quiet again.

"What the fuck was that?" yelled Poplawski, getting to his feet. The Ranger First Sergeant's eyes briefly left the enemy's ambush line in front of him.

"Don't know," replied Captain Robison but that was about to be cleared up with the next radio transmission.

"Valhalla-Six, Pistol Six-X-ray. Over."

"Six. Go, X-ray," said the Ranger Captain.

"A B-40 hit the back of the supply truck. We took out the shooter and a few other *November Victor Alphas* charging at us. We're good, for the moment. We've secured a good perimeter. Over."

The MP sergeant in the gun jeep had phonetically labeled the attackers as NVA soldiers.

"What's your status, Pistol X-ray?"

"Some minor shrapnel wounds from the RPG, but we're good."

"And the supply truck? Is it serviceable?"

"The RPG took out the stacks of rice, splintered some lumber and sheet metal, and knocked out the truck's radio, but there's no real damage to the truck. The Transportation officer tells me it's still operational and Good-to-Go. Over."

"I copy, X-ray. Be advised, the *Duck* is out of the fight and Pistol-Six and three of your people are wounded, so you're it, X-Ray. You copy?"

"Yes...I, I copy, Valhalla."

"Good. Valhalla-six, out."

"Looks like the NVA were waiting on us," said the First Sergeant.

The Captain nodded, thinking the same thing, and something more as he got back on the radio, this time to the gunship.

"Piebald, you got eyes on the jeep up the road?"

"That's a negative, Valhalla-Six. Too much double-canopy. The jeep charging that ambush like that took balls. That was something. Over."

It was *something,* thought Robison and he wasn't yet certain what to make of it.

"Can you bounce a Dust-off bird for us? We're going to need it. We've got at least three wounded that need to be pulled out."

"On it, Valhalla."

The *Dust-off bird* was an Army medical evacuation helicopter, a Uh1-H Huey Medevac model with a big red cross on a square white backdrop logo painted on the nose of the aircraft and along the side doors. The red cross on the white square would make for an easy target for the enemy when it came in. Whether the enemy would honor it as a medical mission was another matter since the large red cross also put it in the enemy's crosshairs and made for an easy aiming point as a stationary or hovering target.

"Roger that, Valhalla. On it! Piebald Two-Three. Out."

Chapter 25

1,500-feet above the small battle, the Cobra attack helicopter was doing lazy circles in a holding pattern. With an eagle eye view over the back road, or at least what he could make out below through thin openings in the canopied covered tree tops, the Cobra pilot was back on the radio calling down something his front seat gunner had seen on their last pass.

"Valhalla-Six, Piebald Two-Three. Over."

"Six. Go, Two-Three," said Robison, readjusting his LBE-web gear that had been skewed during the tumble out of the jeep. A light line of sweat was spilling down into his eyes and stinging. He wiped it away with the back of his hand and then wiped it on his nearest pant leg.

"Be advised, on my last pass my X-Ray caught a quick glimpse of your lead jeep. Looks like it's parked half into the brush just ahead of you where the road comes to an end."

"Our meet-up site. Any sign of movement around it?"

"Negative, but don't take that to the bank. Like I said it was just a quick glimpse. Your lead jeep driver some kind of cowboy or something?"

"Something. Any signs of the bad guys planning any more welcoming surprises?"

"Took some A-K and RPG fire on the last look, but we're good. Also, be advised, it looks like the bad guys are bomb-shelling away. They're scattering. Some November Victor Alphas in green uniforms and pith helmets and some locals in loincloths…"

"Loincloths? As in Montagnards?"

"Roger that, the angry indigenous kind from the rifle fire they were throwing at me and my gunner. Hell, I even think one even fired a crossbow at us! Although, I'm not sure how he would've mounted my Cobra on his trophy wall."

The gunship pilot gave a short laugh and then added, "Not sure how I'll write that up in the After Action Report, either."

"Hostile fire of the oldest kind, Two-Three. Wait one," Robison said, pausing and mulling over what more needed to be done before he got back on the radio to the gunship pilot.

"Piebald Two-Three. Be advised, I'm going to take a ground unit up to the jeep's location. I'd appreciate it if you'd hang around for a bit, and maybe be ready to cover us while we attempt to rescue or recover those in the jeep."

"No problem, Valhalla. My Low Bird made it safely back to Loc Ninh, with another on the way from Lai Khe, so I'm good for a while. I'll stand-by to cover."

"Roger, Two-Three. Valhalla-Six. Out."

"SHINTAKU AND CANTU! ON ME!" Robison yelled to the two former Team Leaders as he handed the radio handset back to his First Sergeant. Guessing at the audible play the Ranger Company Commander was about to call, the First Sergeant moved up his side to join them.

To the two young sergeants the Captain said, "You Good-to-Go?"

"Yes sir," each said, not asking where the *go* would take them.

"Then grab your web gear and get me one more volunteer. We're going after our V-I-Ps."

Poplawski protested the decision, even as Shintaku chuckled at the notion that he or Cantu had *volunteered* as he ran to the Deuce-and-a-half to Shanghai Ranger Bowman.

"Grab your web gear. Follow me!"

The small group had assembled behind the Ranger jeep where First Sergeant Poplawski was reaching in the back of the jeep and grabbing his M-16.

"I'll take them, Sir," said the First Sergeant only to have Robison wave him off.

"No, First Sergeant. I need you and Lieutenant Plantagenet to secure the perimeter here, and see to the wounded. The Medevac helicopter's on its way, so get them safely on it and be ready with a small QRF to come after us if we run into trouble. You copy?"

Poplawski didn't like the decision but complied with a pursed-face nod.

"Not much room here for the helicopter to work with," he said, looking around at the natural clearing and searching for a space large enough to set the Medevac bird down.

The Captain warily nodded.

"More than likely they'll have to hover and drop a rescue basket," he said. "The NVA picked a good ambush site."

"That they did. You sure you don't want me going along with you to find Evans and Quan?"

"No, I need you here."

"Then take this!" the First Sergeant said, handing Robison the backpack PRC-25 radio from the jeep.

The Captain took the radio as he eyed the stream bed and open ground ahead of him. The 90-foot stretch of open ground would be the first challenge.

"We'll make a run on the tree line," he said to Poplawski. "When I give you the signal, Top, I want every gun we have firing it up until we reach the far side of the creek."

"Roger that, Sir."

Poplawski still wasn't thrilled about the Captain leading the rescue attempt by charging the ambush line, but was wise enough to know there would be no arguing it.

"Okay, but if you hit the shit, we're coming across the creek on the road with this jeep and the gun truck guns a-blazing!"

"If you do then stay within Quan's tire tracks. He fortunately seemed to have avoided the land mines the reception committee had planted for us."

"Yeah, he did and will do, if we follow."

With another thought in mind Robison said, "You know, their ambush almost worked."

"Yes sir, but thanks to the Low Bird, it didn't. The rest of us were on this side of the clearing and the creek."

"Uh-huh, and I suspect the bad guys didn't count on the additional fire power we brought with us with our gun truck."

Poplawski nodded. "No Sir, they didn't."

Robison nodded, but there was something more on his mind that was troubling him. Something darker. "You notice in the firefight and when Quan took off like that, the jeep didn't seem to be taking any hits from the enemy gunfire?"

"Come to think of it, I did."

"Might make one wonder if maybe he knew something about the ambush that we didn't know."

The First Sergeant gave a narrowed eyed, quiet nod. The thought had struck him too.

"Which doesn't bode well for Evans," said Robison. "Get the perimeter set up and secured. We'll be back."

Chapter 26

After adjusting the straps of the backpacked radio across his chest and shoulders and cinching them securely, Captain Robison did a quick commo check.

"Piebald Two-Three. Valhalla-Six. Commo check. Over."

"Got you Lima Charlie," came the reply indicating the call was Loud and Clear.

"Roger that, Two-Three. Valhalla-Six. Out."

Robison attached the handset high up onto the left side of his web gear harness near enough to his left ear to hear radio traffic as he grabbed his rifle. Shintaku, Cantu and the third Ranger, Spec-4 Bowman, were huddled around their Company Commander.

"We're going in after Mister Evans and Quan. We'll be staying off the road," said the Ranger Captain, calling an audible as he eyed the far side of the clearing. "We'll advance by leapfrogging out in teams of two. On the other side we'll stagger the moves 10-yards at a time after we reach the road across the creek."

This wasn't in the playbook, but the game clock was ticking down. "Sergeant Cantu, you're with me." To the other two, he added, "Sergeant Shintaku, I want you and Specialist Bowman to take the left side of the road. We'll take the right. Once you get there, take a knee inside the tree line and underbrush and hold. We'll take the lead and then cover your go. Oh, and I want you, no, I *need* you to maintain visual contact with either myself or Sergeant Cantu. Same-same for us. Everyone copy? Everyone on the same page?"

"Copy," said Shintaku and Bowman and Sergeant Cantu echoed the comment.

"Good."

Robison turned to the First Sergeant and said, "Top, we're gonna need some cover fire on the ambush line before we make our run."

Poplawski grimly nodded and belted out the command to provide the cover fire.

"ON MY COMMAND, GIMME A MAD MINUTE ON TARGET!" he bellowed, directing those in the gun jeep and fortified truck to fire up the ambush line and flanks with a heavy amount of heavy machine gun and small arms fire. "FIRE!"

Several thousand rounds of the gun fire and high explosive grenade rounds hit the jungle foliage facing them in a penalizing toll. Splintered leaves and branches broke and flew back into the rainforest along with kicked up dirt and rocks that tore into the greenery like natural shrapnel. The suppressing cover fire was devastating in its ferocity and timing, and the quiet that immediately followed was once again, unnerving.

"OUR TURN!" said Robison to his ground team. "NOW!"

In a fast run the makeshift two-man Ranger assault teams came out from behind cover, sprinted across the clearing and the creek bed, and made their way into the far tree lines on opposite sides of the road. They met no return fire and just inside the carved up brush they took a knee. The awkward quiet was unnerving. With adrenaline pumping and their breathing heavy from the run, they waited, watched, and listened to the jungle in front and around them for any sign of the enemy. The smell of gun smoke and churned up ground and bleeding greenery lingered and permeated the air, along with a growing haze of smoke from the growing brush fire off to their left side of the clearing.

If all was good, they would move forward, leapfrogging and staggering their moves, and dealing with who and what they did or didn't find.

Once Robison had visual contact with Shintaku and Bowman, the Captain gave them the closed fist hand signal to hold in place and standby while he and Sergeant Cantu carefully started forward.

Robison took the lead. Leaning forward at the waist with his rifle ready he slowly began moving through the brush. Cantu followed a few yards behind him keeping an eye out to the right as he went. Like seasoned hunters they quietly crept through the jungle brush with slow and deliberate steps, all the while paralleling the thin road so as not to draw attention or give themselves away. Jungle scrub and underbrush make for good concealment, but lousy protective cover. The one lane road just a few feet away offered a better line of sight for the other team's line of travel as they moved, so Shintaku and Bowman covered their advance while keeping watch on their left and what had been to the main ambush line.

Nine to ten yards on Robison and Cantu held up. When they were set and ready, the Captain gave the hand signal for Shintaku and Bowman to move out on the far side of the roadway.

They were barely a few yards into the now quiet tree line when Shintaku gave an upraised fist stopping Bowman behind him. He couldn't see the Captain, but Cantu was in his line of sight. Shintaku signaled to Cantu that something had caught his eye. He pointed to his eyes with his index finger and then in the direction of what he was looking at to the left of him. Cantu passed along the quiet message to the Captain as Shintaku whispered back to Bowman to hold in place as he crept forward to check it out.

With the selector switch on his M-16 on AUTO fire and finger on the trigger, he was ready to pray-and-spray the chewed-up ground around the enemy fighting position he had spotted and anyone in it. He was pretty sure this was close to where the armored car took the RPG fire, and the next few steps confirmed it when the dead body of the North Vietnamese soldier who had fired it lay crumpled in the brush. Burke's machine gun fire from the *Duck* had taken him out.

A few more cautious steps on and to his left, where the convoy had taken the bulk of the Soviet RPD machine gun fire and where he'd aimed in the shoulder-fired LAW, two more bodies of the attackers lay in a small trench line where they fell. The wooden stock of the Soviet machine gun was splintered and its Chinese 25-round, belt-fed ammunition bands lay shot up, twisted, and scattered. What the gunship rockets and the gun truck's machine gun rounds maybe had missed, the anti-tank LAW rocket had scored with vengeance. Black bottles flies were already dancing across the crumpled bodies and touching down on the dark, sticky pools and splotches of blood.

Taking slow, deep breaths, trying to calm himself, Shintaku began tracking a slug-like blood wash made from a fourth ambusher who had crawled out of the trench line back toward a nearby dug-out, L-shaped fighting position. The ambusher never quite made it. The soldier lay in a fetal position clutching what was left of his stomach and bowels. A pale green pith helmet lay where it fell shy of the bunker he was hoping to reach. The bloodied drag marks showed serious blood loss with a long, dark maroon scrape from the dying crawl.

A quick breath in and out kept the Ranger from being rattled as his eyes were now scouring the surroundings looking for any more enemy soldiers or fighting positions. This wasn't the time to rush things or to be careless.

Satisfied he wasn't about to be a target himself, he signaled to Bowman that four of the ambushers were down before he moved on at an even more cautious pace. Snaking his way forward, he came to an abrupt halt at what looked to be the body of a fifth dead ambusher. The ground in and around the fighting position was badly chewed up where the gunship's minigun had finished what those weapons in the convoy had started.

The fighter, though, wasn't dead, and his face was locked in the weary resignation that the horrific wounds were his and that he wouldn't survive the rest of the fight. This ambusher, though, wasn't a North Vietnamese soldier. The black vest-like top and adorned loin cloth showed he was a Montagnard, one of the villagers they had come to see and help. Shintaku could see that the man's left hip and leg were gone, leaving a large bloody hole of torn muscle and shattered bone. From the deep claw marks in the ground, the Montagnard had used every ounce of strength he had left in his upper body to retrieve the missing pieces and had failed. The man was dying but at the sight of the Asian-looking enemy staring down at him, he still tried reaching for the American-made M-16 beside him.

"Uh-uh," said the Ranger, kicking it away. Reaching down, Shintaku scooped it up, thumbed the selector switch on SAFE, and then slung it over his shoulder.

The man was dead even before the Ranger moved on to the next ambusher he spotted laying only a few feet away. This sixth man was a North Vietnamese Army regular, who appeared to be comfortably laying back against the base of a tree with his pith helmet lowered over his eyes as though he was taking a nap. His green uniform, helmet, and backpack were flecked with pieces of leaves and severed twigs and his AK-47 assault rifle was laying in the nearby fox hole. A closer look showed where a .50 caliber machine gun round had punched a fist-sized hole through his thin chest and blew what had been there out his back.

Shintaku grabbed up the assault rifle as his eyes tracked a small path and blood trail leading away from the fox hole. Following the blood trail, he soon found the next dead enemy soldier laying in the underbrush. His weapon was missing and judging from the tramped down brush and ground and the pulled vines leading further into the jungle, it was likely he'd been scooped up and taken away from the ambush line by one or two of the fleeing ambushers and left where he'd died. Keeping to the Captain's ten yard rule about keeping the others in sight, and knowing he was pushing his luck if he pushed on alone, he made his way back to Bowman.

"Seven down," he whispered to Bowman, who nodded and covered him as he edged his way over to the road to signal the find and this time made eye contact with Captain Robison. The Staff Sergeant held out an open hand with fingers and thumb spread wide and then raised two more fingers making a throat slashing gesture with a thumb.

Seven down. K-I-A.

Robison nodded and then slowly rose to his feet and gave Sergeant Cantu the hand signal that it was their turn to move up. Something, though, out on the road caught the Ranger Captain's attention and he gave an upraised fist halting the go. Out on the poor, back country roadway two semi-ovals showed where the NVA had planted two more anti-tank mines. The churned up ground and dark discolored lumps stood out against the paler dust-covered road. With only a few open spaces in the treetop canopy overhead nearly covering the road there wasn't enough direct sunlight or time since the mines had been planted to bleach and dry out the darker soil to blend it in.

'*Half-assed job*,' thought Robison, which explained the tire tracks on the road from Evans' jeep where Quan had easily driven around them.

The Captain moved on only to stop again when he came across a dropped NVA canteen left behind during a hasty withdrawal. He brought his rifle up readying to fire as he squinted and scanned the immediate area a little closer. Behind him Sergeant Cantu followed his lead. There was a blood trail, but not the wounded or dead enemy soldier who'd made it.

With his M-16 low and ready the Captain crept forward with even more caution knowing that wounded soldiers, like wounded animals, would be even more vicious and unpredictable when cornered or suddenly encountered. Ferocity in a war zone was always in play or waiting in the wings. A line of sweat was beading down Robison's forehead. He wiped it away with the sleeve of his free hand while keeping a grip on the pistol grip of the rifle ready to fire. He didn't need stinging or blurry eyes. No, not now.

The body of a dead enemy soldier was sprawled just off of the road like a badly tossed rag doll. The enemy soldier was trying to make a run for it on the road but the four to five machine gun rounds through his back left horrible exit holes in his stomach and chest. Another blood trail showed signs where several others had carried away another wounded man. The escape route was wider here with heavily tramped down grass, broken branches, and a small, almost tunnel-like opening in their hurried direction of travel.

Robison halted and gave Shintaku the hand signal for his two-man team to move up. The staggered moves by both teams on both sides of the road gave each team a better look and angle at what lay ahead of them. It wasn't much of a look, but even a small advantage provided an edge in combat, and at the moment it was all they had.

There was more tramped down grass, brush, and broken branches on both sides of the road, a lot more, leaving the two-man teams of Rangers following the much wider and more open paths the main ambush party had made in their rushed retreat. By staying off of these newly created lines of travel, and slowly paralleling them inside the brush and tree line, the four Rangers would hopefully avoid any direct small arms fire as well as any potential boobytraps. The four moved in silence or as silently as they could knowing any noise out of the ordinary would draw fire. The sound of small branches and thin limbs suddenly snapping and breaking by them would give away their positions and draw fire, so they watched where they walked.

They were still tracking the spoor and sign through the much too quiet jungle and only stopped again when Shintaku caught something glistening in the brush a few yards ahead of the other two on the far side of the road. Muddled sunlight was reflecting off of the spiked metal bayonet of an AK-47. But from Shintaku's angle and against the green and brown jungle backdrop, it stood out like a beacon.

Shintaku couldn't see the enemy soldier who had done a pretty decent job of hiding and lying in wait in the tall weeds and brush, but the shining steel spike that was angled toward the approaching Ranger Captain had given his position away. The enemy soldier just three yards ahead of the American had planned on making a quiet kill or two before he fled in retreat. It was either a rear-guard or a wounded soldier's last defiant act.

Across the road Shintaku could also see that the Captain and Cantu hadn't seen the NVA soldier in hiding nor the bayonet in their approach, and were unaware of the imminent threat. Knowing he couldn't snap his fingers to get their attention without the enemy soldier hearing it too, and with no time to warn Robison or Cantu, Shintaku brought up his M-16, sighted down the rifle's iron sights, and fired a three round burst a half a foot and down behind the bayonet. The copper-jacketed bullets slammed into the brush and the NVA soldier behind it. Although the M-16's .223 round wasn't known for its knockdown power, at less than 15 yards the man in hiding was blown back into the weeds around him from the muzzle velocity and where the rounds hit.

With his finger on the trigger of the A-K, and as he fell the dying fighter sent a wild burst of automatic rifle fire into the jungle as he fell but the rounds flew well away from the two Americans. The rounds that went high and wide of Robison and Cantu sent the two to the ground as they dropped and returned fire toward the sound of the discharged AK-47. If the enemy soldier wasn't dead when Shintaku hit him, then he was dead a few times more from the return fire from the other two Rangers.

When no return fire came back at them, and the jungle got awkwardly quiet again, the Captain slowly stood and looked across the roadway to find Staff Sergeant with his rifle still aimed in on the dead ambusher's position. Shintaku raised up one finger as he pointed ahead of Robison and Cantu where he'd shot the ambusher, signaling that the man was down.

Robison gave Shintaku a thankful nod, inhaled slowly through his nose, and then blew out the air through his teeth a few times using the calming breaths to steady himself.

"Valhalla-Six, Valhalla-Six. Valhalla-Seven. Over?" This from a worried First Sergeant was making the radio call.

With the volume set on low and the handset high attached on his shoulder harness near his left ear, the incoming call could only be heard by the Captain. The radio's handset made it easier for Robison to respond as he kept watch on his surroundings while holding onto his rifle. All that Cantu could hear was the Captain's whispered response.

"Six, Go."

"Valhalla-Six, you good?"

"We are now, Seven," Robison said quietly into the handset. "All's good. Six out."

With the radio call ended it was time to move out again. Several tense moments and a few yards later Robison found the dead enemy soldier sprawled out in the brush. He had been hit in the right shoulder, chest, back, and neck. Blood was still pumping out of his severed carotid artery, but it was a slow spill that stopped with a death rattle.

"Rear guard, Captain?" whispered Cantu coming up next to Robison, eyeing the dead ambusher and the extended spiked blade that pushed out from under the rifle barrel.

"One of them, anyway."

"Looks like he wanted to bayonet us."

"His mistake. We'll take it slower and avoid any more little surprises," said Robison, grabbing up the AK-47 and slinging it over his right shoulder.

The next go brought the two in the lead to another dogleg bend in the road. Sneaking out toward the edge of the jungle for a better look at what lay ahead to the right, Robison took a knee and gave the hand signal for the others to hold up.

Through the leaves, just inside the tree line he could make out the proposed meet-up site where the road ended 30 to 40 yards ahead of him. The back end of the MP jeep was sticking out of the jungle on the left side of the road in the natural cul-de-sac. The jeep appeared to be abandoned. Evans and Quan were nowhere to be seen. The five crates and the mounted machine gun were missing too, but he wouldn't know for certain until they got closer.

There were no enemy soldiers in sight, but that didn't mean they weren't there. The NVA soldiers may not have been Southeast Asian Daniel Boones, but the *Dega* were. The heavily wooded jungle was their well-trodden ancestral home. It always had been, and the Ranger Captain had little doubt that even now they were quietly keeping an eye on the Americans, just as they previously had on the North Vietnamese Army movements as trail watchers prior to the *Friendly Fire* incident that had turned their loyalty.

With the jeep partially in sight there was no need to get sloppy and make a run at it. Robison gave the hand signal to move out and the two teams continued on working the sides of the road in the ten yard moves. By the third leapfrogging maneuver the Ranger Captain had a closer and much better look at the jeep.

It wasn't abandoned. Quan wasn't there but Evans was. He was slumped over in the passenger's seat with his chin to his chest and he wasn't moving, nor was there any movement in or around the jeep. The mounted machine gun was gone. With the body in the jeep, it appeared that the NVA ambushers had left a calling card, or perhaps, were waiting to draw in the rescuers when they tried to retrieve the body.

Because the old road had curved to the right, Shintaku and Bowman would have a further way to go to catch up to the two others on the other side of the road before they secured the jeep and the body in it. Just after the Ranger officer gave Shintaku the hand signal for the final move, sudden movement out on the road caught the Captain's attention. Something broke out of the brush ahead of him and began crawling across the dirt road.

The Captain snapped his fingers a few times as loud as he could make them until he had the Staff Sergeant's attention. With an up-upraised fist the Captain pointed at him and signaled for the two Rangers to halt in place and not move any further. With the same free hand, he pointed to his eyes with two fingers, pointed out to the road and then wiggled the hand trying to get across what he was looking at. The wiggling hand gesture wasn't in the Lurp training manual, and the now confused Shintaku was trying to figure out what the hand gesture meant. It also had him carefully brushing aside the large *Bac Ha* elephant ear leaves so he could get a look at what and where the Captain was pointing. The threat was there, a dangerous one and Shintaku slowly brought up his rifle.

When the rifle went up Bowman quickly took a knee and brought his rifle up too as he peered through the foliage trying to identify this latest threat and troubled because he couldn't see it. He wasn't sure of what or where the threat was, so he kept his eyes locked on the jungle to Shintaku's left ready to fire, if it came to it. From where he was kneeling he couldn't see the 17-foot-long, green scaled King Cobra slithering across the opposite side of the road in the direction they were heading, but Shintaku could. Nor could Bowman see that the large snake that had stopped three-quarters of the way across the road or that the deadly reptile warily raised the front third of its body six feet off the ground, flared its round, boot-sized head into a wide threatening hood and slowly began a calculating sway. The snake's tongue flickered as it tasted the air at the dangerous human scent it had detected.

The big snake hadn't seen the humans, but it had already tasted trouble. Agitated by the noise and chaos of the firefight and the latest gun play, and especially at the humans that had caused it, the huge snake was now searching for safer ground and a way away from the always potential trouble.

After a long moment the hesitant reptile drew in its hood, lowered its head back down to the ground, and then slithered the rest of the way across the road. To Shintaku's horror it disappeared in the jungle underbrush barely three or four yards from where he was standing.

A chill shot through the NCO's body, brought on from knowing that a bite from a King Cobra could bring down a water buffalo, and in rural farm communities often had. Farmers had fallen in their fields unable to reach their villages or loved ones before the deadly toxins shut down their nervous systems and left them dying. He'd given a class on the poisonous snakes the Ranger trainees could expect to find in the jungle, but this was the first time he'd ever seen an actual King Cobra and he was momentarily rattled. The deep gutter the snake left on the dirt road was the width of a softball bat.

Back across the road, Robison signaled for a change of strategy. Knowing the deadly snake was somewhere up ahead of the other two-man team, he waved Shintaku and Bowman over to his side of the road. The hand signal didn't need to be repeated.

"*Roger freakin' that, Captain!*" said the normally unflappable Shintaku to himself.

Turning back over his left shoulder, he snapped his finger twice, and by the second snap, he had Bowman's attention. Pointing toward the direction he wanted him to go, Shintaku double pumped his upraised fist. The double-pump meant *double-time*, which in civilian speak meant, *haul ass and run*.

Sweet Sorrow

Bowman sprinted across the open road towards the Ranger officer's position while Robison and Cantu covered his go. Shintaku quickly followed and both were taking a knee behind the two other Rangers inside the cover of the still awkwardly quiet jungle.

With a little nervous laughter and a slow shake of his head, Shintaku gave the Captain an appreciative nod. No words were necessary.

With no incoming fire before or after the two had crossed the road, the Captain suspected the ambushers were long gone. Any remaining action would only be more rear guard attacks or harassment fire. The large snake, though, told them there were other dangers lurking and that they still needed to be careful.

Sergeant Cantu eased forward and asked to take point. Robison nodded, and then in a staggered Ranger file, the four quietly moved, stopping just shy of it in the natural cul-de-sac. The jeep that was half in the bush was less than ten yards away. Evans' body was slumped down in the passenger seat.

To the right of the jeep where the dirt road ended, a smaller, sinister looking tunnel-like path led deeper into the jungle. The thin, dark path in the even darker part of the rainforest was ominous and foreboding. It was designed that way. Entering it, and especially now, only invited more trouble. This was the doorway to, and the domain of, the hill tribe that took part in the ambush.

"Keep to the left side of the jeep and well away from that path beyond it. You copy?"

Cantu understood why and nodded. It presented too much of a shooting lane.

"We'll cover you and when you reach the jeep, drop down behind the engine block or wheel. We'll be moving up from the right. Don't move the body. Could be its booby trapped."

Cantu nodded a second time, but from where he was crouching, he couldn't see the path or get a good look at the V-I-P. Moving a few steps to his left he paused for a moment when he caught sight of the baleful looking trail and the danger it presented. The first thought that came to mind was fish in a barrel with the bad guys doing the shooting.

"Take it slow," whispered the Ranger officer. "Really slow."

"Roger that," he whispered back to the Captain. He was hugging the tree line as he crept forward just inside the brush line edge of the jungle, ready to shoot any damn thing that moved. Covering his advance, the three others had guns up and ready.

The trouble was that when Cantu slipped into the jungle to work his way around the green and brown cul-de-sac he moved so quietly and stealth fully, he not only went unnoticed by any enemy soldiers that might've been waiting in hiding, but he also disappeared from sight of the three Rangers. They weren't sure where to aim or where he was until a few moments later when he eased out of the dense foliage just to the left of the parked jeep.

Robison couldn't help but smile. Rangers lead the way, he thought, and Lurps like that do it best.

Cantu did a quick look around the jeep and the dead end road before he slipped in and crouched down behind the engine block where he got his first look at the body slumped over in the passenger's seat. The civilian's head was flopped down on his chest. A blood trail from a deep gouge over his left eyebrow spilled down over his nose, cheek, and chin and onto his once sterile jungle fatigues. The eye below the cut was swollen shut and a badly bent nose had dribbled blood and snot down and into the mix.

The dead man's hands and feet were bound with some kind of hemp rope. Then, to Cantu's surprise, the dead man tried to lift his chin, failed but groaned in the attempt. He was still breathing, even if he was barely conscious.

The Ranger sergeant raised a fist above his head and pumped it up and down, fast and with the purpose that brought the rest of the rescuers quickly moving up to the jeep. While Shintaku took a knee covering the entrance to the dark trail, Bowman went prone on the right to provide protective cover to those at the back of the jeep as Captain Robison took a knee next to Cantu. Three sides of their position were now covered.

"He's alive," Cantu whispered to the Captain. "But there's no sign of Mister Quan."

Or the M-60 or the crates, thought Robison, which really didn't surprise him. He didn't think they would be. He was more surprised that Quan had left Evans alive. When the sergeant rose up to untie the ropes, Captain Robison stopped him.

"Careful. Check for boobytraps."

Cantu nodded and did a prudent visual search of the seat, and was satisfied there wasn't a pressure plate or loose grenade beneath or behind Evans waiting to explode when they moved him. Dropping down low to the ground he checked underneath the jeep for tripwires rigged to explode. Again, there was nothing that looked threatening or out of place.

Giving a thumbs-up to the Captain, he stood and watched on as his Company Commander untied the ropes and began checking the V-I-P for any other injuries or wounds that weren't so visible. Other than the thumps to his head and possible concussion, Evans appeared to be okay. That too surprised the Ranger Captain, but then again maybe not, he thought, as something else crossed his mind that brought on a smirk.

The *something*, he was thinking was that here in Southeast Asia you didn't need to kill a man to beat him, you just needed to humiliate him and make him lose face, something Robison suspected Quan would very much savor.

"We following them in?"

This from Shintaku who was eyeing the shadowy path leading towards the *Dega* village. The village was less than a klick away and Robison suspected the rest of the way into the living, gloomy abyss would only be a foolish and costly undertaking.

"No," the Captain said, finally. "Not without a Battalion backing us we're not. The NVA were sloppy with their ambush and the poorly placed mines on the road, but I doubt the *Dega* will be with anything they've set up to slow us down if we try to move on their village. We have Evans and the jeep. That's good enough. We're heading back."

He set the A-K he had slung over his shoulder in the backseat of the jeep and then removed the backpacked radio and placed it on the jeep's passenger seat while stretching out the cord of the handset.

"Valhalla-Seven, Valhalla-six. Over."

"Seven. Go."

"Be advised, we have one injured Victor India Papa," radioed the Captain. "We're on our way back to your location. Watch for the jeep and our people coming in."

"I copy, Six. Eyes wide open. Seven out."

Robison climbed into the jeep behind the steering wheel, started up the engine and shoved the floor shift into reverse. Easing his right foot on the gas pedal he let out the clutch and slowly backed out of the brush. Cranking the steering wheel hard to the left he pointed it back down the way they had come. Shoving the floor shift in neutral he let the engine idle as he called Sergeant Shintaku over to him.

"I spotted two more possible anti-tank mines planted on the road on the way in," he said. "Give me a good lead in case I roll onto a third I didn't see, then get the others back to the convoy A-SAP."

A-SAP meant *as soon as possible* but in combat it also required a certain amount of caution and luck while hauling ass.

"Yes sir, but are you sure you don't think maybe I should drive the jeep back?"

The officer gave him the side-eye and then smiled and said, "I need to get our V-I-P back to safety, and besides Sergeant Shintaku, didn't anyone tell you that rank has its privileges?"

Robison grinned at his own little joke and Shintaku gave a not-quite convinced nod back. The possibility of running over a third anti-tank mine didn't sound like much of a privilege to him.

A light wind was pushing the growing wildfire well south of the stone bridge and the clearing, and the smoke of the burning rainforest was pushing up through and over the treetops. Before long it would carry well beyond the contact area and become a full-fledged forest fire. Any ambushers remaining would be fleeing the path of the flames and away from the direction it was heading.

"Oh, and stay on my tire tracks. If I'm safe then you should be safe."

Pushing in the clutch and easing the floor-shift into first gear, the Captain started forward. Thanks to the seldom used road the tire tracks the jeep made going into the jungle cul-de-sac stood out like light orange painted ribbons. He used them as his guide on his way out.

Before long he came to the dull pie plate size patches of ground that showed where the Soviet anti-tank mines had been poorly placed. Steering around the first patch of disturbed ground and staying on Quan's tire tracks, Robison also kept an eye out for any tripwires or signs of other secondary hidden explosives. He was driving so slowly in first gear that he almost killed the engine. A nagging thought was telling him that with no one riding shotgun, and with his concentration focused on the road to avoid the anti-tank mines, any enemy soldier lying in wait could easily pick him off.

"*You are soooooo right, First Sergeant,*" he said to himself. "*I'm taking the R&R to Hawaii!*"

Just as he was approaching the second anti-tank mine, Evans was slowly regaining consciousness and was still more than a little groggy. Like anyone after having been knocked out, he woke up in a confused and combative panic. Unsure where he was or what was going on, and crying out, he reached over with flailing arms trying to pull on the steering wheel.

"Quan! Wha...what are you...NO!"

Robison shoved his hands away and regained control of the steering wheel.

"I'M NOT QUAN! STOP IT! STOP GRABBING AT THE WHEEL!"

Only the half-conscious and badly rattled Evans grabbed and pulled on the steering wheel a second time, and had steered the right front tire of the jeep dangerously closer to the anti-tank mine. There was no yelling or trying to reason with him, so the Ranger Captain knocked his arms away with a pounding hammer fist and then swung it hard across Evans' nose when he once more tried to grab at the steering wheel.

The backhand blow broke what was left of Evans' already broken nose and sent him falling back against in his canvas covered seat and groaning. The now even more dazed and moaning Evans was holding his bleeding nose with both hands. Blood was dripping through his fingers and spilling onto his shirt. With Evans seeing stars and maybe the cosmos, Robison managed to steer away from the second anti-tank mine just in time as he concentrated on getting the jeep back on the original tire tracks as near as he could.

At the final dogleg bend that brought the jeep to the clearing he was happily surprised to see the First Sergeant and several of his people covering the clearing from the enemy ambush line. In front of them were a handful of AK-47 assault rifles, a badly broken RPG-7, and a Soviet RPD machine gun that had been gathered up from the ruined trench line. Nine dead NVA and Dega bodies had been dragged out from the brush. Any of the dead soldiers' weapons were stacked in the back of the Ranger's Deuce-and-a-half.

PFC Sanchez gave him a nod as the jeep passed.

In the clearing Robison gunned the gas pedal and picked up speed before the creek bed and then splashed across the stream with tires kicking up mud as he went. On the far side he drove the jeep behind the Ranger Company's Deuce-and-a-half where he stopped. As he shut the jeep's engine down Evans was laying back against the passenger's seat groaning and looking pitiful.

"Doc, when you can, will you check him out?" Robison said to Doc Moore, who was working on the more critically injured and wounded MPs in the truck bed.

Peeking over the tailgate of the truck, the overworked Moore could see that Evans, with the battered nose and trashed eyebrow was in no immediate danger, but nodded to the Captain anyway.

"Will do, Sir, but I'll need a minute."

"No problem, Doc."

Grabbing up his M-16 Robison turned back toward the creek bed and joined the First Sergeant, PFC Sanchez, and the red haired new guy.

Waiting for the three remaining Rangers that were following he whispered, *'Come on! Come on! Come on!'*

The whisper was in time. The three Rangers were double-timing their way around the last bend in the road. Once they joined the waiting Rangers, they all crossed back over the creek using the stone bed bridge. Soon they were all behind the big truck huffing and puffing. Dark patches of sweat lined their underarms and lower backs as beads of dust tinged sweat dripped from their foreheads and faces. First Sergeant helped his Commanding officer out of the radio harness.

"Trenches, spider holes, and reinforced fighting positions," said the First Sergeant to the Captain, staring back at what had been the ambush line. "Looks like they had time to prepare for us."

Robison grunted. "Like maybe we were set up by someone."

Poplawski gave a thoughtful nod. "That'd be my best guess, sir," he said. "I see you brought back Mister Evans. Any sign of his protégé?"

"Quan with the wind. As are the MP's mounted M-60 and the mystery crates Evans had in this jeep, and frankly, I don't give a damn."

To Shintaku, Cantu, and Bowman who were winded and sweating he said, "Good job. Now get something to drink. Stay hydrated. Then do an ammo check and stay alert. We may not be out of this just yet."

The three nodded and made their way to the Deuce-and-a-half where they climbed in the truck bed, took long pulls of water from their canteens, rearmed, and then took up guard posts behind the steel plates.

The Captain turned back to the truck bed studying the damage from the ambush. "So, what are we looking at here, First Sergeant?"

"Three with serious injuries in the initial explosion and roll-over, including the MP Major. The helicopter is ten minutes out. There's a Quick Reaction Force on stand-by if need be. It's your call, Sir."

"Naw, I think we have this handled unless we run into something heavy on the way out."

"I'll radio that it in, Sir."

The Captain nodded. "You said the Medevac's on its way in?"

"The fire will probably keep them from trying to touch down."

Lieutenant Plantagenet joined them at the back of the truck as the wood smoke began overtaking the sulfur and metallic rotten egg smell of the gunpowder from the firefight and permeating the surroundings.

"We'll need to start back after we get the wounded out in case the wind shifts again. Any of our people wounded or injured, Lieutenant?"

"Four or five suffered some minor wounds, cuts, or dings from shrapnel from the RPG and whatever else that came at us. Doc Moore looked them over, bandaged the ones that needed bandaging, but they're all swearing they're Good-to-Go and ready to kick some more ass."

Robison chuckled. Of course, they were.

"And the armored car?" he asked, turning to the First Sergeant.

"It's toast. Our jeep and both trucks took a bunch of hits, but thanks to the Engineers and their add-on sandbags and steel plates, they're still operational. As for our jeep, the windshield is gone, both headlights, and the left front tire are shot to shit. Oh, and the side mirror is dangling like a broken branch fixing to fall. Once I replace the tire with our spare, we'll be ready to roll. It ain't gonna look pretty, but we'll get back to Camp."

"Good. Then let's get whatever's valuable out of the armored car in case we get the okay to torch it."

"Done and done, Sir. The MP buck sergeant, now in charge of the Major's people crawled in and removed the map, weapons, and whatever else that wasn't nailed down out of the hulking mess after he got permission to destroy it in place, which won't be all that hard to do seeing how the fuel is still spilling in and around it. He's got a Thermite grenade ready to use on it once you give the nod that we're ready to roll."

"Well, that should get it cooking."

"How's James Bond doing?" Poplawski asked, tilting his head towards the still groaning Evans in the jeep.

"Shaken and stirred."

To the junior officer he said, "Lieutenant, round me up two people to help our V-I-P out of the jeep and get him over to the back of the Deuce-and-a-half."

"Yes sir."

The command was relayed and two Lurps lifted Evans from the jeep and hauled him over to the right of the truck that was serving as Doc Moore's makeshift triage area, so they set him down against the big truck's back wheels.

When he was done bandaging the seemingly indestructible Sergeant Burke, Moore started in on his assessment on the semi-conscious civilian. Robison walked over and waited for the Medic's diagnosis.

"His injuries don't look life threatening," Moore said to the Captain of his evaluation. "A concussion, from the looks of it. His left orbital bone and nose looks fractured. He hit the dashboard or something?"

"It appears his not-so-counterpart smacked him hard a few times with his pistol," said the Captain, leaving out that perhaps his own swipe and heavy backhand bloodied and broke the nose in a few more places. Robison knew it would've been a whole lot worse if he hadn't smacked him a good one on the drive back when the panicked Evans was tugging on the steering wheel that threatened to run the jeep over the Soviet mine.

"So, the Vietnamese spy guy was working for the other side, a double-agent, I take it?"

"Looks that way, Doc," he said. "You know, I read an article that some hotshot journalist wrote for the New York Times awhile back stating how Viet Cong and North Vietnamese agents had infiltrated every level of South Vietnam's government."

"Is that right, Captain?"

"Estimated to be in the thousands, from the low man or woman on the totem pole all the way up to some in their high office command."

"Well, isn't that just peachy."

"A good part of the orchard anyway."

"The Medevac's two minutes out," yelled Lieutenant Plantagenet standing at the cab of the Ranger's Deuce-and-a-half holding a radio handset to his right ear. "They can't land, so they'll send a basket down."

"Roger that," said Robison. "Pop a smoke and guide it in."

As the Lieutenant retrieved a smoke grenade for the incoming Medevac helicopter the Ranger Captain turned back to the medic.

"Who goes out first, Doc?"

"I'd say the MP Major, Captain. He took the worst of it. He's got a few broken bones; left wrist, arm, and pelvis in the rollover, with what I'm pretty certain, some internal bleeding. He's critical. The gunner lost a toe and suffered a leg cut to his thigh, a broken shoulder too, and the armored car's driver has a crushed ankle, a knee that's going to be tough to repair, some cuts and burns from the explosion. Might not be a bad idea to send Mister Evans out as well."

"Anyone else?"

"Specialist Taras got grazed by a bullet to his scalp and got peppered with some small shards of glass from the windshield. Nothing serious. I mean, not like it could've been. I don't know how they missed hitting him except that maybe he's skinny as a fence rail and Charlie's bullets are too fat. I bandaged the head wound and plucked out the windshield fragments. Says he's Good-to-Go."

"What do you think?"

Moore's answer came with a shrug.

"He'll be okay. A Purple Heart, for sure but the kid's tougher than he looks."

Captain Robison turned and looked around until he spotted the young Ranger still standing stern-faced as he went back to the jeep and placed the M-60 machine gun on the mount and locked and loaded the linked machine gun rounds back into the feed tray. Like Hernandez and Bowman who were scanning the road and the jungle across the creek searching around for another target with their machine guns, Taras was ready for whatever came next.

With the bandage covering the grazing head wound and his Tiger fatigue trousers showing a few holes and blood stains from the flying glass from the shattered windshield, Taras had survived the firefight pretty well, considering what all came at him.

"Taras, you Good-to-Go?" the Captain yelled to the Spec-4.

Taras turned briefly from behind the machine gun, nodded, and gave a thumbs up to his Company Commander. "Yes sir, roger that," he said.

The Ranger officer returned the nod.

"What do you think, Doc?" Robison asked the Medic just to make sure.

Moore shrugged. "I think the bandage will hold until we get back to Camp Mackie. His eyes are clear and other than being 18 he doesn't sound too confused. But it's his call, Sir."

"Let's keep an eye on him on the return ride home."

Robison started to head back to the First Sergeant only to turn back to the medic.

"You rode in the back of the truck on the way out here, didn't you, Doc?"

"Yes sir."

"Then you'll take Mister Evans' jeep back. It's all yours. Find someone to ride shotgun with you."

Doc Moore grinned. The jeep would be a more comfortable ride than in the back of the shaky Deuce-and-a-half.

"Yes sir!"

Chapter 27

The wildfire that was pushing to the southwest and away from the convoy in the small clearing allowed for the Medevac helicopter to come in low over the trees from the opposite direction. The Rangers stood ready to provide cover fire for the Medevac extraction as the Dust-Off helicopter settled into a hover. The Huey that was loudly chopping air hugged the northeast side of the clearing with the co-pilot keeping a cautious eye on the growing forest fire while the pilot held the aircraft in place. In the cargo hold the helicopter's crew chief lowered a stretcher-like metal rescue basket to evacuate the wounded.

One after another the three seriously injured and wounded MPs, and the lesser injured Mister Evans, took the swaying, twisting, and turning cable rides up to the open cargo bay where the on-board medic pulled them in. When the last of the four was safely in the belly of the aircraft, the rescue basket was stored, the Medevac helicopter pivoted, dipped its bulbous nose, and roared away.

The rotor noise from the helicopter was replaced by the fire spitting and cracking clamor of the burning brush and trees, and an occasional whump of flames from the wildfire that was climbing higher in the dry forest. The wildfire was growing dangerously in size. If the ambush hadn't set nerves on edge, then the caustic smoke and fire did, because the convoy, remaining in place, was once more under another kind of dangerous threat. Shifting winds could easily send the flames back toward the clearing and woodcutter's road and block their only way out. The Ranger Captain well understood the dilemma it presented and suspected that the NVA commander might reach that same conclusion and try attacking again with mortars to keep them from moving and letting the flames accomplish what they couldn't.

Fielding yet one more radio call from the gunship pilot confirming a turn-around time, Captain Robison called for an impromptu briefing to lay out the convoy's exit strategy. With only one way in and out of the jungle back to Highway QL-13, there was still the strong possibility of a second ambush and that would dictate much of what he had to say.

There was more from the radio call that he would share with the key players as they gathered in a semi-circle around him. Captain Robison didn't need his compass or map for the outbound journey. The to-and-from was a given. What might happen in between, though, wasn't.

"Listen up, here's how it stands," he said, making sure he had their attention. "Another Pink team is refueling at Lai Khe. It's on its way. They'll cover our exfil from here back to the main North-South highway once they get here, but with the fire growing there's a strong possibility the fire could turn, which means we can't wait."

There were a few looks of concern with that last bit of news just as he knew there would be, so Robison offered some verbal salve to ease some of the rash apprehension.

"Here's the new order of travel."

He explained that the convoy, now minus the armored car, needed a vehicle to take point. Robison suggested shifting the vehicles so that his jeep would now be in the lead. That, though, drew an interrupting cough and head shake from his First Sergeant. Robison turned to Poplawski who, in turn, turned to the MP buck sergeant, who looked like he had something pressing to say on the matter.

"It's okay, Sergeant. He won't bite," said Poplawski. "Tell the Captain what you told me earlier. Go on. Tell him."

"Pistol-Six X-Ray, I take it?" said Robison.

"Yes sir," said the early 20-something NCO sergeant finding his voice for the proposal he would be making. "Sir, my jeep covered the convoy's six all the way here, so, if it's alright with you, I would like to take the lead on the way out."

"You would?"

"Yes sir. I…well, I mean, we would appreciate it," he said. "We owe it to our Major and our buddies to see the task through."

It was an obvious matter of pride to the buck sergeant and the two other MPs. As Military Policemen, they were professionals. They had a job to do, and wouldn't shirk their duty or dodge the responsibility. They hadn't so far, and they had shown their grit during the ambush and following firefight, so the Ranger Captain's decision was an easy one.

"Okay, Sergeant," said Robison. "You'll take the lead. Take it slow and keep an eye out for any new churned-up ground that shouldn't be there on the way out."

"Landmines?"

"Or Anti-tank mines, boobytraps, or tripwires. We encountered a few mines they'd placed up the road when we went after Mister Evans, so be cautious as you go. I don't like the fact that we have to take the same route out of here that we came in on. Charlie and his new found *Dega* buddies know that too and might have something else nasty in store for us, so as I said, take it slow and keep a good eye out for anything suspicious or out of place on the road.

"Oh, there's a little bit of good news. I'm told there's a lot of military traffic on the road heading up to Loc Ninh with gunships escorting the vehicles, so we should, and let me emphasize that word, *should*, be good this time of day. However, we won't let our guard down. Do a weapons and ammo check and let's get ready to roll in five mikes."

Robison glanced at his watch and then checked the overhead sky. The day was wearing on and, despite the growing fire, the temperature was cooling. There were cumulus clouds pushing in from the South China Sea. If they pushed in lower there might be a shower, but nothing heavy. A light shower about now, he was thinking, would actually be welcomed. Any rain would curb and perhaps control the wildfire. If it didn't then the fire would burn out of control for miles.

"We should be at Camp Mackie's back gate well before sunset. Alright then, everyone move back to your vehicles and be ready to move."

There was better news. The sound of approaching helicopters told them that the Piebald Pink Team was arriving on station earlier than expected. The radio call that followed confirmed it.

"Valhalla-Six, Piebald Two-Three. Over."

"Valhalla-Six. Go."

"We're refueled, rearmed, and ready to rock and roll. By the way, that fire down there is still moving south and west and away from the road. You should be good to the highway."

"Roger that Piebald Two-three. Glad to have you back. We're Good-to-Go. Valhalla-Six, out."

"Happy trails," came the reply. "Well, happier anyway."

With the Scout helicopter flying well out in front of the wood cutter's trail, Captain Robison gave the order to saddle up. Once the vehicle engines rumbled to life, he gave the radio order to '*Go*,' and the convoy was on its way and rolling.

Using the clearing as a quick turnaround, the vehicles rearranged the convoy line. The MP gun jeep took the lead, followed by Robison's jeep 15 yards behind, then the Supply truck, Doc Moore's jeep with Staff Sergeant Shintaku riding shotgun next in line, and finally the Ranger's modified gun truck bringing up the rear. Behind them the armored car that was on its side in the clearing was engulfed in flames and melting paint and wiring and destroying anything else inside the vehicle that could burn. At 4,000-degrees Fahrenheit the thermite grenade had turned the engine block into molten metal while the spilled fuel ignited the fuel tank with a muffled whoomph! There would be nothing left for the enemy to salvage.

The remaining vehicles in the convoy weren't much to look at either. However, even with its dinged-up steel plates and bullet ridden sandbags the convoy still presented a formidable fighting force, given that Hernandez was still on the .50 caliber heavy machine gun, Taras, Daley, and Sanchez, and an MP were up behind their M-60 machine guns. Not to be left out, the new FNGs were looking to use their M-16s, grenade launcher, and their last M-72 LAW. Adrenaline, balls, and just the right amount of savvy had them ready for any new fight that might come their way.

If the Transportation Officer or the MPs weren't on edge on this part of the journey, then the veteran Lurps gut instincts told them they needed to be. They were all painfully well aware that the route they were on was the same route they had taken from Highway QL-13. It was always deemed a big no-no and violated one of the primary rules of Rogers Rangers, and something that had been drilled into them during their training, and even more so on combat patrols. It was a 200-year-old tried and true rule, which was, you don't go back the same way you came in.

Period.

In 1757, during the seven-year French and Indian War, Major Robert Rogers sat down on Rogers Island on the Hudson River near Fort Edward and penned his twenty-eight rules and guidelines for Ranger patrolling and guerilla warfare operations. Those rules and guidelines became chapter and verse for all Ranger operations and served as the genesis for U.S. small unit guerrilla warfare. That Rogers remained loyal to Great Britain several years later during the Revolutionary War also provided the British with the foundation for their own special operations rules and guidelines. Good tactics were good tactics, regardless of whose flag they fell under.

Because of the strong possibility of a second ambush or newly placed landmines or other boobytraps, the going had to be slow, with all eyes and ears out scanning and listening for anything that looked or sounded hinky. Nerves were on edge with good reason from the primary ambush and the attack to the rear of the column. It paid to be suspicious, or you bled the cost of naivety.

The better advantages for the convoy were still the Cobra gunship and Low Bird helicopter that arrived just as the convoy moved out. Targeted retribution from above had those potentially waiting in ambush nervously thinking twice.

That the going was always in first gear proved effective when the lead MP vehicle slowed to yet one more stop to check out a suspicious looking patch of ground on the road a mile into the return ride. The patch was newly churned ground, dead center on the tire tracks the convoy made on their way in. The patch was slightly darker in color and in the shadows from the trees, it almost went unnoticed. Brush marks away from the patch told the rest of the story. Brush marks may have worked well in movies but in real life the Sergeant knew the scrapes stood out like raked-over scars.

The MP sergeant had his driver stop the vehicle well in front of the dark oval. The jeep engine was knocking as it idled as he radioed back the suspicious looking find to the Ranger Captain.

"Valhalla-Six, Pistol-Six X-Ray. Over."

"Go, X-ray."

"Be advised, I think we have a mine ahead of us at twelve o'clock. I'm going to move up on foot and check it out."

"Roger that, X-Ray. Easy does it. Break. All vehicles remain and hold in place and watch your surroundings. Valhalla- Six out."

The radio commo that brought the rest of the convoy to a halt, now had the column once again on high alert.

"Cover me," the MP sergeant said to the two other MPs in the jeep as he climbed out and took out his Colt 1911 handgun. You didn't need a lot of rounds when one of eight rounds that the .45 caliber sidearm carried could easily slam into a human body and tilt the nervous system out of play. Game over.

The MP on the jeep mounted machine gun gave him a chin-up nod while the jeep's driver began scanning the jungle along both sides of the woodcutter's road. With the heavy sidearm in hand, the MP buck sergeant crept forward to check out the disturbance with the two MPs covering his go.

Six feet in front of the ground disturbance he stopped and took in a deep breath. The pucker factor tensed his abdomen and gurgled bile at what he was looking at. Off to the side of the road was a broken broom-size branch of brush that had been used to try to conceal any sign of what had occurred here, but the placement of the anti-tank mine and the cover-up was hurried. Convoy runs in the past had taught him something more of VC tactics. The disturbed piece of ground, the size of a large dinner plate, might only be a ruse for a better placed and better concealed landmine or boobytrap like the one that took out their armored car, so the sergeant studied the road around him for anything else out of the ordinary. Thankfully, there wasn't, and he breathed a sigh of relief that only lasted until he turned back to the problem in front of him.

Dropping down to his knees the MP sergeant went prone as he crawled and inched his way forward. Taking out his Buck knife he opened the three-inch blade and began probing the dirt around the churned oval shaped dark patch.

The third poke with the knife touched against buried metal, as did a careful fourth and fifth. It was a Soviet anti-tank mine, a big one. A TM-46, more than likely, with enough explosive charge to turn the jeep and everyone in it into human confetti. A careful check around the buried mine didn't show any hidden tripwires or manual detonation wires. Thankfully, nobody was hiding in the bush ready to trigger an explosive. Putting his knife away, the MP sergeant took in a deep breath, scanned the road ahead for any more dark patches, found none, and then stood and made his way back to the others.

"It's an anti-tank mine," he said to the others in the lead jeep.

The Ranger Captain was right. After the convoy had passed the NVA had quickly planted another nasty little surprise.

"Valhalla-six, Pistol-Six, X-ray," said the MP sergeant getting on the radio.

"Go, X-ray."

"We have a Soviet anti-tank mine in front of us, Sir. A TM-46 or a Chinese equivalent, I'm guessing. It looks to be a 20 pounder from the size."

"Roger that. Back away slowly, and put some distance between you and it and then get behind some good cover. Be ready for another ambush too. I'll send up one of my people to place a charge on it. We'll blow it in place. You copy?"

"Copy," came the reply. "Pistol-Six X-Ray, out."

Staying on the radio the Captain shifted the audience. "Break! Break! Piebald Two-three, Piebald Two-three, Valhalla-Six. Over."

"Piebald Two-three. Go, Valhalla."

"Be advised, we have a landmine in the road holding us up. Give us ten mikes to blow it in place and have your Low Bird steer clear of the immediate area for a bit. You copy?"

"Affirmative. Break-Break. One-Eight, you copy?"

This from the gunship pilot to the newly arrived Low Bird.

"Roger that, Two-three," radioed the Scout helicopter pilot clearing the area and moving further down the road and away from any potential shrapnel once the landmine was blown in place. After a few buzzing passes and some serious eyeballing up ahead, the Low Bird gave its report.

"Valhalla-Six, One-Eight over."

"Six. Go."

"Be advised, there's no movement on the ground down below. From what we can see, all looks to be quiet. You're Good-to-Go."

"I copy, One-Eight. Thank you. Valhalla-Six out."

The Rangers were up and ready for another fight while the small Scout helicopter buzzed over the trees seeking out any enemy that still might be in hiding. Underestimating the tenacity or resolve of the Viet Cong or North Vietnamese soldiers could get you killed in a myriad of ugly ways. When no ambush or other threats were detected, Captain Robison realized that the landmine was just a bad '*goodbye*' parting gift left behind by the ambushers.

It was a gleeful Sergeant Cantu that Captain Robison sent forward to set a charge on the landmine. Grabbing a quarter pound of C-4 and a one-minute timing fuse and blasting cap from the truck, Cantu made his way back down the road on foot to the MP jeep.

With a chin up nod to the MPs who were readying to back up their jeep to find some distance and better cover, Cantu asked the MP sergeant what he'd found.

"Thirty feet up the left side of the road. Directly under our old tire tracks," said the sergeant, pointing to where he found the anti-tank mine. "I didn't see a detonation wire or tripwires, and I didn't try removing it either since Charlie sometimes plants the mine over the prongs of a Bouncing Betty landmine."

"You've seen that before?"

The MP sergeant gave a slow nod. "Oh yeah. Lost one of my guys a few months back on another convoy. You think you're safe taking one of the mines out of the ground and then another one beneath pops up and ruins your day at groin level."

In the shadows from the tree branches and jungle laying in patches across the roadway Cantu couldn't see it yet but at least he had a head's-up where it was.

"I'll cover you," said the MP sergeant. "My people will do the overwatch."

"Good. You watch the right. I'll take the left." Cantu turned and gave a nod to the MP behind the M-60 machine gun.

In a slow walk the Lurp started forward with the MP sergeant trailing. 20 feet out the MP sergeant pointed to where the anti-tank mine had been placed. It didn't stand out as much as Cantu had expected. The color change of the dirt concealing the mine was minimal. The MP sergeant had a good eye. Just a few feet in front of the mine the Ranger could make out the faint scrapes and scratches from where an enemy soldier or two had tried brushing any sign away of what they'd placed. A two-foot long broken branch with leaves lay next to the road where it had been discarded.

"Sloppy, sloppy, sloppy," he muttered, shaking his head at the tree branch all the while keeping an eye out for wires leading to unseen and better planted secondary devices.

He'd check out the broken brush first to make sure there wasn't a captured Claymore anti-personnel mine ready to blow on them while they were focused on the mine in the road.

Back at the Ranger jeep there was time to talk and that is exactly what First Sergeant Poplawski was doing over his right shoulder.

"So, Specialist Taras? You have a first name, do you?"

"My name, First Sergeant?"

"Yes, your first name. What is it?"

Captain Robison turned in his seat and smiled at the painfully young looking Ranger who was standing back up behind the jeep-mounted machine gun. His jungle fatigues were flecked with half a dozen small, bloodied spots and the bandage that was wrapped around his head was beginning to droop. Just above the bloodied gauze a bump was forming.

"It's... it's...eh, Gale, First Sergeant," he said, quietly. The growing blush on his cheeks said Taras was more than a little embarrassed by the admission.

"Gale?"

"Yes, First Sergeant. It's my mother's maiden name. I just...I..."

Poplawski raised a hand palm out in submission. "Got it! Got it! No problem!" he said, and started to chuckle.

Taras, though, didn't find it funny, never had, but Poplawski kept chuckling regardless, but when he noticed the young soldier's set jawline and furrowed brow reaction, he stopped laughing.

"Wait one. I ain't making fun of your name, young Ranger," he said, holding up both open hands to placate the soldier. The First Sergeant pointed to the mounted machine gun.

Sweet Sorrow

"I'm chuckling because of your name being Gale and you standing at that M-60 during the firefight like another kind of gale to be reckoned with! Nice job, *Hurricane*. Ya done good!"

"*Hurricane*? I like it, It's fitting!" agreed the Captain. "So, *Hurricane* it is!"

Taras hadn't expected the compliment, and any pain he might've been feeling from the small grazing wound he took in the ambush or self-consciousness he felt about his first name, vanished.

Taras smiled and nodded back to his Commanding Officer and the First Sergeant. *Hurricane* wasn't a bad nickname to have.

The kid had grit, thought Poplawski, thinking that Taras also had saved his ass given the kick out of the jeep just before the incoming enemy machine gun rounds tore through the driver's seat where he'd been sitting.

When they got back to Camp Mackie he'd speak with the Captain about putting Taras in for a medal, a Silver Star for Gallantry at least, because when the shit hit the ambush fan, and it certainly did, the kid stood tall, and stayed in the fight, toe-to-toe. Christ, he was gallant in the best sense of the word. He never wavered even when the rest of us were ducking and jumping for cover! He saved some lives and bought some much needed time for others like my dumbass when we desperately needed it. If that didn't meet and merit the criteria for the medal then nothing did.

Poplawski also knew that if the Silver Star somehow got kicked down by command as it sometimes did with Enlisted men, then at least Taras would get a Bronze Star for heroism. There were allocations for awards in any given After-Action writeup, just as there were those in the positions power to say *yea* or *nay* for any medal nomination. With the First Sergeant and Commanding officer witnessing the act and championing the writeup, the odds would be in favor of Taras, if the BIG-TOC wouldn't shoot down the medal requests because of the way the mission turned out.

Still, Poplawski would submit the request anyway and there was little doubt that it would certainly be with the Company Commander's full blessing. There were others worthy of awards as well for their actions that went above and beyond today, and he knew that Captain Robison would recognize and praise their valor, too. The Captain was well ahead of the thinking and said as much.

"We'll need some award write-ups when we get back," he said to Poplawski.

"Yes sir."

"Let's make a list of some names, compare some notes and recommendations, and then have Lieutenants' Marquardt and Plantagenet do the write ups."

Poplawski nodded and understood why. With the two Lieutenants writing up the award nominations for the Company Commander to look over and sign off on before sending them up the chain of command, the nominations stood a better chance than anything he could put down on paper. The First Sergeant knew that perhaps he was too earthy and succinct when it came to the wording for the award write ups. Captain Robison smiled at the thought as well, remembering when Lieutenant Marquardt had once offered to *'eh...better rephrase,'* the First Sergeant's write-up for the brave actions of several Rangers after one of their hard-fought long range patrols.

"Why, Lieutenant?" he recalled Poplawski asking, seemingly confused by the offer while Robison, watching on, had tried to suppress a chuckle.

The Ranger Company's Executive Officer who had handed his boss Poplawski's write-up was doing his best not to chuckle as well. The citation gave a brief account of their actions in a tense firefight and ended it with, *'They kicked ass when it mattered, Ranger style. Now give them something shiny. They were out-fucking-standing!'*

"Well, he's not wrong, Lieutenant," Robison said at the time, reading over Poplawski's work. "But why don't you massage it some and make it a bit more BIG-TOC palatable with the correct military awards jargon? First Sergeant, you don't mind if the X.O. helps you with the wording."

"No Sir."

"Good," Robison said nodding, thinking that while the First Sergeant's take was likely more straightforward and to the point, the award would never see the light of the proverbial day. The Lieutenant's modified version would get the job done. It was like his Grandmother once told him; *'You can't sing in the choir unless you know the words and can carry a tune.'*

He would get Marquardt working on the write-ups and between them they would find the right tenor and tone. They would use the Executive Officer's editing again for these new award recommendations.

"Ya done good, *Hurricane*!" said the First Sergeant, complimenting Taras one more time.

"Roger that," said the Captain, hoping that the storm was over, while the hold up from the Soviet Anti-tank mine said otherwise.

Of course, it did. It wasn't going to be an easy day and the sun was still shining.

Chapter 28

Sergeant Cantu was laying prone directly in front of the buried Soviet anti-tank mine humming to himself as he carefully probed the ground around it with his bayonet. To the MP Sergeant it sounded like *Mary Had a Little Lamb* as he worked. Christ! He was smiling too!

An almost inaudible clink with the knife blade told Cantu he'd located the large, circular metal canister before he had made a series of similar taps around the circumference of the canister. The diameter of the mine was the size of an old Chrysler hubcap, only a lot thicker in depth and packing more explosive mileage. Taking in a short, quick breath, he probed a little deeper beneath the canister to see what, if anything, was there. The tip of the knife touched a second metal canister.

"Well now," he said. "Helloooo to you too!"

The MP sergeant was right about his warning. Beneath the anti-tank mine was a second smaller mine. Whether it was a Bouncing Betty anti-personnel mine or one that would detonate when anyone removed the one above it was anybody's guess. The first explosion would set off the second one a second or so later, not that he'd be around to hear it. He knew he'd be pink mist and jelly sticking to the leaves and trees in the surrounding jungle.

Cantu wisely didn't attempt to remove or move either mine.

"Good call," he said to the MP sergeant over his right shoulder. "They left us another one underneath it. Go ahead and move back to cover."

As he was speaking Cantu began stuffing a Claymore blasting cap into the small charge of soft, malleable C-4 explosive putty and then placed it snug up against the anti-tank mine. The charge would take out both mines.

Setting up the charge he slowly began reeling out the blasting cap wire as he made his way back to the jeep.

Plugging in the wire to the charging device he turned to the MP sergeant he said, "We're ready to rock n' roll. Call it in!"

The information was relayed to Captain Robison who advised everyone in the now even smaller convoy to get down behind good cover and hunker down. The MP sergeant as the MPs lowered themselves down behind their jeep as Cantu shouted out the warning.

"FIRE IN THE HOLE!" he yelled three times as he squeezed the hand-held clacker three times quickly.

There were two enemy mines but the blast that came produced one booming eruption that sent a rising geyser of orange tinged dirt, rock, dust, and metal fragments bursting up through the canopy-covered trees with the bulk of it raining back down on the road. Shrapnel whizzed overhead and into the MP jeep, but the four GIs on the ground were safe. The blast left a sizable crater roughly five feet deep and wide in the already bad road. The crater wasn't anything any of the vehicles couldn't steer around and avoid but there would be some roller coaster and bouncing maneuvering to move beyond it.

"There it is!" Cantu said getting to his feet and walked back to the Ranger's Deuce-and-a-half where he gave the Captain a wide smile and a thumbs-up. The Ranger Officer nodded and gave the radio call to *'Saddle Up.'*

The convoy rolled on, and with no more ambushes or buried mines to halt or hinder it, they reached the main highway less than 15 minutes later.

"ELVIS HAS LEFT THE BUILDING!" Hernandez yelled to the Rangers in the truck bed as the Deuce-and-a-half made the turn onto QL-13 and had picked up speed.

"Well, Suspicious minds aside, Hound Dog, we too were caught in a trap," laughed Daley.

"All shook up, but rockin' all the time!"

"Yeah, we were. Good job, people! Even you new guys didn't do too badly!" This backhanded compliment was aimed at PFC *Ironic* and Sanchez.

"My mama really likes Elvis," said Sanchez, joining in on the conversation.

"Then your momma has great taste in music," said Hernandez. "My respect for you, maybe, has grown."

Sanchez grinned at the compliment while Hernandez dismissed it with a shrug and a semi-loud, *meh.*

"You're still new, so we'll leave it at *maybe.*"

"You know, we had a guy in my old Ranger Company named Elvis," said Daley.

"Seriously?"

"Yep, Good dude."

"You guys fuck with him because of his name?"

"Oh yeah, we did, but he had a good sense of humor. Took it good naturedly, for the most part, as long as you weren't being an asshole about it."

"For the most part, huh?"

"Uh-huh, and offered up his thoughts on the matter, especially to one dumb sonofabitch in our unit who ragged him one too many times about it in the chow line."

"What he'd do?"

"He just turned and smiled at the fool and said, quote, *'Don't be cruel, or I'll kick your ass, comprende?'* Unquote. Then he did one of those Bruce Lee Kato sidekicks that stopped a few inches from the guy's nose."

"In jungle boots?"

"With the Vibram pattern sole bringing home the message."

"That'd work. Always good advice too!"

"And, of course, he followed that up with, *Thank you, very mush.*"

"Funny dude."
"Yep, and a good Ranger."

The remainder of the drive back to Camp Mackie was uneventful, although there were a few tricky maneuvers hugging the shoulder of the road, along with another *'pull over and give'em room to pass'* side of the road delay, when one more long convoy of trucks filled with ARVNs, supplies, and interspersed with track vehicles and tanks, were headed north toward the border on the highway.

As they waited on the literal sidelines for this latest convoy to pass, First Sergeant Poplawski commented to Captain Robison on the day's events.

"You know, I kinda liked having the gunship and Low Bird along with us today. Makes me appreciate those *'Blues'* recon platoons, and how they all work together with their own eyes in the sky. I think maybe they've got it all figured out."

Robison agreed. "Yeah, they do, don't they? You know, when we get back what say maybe we pass along one or two of the A-K's or extra SKS rifles we have to those pilots along with our thanks? We'll need to get them removed from our inventory anyway since they're officially not on our books. Maybe a bottle of whiskey too. I'll spring for the booze."

"Roger that, Sir."

When the road traffic finally cleared twenty minutes later the small convoy rolled further south. Although it was only mid-week the rest of the way proved to be a quiet Sunday drive.

Chapter 29

By the time the small convoy reached Camp Mackie's back gate, halted, and waited for the MPs to unlock and unchain the barrier, both the last light of day and the last bit of remaining adrenaline of those in the convoy were beginning to fade. It had been a long trying day, and it wasn't over yet.

"Valhalla-Six, Piebald Two-Three. Over."

"Go, Two-Three."

"A pleasure working with you today, Valhalla," said the Cobra gunship pilot.

"And with you as well, Piebald. We'll send a thank you bottle of Jack over your way in the morning," said Captain Robison. "You and your team earned the drinks on us."

"Wait one," came the response from the gunship. A moment later the gunship pilot was back on the radio.

"Valhalla-Six be advised, like all outstanding pilots we always have a healthy supply of good liquor back at our A-O. However, what we don't have are any of those fancy Ranger scrolls you guys wear that'll look nice on our pilot's briefing room. Any of those you could spare would be appreciated."

"Done! Two-Three. We'll send a bunch. Valhalla-Six out."

The helicopters had already veered off over the Camp toward the main flightline towards their assigned revetments as the Military Police guarding the Camp's back gate came out of their bunker and were unlocking the padlock on the links of the heavy chain that secured the massive gate. This gave Captain Robison time to call the day's principal players; MP sergeant, Transportation officer, and Lieutenant Plantagenet over to his jeep for one last word. With dusty faces, tired eyes, and in some cases, gun smoke residue showing in the creases of their faces like broken spider webs, Robison decided to keep it short.

"First of all, let me say, and stating the obvious, it's been a long and difficult day," he said, "but thanks to all of you, and the genuine teamwork involved we survived the ambush that was designed to take us all out. That didn't happen because you didn't let it happen. You didn't just do well under the circumstances, you did very well, and I intend to let the Base Commander know that and more later during the mission debriefing. If you're intending to write up any of your people for awards for their actions today, then I'll be glad to endorse them with some of my own comments from what I witnessed. I'll also be writing you up for awards as well for your leadership. Finally, if you or any of your people have any injuries or wounds of any kind from the firefight today, then get them checked out at the Aid Station. Don't let macho get in the way by saying, 'Naw, *it's just a scratch.*' Small cuts and wounds tend to fester and turn nasty from the jungle and the heat. You copy?"

'Yes sirs' and head nods followed.

"Good. Now, head back to your units and let your commands know what's going on, although, I suspect they've already received word of the events that played out. Statements will need to be taken, so I would advise you to sit down with your commands and iron them out, because if we're not called to the BIG-TOC later this evening for a debriefing, then I'm sure we'll be called there tomorrow morning."

That was met with a round of much better, *'Yes sirs,'* and nods.

"Dismissed."

The soldiers offered a collective salute and Ranger Captain it. Once the big gates were pushed open, the vehicles in the small convoy entered the Camp and then broke away toward their home units and compounds. The Ranger jeep with its shot out windshield and headlights, along with its many paint scrapes and dings from enemy machine gun rounds and small arms fire, led the way like a tired boxer going back to the shower room after a tough bout. The Deuce-and-a-half truck that had fared better solemnly followed. It was a short drive to the Ranger Company compound.

For the Lurps of Romeo Company-Ranger there were cuts and other wounds to be better treated at the Aid Station, weapons to be cleaned and turned in to the company's Armorer, vehicle log books to be updated or pretended to be updated, and showers to be taken, if there was enough water in the two 55 gallon drums that served as the company's shower point.

As those Rangers that took part in the convoy and firefight climbed out of the vehicles, First Sergeant Poplawski, at the request of Captain Robison, called for a small formation. As they formed a half-circle gathering around the Company Commander and First Sergeant, Robison was staring at their sweat-stained and tired faces before checking his watch.

"First Sergeant!"

"Sir?"

"What time does the Mess tent close?"

Poplawski checked his watch. "Half an hour by my Rolex, Sir."

Robison grunted and to the ten Lurps he said, "If Doc Moore clears you, then get some hot chow. But, if, and only if Doc deems any of you needing more medical treatment or a look-see by the Aid Station Doctor, then do it. Once you're done with Doc get some chow, then clean your weapons, and get a shower. Lieutenant Plantagenet?"

"Sir?"

"Let the Mess Officer know what's going on and if they can keep the Mess Tent open for any of those coming back from the Aid Station, or maybe see if they'll let you have some take-out. You copy?"

"Yes sir," came the response. "You want me to bring something back for you and the First Sergeant?"

"A sandwich, would be fine."

"A sandwich, Sir. Is that all?"

"Yep, just slap whatever meat they're serving on some bread with a little mustard that'll work just fine for me," Robison said, turning to the Senior NCO. "Top?"

"No Sir, I'm good. I have my coffee and a can of some lovely Beef and Potato C-Rations. That and a few dabs of Tabasco sauce makes for a little bit of Heaven, it does."

"I worry about you at times, First Sergeant."

"By sheer coincidence, Captain. I worry about me as well!"

Back to the others, the Captain added, "Gentlemen, just so you know, you all made me and the Company proud today, and proved why Rangers lead the way. First Sergeant?"

"Sir?"

"They're all yours."

Robison turned the men over to Poplawski.

"Right! The Captain was being way nice calling you hooligans and filthy animals, '*Gentlemen*.' Could be his West Point manners or quite possibly, sun stroke. Anyway, you heard him, see the medic, and if he clears you, then get some chow. Oh, and you got the rest of the night and tomorrow morning off. Dismissed."

The call came into the unit's Orderly Room a few minutes later as they were stowing their gear and settling in. Robison took the call, which was mostly listening, and then replied, "Roger that," to whoever was on the other end of the line before he hung up the phone.

"That was Colonel Becker's aid saying that there will be a mandatory debriefing in the BIG-TOC tomorrow at 1300 hours. They need a statement for the After Action Report," the Captain said to the First Sergeant as he was using a P-38 to open his can of C-Rations.

"Good news, travel fast."

"And bad news even faster."

"Seems late in the day for a debriefing, doesn't it, Sir?"

Robison shrugged. "Could be they want to read all of the statements and hear from all the key players, and maybe hear from Saigon first on why it all went south."

"There's that," agreed Poplawski.

Lieutenant Plantagenet was back carrying two sandwiches on paper plates, along with paper coffee cups filled with fresh peaches.

"Turkey sandwiches, Sir, and some peaches," he said, handing one of the sandwich plates and cups to the Captain.

"Thank you, Lieutenant."

"You're welcome, Sir."

"We have a few cold beers in the fridge, Captain," said the First Sergeant. "Want one, Sir?"

"Sounds good, Top."

"How about you, Lieutenant?" offered the Captain to the junior officer.

The surprised Plantagenet, who was on his way out the door, turned back, and nodded. This was a first; a welcomed one.

"Yes sir, thank you."

Poplawski retrieved three cold cans of Budweiser beer from the mini-fridge and handed one to his Commanding Officer and another to the Platoon Leader, who both gave a tired nod of thanks. The First Sergeant handed the Ranger Company Commander a church key can opener and the three opened the small cans.

The weight of the day was taking over, after the Company Commander gave a salute holding up his can of beer, the two others returned it. Afterward, they ate and drank in silence.

Plantagenet was quietly pleased just to be included in the mix while the Ranger officer and First Sergeant were quiet for another reason. The Higher-highers both in Saigon and the BIG-TOC would be looking to assign blame.

But that was tomorrow and in combat you dealt with what was in front of you one fight at a time.

Chapter 30

Captain Robison was right about the mission debriefing being delayed, but wrong that the new time of 1300 hours would be set in stone. A second call from the Colonel's aid at 1100 hours informed him that the debriefing would now be held the following day.

"The debriefing is now scheduled for 1500 hours tomorrow," Robison said to his First Sergeant.

"Hmm. Delayed again," said Poplawski, mulling it over what this new holdup might mean. "No worries, Sir. I'll gladly be ready with my two-cents worth."

"Officer's only, this time around, I'm afraid. Lieutenant Plantagenet will be going with me. They want a statement from him as well."

"Ah!"

"Apparently, they're interviewing and taking statements from the wounded MP Major at the 24th Evacuation Hospital in Long Binh, and from Mister Evans from his hospital bed in Saigon."

"Saigon? Oh, that's right, he's a civilian, sort of. Sort of an asshole, too."

"The BIG-TOC wants my statement by no later than 1800 hours today."

"Do they need one from me?"

"No, just mine. They said that they'll add it to the others from the Lieutenant from the Transportation Company, the MP Sergeant who had taken over the MP contingent after the Major was wounded, and from the pilots from the Piebald team."

"Then you and Romeo Company should both fare well. Evans and Quan, maybe not so much so."

The Captain shrugged. "Maybe being the operative word."

"No worries, Sir," Poplawski said, bolstering his confidence. "I'll drive you two over and wait. In the meanwhile, I'll get started on finding new homes for any of our, eh, borrowed items and things that aren't on our books."

"Good."

"I'll pick you both up after the debriefing."

The Captain nodded. His mind was on the written statement and whether it needed another draft. He'd already gone through a few rough drafts the evening before and eventually settled on the final one that he typed up and had ready to submit. He thought he'd told it like it was and how it played out from start to finish, Dragnet style. *Just the facts, Ma'am.* Lean and mean. He had read over Plantagenet's statement when the Lieutenant submitted it to him earlier that morning. The statement pretty much mirrored his own with perhaps a few more references of the significant actions of those involved that turned the ambush, under what Plantagenet wrote were *'the brave leadership of Captain Robison.'*

Plantagenet's words brought on an appreciative nod when he read them. And a chuckle.

"You do realize I got dumped on my ass out of the jeep, right, Lieutenant?" laughed the Captain reading over the statement.

"Yes sir, but I was always taught that it's how you get up afterward that counts. I'm proud to serve under your command, Sir."

"And I'm proud to have you on my team, Ranger. And I thank you for this," Robison said, waving the junior officer's typed statement. "It's appreciated."

The statement might help but because it was a failed mission, someone was likely to be held accountable, which really meant hung out to dry, for its failure. He would accept his responsibility in the mission, but he wasn't about to fall on his sword for what clearly had been a compromised mission. That blame belonged to Quan and his role in planning and setting up the ambush. To that end Robison was determined to stand up for his Lurps, his Rangers. They not only did their best, but they also did what was necessary, and at times, exceeded any definition of that critical requirement.

From the gathered interviews and statements, and what would be learned in the official debriefing, there would be an Official After Action Report generated where the inevitable fault would not lie in the stars, but be brutally assigned.

After all, the mission had indeed failed. The gold and silver reparation, ala bribery payment, was gone, the particular Dega/Montagnard tribe was no longer an ally of, or for the Saigon cause, and Quan, the former top-level and once highly regarded spook in the South Vietnamese government's CIA counterpart, the *Phu Dac uy Trung uong Tinh Ba-* their Central Intelligence Office, proved to be a top-level spymaster for the North Vietnamese.

Besides the planned ambush Quan had a big hand in arranging, and the precious metals and MP machine gun he and the ambushers had walked off with, there was little doubt that he had also taken some critical Top Secret intel, such as the names of spies conducting on-going missions and safe house locations in the North, and operational strategies and codes with him that would set back intelligence gathering in the war for years.

Quan's deception would most likely be singled-out for the failure of the mission, as would the *'inactions'* of those other key players roles that Evans might point to during the ill-fated mission. Where the dice would tumble, though, was always a crap shoot.

Once the witness statements were objectively pored over and scrutinized by Camp Mackie's Command the results would be disseminated in the debriefing to the convoy's key players, or because of their injuries or wounds, to their assigned representatives. What remained and was finalized would be delivered to the Higher-highers at MAC-V Headquarters Command.

The process took two days, and after rescheduling the debriefing once again, it would now take place on day three at the BIG-TOC at 1500 hours.

At 1445 hours, First Sergeant Poplawski had the jeep idling in front of the Ranger Company's Orderly Room. A few minutes later a stern-faced Captain Robison and worried looking Lieutenant Plantagenet emerged from the Quonset hut office and climbed into the awaiting jeep.

"Let's get this done," Robison said to Poplawski.

"Roger that, Captain," the First Sergeant said, shoving the jeep into first gear and to make the short drive over to the BIG-TOC. Because it was a failed mission, it was also a quiet ride.

Facing the music seldom meant there would be easy listening.

Chapter 31

With his head tilted skyward a very bored First Sergeant Walter *'The Brick, as in Wall, just don't ever fucking call me Walter'* Poplawski was leaning back in the driver's seat of the Company's *borrowed* jeep and slowly blowing smoke rings from his cigarette into the bright blue Vietnamese sky.

The first, and larger perfectly formed circle of smoke, was dissipating as the following two smaller smoke rings blew through its center when Captain Robison and Lieutenant Plantagenet came out of the BIG-TOC from the debriefing.

Sitting up straight in the canvas cover seat, Poplawski field stripped the cigarette and pocketed the filter as the two officers made their way over to the vehicle.

"How'd it go, Sir?" he said, addressing the Captain, as the two officers climbed into the jeep and took their seats.

"A little better than we'd hoped," said Robison as the Lieutenant smiled and nodded. "As expected the Colonel shared his displeasure with how it all went down. Said Saigon wasn't happy. Same-same with two of the finer minds of the government officials still inside the BIG-TOC, who swore they're also from the *'Civil Operations Rural Development Agency'* and not from Langley, especially since the five crates of what they only described as *'materials'* were lost in the hubbub."

"*Materials*? Seriously," he said, They said, '*materials*?'"

"And *hubbub*," said Robison. "Even when the curious Colonel pressed them about what exactly those *'materials'* were, the agency boys quickly changed the subject and went on about the more critical loss and support of the Dega."

"No kidding, Sir. That was the more critical loss."

"True. He also said when they spoke to Evans in the hospital, he laid the fault on the South Vietnamese Army for shelling the village, which set the stage for what followed…"

"Ya think?"

"And, of course he bitched about the delays on the road with the convoy."

"What? He was looking to get to the ambush sooner. You mention that his amigo, and handpicked Vietnamese secret squirrel counterpart, Quan, sold us out and likely planned the reception?"

"Didn't have to! Surprisingly, Colonel Becker brought up that very point to the representatives of the C-I-A…."

"Eh, don't you mean, the *Civil Operations and Rural Development Agency*, Sir?"

"Oops, my mistake!"

"By any chance are the names of those two civilian representatives Burger or King?"

Robison chuffed and shook his head.

"No, but one of them pulled me aside later and privately mentioned to me that Evans has some kind of legacy clout with the Agency. Apparently, his father worked with Donovan and the OSS back in the day. But, many of those who have worked with junior at the C-I...eh, *Civil Operations and Rural Development Agency*, hyphen A, here in-country, including the station chief, think he's an asshole."

"Then I might have some new found respect for the hyphen-A's," said Poplawski.

That brought a chuckle from the Lieutenant in the backseat, who, like any good audience member, was quietly enjoying the exchange.

"Overall, we didn't fare too badly. Turns out MAC-V Headquarters had some of their people interview the MP Major and the wounded turret gunner in the hospital to get their statements."

"Command looking to hang us out to dry?"

"Naw, due diligence, I suspect. Both the MP Major and the wounded gunner said we were the ones who actually saved the convoy by breaking the ambush, rescuing, treating, and evacuating the wounded, including them as well as Evans- all under heavy enemy fire. The Piebald pilots praised us highly too, as did the Transportation officer in their statements. Said we went above and beyond."

"They said that?"

"They did, and apparently the MP Major added that we deserve official recognition for it, so it looks like we gained better status in both MAC-V's and Colonel Becker's eyes. The funny thing is, Colonel Becker isn't exactly our biggest fan..."

"So, I've gathered."

"Surprisingly, though, and to his credit, he stuck up for us today. Said, *'My Rangers more than held up their end,'* he said in no uncertain terms. I mean, he was direct."

"He said, *'My Rangers'*?"

Robison grinned and nodded. "Thought you'd appreciate that."

"Wonders never cease!"

"There's more! He even took me aside to congratulate me on making the Major's list, saying, quote, *'You are a credit to your race.'* Unquote."

"Oh, Hell Captain, you're a credit to anybody's race," said Poplawski. "Don't suppose he said anything about your wonderful and amazing Pollock First Sergeant, did he?"

"Nope, I'm afraid he didn't, but if it's any consolation, I think you're pretty damn spiffy!"

"Spiffy?"

"Okay then, how about out-fucking standing?"

Poplawski brightened. "I am, aren't I."

"That you are. However, on the downside, there won't be any more Lurp missions for us. Officially we're on stand-down."

"It's been an interesting run, Sir."

"It has. However, for the next few weeks Colonel Becker plans on using some of our people and our modified gun truck to supplement any MP road escort duty. The MP Major and the MP sergeant who was wounded apparently told him we're good to have around in a gunfight."

"No shit, Sir. We are!"

"Uh-huh,. Curiously enough, so did the Piebald Pilots."

"Insightful people, they are. Truly!"

"So, eh, what did you give them to speak so highly of us, Brick?"

The Ranger Captain stared at his First Sergeant and a long moment passed before the First Sergeant smiled.

"You mean, besides our thanks?"

"Yes. Beside our thanks."

"Two birds with one stone, Sir."

"What kind of birds?"

"Well, it's possible that along with our thanks for their fine air support and those scrolls you gave me to give them I might've also presented the Piebald pilots and crews with a few of our captured AK's and SKS rifles. As you know and made me well aware of, they aren't officially on our books, and we needed to get out of our inventory."

"True, I did say that. And the MP sergeant who took over after the Major was injured?"

"A shiny Tokarov pistol and NVA holster."

"Before or after they wrote up their statements?"

Poplawski's grin grew wider. "Before, because as you well know, Sir, Rangers lead the way."

"That we do, my friend. That we do. By the way, one of the visiting civilian eh, agency workers informed me that Mister Evans apparently is being sent back to Langley once he recovers, and you're going to love this!"

"Love what, Sir?"

"He's getting promoted!"

"Of course, he is," clucked Poplawski, lowering and slowly shaking his head. "And thus explains this whole circus as we know it."

"Why First Sergeant, I do believe you are a cynical man?"

"Once again, Sir, you are spot on."

"In its time, Romeo Company did some good."

Poplawski nodded. "A shame it ain't later in the day," he said, cranking the jeep engine up to life as he studied the position of the sun in the late afternoon sky.

"Why is that?"
"The good guys should always ride off into the sunset."